WAR AND WIND

TIDES BOOK 2

ALEX LIDELL

DANGER BEARING PRESS

WAR AND WIND

Copyright © 2017 by Alex Lidell.

ISBN: 978-0998760421

For information contact :

alex@alexlidell.com

www.alexlidell.com

Sign up for news from Alex Lidell: www.subscribepage.com/TIDES

First Edition: June 2017

ALSO BY ALEX LIDELL

TIDES

FIRST COMMAND (Prequel Novella)

AIR AND ASH (TIDES Book I)

WAR AND WIND (TIDES Book II)

Untitled (TIDES Book III)

TILDOR

THE CADET OF TILDOR

SIGN UP FOR NEW RELEASE NOTIFICATIONS
www.subscribepage.com/TIDES

Reviews are an author's lifeblood. Please consider saying a few
words about this book on Amazon.

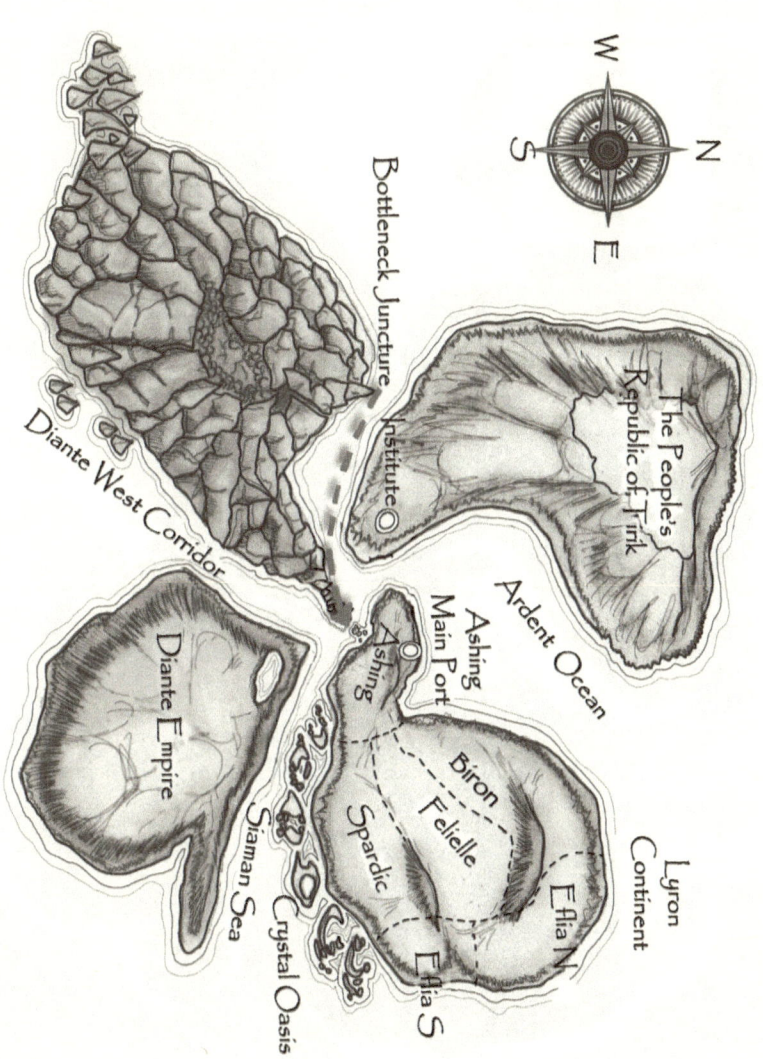

Bottleneck Juncture

Institute

Diante West Corridor

The People's Republic of Tink

Ardent Ocean

Ashing Main Port

Ashing

Diante Empire

Biron

Felielle

Spardic

Eflia N

Eflia S

Lyron Continent

Siaman Sea

Crystal Oasis

N

W

E

S

CHAPTER 1

QUINN

Captain Ral Quinn of the Tirik Ship *Hope*, The People's Republic of Tirik Navy, knew his good fortune would run out at some point. And it had. Two months ago. By boat.

"Commissioner Jaquis." Quinn bowed to the well-dressed man as if nothing could have made him happier than his political watchdog's appearance on the quarterdeck. Really, the year he'd spent running with no more than nominal supervision was much more than any Republic officer dared hope for. It couldn't have lasted forever.

Quinn had served in the Tirik People's Navy since he was ten, before the war with the Lyron League flared up in full glory. It was Quinn's way of giving back to his countrymen who'd spilled their blood to ensure that he, an orphan with no lineage or royal blood, had a chance at opportunity and prosperity. Now the People's Republic of Tirik fought for the freedom of their brethren, who writhed under royal thumbs in the six kingdoms of the Lyron League—Ashing, Spardic, Felielle, Biron, Eflia North and South. Once the gluttonous Lyron kings were dethroned, the resources the Lyron royals hoarded for themselves would be distributed to those whose needs were genuine.

But there was much to do between now and victory. Quinn's current mission was humanitarian and as vital—in its small personal way—as any fleet battle. Ironically, the greatest obstacle standing between Quinn and success came from his own government.

It little helped that since picking up Commissioner Jaquis, everything that could have gone wrong had. First there was the *Devron* attack, then the earthquake, and then an idiotic directive sending them right back into the Siaman Sea to pick up additional passengers before dropping off the ones already in the hold. "I trust you've slept well, sir?"

Jaquis pressed his lips together and surveyed the deck. Small for a man, with a bald head, thin mustache, and a proverbial rod up his ass, Commissioner Jaquis made up in self-importance what he lacked in brains. Taking a journal from the inside pocket of his coat, the commissioner made notes. Sour ones, if his face was any guide to the matter.

Quinn supposed that most of a commissioner's job involved finding fault with his charges. Putting his hands in the small of his back, Quinn waited patiently for Jaquis to spit out whatever brilliance entered the commissioner's mind this morning. At twenty-five, Quinn had been at sea for fifteen years and had seen many commissioners come and go. Quinn also understood the importance of the *Hope*'s current mission.

"Might I ask, Captain"—Jaquis spit his words from the thin line of his mouth—"whether we are on the same heading as we were last night?"

Quinn hesitated. Technically, they had made a small adjustment to gain the most advantage from the wind. But the commissioner might find the technical answer condescending, or worse, evasive. Quinn bowed slightly, his woolen coat whispering as he moved. "We are continuing on the same path, yes. North, across the Siaman Sea toward the Lyron archipelago."

To Quinn's pleasure, the crew gave no reaction to their captain's un-seamanlike words. They were a good lot and had taken Jaquis's measure early on.

"And why would that be?" the commissioner demanded, his eyes narrowing to slits.

"The shore hasn't moved, sir." The words came out before Quinn could catch himself, but Jaquis was pushing Quinn's patience to the limit. They were on the quarterdeck, damn the man. And though Quinn was in civilian garb for the sake of the mission, he was the ship's captain.

"Is that meant to be funny, Mr. Quinn?"

This time, Quinn checked himself. Hard. He had to if he knew what was good for his health and that of his crew. The recent appearance of the *Devron*, a Tirik man-of-war that had attacked the Lyron League's *Aurora* and the merchantmen she had under escort, including Quinn's own *Hope*, had been a serious setback. Quinn little blamed the *Devron*'s commander, who'd had no way of knowing of Quinn's mission, no reason to suspect that one of the "Lyron League merchantmen" under *Aurora*'s wing was secretly Tirik. But someone in the admiralty who *should have* known had plainly botched everything up. Royally. But without knowing the source of the error, Quinn decided against steering the discussion that way.

"Now that we made the additional pickup from the Diante, we will need to head back toward the Bottleneck Juncture,"

Quinn said patiently. The Siaman Sea flowed between the archipelago at the south of the Lyron continent and the northern shore of the Diante Empire—a bizarre nation that remained neutral in the Tirik-Lyron war. To exit the Siaman Sea and return to the Tirik mainland, Quinn would be obliged to traverse the narrow opening known as the Bottleneck Juncture, which permitted only a single ship to pass through at a time. "Crossing the Siaman and approaching the juncture alone would put us and our passengers in greater danger than maintaining present course, meeting the *Aurora*, and having her escort us there. It is a longer route, but the safer and wiser one."

Jaquis shifted his weight. On paper, the political overseers attached to naval operations had some experience at sea. In practice, the Committee for Patriotism had other priorities, and the People's Commissioner was often busy being sick over the rail. Quinn supposed *Devron*'s attack was the first action Jaquis had seen in any proximity. It had been all Quinn could do to keep the commissioner from running up Tirik colors and blowing Quinn's cover out of the water. Which would have been a disaster on several levels. Not least of which being Quinn's passengers. For many of them, this covert passage was the last hope for life.

Jaquis was as skittish as a fresh-faced middie, but infinitely more dangerous.

"The *Devron* may still be in these waters, and she does not know we are on the same side. She might return to finish the job. If we are with the Lyron ship, we will hardly be able to signal our heritage to the *Devron*!" said Jaquis. "Can we not disappear into the greatness of this ocean?"

"We can, sir," Quinn said agreeably, not bothering to point out that the Siaman was a sea, not an ocean. "Any time you wish. Though I must point out that the Siaman Sea poses greater danger in the form of privateers, Diante patrols, and possibly other Lyron vessels. While I've the fullest faith in my crew, we are sailing a merchant vessel, not a man-of-war." Quinn shrugged. "As ironic as it is, sir, we will be safest in the wake of a Lyron frigate. Her captain is a typical noble blood who values his own pockets over his nation, and I pay him plenty well to watch over us."

If Quinn had ever needed proof of how privileged birth corrupted a soul, Captain Rima of the League Ship *Aurora* had provided it in spades. When Quinn's mission ended, he was going to sink the despicable frigate and leave the world better for it.

CHAPTER 2

I stand frozen in the passageway before the infirmary, the Lyron League Ship *Aurora* rocking beneath me. My tight braid sways like a pendulum, drumming a soft *tap tap tap* on my shoulder blades. A fourteen-year-old midshipman named Thatch Lawrence is at the infirmary door already, his skin pale and hands clenched into fists. He'd heard the news too, then. Thatch Lawrence gives me a single terror-filled glance, his curly hair and freckles making him look much too young.

The infirmary door opens before the middie touches the handle. Thatch Lawrence flattens himself against a bulkhead to let First Officer Domenic Dana and Marine Lieutenant Catsper walk past him. The sight of Domenic makes my chest tighten and burn. His face is hard, his sea-blue eyes are cold and unreadable. Beside him, Catsper is fury made flesh. Catsper's dog, Rum, trots beside his master, baring teeth at everything.

Thatch Lawrence slips into the infirmary the men just vacated. I hold my place, waiting for them. My hand presses against the wooden bulkhead for balance, my ankle unstable from a recent fall. Rum's nostrils flare as he passes by me. The dog can smell my magic and little likes it.

"A pleasure to see you too, Rum." My voice is flatter than I wish.

They stop beside me, Domenic taking up most of the narrow passage. Too tall to stand upright, Domenic braces his hands on the overhead beams and hunches. His presence fills the space around us with crackling power. Close. So close. I swallow and take a step back from him.

Domenic's gaze tracks each of my movements.

"Someone put a bag over Midshipman Kederic's head and beat him unconscious. I set two bones and a dislocated shoulder," Catsper informs me. With no doctor aboard the *Aurora*, the lieutenant of the marines lends his battle-earned skills to the injured. "Luckily for young Mr. Kederic, he remained unconscious through it all. I place his chances of waking up at all at fifty percent." The marine crosses his arms, the movement feline and controlled. Catsper and Domenic are both twenty-two, beautiful in a male way, but different as two lethal blades forged from different kingdoms. Which they are. Domenic rules ships; Catsper rules muskets and blades. The marine's voice drops so low, I can barely make out the words. "In case that was too subtle, Ash, let me be clear. The middie's injuries are a result of an assault, not an accident."

Attacked. A midshipman on a naval ship was attacked. Even with evidence at hand, my mind struggles to accept what's happened. An assault on a middie would earn a severe flogging, if not a death sentence, on any ship. Domenic, who keeps discipline aboard the *Aurora*, punishes for much less. Which means whoever dared attack Midshipman Kederic had the backing and protection of the one person whose authority on this ship exceeds Domenic's—Captain Rima.

Captain Rima is a brilliant, nepotistic coward. He is corrupt. Sleazy. Manipulative. Dishonest. Entitled. But with all that, he's still a captain in the Lyron League Navy, not some pirate commodore. Someone promoted him up the chain to his current rank. He has an admiralty to answer to. But a naval captain who wants to put a middie into place bends the youngster over a gun and canes him before the crew. He doesn't stage an assault by proxy in a dark corner. He can't. Except he had.

Domenic focuses on my face with a mix of harsh condemnation and heart-wrenching concern.

I have the good sense to look down.

Because this is all my fault.

Less than two days ago, I cajoled the *Aurora*'s midshipmen into disobeying Captain Rima and secretly diverted the ship into a bay to shelter against foul weather. We had expected a storm. We got an earthquake. Being close to land as we were—as *I'd* brought us—the *Aurora* fell victim to a great wave that nearly capsized the ship and killed five of the crew.

When the sea settled, Captain Rima publicly proclaimed the course change had been his doing—not to take responsibility for the trouble, but to keep the crew from doubting his control of the ship. I'd let myself believe that Rima had talked himself into a corner, as he could hardly punish anyone for disobeying what he claimed to have been his own orders.

I was a bloody fool. Rima isn't the type to let a challenge go unpunished. I *knew* that. But I hadn't imagined the punishment would take this form. No one in their right mind would have imagined this; a quiet assault with a public smile. It is the kind of thing the People's Republic of Tirik would do. Not us.

9

Domenic's nostrils flare now as he glares down at me. When I organized the course change, I went behind *his* back as well as Rima's. On purpose. I knew that Domenic would never agree to a secret course change—he's too good an officer to disobey the captain's orders.

"*I did what I had to do,*" I'd told Domenic unapologetically an hour ago when we stood alone in the cargo hold, our desire for each other slowly conquering our common sense. An hour that might as well be a lifetime.

An hour ago, the beaten-unconscious Kederic was as yet undiscovered. An hour ago, I hadn't yet tasted Domenic's lips. "*I did what I had to do,*" I'd told Domenic, meeting his gaze head-on. I also told him my suspicion that Rima was using the *Aurora* to run a side business for his own profit, that my course change was for the ship's own safety.

"*And what of repercussions? Or does your righteousness shield those from view?*" Domenic had demanded.

"*I decided I'd rather face your wrath in a bay than risk catastrophic weather in open sea.*"

"*My wrath?*" Domenic shook me. Hard. "*You are bloody smarter than that, Nile. I can make your life temporarily miserable, but you damn well know that I won't make you dead. You think Captain Rima would extend you the same courtesy?*"

Now I have my answer. Except it isn't me who is paying the price, but Kederic. Worse, I fear the injured middie is just a start.

Domenic's rigid shoulders say he agrees.

We are at war, fighting for the survival of the Lyron League's six member kingdoms that the People's Republic of Tirik wants to destroy. Having killed off their own monarchy and nobility, the Tirik People's Party turned their once-vibrant nation into a realm of poverty and ruin. Fear rules there, with neighbor spying on neighbor and innocents executed on charges of having royal blood.

The Tirik newsleafs and politicians claim the Tirik Republic fights Lyron in order to liberate the Lyron people—but that isn't true. The People's Party fights because if the Tirik citizens stop killing us, they will turn on the Party's own corrupt self-proclaimed heads. Plus, having squandered their nation's riches in the wake of the revolution, the Tirik Republic wants to possess ours.

It's the Tirik Republic we are supposed to be protecting ourselves from. Not our own captain.

Catsper pushes between me and Domenic and gets Domenic started toward the deck above. If Catsper suspects that Domenic and I had been kissing when he'd barged into the cargo hold with news of Kederic's attack, he lets none of it show. I start toward the infirmary before I can see whether Domenic ever looks back toward me.

The kiss had been a mistake, and we both know it.

There is little I can do at Kederic's bedside beyond assuring Thatch Lawrence that whatever happens, we'll face it together. After a quarter hour, I leave the boy to sit with his friend and make my way to the open deck in search of another middie involved in our plot, Ana.

There are five middies total aboard the *Aurora*, the sixth having been killed in a Tirik attack two weeks ago. Kederic, seventeen, is the oldest, and a true seaman in the making. Sixteen-year-old Ana hates the sea and is aboard only to support her family's social standing. Fourteen-year-old Thatch Lawrence and twelve-year-old twins Song and Sand make up the remainder of the *Aurora*'s cadre of officers in training. Of Rima's targets, Song and Sand I worry about least as they are Rima's nephews, but Thatch Lawrence and Ana have all the

11

reason in the world to be frightened. As do I. Although I'm not a middie myself, everyone aboard knows I keep close ties with the young officers and share Ana's cabin.

That target now on my back is another reason why what happened in the cargo hold with Domenic must never repeat itself. Intimate relations between an officer and sailor are forbidden, and what Rima could—*would*—do if he discovered us chills my blood.

Emerging on deck, I squint at the bright sunlight, finding Ana clutching the rail with a white-knuckle grip. Her face turns toward me, eyes lined with silver and glistening. She's heard about Kederic, then. I come up to stand beside her and watch the sea.

Ana is only a year younger than me, though her petite stature makes the difference seem more pronounced. Tall, redheaded, with the straight-backed posture drilled into me over the nine years I've been at sea, I tower over mousy Ana. Mousy but smart. And kind. And scared out of her wits, it seems.

"You heard about Kederic?" I ask quietly.

Ana nods, the wind ruffling her dark hair. Ana's lower lip bleeds where she's chewed it with her teeth. "Commander Dana won't release me from deck to go sit with him," she whispers.

"You are on watch now," I say softly. "You can sit with him as long as you wish in a few hours."

Her head whips to me, her nostrils flaring. Around us, the deck crawls with thirsty work parties and bubbling tension. We are short on drinking water, have been for a week now, and the repairs from the great wave's damage are forcing the crew into longer shifts even as the reduced water rations dry their lips. The Spades, a training unit of adolescent marines from the Spardic Kingdom, stand guard with loaded weapons near each water cask. The hands snap at each other with little provocation, and bosun's mates are busy keeping scraps from escalating.

Ana's jaw tightens. "No, Nile. You don't get to lecture me about what one can and can't do on watch. Not anymore. Your naval rules are supposed to protect us. How is that working out?"

"Ana," I whisper, though I've no notion what to say next. "We'll get through this."

Ana wraps her arms tight around her shoulders, a tear sliding down her cheek. I quickly shift my weight to block the crew's view. Ana has been at sea for only seven months, but she is a midshipman, an officer in training, and the crew cannot be permitted to see her cry.

No crying before the crew. That was one of the first lessons I learned when I first stepped aboard a ship at age eight. A different ship in a different world. The youngest child of the Ashing king, I was destined for the admiralty commanding our kingdom's armada. That wasn't how it worked out. When my ship failed at an impossible mission, my father sacrificed my career for his public image, while my mother schemed to marry me off to Felielle's Prince Tamiath.

I ran. Ran all the way to the *Aurora*, where everyone thinks me nothing but a lowly seaman.

Everyone except Dominic and Catsper, who know the truth and keep my confidence.

"I want off this cursed ship," Ana whispers, her voice filled with agony. It's her thirst talking. I hope it's the thirst. There is a haunted look about her, as if the great wave had washed away her spirit and left but a shell behind. "I want my family and my home. I want to marry and raise children. I want to be anywhere but here."

I touch her hand, my long fingers awkward beside her small, pretty ones. "Hold fast." I conjure a smile I hope is reassuring. "We need to hold together now. All the middies do. And the crew needs you too. We've set course for the Crystal Oasis to take on fresh water. It will be not much longer now until we dock. Just focus on that, all right? Focus on getting the ship and crew to water and we'll work everything else out one step at a time."

Ana pulls her hand away from my touch. "I'm no idiot, Nile. I know bloody well the crew needs nothing of me. If anything about this ship was based on the crew's needs, you'd be in bloody command, not playing at being some lowly seaman you are not."

I freeze. It is the first time Ana's called me out on my mysteriously obtained naval knowledge, and her voice is bitter with resentment. After I took command of Ana's gun battery in the middle of battle and spent hours tutoring the middies on navigation skills, anyone with half a brain realizes I've been at sea for some time. But going to sea to escape a past life is a long-standing tradition amid seafarers, and an unspoken sacrosanct rule keeps questions in check. Everyone has secrets they want to keep ashore.

Ana had respected mine until now. But her limits are stretching. Ripping.

I grab her arm. "Please. Let's not do this. Not now. We need to stay together."

She jerks away. "You're a hypocrite."

"What?"

"Forget it."

I shut my eyes and inhale the sea air. Ana is thirsty and frightened and not herself. The happenings on the *Aurora* are nothing either of us expected. The Siaman Sea, where *Aurora* sails, a stretch of water between the Lyron continent and the reclusive Diante Empire, is far from the Tirik Republic and supposed to be a safe station.

It isn't working out that way. The Tirik ship *Devron* attacked us two weeks ago, taking as prize two merchantmen we had under our protection. Then the earthquake and the great wave that nearly capsized our ship last night. And now Kederic...

"I'm going below," I tell Ana, and start to the companionway ladder without waiting for a reply.

I sense *it* a heartbeat before it happens. The sudden, too familiar fear pulsing through my body. The racing heart rate. The shallow breaths. My body is about to betray me, and I've nowhere to hide.

Blood drains from my face.

"Nile?" Ana's voice is distant. Concerned. "Nile, what's the matter?"

I can't answer. The first of the green lights flashes before me.

CHAPTER 3

I'm grateful I am able to fall to my hands and knees before the familiar convulsions rack my body. The impact of my knees hitting the deck reverberates through me even as I use my last strands of control over my body to thrust my head through the sideboard rails. I tuck my right hand into my belt. As before, the right side of my body tightens involuntarily, only the belt keeping my arm from flailing like a deranged rag doll. My back slams against the rail.

"Nile!" Ana kneels beside me, the *thrash thrash thrash* of my right side colliding with her hand.

My head shakes. I don't intend it to, but Ana extracts a meaning from the motion. "It's all right," she says quietly. "You just look as if you're seasick. Again."

The part of my mind that can still think thanks her, though I've no way of telling her that. The convulsions will stop when they deign to and not a second before. I've learned that much.

"What's going on here?" Domenic's low voice demands from somewhere close. Too close.

Ana puts one hand on my forehead, the other holding my hair back for me. "Ash's stomach is rolling again, sir," she says with an exasperation-filled voice. "I'll take her below just as soon as I'm certain she won't sully the berth."

As if on cue, my jerking spells end, and I do throw up over the rail. Horribly. With Domenic watching every moment of it.

Behind us, the hands snicker at me. My face is hot as I swipe my sleeve across my mouth, but better the crew laugh at my belly than think too closely on what happened.

"Enough," Domenic barks at them before looking down at Ana. "Take her below, Lionitis."

More chuckles follow us as Ana helps me navigate the steps of the companionway and silently helps me to our berth. The tiny room is the length of Ana's cot and the width of three steps. The hammock I sling up at night is rolled up, leaving just Ana's sea chest and a tiny hanging desk. Small canvas smelling sacks of dried apple skins and ground cinnamon fight a losing battle against stale air.

I squeeze Ana's hand in gratitude.

"It's getting worse, isn't it?" she says quietly, closing the door. "Whatever it is that's causing these fits of yours."

My chest burns. I sit on her sea chest, both because I cannot stand and to cover my shock. I hadn't realized she'd noticed the convulsions before today, saw them as anything but the seasickness I claim them to be. A naïve, ridiculous hope given we share a berth. "It's just the stress," I mumble. "I'll do better once we take on fresh water." That much is true. I swallow and look up, needing to know what exactly she thinks she saw.

"By the Goddess," Ana hisses. "You've asked me to respect your secrets, but there is a line between discretion and daft blindness."

My strength is drained, and my heart pounds so hard, I barely hear Ana's words. "What do you want me to say, Ana?"

"Why do you suffer these fits?"

Because I have magic in my blood, magic that calls to air and leaves me with convulsions as a side effect. I'm *Gifted*, like my twin brother. And if anyone finds out, I will get kicked off the ship in a heartbeat and shuffled off somewhere out of normal people's way. Gifted are unpredictable, too dangerous to others and to themselves. I had come aboard the *Aurora* to search out a cure for my twin's Gift, but now I am seeking one for both our sakes. I swallow, my mouth dry. "I don't know."

Ana scowls. "I don't believe you."

I shrug.

Her nostrils flare. "Fine. To be frank, I little care. I covered for you just now because I know you wish to keep whatever *this* is quiet. And now I want answers to my real questions. No, not just want. I deserve answers." Ana's face is hard, and she crosses her slender arms across her chest. For the first time since I met her, her petite frame dwarfs my taller build. "And I'm tired of hearing your ballads about duty and responsibility while your actions reflect anything but. Or will you tell me you followed those very virtues the night you ran from Ashing to join the *Aurora*?"

I rub my face and stare up at her. Ana... This Ana, she isn't the girl I first met. Her skin is dull, her lips cracked, and her eyes have sunken into her once-delicate face. If the battle with *Devron* and the night diversion of the *Aurora* have fed my spirit, they've emptied hers, leaving nothing but desperation.

"What specifically do you care to know?" I ask. *What exactly are you accusing me of?*

"Do you recall last week's dispatch ship?" she asks.

Of course I do. Probably better than Ana does because of

the news the ship carried—news that I learned from Catsper, but Rima keeps from the crew. While the *Aurora* kept to her backwaters station, the Tirik Republic engaged the Lyron League fleet in the Ardent Ocean that separates our two continents. Engaged, and enjoyed the greatest victory in the dozen years of our war.

In a single day, the joint Lyron League fleet lost twenty ships. With the joint League fleet nearly crippled, the six kingdoms on the Lyron continent will soon be left to rely solely on their own private armadas for protection. My kingdom of Ashing, the smallest of the six and the one closest to the Tirik, will be the first to fall.

"I remember," I say carefully. "What of it?"

"My mother's letters were included with the mail," says Ana, as if letters from a Felielle Kingdom noble should somehow raise my suspicions. "My mother includes newsleafs with her correspondences," Ana continues. "The last had a note of a missing girl. It struck me as odd. A girl matching your description went missing right at the time and place I met you. A girl who was once destined for the Ashing Admiralty, until the ship she was on went against orders. Like *Aurora* went against orders just recently. Both diversions ended in disaster."

Storms. The newsleaf. Only my quarterdeck practice of masking my thought keeps the fear and anger from my face. Fear for what Ana might be thinking and anger over the suggestion that the *Aurora* and *Faithful*, the ship I had served on and lost due to my father's scheming, are anything alike.

Ana leans forward, looking down at me. "Are you Nile Greysik, Princess of Ashing?"

I chuckle. "If I was an Ashing princess, don't you think I'd have found berth on a higher-class ship than this backwaters rubbish?"

She weighs me.

I make myself breathe. In and out. In and out.

"No," Ana says after a few moments, shaking her head for emphasis. "Someone else, yes, but not you, Nile. There is too great a chance of exposure on a better ship." Her jaw tightens. "I'd once have thought that a missing princess must be a victim of misfortune or kidnappers, for surely no girl would care so little for her parents' feelings and the surname she owes her children. But you... You've no notion of family honor. While I left behind all that is dear to protect my family's dignity, you care for no one and nothing beyond your enjoyment of the sea." She pauses. "No one else might consider that a late-night conscript from the Ashing shores is anything but a runaway from a foul life, but I know you better than they do. And you are just that ruthless."

I'm ruthless because I've no worry over the surname of my nonexistent children? I blink at Ana's words and sigh in feigned boredom. "I saw the newsleaf, Ana. Prince Tamiath of Felielle, the princess's intended groom, is the one who wrote the notice. He is offering a reward for the girl's return, as I remember." I raise a brow. "The thought of gold is making you see things, I think. You'd not be the first to fall victim to an expensive imagination."

Her brows narrow. "I don't believe you."

"If you wish to believe you share a berth with the missing bride of a Felielle prince, go right ahead. I would keep your delusions to yourself, however, unless you wish to become the laughingstock of the crew."

She smiles without humor. "Oh, I'm already the laughingstock of the crew."

This morning, I would have told Ana that wasn't true. That every day she is making strides toward earning their respect.

21

But now I keep my silence lest she use any of my words against me.

Ana steps forward, her lips brushing my ear. "Don't you ever instruct me on duty again, Nile Greysik of Ashing," she whispers. "Not when you abandoned your family, your husband, your people, and two nations. Make no mistake, you are the hypocrite I named you."

CHAPTER 4

I am nauseated all night, and the lingering effects of the convulsions are only partially responsible. Ana's words haunt me, her anger a nail in my flesh that joins too many others. I give up on sleep altogether with the first rays of dawn and seek out Catsper. To talk, to fight, to do anything but wait for my mind to explode into shards. The marine is busy with his own work however, and I'm not about to interrupt him to babble about feelings. And even if I did, there is one matter that would still remain unvoiced.

That matter is currently striding along the circumference of the deck, inspecting the tied-down great guns, the stone-sanded wooden deck, the set of the sails. My jaw tenses as I see a knotted rope's end in Domenic's hand, a reminder to the crew to behave. Domenic taps the rope absently on his thigh, his face a mask of icy harshness. And it *is* a mask, I realize. The more willing the crew believes Domenic is to hand out punishment, the less he must actually do so.

I wonder for the first time whether Domenic minds it, being

feared. Hated. Thought of as a savage monster who savors pain and blood. An image he's carefully constructed for himself here on the *Aurora* and one that is at odds with the man I met on the Ashing beach that month ago. The man whose gentle, calloused fingers caressed my skin yesterday.

I try to make myself busy, but each time I try to focus on checking canvas for tears or line for wear, my thoughts stubbornly sneak back to the hot press of Domenic's lips, his stubbled chin sliding across my face, his hand pressing hard against the small of my back. It is as if Domenic's kiss awoke a sleeping girl inside me and now she is yawning and stretching, and shoving Nile Ash to and fro like a fresh wind. It is an effort to avoid looking at the man, a losing battle to concentrate on anything else.

Domenic's trained gaze finds me across the deck and narrows.

My chest tightens. The last time he saw me, I was hurling my guts into the sea. Suddenly, I want nothing more than to disappear before Domenic's steady steps reach my workstation, but my body holds fast of its own traitorous accord. My mouth dries, my limbs wanting to run toward him and sprint away at the same time.

I beg the stars he doesn't speak to me, for I'm at a sudden raw loss for words to utter back. My heart strikes hard against my ribs. If Domenic regrets yesterday's kiss... One word from him will cut me to the quick, and it's my own damn fault.

Like a coward, I throw a glance over my shoulder, begging for someone to interrupt the impromptu meeting before it happens. No one does.

"Ash?" Domenic's voice is a soft rumble. He steps toward me, close enough that I feel the heat of his body mixing with my own, the salty sea smell that clings to his clothes filling my lungs. Close enough that if he lifts his hand, he'll touch me. Domenic crosses his wrists behind his back. "Are you well?"

Am I *well?* The absurdity of the question hits me like pelting hail. Ana. Kederic. The fleet. Whatever this thing is between Domenic and me. The list of things standing between me and *well* is too long to count. I long for Domenic's hand to reach forward, for the calloused, powerful fingers to brush my cheek. The image alone sends enough energy through me that I half expect lightning to crackle through the deck.

A kiss. It had been one illicit, illegal kiss. The first for me, but likely one of dozens for him. Of hundreds, perhaps.

Domenic frowns, and I realize I'm yet to give him an answer.

"Aye." I swallow, placing my own hands behind my back in mirror of his, aware of the rest of the deck's crew going about its business. "Aye, sir."

He surveys every inch of me, then jerks his chin at the canvas that's now pooled on the ground. "Is there a reason you've tortured the same bit of sail three times now?"

I reach for my work reflexively, tripping over a nearby coiled rope.

Domenic grabs my elbow to steady me before I fall. Plainly, there are no problems with concentration on his end. "Are you drunk, Ash?" he asks, the corners of his mouth twitching.

I swallow, longing for some part of the deck Domenic is not at. Coward. That's what I am.

"I've seen rope get in a seaman's way before," he continues lightly, his hand still on my elbow. "But I believe this is the first time I've witnessed one chase and attack a sailor from behind."

"Yes, well, it's a very...resourceful rope, sir."

Domenic presses his lips together. Composure recovered, he

releases me and straightens once more. "I see. Very well, be about your duties."

I swallow a sigh of relief and scurry off like a deranged weevil, leaving the canvas to be someone else's problem. Domenic's, if there is any justice in the world.

Taking measure of the sea, I find it calm today. The shore visible on our larboard side is a bit of a mess, but not as bad as I feared, and much of the forestry is intact. The open water on starboard sparkles under the clear skies. A now-familiar merchant ship, the *Hope*, had joined us during the night and currently holds position in our wake. The Lyron League Merchant flag on its mast flaps in the breeze.

"Ms. Lionitis," Captain Rima calls, emerging from the companionway ladder. He wears enough gold chains, bracelets, and rings to keep several families fed for a year. The jewelry's shine matches the Eflian's yellow irises and jingles as he walks, his gait no less confident for being slightly pigeon-toed. "Signal our intended course for the Crystal Oasis to our charge."

Ana moves through the motions with vacant eyes. "The *Hope* acknowledges course, sir," Ana says after a few minutes of hoisted flags.

Rima nods, unsurprised, and rubs the tribal tattoos etched over his cheekbone. Wherever the merchant ultimately needs to go, it's in her best interest to await our readiness instead of weathering the waters alone. I don't even blame *Hope*'s skipper for paying Rima extra to escort his ship out of turn. I do blame Rima for accepting the bribe.

"Mr. Dana," Rima calls, his voice carrying over the deck like a rooster's call. "Have you found the culprit behind Mr. Kederic's misadventure?"

"No, sir," says Domenic. "Not yet."

"Hmph. I've a name or two of hooligans I suspect. If you

26

remain empty-handed much longer, I shall be glad to assist in your investigation."

My mouth dries. Innocents. Rima will find convenient, innocent scapegoats and order Domenic to punish them. The threat, or perhaps promise, hangs in the air above the deck, poisoning my blood.

"Aye, thank you, sir," Domenic says with no trace of emotion.

Rima smiles and twists his mustache between his thumb and forefinger. "One other matter I hope you will assist me with, Mr. Dana." Striding back to the companionway, the captain snaps his fingers. Moments later, twelve-year-old midshipmen Song and Sand climb onto the deck. The boys' heads... the boys' heads are shaved smooth, the diamond pattern that marked them as members of Rima's clan gone to reveal smooth, pale skin. "Mr. Song," Rima barks, and the shyer, quieter of the two boys steps forward, his head bowed.

"Mr. Song, here," Rima says to Domenic and the watching crew, "has had trouble keeping up with cleanliness. He has lice, Mr. Dana. *Lice.* Aboard a ship. Let's have a pump rigged and soap located." The captain turns to the wide-eyed boy, who is shaking his head in denial that comes off as a plea. "Strip, boy."

Song stands frozen, his arms limply at his side.

"Now, Mr. Song," Rima croons. "Unless you wish to be bent over a gun first?"

Domenic motions a pair of sailors to bring a pump from below and quietly finds work for several of the female crew off deck, but there are too many women working this shift to make us all disappear without bringing attention to it. Around Song, seamen grin self-righteously at each other. Middies go to sea at a young age, learning the basics of ship handling and command while their enlisted counterparts learn the physical aspects of the trade. The custom inevitably translates into grown seamen taking orders from youngsters, and thus they are quite glad to observe those same youngsters humbled. A poetic justice. If only justice had anything to do with it.

Within a few minutes, a pump is rigged to pour cold ocean water over the now-naked boy standing miserably before the entire crew. A few paces away, his twin brother's fists are clenched tight at his sides. Just the thought of my twin Clay being tormented makes blood boil inside me, but for Sand to watch his brother's suffering must be torture in itself.

"Today, Mr. Song. Have you not seen soap before?" Domenic barks at the boy, trying, I realize, to pin both Song's and the crew's attention on himself. Let them talk about the monster in the officer's uniform, perhaps even side with the boy against the better target.

It almost works, until the water starts and Song yelps in surprise at the chill and pressure. The whole damn ship erupts in laughter. And then not even Domenic's attempts to anger or frighten the boy succeed in hurrying Song through his ordeal. Sitting his naked body on the deck, twelve-year-old Song cries out his heart.

CHAPTER 5

QUINN

"What is the holdup *now*, Mr. Quinn?" Commissioner Jaquis demanded, puffing out his chest like an adolescent rooster.

"The *Aurora* intends to refill her water stores, sir," Quinn answered, tapping two fingers against his thigh. Freshwater sources were few in the Siaman Sea, and Quinn considered whether there might be a way of topping off his own water barrels without showing their hand to the frigate. Unlikely, but worth the consideration. The delay for resupply would also allow him a better view of the islands and the damage the recent quake had wreaked here. He had been nothing short of fortunate that the *Hope* had been in deep enough water when it happened to have ridden out the disaster without injury. Had he been close to land...

Quinn shook the thought away. What was important now was not what *could have* happened, but what *did* happen. How far did the earthquake's damage extend? All the way north through Lyron? Up to the Tirik continent in the west? Were ports lost? Ships? Cities? The wood needed to build and repair ships grew near the coastlines on both the Tirik and Lyron continents. If those forests were damaged, they were in grave trouble. Quinn had no way of knowing any of it, though. He could not even say whether the quake in the Siaman was the worst of the event, or a minor side effect of a greater disaster elsewhere.

"Are you not paying her enough to keep to schedule?" Jaquis demanded, jerking his chin at the Lyron frigate. He opened his mouth to say something more, but at that moment, a flushed middie raced up the companionway and made haste toward Quinn.

Quinn hoped the boy would remember to pay respects to the commissioner first, but it seemed unlikely. Even more so when the ship suddenly swayed.

"Captain Quinn!" the middie panted. "There's an episode in the hold!"

Quinn turned and hurried after the boy, leaving Jaquis to make his own way down. Nodding to the marine sentry outside the door, Quinn pushed his way inside. The wind hit Quinn's face at once, and he put his forearm up to protect his eyes.

Dozens of Gifted within pressed themselves against the bulkhead. In the small, cleared space in the middle, two men held down an adolescent boy. The boy's body arched horribly, thrashing and straining against the men's grips while he stared into nothingness. A dark stain spread on the front of the boy's breeches, the stench of urine mixing with the other odors of many bodies confined in too small a space.

"What is this?" Jaquis demanded behind the captain.

"One of the air callers is having a fit," Quinn answered

without turning around. He pointed at the men holding down the child. "Let go of him at once."

"He can't control it, sir," one of the men said, his own face full of fear. "He'll hurt himself bad."

The boy's body contracted again, and a sickening snap sounded as the arm being pinned to the deck broke under the torque.

"Let go," Quinn snarled.

This time, the men obeyed without question.

Quinn ran his hand over his face. In the year Quinn has spent transporting Gifted to the Institute, he'd learned all he could about the poor sods' ailments. Holding down a convulsing air caller did little good and much harm. There was nothing for it but to let the spasms ride out their course and hope the victim was still alive at the end. The boy was already blue around his lips, whether from choking on his own tongue or the air current destroying his lungs.

The wind circulating in the hold picked up and rocked the ship.

Quinn swore.

It was a bad sign when the convulsions and the wind came together. He pulled his gaze away from the boy and scanned the others. The three water callers had tucked themselves into a corner. Their blood was too thin to clot—they'd be as good as dead if anything struck them. They'd lost one poor soul on this trip already.

"Listen up." Jaquis's voice suddenly filled the hold. "I am the People's Commissioner Jaquis, of the Patriots Bureau. Whichever one of you is responsible for this wind, raise your hand now."

The Gifted stared blankly at Jaquis, then murmured among themselves.

The ship shuddered violently.

The commissioner's face darkened. "The Tirik Republic is doing you a great service," Jaquis bellowed. "At great cost to ourselves, we are taking you to the Institute to cure you of your ills. Now, which one of you is putting this ship and all its passengers in danger?"

Quinn saw the wave of fear rush over his charges. The poor souls had enough trouble without this. With a sure step, Quinn planted himself before the commissioner. The ship bucked again. Quinn grabbed hold of the overhead beam with one hand and used the other to steady the politician on his feet. "Sir," Quinn told Jaquis quietly. "It isn't any of them. The magic in the lad's body is calling air to itself. That is how the disease works."

Sweat beaded on Jaquis's temple. He stared at the convulsing Gifted, the wind whipping around them. "He cannot end it?" Jaquis's voice rose.

"No." Quinn forced the commissioner's gaze to meet his own and spoke softly. "The boy is in the midst of a convulsion, but he is still conscious. The windstorm will end when the boy regains control of his body, loses consciousness, or passes from this world. There is nothing we can do just now but care for the others. I will have one of the men escort you to your cabin to rest, sir, and inform you when this is over."

Jaquis pulled away from Quinn's hold. "This Gifted is endangering the ship!"

Quinn tightened his jaw. "With due respect, sir, *I* will care for my ship."

The commissioner's eyes flashed. His hand reached into his waistband, and he spun away from Quinn. The captain had a moment to register the flash of metal before the report of a pistol pierced the hold.

The wind died at once, together with the air caller.

"The *Hope* is not *your* ship, sir," Commissioner Jaquis told Quinn in the bloody silence. "It belongs to the people of the Tirik Republic. And it will act in the greater good of all people, not just one boy."

CHAPTER 6

"Nile." Domenic's voice spins me around, my heart jumping at the sound. We are in one of the *Aurora's* narrow passageways, me heading toward the boys' berth, and Domenic—I don't quite know what Domenic is doing here. Passing by or... Was he waiting for me?

I don't allow myself to consider that beyond a heartbeat and knuckle my forehead instead. "Sir."

Domenic reaches out and straightens my shirt collar, which has slipped out from beneath my jacket. Domenic's own shirt and jacket are as perfect as always, the tight muscles beneath unyielding and coiled.

I can't move, like a rabbit caught in a snake's stare. Domenic's hand lingers on my lapel a moment longer than necessary, and the thump of my heart vibrates through me. It is such an illegal and dangerous game we are playing. The admiralty would put Domenic and me ashore if we were caught. But even that is a small sting compared to what

Domenic could do to my soul, which is stripping bare before him.

Domenic frowns as he pulls away, and jerks his chin toward the hatch leading to the lower hold, where we could find privacy.

My body almost answers before my mind, but reason catches up at last, and I shake my head, though the effort to move my muscles is nearly insurmountable. "I need to see the middies," I say quietly. "What happened to Song on deck—"

"I know. I was there." There is an edge to Domenic's voice. Not anger, exactly, more like tightness. As if he is struggling to keep his heart from his voice. "Are you afraid?"

"Of what?"

"Of being next," he says bluntly.

My shoulders pull back. "No."

"You should be." Domenic grips my arm hard enough to get my attention. "There is bravery and there is ignorance. You need to be careful."

I lower my voice so even Domenic, standing inches away, must strain to hear. "I don't have time to fear a petty, ignorant tyrant in a captain's coat, whose mere existence is an affront to the navy."

His jaw tightens. "Make time. Because *I* fear for you. And Nile..." He pauses to ensure he has my full attention. "The words you say about the captain border on mutinous. Keep them to yourself."

"Always the dutiful first officer, aren't you?" I shake off Domenic's grip. "Do you like it? Strutting around this floating disaster in the name of discipline?" It's a low blow, but Domenic doesn't flinch.

"I like *not* having to flog seamen, I like having a functional ship, and I like protecting those who serve under me from greater danger. If keeping the crew in fear of my discipline will keep me from having to dole it out, I will keep both the fear and my reputation of being a savage, blood-thirsty bastard burning as brightly as I must." He steps close to me until but a hair's breadth remains between our bodies and looks down at me from his greater height. "And if I'm ever faced with a choice between you being safe and you liking me, make no mistake about which way I will sway."

I stare back at him on principle, but I know there is a cost Domenic pays for the game, and I wonder if he'll ever tell me what it is.

The deck creaks, footsteps nearing from the deck above. Before either of us can say anything more, I pull away and hurry into the middies' berth without turning back.

The three boys are there, Song and Sand huddling under blankets and Thatch Lawrence sitting beside them. As I enter, Thatch Lawrence comes to his feet. The boy's freckles are stark against his pale face, and his body quivers with rage.

"I'm not sorry," he tells me by way of greeting, his shoulders pulling back defiantly. "I hate Captain Rima, and I'm scared of the bastard, but I'm not sorry for taking charge of the ship. None of us are. None of us who are here, I mean."

Ana is not.

My throat tightens as the middies' heads nod one by one. The bastard calling himself captain doesn't deserve these youngsters. Not by a long shot. I check my tone to an officer's slow, confident drawl. "Very good. Because we still have a ship to run. All of us. And if the Tirik attack again, it's you who will keep the *Aurora* afloat and fighting." My voice drops, my eyes meeting each of the boys' in turn. "And meanwhile, no one goes anywhere alone, all right?"

The following morning, I take one look at Catsper's cocky

swagger and know, just know, that the marine has something up his sleeve. The morning routine of cleaning the deck and setting the crew about breakfast is finished, and the hands now go about trimming sails to Domenic's satisfaction. My still-sore ankle keeps me rooted to deck, though it's healing faster than is convenient, since it's the unpredictable convulsions and not the tweaked tendons that are really keeping me from the shrouds. I can't risk going up until I have a handle on the jerking spells. I make a point of limping.

Domenic frowns.

My jaw tightens. I'm overdoing it, and he's noticed.

"Mr. Dana," Catsper hollers across the deck, turning a hundred eyes and stilling conversations. Outside the privacy of the Cove—the Spades' nickname for their berth—Domenic and the marine talk as little as duty allows, and when they do, their voices are quiet and businesslike.

Domenic's attention snaps to the marine lieutenant, who stands on the high poop deck, his blond hair whipping in the wind, his hands tucked arrogantly in his pant pockets. Behind Catsper, a squad of young Spades stands at attention. At least that's still normal. Domenic squares his shoulders and looks up. "Lieutenant," he says, managing to make his voice carry all the way to the poop without the appearance of shouting.

"I just heard we have a lice problem aboard, Mr. Dana," Catsper calls. "And I'm most distressed."

Song pales, stepping closer to his brother as the hands on deck grin. My stomach clenches. Ana, who has spoken not a word to me since our confrontation, grips the rail.

"The situation is handled," Domenic says with a deathly calm that would have anyone sane shutting his mouth at once.

Catsper rocks back on his heels and grins. "Still, I think one can't be too careful on a small ship like this. Might I beg for a pair of seamen to work the pump for me, seeing as it's still on deck?" He pulls a square brick from his pocket. "I've even brought my own soap."

The ship is silent as Catsper jumps over the rail of the poop deck, landing on the quarterdeck below with feline grace. Anyone else would have broken a leg in that jump, but Catsper barely blinks at the impact. The pump is indeed still here, Rima having contradicted Domenic's order to have the damn thing removed. A reminder of Song's humiliation that Catsper...

Waves and hail.

I choke on nothing as the marine grins and begins to unbutton his clothes. The black jacket is off first, folded neatly and handed to one of the marine boys who Catsper summons with a single glance. The shirt comes off next. Catsper's lithe, hard torso is covered in tattoos and scars. And the marine owns every honed inch of it.

Standing a few paces away, Domenic stares at Catsper, everything about his posture shouting *Stop it* as loudly as if he'd given the words voice.

Catsper grins and pulls the top lace of his pants loose.

CHAPTER 7

For the first time ever, I see Domenic close his eyes on the quarterdeck and take several overtly calming breaths. When he opens them again, Catsper is fully naked, utterly comfortable, and waiting patiently for the two seamen already poised at the pump. Rum, the damn animal, trots up to his master and sprawls lazily on the deck as if to say, *If you are having a bath, I want one too.* Of course, *of course,* Catsper owns the only dog in the universe who doesn't hate water.

I catch Johina sneaking off deck moments before the dreaded thump of Captain Rima's footsteps clanks up the companionway. The already silent deck holds its collective breath. Even the seamen at the pump stop working, leaving a soaped-up Catsper standing in a puddle of water without more coming.

"Mr. Catsper." Rima's nasal voice is a deadly purr. "To what might we owe the exhibition?"

Catsper wrings out his hair before answering. "Lice, sir. Better safe than crawling, wouldn't you say?"

～

"Are you insane?" Domenic grabs the lapels of Catsper's jacket and slams the marine into the Cove's bulkhead.

Catsper lets him, not even wincing at the impact. The rest of the Spades give the quarreling pair little attention. Their commanding officer can take care of himself. Penn, one of the younger marine boys who has taken a liking to me, tosses me a dagger.

I raise a brow.

"Start carrying it with you, Ash," Catsper calls over his shoulder, then nods to Domenic to continue the pummeling all he wishes.

Domenic steps back and sits on one of the boys' sea chests. "Are you insane?" he repeats, this time in a reasonable tone, as if inquiring after the weather.

"Oh, most certainly," says Catsper, straightening his clothes. "And clean too."

"You think Rima—"

"I think I can handle Rima a bit better than a handful of children," says Catsper, and suddenly there is no more humor in his voice. A chill settles over the Cove at once, Catsper's irreverence only adding weight to what he's done, why he's done it. There is a hunt aboard ship, and if Catsper can't stop it, he'll offer himself as bait.

The marine is trying to mop up my mess by throwing himself into the fire. My face burns. Even Domenic becomes rigid. I raise my chin and meet Catsper's green eyes and then Domenic's blue ones. "It should be me," I say quietly.

Catsper snorts. "Let's get to training with that knife Penn gave you before it *is* you, Ash."

"I thought your ankle hurt, Nile," Domenic says quietly, his brow cocking. "A bit difficult to spar with that, I'd think."

I hide a wince. Behind Domenic's back, Catsper gives me a look as if to say, *Your problem. You deal with it.*

I shrug nonchalantly, but my heart gallops as I say, "I'll manage. I imagine Catsper will tell you it's unlikely the Tirik will inquire about my health before trying to stick a blade between my ribs." My smooth words feel like slime in my mouth. I'm lying to Domenic. Again. After he's invited me to into his confidence, shown me the man behind his cold mask. And just as with the ship's change of course, the thing I'm hiding—my Gift—is not a negligible one.

"You took a fall from the shrouds, Nile. And I've not seen you mount the rigging since," Domenic says softly, and my heart sinks further. He's been watching me. He's been worried. Falling from the rigging is much like falling from horseback—it's vital to get back on before the fear festers.

And, horrid person that I am, I meet his genuine concern with half-truths. "I've not grown a sudden fear of heights." It's getting caught in the midst of a jerking spell and falling from said height that bothers me. "I've been at sea long enough to know fish-bait pitfalls. A little more time to heal, and I will be back in the ratlines."

Domenic's gaze bores into me.

Slime. I am lying slime, and I don't deserve him.

Domenic opens his mouth, and I *know* he's about to suggest we step out together. Before he can utter a word, I turn to Catsper, my blade in my hand. "So, where are we training?"

I STAY out of the berth Ana and I share for as long as I can, eating dinner with the Spades, checking on Kederic and the boys, and staying on deck to mend sail until the darkness forces me below. My magic has been refilling, and since my reserves emptied into the sails, the need to release it soon stirs in my blood. When I confide as much to Catsper during our sparring lesson, he puts me through such training to tighten my mind's focus that I can little tell whether it's the marine's assistance or the recent convulsions that lie behind my screaming muscles. Either way, when I finally stumble down to the shared berth at day's end, I can think of nothing but slinging up my hammock and sinking into sleep.

Opening the cabin door, however, I find myself uncertain I've come to the right place. The ridiculous baubles and ribbons Ana has lying around have been cleaned up. The little apple-cinnamon potpourri sacks are gone. Even the embroidered blanket she keeps covering her sea chest, the one that falls to the deck and tangles my feet each time the *Aurora* hits a wave, is nowhere to be seen.

Ana sits on her cot, the lantern swinging above her as she writes in her journal. Her hazel eyes slip to me as I enter, then return coolly to her work.

"Good evening," I say slowly.

Ana nods briskly, her slender hand making curling motions as she fills the page. The passive anger blossoming from her is powerful enough to back me into the wall. Fine. If the girl wants to brood, she can. Unrolling my hammock, I string it up to the bulkhead with practiced motions.

"Who do you think will be next?" Ana says into my back, her voice cold. "Kederic was two days ago. Song yesterday. A reprieve today, it seems, but the night's not over yet. So who do you think will be next, Nile? Me? Sand? Thatch Lawrence? Not you, though. No, you like to stay behind the scenes, pretend to be something you are not. Play it safe."

44

I sink into my hammock and rest my forearms atop my knees. My head throbs, my muscles ache, my blood boils with magic, and my heart can't slow down for thoughts of Domenic. Despite it all, I force calm reason into my voice for the sake of the girl who'd offered to share her berth with me when I had nowhere else to go. "We are all targets, Ana. If I could protect you and the boys with my body, I would."

Her head snaps to me. "Would you?"

"Of course."

She puts down her pen and meets my gaze. "Then go over to Captain Rima's cabin, tell him who you are, and order him to turn this ship back to the mainland so we can all get off it."

I pinch the bridge of my nose. "I'm no one, Ana."

She snorts. "That's what I thought."

Pushing away my exhaustion, I grab my blanket and limp down to the cargo hold to sleep. Dark, stale, and rat infested it might be, but I will get better sleep lying on coiled rope than in my berth tonight.

I don't get better sleep. I get no sleep, actually, as I nestle amid the ropes and let the motion of the ship stir my thoughts to and fro like stew. I'm tired and thirsty and...and very alone.

"Are you waiting for me or hiding from me?" Domenic's voice caresses the silence an hour into my solitude. I jerk upright as he approaches my resting spot, the covered lantern in his hand letting the barest of light wash over the forgotten space.

"Neither." I'm wide awake now, my hands gripping my rope nest. Despite the poor lighting, I am acutely aware of Domenic's every motion, from the solid tap of his boots against the deck to the slight stoop of his shoulders as he ducks beneath the overhead beams, to the instinctive sway of his body to compensate for the rocking sea. "I'm just, err—"

"If the next word out of your mouth is *sleeping*, then you should devise a better lie."

"Resting?" My heart's insistent pounding muffles my thoughts. "Will you accept *thinking*?" That at least has the added benefit of being true.

Domenic reaches me in two long steps and crouches beside me. "Shall I leave you to your thoughts?"

Yes. No. I don't know. I rub my face.

I don't know what Domenic reads in my eyes, but after a moment of intense study, he hoists himself up beside me and, in a single fluid motion, lifts me into his lap.

His *lap*.

A gasp escapes me. I've seen sailors perch whores on their thighs, and strapping courtiers lift pretty girls, who giggle and wrap dainty arms around the men's necks—but Domenic's manhandling has a different feel to it. Confident and intimate. Possessive. Knowledgeable.

As for me, I've never been with a man, never even kissed one before three days ago when my lips locked with Domenic's in this very hold. *Waves and hail.* I watched Catsper strip himself naked on the deck this morning and felt not a tenth of the awkward discomfort that crawls over my skin now.

Domenic's arms tighten around me. "You don't have to be a warrior just now. Not with me. Tell me what you are thinking."

I couldn't do that even if I wanted to. In any case, it's impossible to concentrate amidst the ensemble of hard muscles pressing against me.

Domenic nuzzles my hair, taking a deep lungful of my scent before exhaling a warm breath that tickles my ear. On the deck above, the bell calls the time. The watch will be changing soon, and Domenic needs to go ensure the transition. There isn't any time for anything on this bloody ship.

"I don't want to *talk*," I rasp, lifting my face toward his.

Domenic's body shifts beneath me, tensing as if readying for battle. Or fighting itself. He inhales again, the tip of his nose brushing my cheek. "We will have time," he whispers, his voice raspy. "We will *make* time—"

My hands clutch his shirt and pull.

The hard angle of Domenic's jaw lowers to align with my mouth, which already prickles in anticipation of his lips' velvety warmth. His lips hover inches from mine, his body stone-still while the air around me is saturated with need. I growl softly, but Domenic remains poised, a captain awaiting the perfect moment before ordering the great guns to life. Inside me, however, the explosions are well on their way. I arch up toward him.

Domenic beats me to it. Like a sail suddenly filled with wind, his mouth descends on mine, his tongue claiming me with powerful strokes that send jolts of energy crackling over my skin. His fingers dig into my flesh, simultaneously crushing and holding me together as the scent of salt and brine fills my nose. It's all I can do to ride the wave of desire and excitement until my lungs burn in demand for air.

I grab Domenic's shirt as he pulls away to draw breath. There is no time to waste, not on a ship where discovery lurks in each shadow. Now that I've tasted him, I can't stop. Even my breasts feel different, full and tingly and altogether like nothing I've felt before. I twist in his hold so that I'm straddling his lap, my face in line with his.

Domenic catches my shoulders, his muscles quivering. "Nile," he whispers, his voice hoarse. He swears softly, and then his mouth is covering mine again, his tongue finding my own, his hands working themselves into the tangles of my hair.

My hands drop to his shoulders, my nails pressing into

muscle. My heart pounds. Closer. I want to be closer. Pushing off my knees, I press into Domenic, grinding my body against his as my hands fumble to open his jacket.

"Easy," he whispers, breaking the kiss to capture my wrists before my hands destroy his clothes.

I stare at him, panting as humiliation drowns excitement. "Why?" The word is out before I can stop them. He doesn't want me. The *why* of it is irrelevant at best and pitiful at worst. "I mean, of course. I—" I start to pull away from him, but Domenic's hold on my wrists tightens.

"I don't want a quick romp atop discarded rope with you, Nile," he says, watching my face. His chest heaves and his muscles are coiled tight as if fighting themselves for control. "The next time we call to port. We will take the day. The night. There will be time, and privacy and a *mattress*, storm and hail. I want to explore and savor you, to show you the pleasure your body can feel, not gulp you down like cheap grog." He drops one of my wrists and reaches for my face, his calloused fingers gentle against my cheek. "And after that... I don't know what we are going to do, Nile, not yet. But I will work it out. I promise. Now, I want to know what you're thinking."

That makes two of us. A waiting silence settles as Domenic gives me the chance to reclaim myself, but ship's bell beats me to speech. Above us, a string of curses and pounding feet announce the familiar commotion of seamen on the verge of mischief.

Domenic glances toward the overhead and curses under his breath.

"You need to go," I acknowledge, giving up my place atop his thighs.

He nods reluctantly. "Are you all right?" he asks, brushing a knuckle down my cheek.

No. Yes. Both. I don't know. I swallow, nod.

He rises in a fluid motion and straightens his uniform, the mask of cool command settling back on his face. A change of costume between numbers in a strange dangerous dance we play.

Especially when one of us is damaged goods and lying through her teeth about it.

"Domenic," I ask, taking cowardly advantage of his averted attention. "What would you think of a Gifted going to sea?"

He turns his face toward me. "Like your twin, Clay?"

I shake my head. "No, not someone so... Not a metal caller. But someone like Price." Saying Price's name reminds me that no one's checked in on the prisoner and his odd weather-foretelling Gift in some time. "Would you've made Price a part of the *Aurora*'s company if you could? You. Not Captain Rima or the admiralty or the Articles of the League. Just you." My shoulders tense as I lay that first stepping stone and await Domenic's answer. Granted, Price is a special case —harmless and more valuable to a seaman than a weather glass. Like I said. A stepping stone.

"No."

I jerk. That was not the hoped-for answer. "What?" I bristle in confusion. I must have misunderstood Domenic. Or he me. "Price foretold weather up to and including the quake. Why in the world not?"

Domenic frowns at the buttons on his coat as he ensures each is turned straight in its loops. "Would you take a terribly powerful gun with a defect into battle? Well," he concedes, "*you* just might. But since you asked for my personal opinion, then it's no. Not only would it upset the crew to have such a seaman in their midst, but also we know too little about the Gifted's magic, how and why it attracts the elements, how it's controlled.

49

The Gifted themselves know too little. It's possible that Price's presence itself triggered the earthquake. That his terrible accuracy predicting the weather is really rooted in his body's influencing the elements to begin with. If I had the choice, I'd have the boy off the ship as soon as it was safe."

I grapple for words and find myself sounding like a petulant child. "Ashing permits Gifted to serve aboard ships." Vetted, tested Gifted doing tasks their disability permits. Crippled sailors sometimes get employment too, if their skill far surpasses their invalidism. The crews never like it, though.

He shrugs. "I know, but Felielle does not. It's a calculated risk, one I think little worth the danger."

Felielle does not. As if that's an endorsement. How can the notions of a nation that is not even mine burn me so? My mother. Prince Tamiath. Ana. Domenic. "Felielle also put ashore its best captain last year upon learning he preferred men over women warming his bed."

Domenic shifts and frowns at me. "What's this really about, Nile? I presume you are neither divining a way of indoctrinating a Tirik Gifted prisoner into the Lyron League Navy nor worrying about your pillow preferences."

No. I'm worrying about your preferences, Domenic... "Nothing. I mean, you were right, I was thinking of Clay. What it might be like when I find a cure."

I rearrange myself in my nest of ropes, nowhere near as comfortable without Domenic's body. At least now I know. And since Domenic wants something more than a *quick romp in the ropes,* then what I'm doing—lying about what I am because I know the truth will make him walk away—it's wrong on the deepest of levels. Domenic deserves someone better than me.

CHAPTER 8

*I*t is one bell into the forenoon watch when Catsper comes to stand beside me at the rail. I feel Domenic's gaze on my back, as it has intermittently been all morning. It's tearing me in two, what he and I did last night in the cargo hold. Half of me, like some awakened primal animal, wants to pounce on him and let the world and consequences and the phantom perfect room in a port of call be damned. Just the thought of his hands on me, touching my back, sliding possessively over my neck, makes my body arc. The other half, the one that still has morals and remembers basic decency, demands I respect Domenic's wish. He wants nothing to do with a Gifted, wants no Gifted on his ship at all. Though he doesn't know it, Domenic doesn't want me.

Perhaps if he'd just wanted fun and physicality, that quick romp, it might have worked. But as it is... As it is, I need to work a way out of this mess with as little hurt to everyone as possible. That private room ashore where Domenic was going to show me all the things our bodies can do, it's as much a mirage as his promise of a plan and future for us. Just as the version of me that he thinks real is an illusion – one that I can never permit him to approach close enough to discern.

I never knew that it could hurt so much to lose what I don't even have yet.

"When will we drop anchor?" Catsper asks, examining the approaching shoreline. The jagged wounds of cracked rocks and uprooted trees left by the earthquake mar the land's silhouette. The Crystal Oasis and its fresh water are hidden from sight, but increasing vegetation confirms our location.

I consider the tide and wind. "An hour or so. It would be wise to stay deeper than we usually might as the quake may have changed the shallows. A longer row for the boat crews, but better that than risk harming the rudder, or worse, running the ship aground."

Indeed, all hands are already on deck, the boat crews at the ready. Hauling barrels of water from Crystal will be brutal, but the men in the work parties will be the first to drink their fill. The thirst in their eyes gives them a wild aura. Thatch Lawrence and Ana, who will each command one of the boats going ashore, inspect the vessels, ensuring that water casks stacked inside are intact. Well, Thatch Lawrence does. Ana goes through the motions. A tension that has nothing to do with thirst hangs over both middies.

"Lice giving you any more trouble?" I ask Catsper.

The marine grins at me. From the corner of my vision, I see Domenic stiffen as Catsper stretches with a predator's lazy calm. "No. I half wish there were. I think I'd enjoy squashing any critters that came my way."

A too-familiar clearing of the throat snags my attention. I turn to see Domenic leaning casually against the shrouds, his attention on me. I wonder what he makes of the distanced morning between us, whether he might be glad for it.

As our gazes meet, Domenic nods toward the ratlines. A small, barely perceptible demand. *Go up.*

Storms. That's what he wants to say to me after last night? Go climb the shrouds? Never mind that I was just thinking about the need to cool things between us. This isn't what I want, Domenic trying to resolve my nonexistent fear of heights. Especially when the truth is so much more damning.

I shift my weight, exaggerating my limp. *Leave me alone. My leg hurts.*

His jaw tightens. *I know you are lying.*

"I could be wrong, but your excuse seems to be wearing a bit thin," Catsper says with quiet dryness. "Or were you planning on asking me to actually break the ankle for you?"

I give him a filthy gesture and make my way to Ana's boat. If she isn't going to check it properly, someone needs to.

Catsper keeps step beside me. "If you are looking for other people's jobs to do, I have a few Spades who'll gladly give you their latrine-cleaning duty."

"We call it a *head* on a ship."

"Well, that changes everything."

I haul myself into the boat. My blood is hot, and I'm grateful for a chance to shove things around without anyone taking great notice.

"Why are you doing Lionitis's job?" Catsper demands quietly.

"Because the alternative is a potential problem with water casks."

"Horseshit."

"No. Truth." I sigh and lean back against one of the casks.

Catsper hops over the side in a smooth arc and lands lightly beside me. Waiting.

Catsper is surprisingly easy to talk to. Maybe because little seems to surprise him. Ever. More likely because I'm not thinking about his lips when I look at him. Plus, he keeps his mouth shut without being asked. "Ana suspects my identity, and is little inspired," I tell him, surprised at the relief my words bring. "In her mind, I'm a hypocrite who abandoned my family. She does not wish to hear me talk of duty, so I'm rather certain my suggestions on checking casks would be little welcome."

"She told you she suspects." The marine's voice snaps, and my relief withers. I'm no longer glad for the privacy of the ship's boat. "When?"

I frown. "Yesterday."

"Then why in the name of storms do I only learn of it now?" he growls, the contained tension of his body as volatile as gunpowder.

Luckily, Catsper isn't the first irate officer I've ever dealt with. I put my hands on my hips. "Why should you?"

"Because I can't protect you if I don't know what I'm protecting you from."

Not the words I expected. "Protect me?" I realize I sound like a daft parrot and shake myself. "Why the hell are you protecting me? And what from?"

"You've at least half a brain. Look at my uniform and work it out."

For an abysmal moment, I wonder if my mother's reach has somehow extended to the backwaters of Siaman, but no. I look at Catsper. A Spade lieutenant in the black uniform of the League's most elite fighters. Catsper's duty is to win the war.

"You need to train with me," Catsper has said upon learning of the Second Fleet's destruction.

"She already trains with you."

"More. You know a lot, Ash. If you are captured, too much is at stake."

Right. Catsper is protecting me because he believes me important to the war effort. I rub the bridge of my nose. "I'm flattered."

"I don't care."

I shrug. "I'm not the princess of Ashing anymore, Catsper," I say without heat. Not an argument. Just simple truth. "The facts in my head must not make it to the Tirik, but as for the rest of my life... Nile Ash is not worthy of a Spade's protection." Without waiting for his answer, I pull myself from the boat.

Ana smiles brightly. At Catsper, not at me. It dawns on me that the elongated conversation with the marine Ana fancies did little to ingratiate me with her. The stiff set of Domenic's shoulders says he isn't thrilled about it either. A historical moment, really, of Ana and Domenic being of one mind. I'd roll my eyes if I wasn't running on thin ice already.

"I have seen little of Rum today," Ana says. "Is he well?"

Catsper stares at her coolly. "He's busy."

Ana blinks in obvious confusion, and Catsper uses the pause to put a hand between my shoulder blades and maneuver us past. His usual stony expression gives no hint as to whether the action is intended as a jab at me or Ana—provided Catsper is aware of what he is doing at all.

Ana's face darkens. "I do not believe we'll require the Spades on a water run, Lieutenant Catsper," she calls after us. Her tone is perfectly respectful, a mix of courtesy due a higher rank outside her chain of command and assertion of a weighed opinion. It is also a transparent attack, launched blindly. Catsper was abrupt with her, and she'll deny his Spades early access to water. *Idiot.*

"When I desire your insight, I'll ask for it, Lionitis," says Catsper.

Ana's brows narrow. She touches her hat in acknowledgment and then turns and walks to Captain Rima.

I curse softly though I little worry for myself just now. The problem with blackmail is that once you make good on your threat, the benefit ends. She will not reveal her suspicions on account of Catsper's rudeness. She will wait for a desired time to play such a card.

Catsper's face is unreadable. He leaves me, and a few steps later, he is beside Thatch Lawrence, talking softly. I catch the words *Kederic* and *stay alert,* on Catsper's lips. Thatch Lawrence looks pale, but nods dutifully to the marine.

Rima walks toward the pair, his hand on Ana's shoulder. "Mr. Catsper."

The marine straightens and inclines his head toward the captain. "Sir?"

"I wish to maximize the room in the boats for our water reserves. The middies shall choose several of the strongest men to take with them. Unless you believe your boys will be able to haul more than men of Johina's and Mic's size, I'd prefer to keep them shipside."

"Aye, sir." The marine manages to sound bored. "I'll recall the detail."

Ana and Rima both smile, but their smiles are nothing alike. Except I don't think Ana sees it.

CHAPTER 9

There is more waiting once Ana's and Thatch Lawrence's boats depart for Crystal Oasis. Rum comes up on deck, looking as friendly as always. I'm tempted to growl right back at him, but I know he's as miserable as the rest of us. Except he doesn't know that water is soon at hand. I've a little water left in my canteen, and I shake it before him. "You can have this if you promise not to bite me for it," I tell him.

Rum whimpers.

Guilt twists me. He thinks I'm teasing him. I open the canteen and hold it low, letting the awful beast lap the remainder of my ration. Once the canteen is empty, Rum gives it a final sniff and swaggers away.

"Ungrateful monster," I mumble.

With Rum gone and no one paying much heed to me just now, I open my magic slightly, just enough to let the worst of the building pressure release. A small swoosh of wind answers, doing a small dance around the deck before scampering off across the waves. It's no candle extinguishing the Diante healer had set as my target, but it's better than anything I could even contemplate before. I'll pay for this in convulsions later, but that can't be helped. Only concealed. I reach for the magic again, this time tweaking it so my stream of air hits chosen targets across the deck. I won't be showing off my skills anytime soon, but—

I freeze, my attention riveted to the figure climbing up the companionway ladder. Dressed in a full uniform, Kederic moves slowly across the deck. His left arm is bound tightly to his body and he uses his right hand to grip the rail as he walks.

Several Spades spread out around him as if by happenstance. Not just him, I realize; they spread around me too. And the twins. Over the whole damn deck. Now that the middie's reappearance brought the marines' subtle guardianship to my attention, I realize they'd been at it for days. Ever since the assault on Kederic. Catsper is taking no chances.

"How are you feeling, sir?" I ask, touching my hat.

Kederic nods at me. Though suffering lines his face, there is also a fierceness of purpose in it. "I heard we had a lice problem while I napped." A corner of his mouth twitches. "I also heard we're unlikely to have one again. I'm sorry I wasn't there to help evict the creatures, but I'll try to make up for it next time."

My answering grin is cut short by movement along the shore's silhouette. The boats are pushing off, the seamen rowing for all they are worth. In another ship, I'd think their extra diligence an effort to impress the officers or answer the plea of a thirsty crew. But on the *Aurora*, sailors don't do that. On the *Aurora*, I think something is wrong.

I am at the rail, waiting for the boats to come close enough to discern what's happened. I count heads and find them short. Ice slithers down my chest. Then there is shouting. Ana's boat pulls by the *Aurora* first, her voice calling for a hoist to be rigged. In her arms, she cradles the ashen body of Thatch Lawrence.

No.

The crews of both boats are shaken, even Mic and Johina, who shove less experienced hands from their way and tie a makeshift harness around the middie themselves. I watch Thatch Lawrence lifted into the air and hear Rima's voice ask the question I've not dared voice.

"Is he alive?"

Ana's voice is admirably stable. "Barely, sir."

"What happened?" Rima demands. His nostrils flare. Either he's a superb actor, or he really has not ordered a murder.

"An accident, sir," Johina says quickly. Earnestly. "A slipped water cask pushed Mr. Thatch Lawrence into the water and his leg got caught in the roots. By the time we managed to pull him out..." His voice trails off, the apple in his throat bobbing as he swallows.

No, Rima never ordered his henchmen to kill Thatch Lawrence. Deaths bring too much attention from the admiralty and in the end, Rima needs an obedient crew, not a dead one. I think Rima wanted the middie frightened enough to be malleable, and Johina had sorely miscalculated. *That's* why he and Mic are fretting so over the accident.

The hands place Thatch Lawrence on the deck. His chest rises occasionally, but the rest of him flops limply. Under Ana's direction, two seamen take him below. I start to follow.

"Ash!" Domenic's voice cuts my steps. "Get this water unloaded, if you please."

I touch my forehead and change course, ordering men into work parties and setting an orderly means of all drinking their fill without ripping open more barrels than we must. Grudgingly, I concede that Domenic is right to have kept me

59

here. There is nothing I can do belowdecks now, and this isn't the time for questions. But that time will come. And from the hard cast of Catsper's face, I know I'm not the only one waiting for it.

I've no chance to speak to Catsper or Domenic the rest of the day, and when I come into my berth that evening, Ana is sobbing into her knees.

Part of me is glad for it. If not for her childish manipulations, Catsper's Spades would have been on the boats. The better part of me kneels beside her instead. We aren't friends. But we used to be.

"Ana."

She looks up over her hands. Her face is puffy and red. Tears stream down her cheeks and wet her shirt. She tries speaking, but no words emerge. Only hysterical gasps.

My heart drops.

"Thatch Lawrence... He died, didn't he?" I whisper, though I already know the answer. Fourteen years old. So full of promise and life. So eager to learn everything he could. Blinking my own stinging eyes, I put my hands on either side of Ana's head, feeling her convulsions of grief through my palms. "I'm so sorry," I whisper.

She jerks, her voice a rising thunder. "An apology won't bring him back. Won't undo what you did."

I lean away from her.

"This is your fault!" Ana shouts. She stands, her teeth clenched together. "Your fault, you hear. You killed him, Nile." The words grow garbled and choked. "You talked us into crossing the captain. You should have known better. Of all people, you should have known better."

Hugging herself, Ana runs from the berth while I recoil from the blow.

THE DAY IS MOCKINGLY PERFECT. Plenty of drinking water, clear skies, seas smooth as ice, a warm brisk wind filling the *Aurora*'s sails. Domenic insists on sweating in his uniform jacket, but everyone else wears shirtsleeves. Including Captain Rima, who swaggers across the deck without a care in the world.

The menace rolling off the captain is so palpable that my pulse quickens in response. He even grins at Catsper, showing the marine a full set of crooked teeth. You'd think the bloody man had just won a battle against the Tirik fleet instead of killed a fourteen-year-old boy. The crew is quiet, though Johina and his ilk are reclaiming their usual enthusiasm at an accelerated pace. None of the middies talk, not even Kederic, though he stands as tall on the quarterdeck as his injuries allow.

The *Aurora*, with the *Hope* under her wing, is heading back west across the Siaman Sea to where it meets the Ardent Ocean and another current, called the Diante Corridor. I'm enough of a mess that when Domenic catches me alone in a momentarily isolated passageway, I let myself collapse into his arms.

"It isn't your fault," he says firmly into my hair, as if he can see right through my mind to the accusation Ana's voice had branded there. His breath is warm, and his hands stroke my back in long soothing strokes. Where my cheek presses against his chest, I feel the strong, steady rhythm of his heart. Despite myself, my eyes begin to sting.

Domenic takes my chin in his hand and forces my face up toward his. "Not your fault," he repeats. "You understand?"

I nod without believing it.

He sighs. "We keep going forward. We have to keep going forward. Right, *lieutenant*?"

I swallow, collecting myself enough to rise to the

expectation and demand of Domenic's words. In Ashing, I had thought a man would make me less of a warrior. But Domenic is doing the opposite, pushing and shoving me to stand upright when all I want to do is curl in on myself and sob. "Catsper's transport may not be coming as planned," I say. My words sound flat, but at least they take root in real thoughts instead of viscous grief, and as I speak them, I begin to slowly reclaim my mind. "It depends how far the earthquake reached. If we lost more ships, there might not be one to spare to collect a training unit."

Domenic nods. "We'll speak with him tonight. In the Cove. All right?" Boots sound against wooden planks, and Domenic steps away smoothly without daring to wait for my reply. "Get back on deck, Ash," he calls over his shoulder. "You've work to do."

It turns out Domenic wasn't just talking for the sake of ship's ears when he ordered me back to deck. Shortly after clearing the companionway ladder, I find Domenic standing beside the mainmast, a spyglass slung over his shoulder and a determined set to his gaze.

"There you are," he says.

My body tenses. "Aye, sir?"

Domenic tilts his face toward the shrouds, a barely noticeable movement that chases clear all my thoughts.

Annoyance and terror filling me in equal measure, I remain rooted to the deck.

"Ash," Domenic calls again. This time, there is nothing subtle about it.

I rub my ankle, then cross my arms, meeting his gaze with a hard one of my own. *I'm not fish bait. Let me alone.*

He furrows his brows and swings his looking glass from his

back, holding it out to me. "Take a turn at the lookout platform, if you please," he says, loudly enough for all to hear.

I freeze. *No.* But it's too late. He's said it. A clear order from the first officer given before the crew. And the last seaman to refuse Domenic's order was Rory, who'd declined to mount the rigging in a storm and was flogged for it. My chin jerks toward Domenic.

Dominic's expression is confident and reassuring. He wants me to climb up, to conquer my fear of heights after an unfortunate fall. And he has no notion of just how wrong he is.

Damn you, Domenic. Damn you to the ocean's depth.

I walk toward him. One slow step after another. My hands are damp with sweat, but there isn't a choice now that he's given an order. No choice at all. I take the offered glass and for a moment meet his eyes, letting anger, fear, and betrayal show in my gaze. I'd asked him to lay off this and trust my judgment, and he refused.

"You'll be all right," he says quietly.

I say nothing. My voice will give me away if I try. My chest is tight, and my stomach clenches into a rock. I settle the glass across my back and walk to the shrouds with the fierce determination of an animal. Others' attentions are on me now. Curious. Confused. Excited by the smell of fear and boiling blood, even without understanding its cause.

My hands close around the shrouds. The ropes' familiar give is inviting. I've climbed this rigging so many times, I can scamper through it in blind darkness. Or with a tender ankle. I can do anything so long as my jerking spells keep silent.

I slow my breaths. I have to keep calm. Once I'm on the platform, I'll tie myself in. Simple and smooth. Just a bit of rope to conquer before then, preferably with body and dignity both intact. With a push, I launch myself into the rigging. My heart is fluttering fast and hard. One step. Two. I falter.

I'd fallen the last time I was up here. That the convulsion struck me when it did and not moments earlier is the only reason I still live. The ropes sway. There is something about the openness, the clear pass to my element that rings a warning in my ears.

Domenic is right, I am bloody frightened of the shrouds now. My breathing races. I am a man's height off the deck, climbing up with reckless abandon as the wind rips around me. Calling to me. Demanding my answer.

Not now, I beg it. But it won't listen. It has me out in the open for the first time in too many days, and it's hungry for me. And me for it. My left ankle buckles harder than I expect, and I catch myself with my right foot. My arms grip the ropes. Something is wrong. I know it in the darkness of my mind, in that space behind my eyes that once threatened to crack my skull with building pressure.

I'm not just frightened. I'm terrified.

I don't know whether a jerking spell waits in the wings or if it's raw fear of it that shakes me. But I know that a convulsion would make my right side useless, and my left ankle will fail if it must support my body weight alone. The spells have hit me twice out here. I grip the ratlines hard, but I still feel the helplessness and see myself falling falling falling.

I'm stalled in place. And shaking. And my eyes are closed.

I open them.

Domenic is staring at me, bewildered. His certain confidence is gone, and his face is begging me to please keep going.

Rima steps up beside him, smiling like a cat with a bowl of

cream. "Is there a problem, Mr. Dana?" he asks. "I was certain I heard you order Ash to the lookout platform."

Domenic is very still and stoic. He knows something is wrong. And he is right.

A numbness settles over me. If I continue now, I think I will die. Not a worthwhile death of battle, but an empty one born of fear and pride. I have a choice. I can die, or I can bleed.

I climb down.

CHAPTER 10

I stand alone in my berth, staring at nothing. I
disobeyed an officer's order. An order I had daftly
lulled myself into believing Domenic would not issue. *Storms.*
His solid presence beside me felt so good that it made me
stupid. It turned me blind to the consequences of my secret, and
the chain of command, and our births. If I'd stayed away from
Domenic, as was right, I'd have long ago convinced one of the
middies to officially assign me deck-only duties.

I swallow and rub my sweaty palms over my trousers. Too
late for that now.

The door behind me flies open and shuts with a slam.

I flinch.

"Nile."

I turn, registering Domenic looming over me.

"You lied to me." A storm rages in his face. "I asked you,
Nile, and you looked me in the eyes and lied. You think you're
the first seaman to grow wary of heights after a fall? I would
have helped you. We would have worked through it together."

67

"I told you I needed to work through it myself." I cross my arms, my anger rising to meet his. "Instead, you decided you know better than I what's good for me. Again. You are like my mother, thinking that if you force me to follow your version of propriety, I'll realize my previous folly."

"I'm not your mother—I am the first officer of this ship," he growls. "And I'm responsible for this crew, of which you are a part. Taking you into my arms didn't change that."

"So you send me to the lookout platform with a glass, like you would fish bait. Like Catsper did to young Penn."

"It's a proven and humane trick," Domenic snaps back at me. "And it works."

"Clearly."

Domenic pinches the bridge of his nose, his other hand balled tight at his side. When he looks at me again, his face is stone. "We shall hold Captain's Mast at noon tomorrow. Present yourself to deck then."

The door shuts behind him, and I sink to the deck, shaking. I'd wanted his arms around me, whispers of courage. Of love. But that isn't what happened. It was my fault. Had I been smarter and stronger, I'd have ensured Commander Dana never looked at Nile Ash long enough to notice anything amiss. But I was neither.

The door creaks open sometime later, and Ana steps into the berth. She hugs her shoulders and looks at me as if deciding what to say.

My face is blank as I stare back. The friendship we'd once had was a mistake. It is time to plug what leaks I can before my ship of life sinks.

"Captain Rima would like to see you," she says finally.

I don't ask why. She would have told me if she wished. "Thank you, ma'am," I say instead and walk past her down the passageway, my stomach telling me that the day is bound to get worse yet.

~

"Ms. Asʜ." Rima smiles when I enter and points an open palm at a high-back chair. *Relax and lean back while you still can.*

I sit on the edge, each of my senses as alert as a hawk's. No. As a hawk's prey. "Thank you, sir."

"I was sorry to see your difficulties today," the captain says with that compassionate voice I know better than to trust. "Had I known Mr. Dana's intentions, I'd have pointed out your injury to him before things got out of hand."

I keep my face politely attentive. There has to be a reason for this meeting beyond demonizing Domenic, which can be accomplished before a larger audience at tomorrow's Mast.

He taps his hand against his table. "Perhaps..." Rima pauses as if the thought he is about to share is just occurring to him now. "Perhaps we've placed you at an ill-suited post. I understand you read and write quite well and can give even the middies a run when it comes to mathematics. If what I've heard of these achievements is not inflated too greatly, perhaps a clerking position would answer better than your present tasks." He smiles slightly. "I've no clerk now, you see, and I suffer terribly for it."

The hair on the back of my neck rises with each of Rima's easy words. Rima despises me. He knows damn well I played a hand in undermining his authority the night of the quake and that I've disturbed the plans of his precious Eflians more than once. So what game is he playing? Why offer me an intimate station? And why now, instead of waiting until after tomorrow's Mast, when I'm weakest?

Because today he has leverage. He knows I fear what awaits me at Mast and that he can protect me from it. Because he wants something specific in exchange.

"I will serve the *Aurora* in the best way I can," I say with a bow. "What would you have me do, sir?"

His smile widens. "Well, first, let us examine your knowledge of the basics. Will you point out the kingdoms and their ports on my chart?"

I knuckle my forehead and carefully do as instructed, keeping my answers to the major dockings any merchant would know of. The rules of this game are a mystery still, and I know I better find them out quickly.

"Surely you can do better than that," Rima chides. "I presume you've spent time on a naval vessel before coming to the *Aurora*?"

I can hardly deny that after my recent performance. "Aye, sir. On the *Maylian*." Named after my late aunt, I don't add. My answer is true enough. I did serve on the small *Maylian* for a spell, before she was decommissioned. It was a short, safe stint ferrying messages all over the Lyron waters—the only duty that placated my mother after my brother Omar's death.

Rima nods, unsurprised. "And show me the ports the *Maylian* docked in."

The military ports. I hesitate. As a League captain, Rima would be privy to the location of these already. Most of them, anyway. I bow and trace my finger along the military routes, skipping over only the handful of the most sensitive Ashing holdings.

"Where else?" Rima snaps. "I'm in little mood to repeat myself. *Maylian* is an Ashing ship. Certainly she docked in more places. Or is your memory too faulty for such simplicity?"

I understand the message well. *Identify the sensitive ports or declare yourself unworthy of being my clerk. And of my protection.* But is he testing me for information he knows or fishing for insight the admiralty did not condescend to give him? His wife's portrait looks down at me, and I lean toward the latter option. The lady is forever maneuvering for admission to courts she has no standing in, and it would little surprise me to believe the same of her husband.

"That's all I recall, sir," I say with what I hope sounds like apology. I may have run from Ashing, but I'm not about to discuss our secrets. "If you give me the evening to research, I will have a better answer for you at once." It's a lie, of course. There is no better answer to be found in Rima's manuals, but it seems fitting.

Rima sighs and steeples his hands on the tabletop. "I need a clerk who will know her duty and her environment, Ash. I have little time for instruction or research projects." He tilts his head, studying me. Weighing. Deciding what value I might have, what I might be able to offer in return for his patronage.

"Well," he says after a few moments. "Discretion is the better part of valor. I value discretion." His hands lower, his fingertips drumming the table. Then he stops and nods to himself. "Very well. Let us speak of something else. It is important for a captain to feel the pulse of his crew, to know its irritations before they become conflicts, to resolve discord before it requires discipline. Would you agree with that?"

I follow the change in direction without moving a muscle. A new proposal. I need not betray Ashing's secrets - I can betray those of the *Aurora*'s crew instead. *Storms and hail.* This won't end well.

"Ash?" Rima prods gently. Almost kindly. "I asked you a question."

"Aye, sir," I make my voice high and obliviously perky. "Very important, sir."

His mouth twitches. "Are you observant, Ash?"

"Oh yes, sir. Very much so."

"Let us see." The captain leans back in his chair. "What can you tell me of..." He studies the overhead beams as if deciding which inconsequential name to throw my way, while I play the game, waiting to find out whose confidence Rima would demand I betray to save myself. He snaps his finger. "Of Lieutenant Catsper, let us say. What can you tell me of him?"

CHAPTER 11

"*And* what did you tell him?" Catsper asks beneath the constant rumble of boys' voices that give the Cove its ironic privacy.

"That you have an evil dog who wishes him dead." Sitting on the deck, I cross my legs beneath me. Rum rubs his ear against my knee, but growls when I try to pet him. I rub my temple instead. Captain's Mast is two hours away, I've not slept the night, and I am more terrified with each bell. "Bloody hell, Catsper, what do you think I told him? That I would be his bloody informant? I played a daft imbecile until he threw me out of the cabin."

Catsper's face is dark. "Did you tell Dana?"

A new wave of anxiety hits my gut. No. I've avoided so much as eye contact with Domenic since he'd left my berth. Point of fact, with the notable exception of the captain, I've spoken to no one but Catsper. I shake my head once and study my boots.

Catsper sighs and leans back on outstretched arms, studying me lazily. "Did you two get stupid?"

I should know better than to be surprised, but my chest clenches despite itself. "You think hauling someone before Mast is the latest fashion in courting?"

His expression remains steady. "I think that Dana's recent pallor has nothing to do with a lack of sunlight."

I twitch in surprise. "It little matters now," I say. A catch in Catsper's brow suggests he may not agree, but I can't bear to continue speaking of Domenic. "What make you of Rima's summons?"

"The offer of protection doesn't shock me. Rima takes pains to ensure the core of the crew is loyal to him personally. The specific questions he asked I must think further on."

I'm certain Catsper's *thinking* will happen outside the Cove, but I find myself unable to continue the conversation. My thoughts struggle with the growing nagging in my chest and stomach and such that even most basic logic slips from my grasp. I chew my nail and give the marine an ambiguous nod.

"You are frightened," he says with irritating calm.

"Wouldn't you be?" I snap. Though for all I know, maybe not.

Catsper raises his brows. "I would little look forward to it." He angles his chin up and calls out to one of the Spades on the other side of the room. "Penn! Remove your shirt."

The boy unquestioningly bares his torso.

I inhale sharply. Thin scars cross his skin. *Waves and hail.* He is just a boy. "What had he done?" I ask Catsper.

"Nothing." Catsper motions Penn to get dressed. "It is part of Spades' training to learn to endure pain. As you can see, we are all still alive. As you will be."

"You're all mad," I whisper.

74

"Perhaps. But we fight well." Catsper crosses his arms. "You've landed into this predicament of your own choice, Ash. Whether you succumb to or learn from it is your choice as well."

"Learn what?" My voice drips venom. I didn't expect Catsper to patronize me, of all things. "The concept of an order? Or action and consequence? Or maybe the rules of the navy?"

"Learn to survive." Catsper rolls to his feet and holds his hand out to me. "Enough talking. We've an hour to work on your wrestling before festivities begin."

He never asks me why I defied Domenic's command in the first place.

I STAND before the entire ship's company, my heart pounding in my ears. *Survive,* Catsper's voice says in my mind. *Survive.*

The officers look down at me from the poop deck. Rima. Kazzik. Domenic. Catsper. The middies. A boy with a drum. Behind me, separated by a line of black-clad marines, the seamen press together. Around me, though, there is space. So much space. I clasp my hands together behind my back, squeezing as tight as I can. My heart pounds so hard, I'm certain the whole ship hears the beat.

"And what have you now, Mr. Dana?" Rima asks. His voice is that steady, careful mixture of firmness and compassion that doesn't reach his eyes. He knows exactly what's before him. And he loves it.

My gaze shifts to Domenic. His face is stoic as it always is, but his fists are curled tight at his sides. In spite of what Catsper said, I am afraid. Very, very afraid.

"Seaman Ash refused a direct order to ascend into the rigging," says Domenic.

ALEX LIDELL

Rima waves his hand. He wants Domenic to continue presiding over Captain's Mast. I'm little surprised. Rima knows how to extract the greatest benefit from agony.

Domenic's throat bobs.

You know what scares me? That one day you will do something in front of the crew, or fail to keep your mouth shut, or bloody forget where you are, and I will have no choice but to hurt you.

Except he had a choice. Not now, but yesterday, when he chose to treat me like a middie, to send me up into the rigging for my own bloody good. When he thought he knew better than me.

"Have you anything to say, Ash?" Domenic asks.

I think I catch a slight emphasis on *anything*. Domenic is throwing me a lifeline, but I've nothing to grip it with. A bead of sweat trickles down the side of my face. The grating is already rigged in the middle of the deck, and the smoldering fear in my chest flares through me. This can't be happening, my stomach pleads with me. Not to me.

But it can and it is and it will. Princess Nile of Ashing would never suffer such a fate, but Seaman Nile Ash opened herself up to it when she enlisted. Of all people, I well knew the discipline common sailors in the navy live under when I chose to make my stand among them. This is a test. If I cannot face this, there is little point in pretending I can sustain the naval future I've chosen. And even less point in everything I've done up to now.

"Ms. Ash," Domenic snaps. "I asked if you had anything to say."

I tighten the hold I have on my wrist and hold up my head. "No, sir." I'm pleased at the steadiness of my voice.

76

"Have the officers anything to say on Nile Ash's behalf?" he asks of his colleagues.

Silence. Then I see Ana shift her weight, leaning out to look at the captain. Her eyes are wide. She's expecting something she is not getting. Ana's gaze flickers between Rima and me, and I see her draw breath.

Catsper's hand closes around Ana's wrist, so subtly that I would have missed it had he not taught me the move. He is pressing a pressure point, and by Ana's sudden gasp, I know he has hit it perfectly.

She snaps her mouth shut.

A momentary relief washes over me. Like Catsper, I little trust whatever Ana was about to say to be of aid. The moment is over too quickly, though, as Domenic speaks again.

"Very well. One dozen lashes," he says clearly from behind a mask of duty. "Remove your coat."

My head swims. I numbly pull off my coat, leaving a thin white undershirt that flaps in the wind. By custom, women are permitted to keep a thin shirt on through punishment for modesty's sake—though wearing a chest band beneath is forbidden. Two Spades stride up and secure my wrists to the grating. "You'll be all right, Nile," Penn whispers quickly, before he has to step away. "The waiting is the worst part."

I hope he's right. I've witnessed many seamen take a dozen cuts without making a sound. I've no choice about the fate of my back, but I do have a say in holding together my dignity. *Survive.* I find Catsper's gaze, solid and reassuring, and hold on to it.

Domenic clears his throat and turns toward the bosun's mate I know is behind me, holding the red cat-'o-nine-tails satchel. "Do your duty," he says coolly.

I lean my forehead against the metal and tense.

77

"Hold!" Rima's voice calls.

My breath catches. I strain my neck to see what's happened, but find only officers' and middies' puzzled expressions.

"Johina," Rima says with cold, pleased calm. "You wield the cat, if you please."

Storms. My heart refuses to beat as feet shuffle and murmurs prick the silence behind me. Footsteps approach and Johina's breath heats the back of my neck. He makes a show of checking my bindings. "I'll make you scream, girl," he whispers. "Scream and beg for your mother."

I'm not so daft as to answer back, but I grit my teeth and promise myself silence. Johina will not be the only one paying attention. I've heard muteness at the grating earns respect in the lower decks. I've also heard the hands place bets. I don't want to know what the odds are on me.

Just when I expect Johina to step away, he grabs the top of my shirt and rips the back open down the middle in a single rough tear. A petty cruelty since the threadbare covering would have offered little protection against the cat, but the brush of air against my suddenly exposed skin makes me feel stripped naked. I shudder and grip Catsper's gaze as hard as I can.

I barely hear Domenic reissue the order to start, but the rustling of the cat leaving its bag is deafening.

Survive.

The drum roll starts.

The pressure of the first crack comes before the pain. I gasp. Penn was wrong. Waiting isn't the worst part at all.

"One," a marine boy calls.

Panic rolls through me. I can't do this.

The next strike lands, taking the air from my lungs. I can't look at Catsper. I can't look anywhere. The hold I have on my body slips, exposing something I fear to see. *Wait!* I yell silently. *I need a break. I just need a short break.*

"Three."

I catch the small inflection in the Spade's voice, telling me to hold on. I think he sees the thread I'm hanging by. But I can't. I scream. We are only at three, and I scream like I never have in my life.

Johina snickers.

I imagine Catsper shaking his head, though he stands statue still, and I swear I hear the smiles of the hands who'd bet against me. A bit of blood drips from Domenic's clenched fists, where his nails must have pierced skin. A great deal more blood snakes down my back. It splatters on the ruined shirt hanging off my shoulders and soaks the back of my pants.

I know I must pull myself together, to reclaim what shreds of dignity I have left. But I only yell louder and flail against my bonds, as if escape from the ropes can save me.

When the green lights flash and the convulsions come, I discover that I can howl through a jerking spell.

By the end, I don't yell anymore. I hang limp, unable to fight or scream or hold myself up. The cat continues to fall in its horrid, slow rhythm, but I think it's striking someone else. Blood collects on the deck, the dark red droplets on the wooden planks.

"Twelve," the marine announces, and immediately Domenic orders my bonds cut away.

I crumple. The deck hits my cheek.

The company is dismissed. I am too. But I don't move. I don't even make an attempt to help myself. It hurts. *Storms*, it hurts. And I've no pride left to grip on to.

After a short while, it is Catsper and Penn who slide arms

under me and help me to the infirmary, laying me facedown on the cot. No other patients are there.

But Domenic is.

I turn my face toward the bulkhead.

"I need to bring a few things from the Cove," Catsper says with his usual practicality and leaves with Penn in tow.

I hear rustling. Water pouring into a basin. A slippery sensation as Domenic pulls the bloody flaps of my ruined shirt open. An intake of breath. "Goddess."

His hands are gentle, but tightly reined anger clips his words. "Why, Nile?"

I hope he doesn't expect an answer, because I have none to give him. I swallow, saying nothing as I listen to the splash of washcloth in the basin and feel the touch of salt water against broken skin.

It hurts, and I jerk. "Don't, please," I beg. Yes, beg. As Johina predicted. Domenic was right when he said my princess self would never survive the lower decks. I'd given myself too much credit, and today the bill came due. "Please." I whimper into my arms. "Please."

I don't know what I expect, but the cloth withdraws. A creak of movement. And then Domenic silently pulls me into his arms.

The comfort is too great to resist. I want to be held, to pretend the illusion is real. So I willingly accept the lie and press my face into his shoulder, sobbing as Domenic rocks me until Catsper returns.

And even then I won't let go. My fingers dig into Domenic, resisting any attempt to lay me flat on the cot. Finally, Domenic shifts his arms to keep me against him and still while Catsper rips away the rest of my shirt and tends to the wounds with disturbing competence. I can't even bring myself to care that I'm topless as each sting of salt still cuts horridly into ravaged flesh. I flinch to get clear of the pain each time the cloth returns.

"This will take longer if you fight," says Catsper. Not a rebuke, just a statement of fact.

Domenic's lips brush across my ear. "Can you hear the sea?" he asks softly. Shifting his hold to free one hand, he strokes my hair. "The waves rushing to kiss the hull, then falling back into foam? The heartbeat of the sea. Listen. Can you hear lub dub of the water?" He continues the gentle murmur while Catsper works and I hold fast to Domenic, his voice even when my mind refuses to understand the words' meaning.

I'm shaking with pain and humiliation when the last of the bandages is tucked into place.

Domenic brushes the back of his hand against my tears. "It's all right. It's over now."

No. It isn't. I pull away from him, hissing as I move to claim my own space on the cot.

He extends his hand toward me, but I shift from his reach, and he pulls back, his gaze pained.

"Thanks to Johina's efforts, Ash's back is worse than it had to be," says Catsper, his voice its usual calm self, though he speaks of me in the third person. Perhaps I'm no longer worthy of a direct address. "Rima's intentions were more severe still, however."

Domenic stiffens. "What do you mean?"

"I checked the cat before the Mast and found a steel-tipped one in its place. I took the liberty of correcting the error."

I draw a halting breath. A steel-tipped cat is reserved for thieves, the worst offenders in close-quarter living. It would have flayed me open to the bone. Small as I am, it may have crippled me.

"Rima," Domenic growls. "The dozen were for the refused order; Johina and the steel for manipulating Rima's ship."

Catsper nods. "I want Ash to stay in the Cove for the present."

The Cove? Leaving aside the agony of moving, much less walking, I am not exactly dying for an audience of adolescent boys who think pain is a pillar of solid training. I want to lick my wounds in the privacy of my small, dark berth. But I want to argue with the marine even less.

To my surprise, the Spades are good company. They say nothing of what happened, but shove a mug of willow bark tea into my hands. When the dinner bell sounds, Penn volunteers to bring down our food, and I realize most of my mess has decided to take the meal with me in the Cove. It isn't pity on the boys' faces. It's empathy. I wonder when they decided to claim me as their own.

We are halfway through the dinner when the door to the Cove opens with a bang and the berth falls into immediate silence. It takes me several moments to turn myself around to see what's happened, and when I do, I find my own voice caught in my throat.

Catsper, who'd opened the door with his boot, force-marches Ana inside.

CHAPTER 12

"*E*veryone but Ash, get out." His voice is low and dangerous.

The boys disappear.

Catsper shoves Ana forward, and she lands hard on her knees. Her face is pale and her eyes as wide as a cornered rabbit's.

"Tell her, Lionitis," Catsper orders.

Tell me? Tell me what?

Ana looks between us as if trying to sort out a horrid mistake. Her fingers trace a fresh bruise along her slender cheekbone, and she shies away from the marine.

Ice fills my chest.

"Everything," Catsper growls. "Now."

Ana hesitates until Catsper raises his hand with obvious intent. "Don't!" She throws up her arms to shield herself. "I was trying to keep us safe, Nile. It was going to be for the best. For everyone. I swear it."

"What did you do?" I ask, though my gut tells me I already know.

"I... I told Captain Rima you are Nile Greysik, the Princess of Ashing, who Prince Tamiath is offering a reward for." Her voice quickens, words tumbling out one after the other. "Kederic's attack and then Song's humiliation and then Thatch Lawrence's accident—we would have been next, you and I. We needed the captain's protection. Prince Tamiath offers a...a great deal of gold for your whereabouts, and I traded it to Rima in exchange for our safety. Both of ours. Until you decided to defy Dana, nothing was going to happen to you."

I shut my eyes for a moment. The betrayal shouldn't hurt now, not after all that's happened. But it still does. "When?"

"The night Thatch Lawrence died," she whispers.

I do the math. Two days ago.

"You are the one who'll gain most in this, Nile. When all is over, you'll be a *princess* again. You'll have a husband and bear children of royal blood. Your mother will have her daughter back." Her tone shifts. "When you are mature enough to understand the value of such things, you will thank me on your hands and knees."

"And is your family debt to be paid off as part of this deal?" I ask, raising a brow. Her flinch is answer enough, and I cut off her denial. "It little matters now, as there will be no reward money." Last night's interrogation takes on new light. As does my flogging. "Rima knew exactly who he had strapped to the grating. And I rather doubt he'd wish to explain such treatment of His Highness's bride to Prince Tamiath. He doesn't intend to turn me over to Felielle."

"Perhaps he will claim to have learned the truth only after the punishment and have it both ways, punish the disrespect and collect on the bounty." Catsper jerks his chin at Ana. "All he'd have to do is rid himself of the reporting nuisance."

Ana's face blanches.

Catsper nudges her with his foot. "I've no further use for you. Get out."

"Wait!" She licks her lips, staring wide-eyed. "You believe I may be in danger, don't you?"

I don't really think Ana is in much danger at the moment, not unless she attempts to communicate with the mainland without Rima's sanction—and we're yet to see a dispatch boat on the horizon. A few words from me could put her at ease. It's the right thing to do. Instead, I shrug with cold indifference that Catsper matches with one of his own.

"Get out of my berth," he says and pushes her out.

I don't watch. I sink gingerly onto a sea chest and rest my elbows atop my knees. Last night's interrogation repeats itself over and over in my head. "What did Rima need the location of Ashing's military bases for?"

Catsper shakes his head, his expression grave. "Perhaps Dana might have a guess."

The mention brings my humiliation and stupidity back in a wave of memory. I rub my face. "Will you speak to him?"

"No."

I look at my feet. My back hurts. "Please."

"We've too few good officers left. You are one. So is Dana. With much of the Lyron joint fleet destroyed, I've little idea who's survived on the mainland. So, no, I'm not going to aid you in avoiding him to balm your feelings."

I deflate, a windless sail hanging slack on a mast. "I'm not anything anymore, Catsper," I whisper. "If you're concerned about the information I might give up when captured, you may find it more efficient to slit my throat."

Catsper crosses his arms.

I glance away.

"I'd hoped a trick at the grating would clear your head for you, but it seems that was wishful thinking," is the last I hear before he leaves, and I bury my face in my hands.

Domenic returns to the Cove the following morning, when the Spades are out on duty and training and the noisy berth is oddly empty. I am sitting on the deck, my knees drawn up and my arms and head resting atop them. I flinch as he closes the door behind him.

Domenic's steps are slow and tentative as he closes the distance and sits on one of the sea chests. "How are you—"

"Fine."

He reaches a hand out toward me, and my back shrieks in terror at even the thought of touch. Without bothering to check in with my mind, my body cringes away, my arms coming up in an instinctual defensive barrier that has Domenic's hand freezing in midair.

"I'm not going to hurt you," he whispers, his voice so raw and desperate that it would shatter me if there was anything left to break.

"You had me flogged," I hiss at him. Gone. I want him gone before the pain and humiliation drown me altogether.

Domenic's shoulders fall, and he buries his head in his hands, his elbows braced against his knees. "Tell me what do, Nile," he says quietly. "Tell me how to make it better, how to help. Talk to me. At least... At least let me hold you through the worst of it."

My voice is ice-cold, even to my own ears, as I lift my face and pierce his gaze. "If you want to help, leave me alone."

I REMAIN in the Cove for three days until I can move well enough to attend to the lightest of duties. When I climb to the deck for my watch, holding my forearm up to shield my unaccustomed eyes from the sun, I feel as though I am stepping onto the ship for the first time. Curious glances watch and judge my every move, and everything is different. There are no middies on watch. Thatch Lawrence is dead. Kederic moves about his duties gingerly, his head up but face drawn. Ana, Catsper tells me, has received the captain's blessing to trade her midshipman's post for a surgeon's mate title and is busy setting up the sick berth below. I swallow bile. Selling me out has apparently already paid dividends.

We are still heading west toward the pronged juncture where the Siaman Sea, the Ardent Ocean, and the Diante Corridor all meet. The juncture's narrow neck, which allows but one ship to pass at a time, has earned it the Bottleneck nickname. The name makes up in accuracy what it lacks in originality. The *Hope* is keeping station behind us. I presume she'll separate at the Bottleneck and continue from the Siaman Sea into the Ardent Ocean. If her skipper is smart, he'll pick up a new Lyron escort there. The Ardent Ocean runs between the Lyron and Tirik continents and is the primary battlefield for our navies.

Whatever is left of our navies.

"Where are the twins?" I ask one of the Spades.

"The captain decided they were too young to be running rampant," the boy answers. "Rima has them attending him directly."

As if summoned by mention, Rima notices my presence on deck and smiles benevolently. But I know better than to write the gesture off to simply maintaining his act before the crew. Rima is a darker mystery than I dare imagine.

ALEX LIDELL

"I am pleased to see your return to duty, Ms. Ash," Rima says, weighing me with undisguised curiosity. "Fetch a cup of coffee for me from the galley, if you please." He winks conspiratorially. "Let us keep you free from Mr. Dana's demands for a bit while you heal, no?"

A princess at his beck and call. I keep my face straight and touch my forehead as I start for the galley. "Aye, sir. Thank you, sir."

Domenic moves to the other side of the rail so as to put himself in my path. In that moment, I want to be beside him, smelling his scent and listening to his breaths. And I want him never to touch me again. In either order.

When I refuse to meet his gaze, Domenic takes a step toward me.

Dropping my face, I scurry around the other side of the deck. My heart twists. He might have been the one to order punishment, but I lied to him first. Repeatedly. I'm lying to him still. Because he'll set me ashore if he learns the truth. And because even if he doesn't dismiss me outright for my Gift, I'm broken in a new and different way now. What I felt when Domenic reached for me in the Cove, the instinctual fear and storm of humiliation is still there, riding on my shoulder and cackling.

I crisply turn away from him and don't look back for the rest of the day. And when, the following morning, a lookout calls, "Sail ho!" I barely bother to turn my head toward the broken horizon.

Until, that is, I hear the boom of a cannon echo across the water.

CHAPTER 13

Three shots. Two close together, then a pause, then one more. My chest clenches, a shiver running through my body. I couldn't have heard correctly. The ship in the distance fires again. A burst this time, with pauses before and after the third shot. The Ashing private armada's signal to get the attention of a friendly ship when time is of the essence. An emergency signal thrown into the distance too great for flag-based messages, a hope that someone on the Lyron League *Aurora* can understand Ashing's code.

Something has happened. While I was out here playing seaman, something has happened to my home.

"Deck, there!" the lookout calls from above. "It's a sloop, Mr. Dana! She has every scrap of canvas on her!"

I take Kederic's glass and focus it on the coming ship. "The *Sparrow*." I wheel around toward Domenic, speaking to him for only the second time since the day of the Mast. "She's the Ashing's fastest. And that was an emergency request to intercept."

"All hands to make sail!" Domenic bellows across the deck without hesitation. "Helm, set course for approaching sloop."

"Belay that order!" shouts another voice before the crew manages a single step. Rima.

My chest fills with dread as I turn to see what the captain will do now. Kederic takes his glass back and finds somewhere else to be.

Rima surveys the deck with distaste that deepens as his gaze finds Domenic's. "What are you about, Mr. Dana?" he demands.

"Flag signals!" the lookout shouts from the mast before Domenic can reply.

Kazzik pulls a signals book from its shelf and flips it open, but we don't have time for this.

"Give me your glass," I whisper to Domenic. "It's an Ashing ship. Please. Give me your glass."

Domenic hesitates a moment, but lets the glass swing off his back.

Swiping the glass from his hand, I train it on the *Sparrow's* mast. "She is signaling with Ashing's code, not the League's," I call, reading the flags as they fly up the mast. The *Sparrow* must have left the Ardent Ocean in great hurry, without taking the League book with her. "Urgent message. Attack imminent."

Rima's hand clamps down on my shoulder, pressing painfully into my sore back. "Yes, yes, thank you," he says quietly. "That is quite sufficient, however. I do not need you upsetting my crew with guessed readings and out-of-context messages." His other hand pulls the glass from mine. "Mr. Dana, have the lookout acknowledge the signal and instruct the *Sparrow* to cease broadcasting dirty laundry for the world to hear. I shall meet with her as soon as distance permits."

No. I suck in a breath.

Rima's gaze flickers back to me. "Get her belowdecks, Mr. Dana. I believe our young sailor here has spoken out of turn enough for one day and needs not be tempted into further transgression."

My lips pull back in a snarl.

"Ash." Dana reaches for my shoulder but his eyes meet mine, and he pulls back, showing me his palm. "We need to go. Now."

I stare at him before moving. *You are a dog trotting at your master's heels,* my gaze tells him.

Do as you are told, replies his.

I follow Domenic's silent silhouette down to the officer's gunroom. The long table has rosters and supply lists on it, along with clean paper and ink. He nods toward the paperwork. "Make two copies of each."

The anger simmering inside threatens to consume what shreds of self-control I have left. "The *Sparrow* is risking her life to warn us of an imminent attack."

"I am aware." Domenic's voice is cold, but it's coming through clenched teeth. "There is nothing to be done about the captain's orders just now."

My nostrils flare, blood boiling beneath my skin. I'm sick of this. Of a captain ruled only by his cowardice and his wallet. Of Domenic's dogged obedience. Of my bloody impotence. "You've not the mettle to do anything, Domenic."

Silence.

And then the stone in his gaze shatters. "And what would you do, Princess?" he snarls viciously. "Run away? Or howl and cry and beg the *Aurora* to action? Or maybe it will be your great strength and fearless work aloft that will lead the entire Lyron League to glory and triumph."

I recoil as if burned. Worse than burned. But then I lean

91

toward Domenic and bare my teeth. I want to hurt him. Hurt him so badly he will feel it for days. Weeks. A lifetime. "It's no wonder Daddy thinks nothing of throwing your name on gambling tabs. To be counted as a man in your own right, you'd need a mind and will of your own."

His hands curl into fists, and a vein along the side of his neck pulses, fast and hard and angry.

"You want to strike me again?" I ask, getting to my feet and spreading my arms before him. "Go ahead. What will it be this time? Will you split my lip or bloody my back? You're good at that much, so might as well play to your strength."

He does strike, but not me. Domenic's fist hits the bulkhead. Without waiting for my reply, Domenic turns on his heel and leaves.

I jerk as the door slams in Domenic's wake. Numbly, I walk to the table, pull out a chair, and fling the whole paper pile onto the deck.

A lifetime passes until the bellowed orders to back sail finally echo across the ship. I feel the *Aurora* drop her speed. Then the ship rocks lightly as a boat is lowered over the side, and the last of my hopes vanishes. The *Sparrow*'s officers won't even be invited aboard to deliver their news—Rima will be heading there instead. And I trust his reporting as much as I believe in his benevolence.

My chest is stone heavy as all hands assemble on deck two hours later. *Sparrow* is sailing away, her sails filled. The *Sparrow*'s sudden appearance and quick departure have made an impression. The hands are as volatile as gunpowder, small bits occasionally exploding in sharp remarks and impulsive assaults on ship's boys and smaller hands. In their anxiety, the crew is reverting back to their primal form.

If the *Aurora* ever truly deviated from it.

"All hands present, sir," Domenic says when the decks swarm with sailors and the marines line the poop deck in a crisp black line. He doesn't look at me. No, he moves as if he has not a bother in the world. Like he always does.

"Very good." Rima holds up his hands and smiles. "Thank you, Mr. Dana."

Domenic nods and steps back.

Rima looks around slowly. "You've no doubt noted the dramatic arrival of the Ashing sloop *Sparrow*," he says with the tiniest hint of mockery in his voice. "With the canvas she carried, I half expected to see a Republic squadron on her stern. Didn't you?"

It's a rhetorical question, but many of the hands nod, and I sense a small exhale of relief from the men around me. This routine is familiar to them, and Rima's smile is encouraging. Whatever else he is, whichever breed of corruption and cowardliness lives inside him, Captain Rima is the master of his crew.

"There was no Tirik squadron, of course," Rima says ruefully. "No squadron, no frigate, not even a fishing boat. The Ashing fleet, superb seamen as it has, does have its showmanship flair. We saw it when *Faithful*, the infamous Ashing flagship, sank thanks to its own glory seeking. When the Ashing king proclaimed its fleet the mightiest in the League only to fold before the Republic's assault. And we saw it now, when a little dispatch ship raised havoc in an attempt to assert the importance of its own meager existence."

Rima pauses, scanning the crowd with his gaze, which lingers on my face a heartbeat longer than necessary.

ALEX LIDELL

I know that Rima is walking all over Ashing on purpose and that my anger only feeds his pleasure. My face burns behind a neutral mask as I wait for his broadside. Now that he's laid the groundwork needed to destroy the *Sparrow*'s credibility, he must move on to the message the little sloop has risked herself to deliver.

"You are wondering what the *Sparrow*'s urgent dispatch was, no doubt," Rima says, reading the crowd. "I will tell you. No, I'll do better than that. I will read it to you. Because I need not put on a theatrical performance for my own crew." He reaches into the breast pocket of his tunic and removes a parchment, the official seal broken across its edge. With the ceremony of unwrapping orders, Rima straightens the page.

"*Lord Captain of the Lyron League Ship* Aurora," he reads aloud. "*It is with sorrow that I inform you of the dire situation in the Ardent. The League fleet suffered grievously during last month's engagement with the Tirik Republic and our economy is fragile. We believe the Tirik Republic will actively harass Lyron merchants in hopes of destroying our trade. As the only ship in the Siaman Sea, it is thus vital that you do your utmost to protect the merchant convoys and remain vigilant for the enemy's likely assault on the defenseless vessels. Faithfully yours, Admiral of the Blue, Lord Hector Delion.*"

Rima lowers his parchment to rub his hand over his face. "In plain terms, the *Aurora*'s mission to protect League merchants is more vital than ever. An important point, to be sure, but perhaps one that required little of the pomp and flair the Ashing ship decided to put forth. We know our duty and are, in fact, en route to pick up a merchant now. The sloop's needless excitement does nothing but give way to rumor." He shakes his head in disappointment. "You can see why I sent the *Sparrow* away at once, I hope?"

94

A murmur passes over the crew.

I struggle to get air into my chest. Rima is good. Very good. Except that he has no reason to know that Admiral of the Blue, Lord Hector Delion, quietly turned in his letter of resignation several days before *Aurora* set sail from Ashing docks.

CHAPTER 14

The letter Rima just read is not from Delion, I'm certain of that much. Either the dispatch was forged or Rima lied as to its contents.

And I have more faith in the *Sparrow*'s skipper than I have in the *Aurora*'s.

"You may return to your duties," Rima calls out, dismissing the crew. The men leave in lighter moods than they were in when gathered, and I am soon the only one still standing rooted in her place. Rima sees me and smiles a cruel, self-satisfied grin. *Did you enjoy that?* he seems to ask silently. *I did.*

Anger pulses through me in hot streaks. I stare at him, at the parchment in his hand, at the rotten satisfaction in his face, and I feel my shoulders roll back, cracking healing skin and opening my magic to air. The magic bubbles and burns, excited to come play after being denied, and I throw myself into shaping it like a sail. The air comes in a great gush, and the wind sways, hitting the deck with an energetic burst that ruffles tunics and flogs the flag.

The seamen curse, more than one losing his hat in the sudden gale. But I don't care about them. I want the dispatch in Rima's hand. I need the dispatch. The wild breeze twists around itself. My gaze burns into Rima's hand while the captain frowns in confusion at the treacherous skies.

I feel Domenic's gaze on me. But I can't help that.

My body stills. I watch the captain, waiting for the moment his grip is loosest. And when I see it, I call my breeze home with a sharp jerk.

Domenic gasps.

Rima squawks as the parchment flies from his hands, carried in the wind. Fast. Too fast. Heading... *Storms.* Heading overboard, to sink away without ever revealing its truth.

I rush after it, skidding along the planks. With a leap that makes me gasp in pain, I lean over the rail and snatch the message.

"Give that to me!" Rima orders, striding toward me with his hand outstretched.

My pulse races. I've mere heartbeats until the captain or his cronies are on me. As fast as my fingers can move, I shake open the document and drink in the words. I've not the time to read aloud or even take in sentences. But the main words, words written in my brother Thad's hand, jump at me from the page.

Earthquake... Mainland shoreline destroyed... Lyron and Tirik. No approach for large frigates to either mainland.... Archipelago vital for timber, food, fresh water... Tirik fleet heading your way... Attack imminent... AURORA MUST HOLD THE BOTTLENECK... Ships on the way.

Air leaves my lungs long before Johina's fist lands in the pit of my stomach. My mouth is dry as I stare up into the thunder of Rima's face. And then I yell as loud as my spasmed middle allows. "Coward!" I struggle to fill my lungs. "The captain lies!

The Republic fleet heads our way! *Aurora* must hold the Bottleneck! The—" That's as far as I get before Johina slams me to the deck and I taste blood. The seaman's forearm presses into my windpipe, and I can scarcely breathe, much less scream.

Slowly, Rima bends down to pick up his letter. He opens and scans its contents. Tucking the dispatch into his coat, he stares down at me.

"You are unwell, Ash," he says gently and loudly enough for all to hear. "I've seen such hysterics in women before, and I fear yours are getting worse each day. I do believe ship's discipline has sent you over the edge. A seaman would have recovered long before now, but a woman..." He shakes his head, while I struggle beneath Johina's hold. "What will you tell us next? That the Republic fleets are abandoning the Lyron Continent to suddenly capture the Siaman Sea?" He glances around, playing to the gathering crowd. "Or perhaps that you are really a princess? Or that you see the future in your dreams?"

The men gathered around us laugh.

Not Domenic. His face dark as a storm, he lunges toward me—only to find himself held fast by Catsper's brutal wristlock. Domenic shoves the marine, who silently increases the pressure until Domenic is frozen in place.

I choke out a growl. My hate for Rima burns hot in my chest. He's pinned me in from all sides. The bastard bloody pinned me in.

"Silence!" Rima barks, and the deck falls quiet. When he speaks again, his voice is cutting. "No one shall make jest of the girl's hysteria. But neither will it be permitted to damage the operations, safety, and discipline of this vessel. Johina, put the wench in irons for the remainder of the voyage."

Johina takes his arm away from my throat, and I have an

instant to draw a lungful of air. "No! He—" I try to shout, but Johina slams me against the deck again.

"Enough of your cheek," he growls and forces his neckerchief into my mouth until I gag on the rancid cloth. Then, grabbing me by my shirt, the Eflian half carries, half drags me into the holding cells. No, not them. He drags me farther down into the bilge, the lowest part of the ship where the refuse liquids of the upper decks naturally find relief. There being no irons here, Johina makes do with a rope around my ankles and wrists. Then, for good measure, he connects the two behind my back and leaves me flopping and gagging in the refuse. I scream despite the gag. I scream for my body, my duty, my failure.

BELL. Bell. Bell. The ship's sounds mark the passage of time that my body counts breath by breath. I hurt. My back, my arms, my lungs. It takes an hour to work the gag from my mouth. Another hour of yelling leaves me hoarse. With each minute, I matter less and less, while the great coward moves the *Aurora* farther from where she has to be.

I plead with the dark that someone comes soon. Someone who will hear the truth. Catsper. I'm a prisoner; surely the lieutenant of the marines can check on a prisoner. Or send one of the Spades. Or... Or Domenic. If he can bear my company after the unforgivable words I threw at him. And after what I'm certain he'd worked out in that moment on deck.

But Domenic doesn't come. And neither does anyone else. Not at the end of the watch, or at mealtime, or when the ship goes dark for the night. Hunger and fear and pain soak through me. Does no one know where I am? Can no one hear my screams? Or am I simply not worth the effort?

What would you do, Princess? Domenic's words haunt me in the darkness. *Run away? Or howl and cry and beg the Aurora to action?* If that is what he thinks of me, what reason has he to come? That or the fact that he saw me for the useless, lying cripple that I am.

My head is light. It's dark and airless here and the stench chokes me. A rat scurries across my shins. I flail to get it off, pulling against my ropes and succeeding only in cutting my skin on the harsh hemp.

I've heard prisoners scream before. I've seen the raw skin on their legs where they fought the restraint. And I've never understood the pointless efforts. What good is screaming on a ship when everyone knows where you are? Or injuring yourself against iron when no further escape routes exist? There is no point to it, I realize now. But down here in the darkness, there is no point to anything. Not when the walls feel as if they are closing in on me. Black and suffocating. And especially when I realize that even if Johina was to return and let me out of the bilge this instant, there is nothing for me to return to.

I've failed. I failed as an Ashing officer when I lost the *Faithful* and its cargo. I failed as a princess when I absconded from my home. Failed Domenic when I chose lies for fear of losing him. And I've even failed as Nile Ash, who's dissolved from a sailor into a pathetic, hysterical wench.

I sob. Nile Ash is dead. She is dead, and in her place, there is nothing, only a useless, crippled Gifted.

I release my control on my magic and let it use me as it pleases. I little care whether the magic burns itself out or burns me dead. The putrid air of the hold chases itself round and round, draining my strength like a sieve. Another meal bell sounds as I lie with my cheek soaking in bilge water, my clothes drenched and my body trembling. Fear. Panic. The too familiar green lights. The jerking spells twist my body so it's straining against the ropes.

And again. Again.

There is barely a heartbeat's pause between the spells. The brewing fear in my gut is no longer a phantom precursor, but a real panic that even the little reprieve between convulsions might disappear. I scream in pain as the next set of shocks engulfs me, my body thumping against the sopping deck. It hurts, and I scream through my hoarse vocal cords, knowing no one will hear the croak. The darkness and cold are heavier around me. I hear no bells. Nothing nothing nothing at all.

I little care now. I know no one is coming.

And no one comes.

CHAPTER 15

QUINN

Captain Quinn of the *Hope* stood on the quarterdeck, his arms behind his back, when the foremast lookout cried for attention.

"Deck ho! The *Aurora* is signaling another course change, sir! She wants us to come due east again."

Quinn looked sharply at the Lyron frigate. There was no reason to veer off that he could see, and certainly not due east, back toward the Crystal Oasis. The *Aurora* was escorting them west through the Siaman Sea toward the three-pronged Bottleneck Juncture. Once Quinn was safely through the Bottleneck opening and in the Ardent Ocean, he would set course for the Tirik coastline and the Institute. Except yesterday's course correction was turning into today's full-on change of direction. As if the *Aurora* was disinclined to continue heading toward the Bottleneck at all.

Quinn's shoulders tensed, and he motioned the *Hope*'s single middie to him.

"Get me my glass," Quinn ordered the young gentleman. "And my compliments to Commission Jaquis. I would be pleased to see him on deck."

The middie disappeared at a trot, returning a moment later with Quinn's glass.

Quinn raised it, quizzing the sea. The *Aurora* was, in fact, heading away from the Bottleneck instead of toward it. He tapped his hand against his thigh. Of all the crossings, Rima had to pick the one when Quinn had a People's Commissioner on board for this little game.

Quinn wondered whether the situation had aught to do with yesterday's Lyron dispatch ship or the phantom wind that was making the *Aurora* buck like a horse with a burr under its saddle. If he didn't know better, Quinn would think the *Aurora* had a Gifted air caller onboard, given the oddness of the weather and the ship's motions. He'd transported enough poor Gifted souls to know what they could do to a ship, and the uncontrolled gale so focused on the *Aurora*'s hull was too familiar a motion to ignore. But of course the League would never allow a Gifted on board, so it was unlikely. But then, everything about this whole cruise was unlikely.

"Aloft there!" Quinn called. "Are there any sails in sight?"

"None but the *Aurora*, sir. I'm quite certain."

Quinn nodded, mindful of keeping his face unreadable. At Commissioner Jaquis's insistence, the *Hope* carried double the number of Gifted she was suited for. Jaquis wanted to make his mark by demonstrating how much more efficient the *Hope* became under his care, but the resulting conditions on the lower deck turned Quinn's stomach. As unique as the Institute's treatment was, it would prove useless if the patients died en route.

"What have we here, Mr. Quinn?" Commissioner Jaquis's cool voice reached over the *Hope*'s small deck.

Quinn waited until the commissioner was close enough to converse with in a soft voice. The *Hope* might be playing the part of a Lyron League merchantman, but that did not mean actual sloppiness was to be tolerated. "The *Aurora* has made a course change, sir. One that will lead her away from the Bottleneck Juncture."

Jaquis's brows pulled together into a single bushy line. "I was under the impression, *sir*, the *Aurora* was ignorant of the juncture being our intended destination."

Quinn inclined his head. "That is quite correct, sir," he said calmly. "The *Aurora*'s captain is unaware we wish to pass through the Bottleneck to the Ardent Ocean. He is paid to escort the *Hope* toward the Diante port, which is one of the three routes the Bottleneck Juncture connects. We typically make our departure signal just short of the Bottleneck, veer away to the Diante port, and change course again once the *Aurora* clears the Bottleneck." Quinn stalled for a moment to give the commissioner time to picture the situation. Things would be easier if Jaquis actually understood the geography. "The Diante port and the Bottleneck Juncture both lie due west, sir. And the *Aurora* has just turned east."

Jaquis snorted. "This is a shakedown. The *Aurora*'s captain wants a higher fee." He made a shooing motion with his hand. "Pay it and let us be about our business. I want the cargo delivered sooner than later."

Do not ever call my charges "cargo" again, Quinn wanted to say. But he was too smart to wage war over words.

"Commissioner, if the *Aurora* wished to increase her fees, I imagine she would have made the demand before changing course." Quinn's clasped hands tightened behind his back, but he let none of the tension enter his voice. This was his seventh trip in the *Aurora*'s wake, and Quinn had a fair idea of the kind of man he was dealing with on the Lyron ship. "If not for birth and family money, Captain Rima wouldn't be allowed near a naval ship, much less into uniform. If he is risking his profits—he will earn nothing should the *Hope* refuse to follow—it is because he fears staying his original course."

Jaquis wrinkled his forehead in thought. "Or he may believe greater earnings lie due east. Perhaps from another source."

Quinn gave the People's Commissioner a begrudging nod. "Agreed. Rima is either running from danger or else sailing toward an advantage. In either case, we've little time to make our choice."

"I see." Jaquis brushed his upper lip. "What are my options, Captain Quinn?"

There was only one choice, if they were to be responsible. "We've three options, sir. We can follow the Lyron frigate as she directs. We could abandon the *Aurora* and proceed to the Bottleneck Juncture alone. Or we can turn back to the Diante shore."

"And what would you have us do?"

"Turn back," Quinn answered without hesitation. "The *Hope*'s mission is humanitarian. We must assume that a danger lies behind the *Aurora*'s course change, which would make continuing on our present path foolish. Following the *Aurora* on a merry cruise through the Siaman is likewise impractical with a deck of invalids who may not survive the added days of the voyage. I recommend we turn back and not attempt the passage again until further exploration."

Jaquis bristled like a rooster, his face filling with indignation. "You would have us *retreat*, sir?" he squawked loudly, so others on the deck were obliged to bury themselves deep in tasks to avoid the appearance of having heard anything. "Are you unaware of the *war*?"

"With due respect, Commissioner," Quinn said patiently, "the *Hope* is not a ship-of-war. She is a modified merchant vessel delivering Gifted to a treatment facility. Endangering the very civilians we are at sea to help would be the height of folly."

"Unacceptable." Jaquis's face flushed, making some of the crew flinch away. "I will not discard my mission based on the superstitions of an overbred Lyron captain who can see nothing beyond a coin purse. Lay a course for the juncture, Captain Quinn."

Quinn felt the burn of many eyes. Making for the Bottleneck Juncture was a mistake, but if Jaquis forced him into said course, Quinn was determined to make the most of it. He had to assume the danger of some sort waited near the Bottleneck. And if he took his crew into the fray, he would extract every ounce of advantage their lives—and deaths— would win for the Tirik Republic.

Ral Quinn, after all, owed everything to the People's revolution. He'd been an orphan with a knack for numbers. The Tirik Republic gave him an education, honing his talent into skill, and offering a chance at a naval post once reserved for noble blood. So as much as Quinn hated the likes of People's Commissioners in general and Jaquis in particular, Quinn loved the promise his nation strove for.

"Helm," Quinn called out, his voice clear and sharp. "Bring us due east and close with the *Aurora*."

"Captain! You—" Commissioner Jaquis cut his protest off as Quinn turned toward him and met his gaze full force.

"The *Hope* is a merchant vessel, Commissioner. I will not be taking it alone into the Bottleneck Juncture." He squinted at the sea before nodding to himself. "We will capture and use the frigate *Aurora* for that purpose. If you wish to join the boarding party, sir, I suggest you arm yourself."

CHAPTER 16

*T*he sun reflects off the ocean and sparkles in grains of beach sand beneath my feet. Domenic's face turns to me, sending a warmth through my chest. The water and fresh wind have mussed his hair, and his friendly eyes watch me intently. It's just me he is watching—not a princess or a pawn piece or an officer or a common seaman. And just me is enough.

"You will take on armed thugs with your bare hands, but the notion of puppies sends you hiding?" he asks. His eyes laugh.

I look down to find Domenic petting Clay's dog. She trusts him, this stranger whose coat I wear. The coat smells of salt and sea and him. A familiar smell. His presence is solidness that fits into my soul. I'm not sure if we've just met or have known each other for some time. But I want to stay with him. And so I will, for a bit longer. Until I leave.

"You could tell me your name," Domenic says.

"Nile of... Just Nile."

"Nile! Storms. Can you hear me?" The familiar voice is tinged with panic. "Wake up."

A dog barks and whines. But it's not Clay's dog. I dig my feet into the sand, rooting myself to my beach, where there is no pain.

"Nile. Wake up." Calloused hands run over my exposed skin. "Goddess, she's cold as ice."

"She's soaked," says a second voice, also familiar and arrogantly sure of itself. "Take off her wet clothes."

I'm shifted again, painfully, and someone begins trying to undo my sopping shirt and trousers. Something about it feels wrong, but my mind is too muddled to sort out what specifically is the problem—until I feel a brush of air on exposed skin.

And suddenly I'm not on a beach anymore. I'm on deck, before a grating, and I know what will come next.

Not again. Not again. Not again. Panic. Blind, hot panic rolls through me. My body thrashes against the coming bonds, and I scream into the palm that suddenly covers my mouth.

The arrogant voice curses. There are four hands on me at once now, forcing the remainder of the clothes off me, off my *back*, as I buck and fight and lose.

But instead of agony, something warm wraps around my naked body. It smells of salt and sea and *him*.

"Easy," the first voice orders. The warm air tickles my ear. "Listen to me, Nile. You are all right, and you need to open your eyes. Now."

The demand, the plea, is so visceral, it hooks into my consciousness. The smell grows. The pain does too. Pain and cold and hunger. I inhale the salty musk of *here* and look at the world.

I'm in the cargo hold where Domenic and I used to hide, a coat wrapped around my naked shoulders. *Domenic.* I smell him beside me, though it takes another heartbeat before I realize that he is cradling me against his chest, his forehead pressing into my hair.

I stir.

Domenic pulls back far enough to see my face, his own drawn in fear. "Nile. Thank the Goddess." He brushes my hair from my cheeks.

I lick dry lips. The only dry part of me. "What's happened?"

A second figure comes into view and squats beside me. Catsper's hair is loose and falls to his shoulders as he surveys me with a soldier's professional gaze.

"You attempted a single-handed mutiny yesterday," says Domenic.

Catsper thrusts a flask into my hands. "And then sometime in the middle of the night, you apparently decided to brew up a small storm to keep yourself entertained."

I try to remember. The screaming. The ship's bells. Hunger. Fear. Convulsions. The truth. "It couldn't have lasted long," I say. "I fell unconscious."

Domenic flinches and glares daggers at Catsper. A deep bruise blossoms above Domenic's right brow, and I'm willing to wager its details match the marine's knuckles.

"Rima had people watching the bilge where Johina threw you," Catsper said, ignoring Domenic's condemnation. "He just let up this evening. You'd have been in greater danger if we came earlier." Catsper rises and starts toward the door. "I need to ensure he's still otherwise occupied. Welcome back, Ash. Try not to do anything stupid."

I study my hands while Catsper's footsteps recede above. The memory of my dream still wraps around me, and I want Domenic so badly, it rips me up inside. Until I remember reality. The events on deck. Domenic knows. I'd felt him watch me call the wind. He knows I'm Gifted. A lying, Gifted, dangerous—

"Nile." Domenic's voice orders. "Look at me. Please."

I try to push away from him, though I succeed no more than a wet gerbil might. The coat covering my naked skin, however, succeeds at moving a great deal better than I had. My face flushes as cold air brushes my exposed shoulders.

Domenic's arms tighten around me. "It's all right. Your clothes were wet, and you were shaking." He nudges the coat back into place and exhales slowly. "Talk to me, Nile. Say something."

"It wasn't the cold," I rasp, but my voice is strong despite its roughness. "The shaking. I wasn't shaking from the cold. Not *just* from the cold. You know that, don't you? And when Catsper said I brewed up a storm, you knew what he meant."

Domenic swallows. Nods. "Aye."

I try to read him but can't. "Does the whole ship know?"

"No. Not unless they watched your face like I did. In the wake of the great quake, a rogue gale is easy to swallow. Certainly more logical than thinking a Gifted had hidden aboard all this time." The accusation in his voice is soft but stinging.

I recoil.

"No." Domenic grabs my shoulder and pulls me to him until my cheek rests in the hollow of his shoulder and his strong arms drape around me protectively. "No more running. No more lying to me. Goddess, Nile," he whispers, his voice breaking with an odd mix of comfort and fury. "Tell me everything and bloody trust me to understand."

My heart pounds against my rib cage. My thoughts and words and feelings tangle in my mouth. But I have to speak the truth now, before I lose my resolve.

And so I do. I tell him everything. From how it started, to the Diante woman's wisdom, to meditation exercises, to my actions during the quake. When I get to the convulsions that kept me rooted to deck and the lies I fed him about my hurt ankle, Domenic's face drains of blood. He stares at the deck, jaw tight as I recount my terror of the climb, of the impossible choice, of my feet returning to deck.

Domenic curses softly. His fingers stroke my back with a featherlight touch.

I cringe away, and he stops at once, his eyes pained.

"You asked me about Gifted on ships, and I was... Goddess." His neck muscles tense. "I was so focused on keeping from throwing myself all over you that I spoke without thinking. I should have known better because you don't say things idly. Not like that." He curses and sweeps his hand over my face, taking hold of my chin. "You've my full attention now. No more half-truths, all right? Not between us."

Domenic's words fill my blood. Fill my world. My heart and breath quiver.

"I presume you two are talking once again," Catsper says behind me.

Domenic clenches his jaw and looks over my shoulder with stony calm. "Among other things, yes. What is the situation on deck? I felt the ship alter course."

"Rima called for a course change back east a quarter hour ago. The *Hope* has been signaled to follow. Ash, enough lounging around." Catsper tosses me a rolled-up set of clothes. "See if you can manage to dress yourself."

Domenic reluctantly lowers me to the deck, and the two turn away as I force my body into motion, slipping one foot, then another into a loose set of Spade trousers and biting down a whimper as I maneuver my shoulders into a shirt. In a moment, Domenic's hands are on the fabric, helping to maneuver the cloth into place.

"I presume you did not, in fact, go mad but rather that Rima's reading of *Sparrow*'s dispatch was somewhat creative?" says Catsper behind my back.

"Give her a moment," Domenic growls.

"If you've found a way to stop time and wind, take all the moments you want," says Catsper mildly.

Reality hits me like a pistol shot, and I stop feeling my aches and wounds, stop feeling even modesty as I turn back to the men while still buttoning the tunic. "The letter was from my older brother, Thad. The earthquake destroyed the shorelines of both the Lyron and Tirik continents," I say quickly. "For now, the only place large ships can safely approach to take fresh water is the Crystal Oasis in the Siaman. Everyone is heading this way now—the private armadas, the joint Lyron League fleet, every ship the Tirik can spare." I pause as Catsper hands me a biscuit. A moment ago, I was ravenous, but now my heart beats too quickly for food. "Whoever controls access to the Crystal Oasis will have the winning hand in the war."

"And controlling access to the Crystal Oasis means controlling the Bottleneck Juncture," says Domenic, following along with my words.

I nod. "Thad was writing on behalf of the Lyron Admiralty. Our orders are to sail to the Bottleneck Juncture with all speed and hold the passage... Did you say we've turned *east*?"

"Yes. Away from the Bottleneck," Domenic says, his face hardening. "In fact, our exact point of sail will make us slaves to countercurrents in half a day's time. Once we enter those, we'll be unable to turn around. It will take weeks to circle the current and reach the Bottleneck again."

Catsper stands, his hands in his pocket. "So in landsman's

terms, you two are saying that Rima is ensuring the *Aurora* stays clear of the action. And that in twelve hours, there will be no reversing course?"

My hand clamps into a fist. "A single ship at the Bottleneck can turn the battle. Even if we lack the broadside of the coming vessels, we can delay their passage through the juncture long enough for reinforcements to arrive. And they are coming— ships, soldiers, anyone the six kingdoms can stick onto anything that floats and send this way."

Catsper cocks a brow. "*We* are lacking proximity to the Bottleneck."

My mind spins as if I'm back in Ashing debating contingency plans with captains and admirals. Playing out the war. I lean forward onto my elbows and study the two men. "Then we need a ship of our own," I say. "And we need to head for the Bottleneck without Rima's blessings."

Domenic chuckles without humor. "Mutiny. You don't think small, Nile. I will give you that."

Catsper squats on his heels. "Much of this crew loves both Rima and their own asses. And the former are leading the latter to safety. The best my boys can do is kill off half the hands for you—and you'd still have no command and control of the ship. And there is the small inconvenience that, in the best-case scenario, everyone involved will be executed as mutineers."

I smile thinly. "I wasn't talking of the *Aurora*. Does there not seem to be another vessel presently in our wake?" A small, fat ship with maybe six guns at the most—that's including the small chaser gun. But still a ship. "I propose to press her into service."

CHAPTER 17

"Something is wrong," says Kederic as he climbs stiffly into the hold where Domenic and I are scheming. Along with Catsper's Spades, my plan requires a solid contingent of seamen who could maneuver and fight the *Hope* after we take her. The last four hours of night saw my friends quietly conscript fellow mutineers with surprising efficiency.

"Mr. Kederic," Domenic says with a raised brow, "we are filling ship's boats with marines in the dead of night with the intent of absconding from a naval frigate and pressing a civilian vessel into military service. Your claim of *something wrong* requires greater precision to have any meaning whatsoever."

Kederic swallows, looking between Domenic and me as if deciding who to report to. He finally settles on a spot right between us. "The *Hope* was closing on us much faster than warranted. At first I attributed it to a fear of being left behind when the *Aurora* came onto her eastern course, and then I thought the darkness was playing games with me, but..."

"But it still looks closer than it should?" I finish for him, and

ALEX LIDELL

the boy nods. I turn to Domenic. "I imagine the *Hope*'s skipper intends to come alongside at first light to demand the reason for the course change. How much longer until we are ready to cast off? I little wish to be bow to bow with our intended prize when the sun rises."

"Thirty minutes." Domenic comes to his feet. "I'll see if I can cut that further and will send Catsper down to collect you."

"Very good."

Kederic returns to deck, and Domenic follows, but I catch his hand. There is no time for this, but there never is. Some things are just important. "Together," I whisper to him. "We are doing this together."

He smiles at me, running his knuckles over my face. "Aye, Ash. We are."

I shake my head. "I don't believe there is a Nile Ash anymore. That experiment ended in rather spectacular failure."

He chuckles. "There never was. You make a rather awful common seaman, Nile."

"Well, I'm not much of a princess either."

Domenic takes my face in his hands. "You shaped our young gentlemen into officers while you were scrubbing decks. You've faced injustices of ill fate and worse orders—and yet stayed loyal to the mission. You've reminded me of the navy beyond Captain Rima's petty whims. Whatever title you sail under, Nile, you have the heart and mind of an admiral. And I will follow you into any storm."

A warmth spreads from my heart, enveloping me in its embrace. I look into Domenic's eyes and feel the togetherness of us rising in synergy. He steps closer, letting his hand roam from my face to my shoulder to—

My body recoils. Slightly, but enough that Domenic notices. Too many sensations, from soft and intimate to humiliating and

118

painful, explode together through my veins. More than I can handle just now. "I'm sorry," I whisper.

"You've been through a great deal," he says softly. "There will be time later." He presses his forehead against mine, offering touch without restraint or pressure, offering his strength to feed my own.

I allow myself a moment to close my eyes and breathe.

"Captain on deck!" The shout from up above is so loud, it penetrates the *Aurora*'s planks. As it is meant to.

Domenic and I spring apart. Rima is sleeping. *Should be* sleeping. As he always does at night.

"Stay here," Domenic hisses, rushing to the companionway. "I'll try to talk him back into bed."

I've no chance to respond before Domenic is gone and Catsper swings himself into the hold, not bothering with the ladder at all. He tosses a Spade uniform jacket into my arms and waits for me to throw it over my shirt before pointing to a spot behind him. The humor is wiped from the marine's face, and he moves like a warrior over field of battle. "The marines and weapons are in the boats, under cover of sailing cloth and darkness," he says curtly. "Kederic is having a boat lowered and the crews are standing by."

I follow in Catsper's wake, keeping my head down as I walk. The voices on deck grow louder as we approach, and I can discern Domenic's stoic tones amidst the Eflian cackles.

"Mr. Johina informs me that the *Hope* is bearing down on us, Commander Dana." Rima sounds much more awake than I wish. "Explain yourself, if you please?"

"Aye, sir." Domenic sounds bored. "The merchie fell behind when we first changed course and has been struggling to catch up since. I expect they fear losing sight of us in the darkness. I saw no reason to wake you over such a nuisance."

Emerging on deck, I start forward toward the boat, skirting the quarterdeck with as wide a berth as the ship's confines allow. The weak light bounces off a pair of pistols Rima has tucked into his waist. I dare a glance at the *Hope*'s approaching lantern and frown. She is coming much more quickly than I thought the merchant capable of. Ahead of me, shapes in the shadows stand frozen in mid-movement, afraid of attracting attention. My pulse gallops.

"I've one boat streaming alongside us," Kederic whispers once we are upon him. "But I dare not move the other right now."

I nod and motion for silence, listening to the conversation on the quarterdeck. *Come on, Domenic. Make him leave.*

"And what is the drag on the ship?" Rima's voice asks. "Is that a *boat* in the water?"

My stomach drops.

"It most certainly is, sir," Domenic says smoothly. "Mr. Catsper's marines are doing a drill. I expect the second boat to be lowered any time now."

Exhaling slowly, I nod to Kederic who quickly puts the men into motion doing just that.

"Belay that, Mr. Dana!" Rima's voice rises. "This isn't time for children's games. I want those boats back at once."

"But, sir," Domenic starts, spinning a complex tale of the marine's training plan. Buying us time.

We hurry, swinging the second boat over the *Aurora*'s side.

"That is enough, Mr. Dana!" Rima snaps as the boat settles into the sea. "We will have these boats up now. And then the *Aurora* shall fire a warning shot across that merchant's bow, before the bloody ship crashes into our hull."

"Of course, sir," says Domenic.

The remaining marines and crew slip over the side. All we need now are Catsper, Domenic, and me.

"Mr. Johina," Rima calls. "Get things sorted, if you please."

Footsteps and a lantern hurry toward us from the quarterdeck. "Pull that boat up, you lubbers!"

Catsper steps in front of me, pushing me toward the rail, but the Eflian's light is faster than I am.

"Sir! It's the prisoner!" Johina shouts, rushing forward toward me. "She's going for the boat!"

Catsper's elbow slams into the Eflian's jaw.

I grab on to the rail and swing myself down toward the boat, heedless of the height.

Catsper lands beside me in one smooth motion and turns to Kederic. "Cast off," he tells the middie.

"No." My voice catches. "We wait for Domenic."

"Cast off," Catsper repeats.

I lunge for the rope Kederic is untying, but the marine grabs me and pins me in place, covering my body with his own. A pistol shot sounds on the *Aurora*. In its flash of light, I see Domenic holding fast to Rima's arm, the captain's smoking pistol pointing to the sky. Rima is doubled over as if he'd been struck.

Johina and Mic swarm toward the pair.

"Domenic!" I shout. But it's too late. Domenic's large silhouette falls to its knees as the Eflians punch and kick it. The sea between us widens with each stroke of the oars. My heart constricts into a horrified fist as I struggle against Catsper. "We can't leave him."

"Enough, Ash." Catsper shifts so his face is inches from mine. His eyes are hard and his nostrils flare as he forces quiet words into the void between us. "You have a war to fight. So you will bloody well pull yourself together and fight it."

I swallow. Grief and shock thread through my veins.

"He's alive," Catsper snarls.

"He won't be soon. He assaulted a ship's captain."

Catsper shakes my shoulders. Hard. "Worry about a court-martial if we ever get there."

My gaze shifts to his, and a decade of training finally takes hold of my mind. I have a ship to take, a juncture to hold, and dozens of people to lead. I owe them all of me. I draw breath.

"Let go of me, Mr. Catsper," I say, my voice the emotionless cool that everyone, myself included, expects from me. "And carry on, if you please."

THE GENTLE SPLASH of the oars cutting the darkness of the sea is all-powerful in the moonless night. We carry no lantern, and the marines make less noise than swaying leaves. The boat rises and falls minutely as it cuts the waves in harmony to the lapping sounds of the water.

The boats are fuller than I'd expected. In addition to the marines and Kederic, I find Price sitting beside me and at least a dozen of the *Aurora*'s seamen, including two women. *But not Domenic.* I push the thought away and stare into the dark night. The *Hope* carries lights, but it is hard to judge distance in the darkness. Beside me, Price clears his throat and Kederic grabs his wrist tight in warning to keep the silence.

Price points to the *Hope*'s lantern, which jumps and sways more than the calm sea warrants. I wonder if she is carrying livestock. It would explain the extra jerking and the unusual hold build. I blow a heavy breath from my nose. There is a good chance the ship will sink before we are through with her and I don't want the animals to suffer for it. We'll have to slaughter them if there is no chance of getting them ashore before battle. *Storms and hail.* As if there wasn't enough to worry about.

"Hold oars," I whisper.

The rowing stops at once, and I close my eyes to listen. All is quiet. Too quiet. The sounds of a ship underway skip over the water, but I hear no chatter of men on watch or officers calling orders. The *Hope* is running silent. A clanking that sounds like the scrape of metal reaches me and Catsper at the same time.

Weapons? the marine mouths to me, his brow lifted in question.

My brows tense. The combination of sounds and the *Hope*'s sudden efficiency sit ill with the vision of the helpless merchant we've escorted through the Siaman Sea.

"Pass the word to the coxswain to bring us along the *Hope*'s intended path," I whisper. "Use the oars as little as possible. We wait until she comes to us and pounce from the shadows." I pause, bracing myself for the next order, one that is bound to kill people that might otherwise be spared. "Mr. Catsper, run the assault as if you are taking a hostile vessel, not intimidating a civilian craft into compliance."

The marine nods once and whistles a bird's tune that's quickly returned from the other boat. The boys' calm movements send a shiver down my back. We sit still for the next quarter hour, waiting for our prey, and slide our oars gently into the water to vie for the final approach. Somewhere in the darkness, the second boat of marines maneuvers silently, pulling up beside us as quietly as a cat.

The cutter shifts as Catsper rises, touching his marines to get their attention. My hand drops to the hilt of my own sword strapped to my waist. The marines pass the touch down the line. A few moments later, the Spade sitting beside me reaches back and squeezes my shoulder. Although I knew it was coming, the firm press of his hand sends my heart into a gallop.

The boat rocks as one by one the disconcertingly small, black-clad bodies cast grappling hooks onto the *Hope*'s hull and hop onto the ropes. Our boarding force is a contingent of children for soldiers. Yes, Spade children, the best trained warriors in the Lyron League. But the facts remain— It will be years before most of the Spades will need a razor blade.

I count the disappearing boys. Five left. Four. Rising, I make my own way to the grappling line.

A hand blocks me. Standing with his feet wide apart and his free hand on his sword, Penn shakes his head. "Not you, ma'am."

I don't bother inquiring as to what he thinks he is doing, and push past him.

Penn knocks me back. Hard.

The shock of hitting the bench rattles me, and I swallow a curse. "What are you doing?" I hiss.

On the ship above, voices rise in alarm. Our Spades have made their presence and intentions known. My hands curl into fists. I need to be there beside them, not hiding in the boat. "We are pressing the *Hope*'s people on my authority, Penn," I growl. "I have to be there."

"You are the only one who can captain the ship, ma'am," Penn shouts to be heard over the rising din as he extends his hand to help me up. "Lieutenant Catsper's orders are to keep you safe. It will be my hide if I let you up before he signals."

I curse. The memory of Thomas punches through me like a pick through ice. Keeping me safe. I already know how keeping me safe plays out. "And it will be your hide from me if you don't," I tell Penn with a venomously sweet voice. "You can keep me safe on deck."

Penn hesitates long enough for me to grab the rope. Then, torn between pulling me down or coming along, he hops onto the line beside me. "The lieutenant will kill me," he informs me with a touch of self-pity that lasts only long enough for him to weigh my progress and pick up speed so he is at the rail before me, covering my entrance.

Pressing a ship into service is, theoretically, a nonviolent affair. An officer of the navy informs the captain of the subject vessel of the press; weapons are shown but rarely used. And then a new flag runs up the mast. Given the unorthodox nature of our invasion and the oddness of the *Hope*'s recent maneuvers, I have little expectation of the matter going quite that smoothly.

But nothing prepared me for what I do see. Instead of finding a ragtag flock of screaming merchants armed with whatever lay underfoot when the marines boarded, I walk into a full-out battle with screams of pain and triumph that chill my blood now that I can decipher them. *Tirik* screams.

CHAPTER 18

My initial cold shock morphs to a grounding cool. Fighting the Tirik is more in line with my training than scrubbing decks. My vision clears as I scan the deck, noting the dying and the wounded. The Spades have control and, though the battle is not yet finished, I've little fear it will not end in our favor.

My gaze finds Catsper pointing his sword at a man with a hard set to his jaw and responsibility in his eyes.

"Book!" the man bellows in Tirik, and I hear the tiny splash of journals with lead-weighted pages slip overboard. He wears no uniform, but I am certain he is the captain of this vessel.

Catsper raises his cutlass.

"Belay that!" I yell, launching myself at the Tirik to shove him from the marine's killing blow. "Don't kill him!"

Catsper pulls the blow just in time to keep from slicing my arm open for me. "You're fighting for the wrong side, Ash," he says calmly even as his other hand brings up a pistol to fire at another Tirik seaman, all of whom are quickly becoming extinct.

I turn to the Tirik captain, who is on one knee. "Tell your men to stand down, sir," I say in Tirik. My voice is oddly calm, and the words feel right on my tongue. "We've control of the ship, and there is no need for more deaths." For the first time in a long time, I am speaking the plain truth.

The man's brows twitch, the only surprise he permits himself to show before his gaze runs over the deck in a final survey that I know tells him the same story as it told me.

"It's over, sir," I say.

He nods, tight jawed and stoic. I've seen the look before, I realize. It's the same one Domenic wore when he ordered me flogged. Standing so close to the Tirik captain, I see agony deep in his eyes even as his firm, confident voice rings out over the ship. "Stop! Lay down your arms! The *Hope* has surrendered."

There is a telltale clink of metal on wood. Men's hands rise reluctantly into the air.

The Spades hold their ground, ready for the kill.

"Lieutenant," I say to Catsper, raising a brow.

"Secure the prisoners," Catsper barks to his boys, and I feel a knot loosen in my chest. The marine nods to me once and turns away, counting heads.

I extend my hand to help the Tirik man up. "Captain...?"

"Quinn." His voice is strained but clear and respectful. "The People's Republic of Tirik. Might I know your name, madam?"

I open my mouth and find myself with nothing to say. *When all else fails, try the truth.* "Captain Greysik, of the Ashing Ship *Hope*."

Quinn's nostrils flare suddenly, and it takes me a heartbeat to realize that the reaction is not to my words, but to something behind me. "No!" he shouts as the report of a pistol cracks through the air.

A few steps away, Catsper grunts with pain and turns, blood already soaking the breast of his shirt. His hand reaches for a pistol, but a second shot sounds before he can bring it to bear.

I twist back around to find Quinn discarding the now useless gun with which he had killed his own man.

"I apologize for my man's actions," says Quinn, but I've no time to listen. I let the Spades take him below while I push my way to Catsper's side.

There is much blood. I press the heel of my hand into the wound to stanch the flow. A wound he wouldn't have if I hadn't ordered the cease-fire. I shove the guilt down, knowing it will return with a vengeance the moment I have my mind free. But for now, I have to be here on deck. All of me.

"I'm fine," Catsper says through gritted teeth, but his words slur and his skin feels cool to my touch. He sways, and I slide my arm under his good shoulder, my heart beating as quickly as his must now be.

"Go below," I tell him quietly.

He pulls back. "I said, I'm fine."

"You stay, you die," I hiss at him.

"Then I die," Catsper hisses back.

I touch his shoulder in gentle apology, the reason for which he does not yet understand. Then, boldly holding his gaze, I issue orders for the two Spades beside me to escort Catsper below by any means necessary. And keep him there.

Catsper's rage sears me raw, but I master my face and call out in a tone whose indifference reflects nothing of what I feel, "Mr. Kederic! Situation report, if you please."

The middie appears at my elbow at once, though I must

clear my throat to tear his attention away from the companionway, which Catsper—having thrown onto the deck the two marines who attempted to lay hands on him—has just descended. "Six subjects killed, three seriously injured, eighteen in custody, ma'am."

"And of our crew?" I keep my voice steady.

"Seventeen marines and eight seamen are fit for duty. Price is uninjured as well."

"Ma'am." A female voice I'd heard only in passing before today saves me from having to reflect on the butcher's bill just yet. I turn to Tara, the able seaman Dominic chose for me. Her usually calm features are sharp with rage. "You need to see the *Hope*'s cargo hold," she says, her nostrils flaring. "It's... It's bad, ma'am."

By the day's standards, which encompass discovering that the merchant vessel the *Aurora* has been escorting is actually a Tirik military ship and watching Catsper take a bullet for respecting my cease-fire, *bad* has a bit to live up to. I motion for Tara to lead the way and follow her down the companionway.

But then it's all I can do to keep my composure as Tara grimly opens the door to the *Hope*'s main cargo hold, lying deep beneath the waterline. People. People overcrowded and locked like prisoners. As I lift my lantern to survey the hold, they turn to look at me with their slanted eyes and round, frightened faces. Faces of people from neither the Lyron Continent nor the Tirik mainland.

Diante faces.

"Who are you?" I ask a girl my age.

No answer.

Sweat covers my palms, and I fight an urge to sprint through the hold, freeing the people before they must spend another moment here. Forty faces. The youngest is six or seven, the oldest, forty. One of the boys' trousers are ripped, and I can see emaciated legs through the tears. A woman's eyes stare at nothing, her body jerking and bending beneath her clothes. A little girl draws up her knees and rocks back and forth, back and forth. Like...like Clay.

Crippled. A bloody holdful of Diante cripples. My mouth dries as a horrid dread fills me. "Are you Gods touched?" I ask.

The woman who'd been staring and jerking a moment ago vomits into a bucket, then wipes her mouth and looks up at me and nods. The commotion stirs others from their frightened silence, and within seconds, the Diante voices shout at me. Loud. Angry. Demanding. Begging. Crying.

Thank the waves I didn't free them immediately. An angry mob can sink a ship. Stepping back, I put my palms out in what I hope is a calming gesture. "I am Captain Nile Greysik of the Ashing Kingdom. My people have taken control of the *Hope* from the Tirik Republic."

The woman wails.

"I am not your enemy," I call loudly over the woman's screams. "The Tirik Republic captured you, not us. Tell me how you came to be here."

More Diante begin to sob and curse, so much so that I start doubting my language skills. I don't speak Diante well, but this isn't high diplomacy. One of the men leaps at me, his hands going for my throat. A Spade pushes him back.

Storms and hail. I raise my voice again, searching for different words. "Silence!" I call, waiting until the worst of the shouting settles. "The Tirik took you prisoner. I am not Tirik. Do you understand?" I direct my last question to a Diante woman who holds the rocking little girl, hoping the focus will prompt an answer.

She swallows. "We are not prisoners," she says. "The Tirik are helping us."

I blink at her. "What?"

The woman kisses her little girl's hair. "I am Neera. This is my daughter, Nim, and she is Gods touched." The woman looks down, her face red to the tips of her ears as the girl scratches her nail again the deck planks, as if drawing. "But Nim's metal gift is too great for her to handle. I wanted her free of it."

It takes me a moment to realize the odd hitch in Neera's voice is shame. As if admitting the burden of elemental attraction and the desire to be rid of it was akin to planning to abandon a child.

Dread gnaws my stomach while Neera seeks her next words. The Diante monks at the Metchti Monastery were the ones said to have discovered a means of taming the ailment. How did the Tirik get involved?

"A Tirik man told me that in the Republic, those who do not feel themselves worthy of the Gift the Gods bestow may pass it to another," Neera continues. "I begged for his help, paid all I had. Please, Young Greatness, don't take us from our course. Nim is just a baby. She can't bear the burden. We need the Institute. Please."

The Institute. Price's Institute. *Storms.* I try to make my voice gentle. "Why did you not go to the Metchti Monastery, Neera? Why trust a Tirik man on his word?"

She frowns. "Go to the Metchti Monastery?" she repeats in confusion.

Several of the Diante snicker.

I feel an abyss forming beneath me. "The Metchti Monastery," I repeat firmly. "In your own capital city. Where—"

"Forgive me, Greatness," Neera says, lowering her face.

"But perhaps... The Metchti Monastery translates to Temple of Dreams in your tongue. It is a concept, not an actual place."

The abyss widens. Blood drains from my face. "There is no Metchti Monastery," I say flatly.

Neera licks her lips. "There is, of course. Just, perhaps not in a way you think. Not in a way you might walk into with your body. Not like the Institute."

"But in the capital..." I know arguing with Neera makes me an imbecile. But I can't help my words. I've heard of it spoken of as a real place. A place with a location. And a cure. An imaginary temple has no address.

"Many of our most devout live in the capital, Young Greatness," Neera says. "People from all over our nation travel to study with the monks there. To reach their own Metchti."

No. *NO.*

I take a step back from the Diante. Sweat covers my forehead and slithers into my eyes.

"Are you all right, Young Greatness?" Neera asks. She squeezes her girl's hand. "Will you help my Nim?"

"The Republic has no cure." My voice is harsh, but it is the only one I can find. "They lied to you. Had you made it to your destination, they would have tortured you all." I spin on my heel and walk out before I have to see my words register in Neera's face.

It is all I can do to stay upright. There is no cure. No Metchti Monastery. No promise of relief, not now, not after the war, not ever. My knees buckle. Of its own accord, my head twists around looking for Domenic's solid presence before I remember that he's back on the *Aurora* and likely in shackles. *Storms and hail.*

At least he's safe for now, I tell myself with as much conviction as I can muster. The one predictable thing about

Rima is that he takes the protection of his own ass seriously, and will keep the *Aurora* on whatever course is least likely to see danger. In fact, the damn frigate is already sailing away from us, not wishing to waste anytime that could be put toward getting as much distance as possible between itself and the coming battle at the Bottleneck.

"Ma'am?" Kederic asks.

"Set course for the Bottleneck Juncture, Mr. Kederic." My voice is hollow. "We will work watch detail out en route."

"But..." He hesitates before adding quietly, "what are we to do with the Diante people? Will we take them into battle with us?"

"You've your orders, Mr. Kederic," I snap. "Be about it. And I want to see the Tirik captain in my cabin."

CHAPTER 19

Captain Quinn has more cuts and bruises than when I last saw him. Two of the larger Spades drag him into the captain's cabin I now occupy and dump him unceremoniously onto his knees. Quinn is about twenty-five, with short-cropped light hair, a square jaw, and handsome dark eyes. His coat is ripped, and a gash runs into his hair, which is matted with blood. The rope binding his hands behind his back pulls his shoulders in a way that must be painful.

He looks up at me with a mix of fury and intelligence that makes me ashamed for allowing such treatment of a naval captain, no matter what uniform he wears. But his kind had opened fire on the *Faithful*'s lifeboats, and Quinn's own man shot Catsper after claiming to have laid down arms. Worse, Quinn's ship carries sick civilians—children—for sacrifice to the Institute.

"Tell me about your *cargo*," I demand in Tirik.

His nostrils flare. "I am carrying forty Diante Gifted," Quinn answers in fluent Lyron. His voice is deep and measured. A professional's voice, telling me a fact he is certain I know already. Except professionals don't put innocent people into a floating cage.

"Why?"

"To aid them." The bastard manages to sound like he believes his own fiction. "The Tirik Republic believes that no man should be shackled to the circumstances of his birth. Everyone deserves the same chance and opportunity as their brothers."

"Spare me the Republic's propaganda, sir."

Quinn stares at me in silent defiance.

I circle around him. I've never interrogated a prisoner before and find myself little enjoying the process. My stomach clenches with longing for Domenic and the support his mere presence would provide. "You would have me believe that you are on a humanitarian mission, then, Mr. Quinn?"

"I would not expect any Lyron League officer to believe that a ship and crew might put themselves in harm's way to help those born less fortunate. Your lack of faith makes it no less true, however."

I stop before him and open my arms. "Humor me, Captain Quinn, and pretend that, despite royal blood, I somehow managed to hold on to my soul—you must be practiced in suspending disbelief, given the rubbish your superiors spout—and spell out your intentions for the Gifted for me."

Quinn's jaw clenches before he spits his answer. "The People's Republic would like to see the Gifted cured of their affliction. I was taking my patients to get them help. That is all I am willing to tell you, *Captain* Greysik."

"Then pray tell me why you aren't curing your own Gifted first?" I throw up my hands. "Why do you hide the existence of your Institute and smuggle other nations' people into the clutches of your science men?"

Quinn's face twitches in surprise at my mention of the Institute. He shifts his shoulders, searching for a more comfortable position, though none is to be found. He considers me before speaking. "The cure is not yet perfected," he concedes. "The Diante down there are better off with a trial treatment than nothing at all. Once we are able to isolate the right physic and make enough for the masses, we will distribute it throughout the Republic." He bares his teeth. "Equally and fairly, regardless of birth and wealth."

"You are torturing innocent people, sir!" I slam my palm against the desk—Quinn's old desk. "How dare you call yourself an officer?"

He raises a brow in irony. "I am torturing no one. The Gifted are restrained for the safety of this vessel and themselves." His voice is calm. "I note you've not let them run rampant over your decks quite yet either."

My fingers curl into fists in frustration. The fragile rein that I have on my temper is slipping, which little helps my cause. "What other Tirik vessels cruise these waters?"

Quinn tries to shrug, but the ropes don't allow it. "As an officer of the Republic Navy, I must respectfully decline to answer that."

"Is the *Devron* still in the Siaman Sea?"

Silence.

"When are you expected back at the Institute?"

Quinn blinks at me like a damn owl.

One of the Spades draws a pistol from his belt and silently points it at my prisoner. Darkness clouds the boy's face. Quinn's man had wounded Catsper, and the Spade isn't just willing to shoot the captain, to execute him here and now, he *wants* to.

The Spade cocks the pistol. The small click is deafeningly loud. "Answer Captain Greysik's question."

Quinn turns toward the voice, registering the barrel pointed at him. The boy's finger flexes inside the trigger guard, and Quinn flinches but reclaims himself quickly. His face is blank. Jaw clenched, Quinn lifts his chin to expose his throat. He waits, the artery on the side of his neck pulsing quick and hard.

Storms. What the bloody hell am I doing, threatening a bound prisoner with execution? And not just any prisoner but a naval officer. A captain. Self-disgust slithers over me, made worse by the small part of my heart that still wants to see the threat penetrate, longing for retribution for the Ashing lifeboats the Tirik Republic once fired on.

"Put away your weapon and cut the captain's bonds," I order the marine, clasping my hands behind my back. "It is the custom of the navy to accept a captured officer's parole. Captain Quinn is to be treated with the courtesy due his rank."

For a heartbeat, I fear the Spade will refuse, but Catsper trained his boys to follow orders. Uncocking his weapon, the marine takes out a knife. He nicks Quinn's flesh as he cuts the rope, then reclaims his post, staring straight ahead.

Quinn winces slightly and rubs his wrists.

"Sit." I point to a chair and wait for him to comply. There is little point in pursuing the previous questions, and I do not bother trying. "What is your relationship with Captain Rima?" I ask instead.

A corner of Quinn's mouth twitches up. "I thought you knew by now. Captain Rima is...*was* in my employ."

My mouth dries. The riches of Rima's cabin. A wife with a lifestyle kings could little afford. The frantic insistence to keep a schedule. The attempt to squeeze me for sensitive military information. Rima wasn't running a little side business. He was working for the enemy.

"How much did Captain Rima know of your cargo?" I ask, the mask of professionalism holding itself by a thread.

Quinn's jaw tightens. "Do not do that again."

I frown. "Ask you questions?"

"Call the Gifted *cargo*."

I pull back from his anger. The outburst could cost him much, and he knows it. "The words were ill chosen," I say honestly. "How much did Captain Rima know of the Gifted?"

He nods, accepting the new words. "In such arrangements, information flows one way, Ms. Greysik. I paid Rima four thousand gold coins for each passage. That is all he needed to know."

A yearly salary for a week's worth of work. Even if Rima knew no details, he would have known no one paid such sums for escorting rice. *Bastard.* I take a step back and compose myself. I can do nothing about Rima right now. "How did you come by this assignment?" I ask.

"I volunteered." Quinn turns to look out the window. The *Aurora* is far from sight, and the *Hope* skips forward easily on the waves. "The danger of crossing Lyron-infested waters in a small, minimally armed ship, riding in the very wake of a Lyron frigate..." He smiles wryly at me, and I acknowledge the situation with a nod. "I found it exhilarating with its challenge. And I was helping all our nations. Elemental attraction is a disease that affects us all, Lyron, Tirik, and Diante alike."

"Yes, it does." Despite his allegiance, it is difficult to hate Quinn. I've met officers like Quinn before. On our own side. I sigh and start for the door, glancing at the Spades before leaving. "Bring Logan Price down to speak with Captain Quinn, if you please. I've some things to attend to."

~

THE *HOPE*'s small sick berth was never meant to accommodate damage of battle, but the woman in a bloody apron who rules over the domain has plainly seen worse. Tirik and Lyron patients lie side by side. I briefly wonder whether the Spades intended to leave the doctor with her duties or if not even they could stand between her and her patients. Seeing me, she takes a step forward. "What's the injury?" she asks, examining me with her gaze and already dismissing the complaint as something that can wait.

"I'm Nile," I say in Tirik. "I'm the captain of the *Hope*."

The doctor wipes her hands on her apron, and a wave of tension ripples over her face. "Doctor Mattia."

I nod in acknowledgment. "I am looking for my marine, Doctor. The one shot by a Tirik officer after the ship surrendered."

"Commissioner Jaquis," the doctor replies.

"What?"

"The shooter. He wasn't a naval officer. He was the People's Commissioner."

I blow air through my teeth. "A fine distinction, no doubt. What of my man?"

"In the back." The doctor's hand goes into her pocket and comes out with a bit of bloody metal, which she drops into my palm. A pistol shot she'd dug out of flesh. "He tolerated the surgery well but has been trying to kill himself ever since."

"Thank you." I close my hand around the slug and start to make my way between the wounded.

"For whatever it means to you," the doctor says with quiet but ill-concealed contempt, "when Captain Quinn killed a People's Commissioner, he signed his own death warrant."

My steps falter. "He killed a man who was violating the terms of surrender," I tell the doctor. "That shot saved the *Hope*'s crew from massacre. No one would fault him for that."

The look in the doctor's eyes takes a few heartbeats to sink in. Yes. The Tirik would punish Quinn for raising a hand against the government's watchdog, no matter how good a reason he had for it. It is the reality of Tirik politics. Of all politics. And, as always, it's the decent people who pay the price.

As promised, I find Catsper in the back. Bandages seeping blood cover his left breast and shoulder. For a moment, I think his body is jerking in convulsions, but then see that the marine is struggling against restraints. Grabbing a knife from my boot, I snap the ties holding his wrists and ankles to the cot.

Catsper shoots upright, his face pale. And angry and more vulnerable than I've ever seen. His chest rises and falls steadily, but even I can tell the movement is too quick.

"Easy." I put my hand on his good shoulder. "How do you feel?"

Catsper grabs my wrist, pressing too cleanly into a tender point to be a coincidence. "I'm fine."

I hiss in pain. No wonder the doctor found it simpler to restrain him. "What's wrong with you? We've taken a Tirik warship with two dozen boys as our boarding force, and we've been running to stay ahead of one disaster after another since setting foot aboard. There is more danger looming ahead. Pray tell me, how is asking after your injuries an insult of mythical proportion?"

"I didn't say it was an insult," he snarls. "I said I was fine. You, on the other hand, have a ship to run and a war to stop. So how about we both get to our duties."

"You are injured, Catsper."

141

"It doesn't matter." His jaw clenches. "I'm a weapon. And I am functional. Don't humiliate me again."

"The order to remove you from deck." I sigh and sink onto the cot beside him. "I'm not apologizing for that. But please"—I wave my hand—"feel free to bleed to death now. I'm certain I will find it most useful when the fighting starts up again. *If* it starts."

"If?"

I run my hands over my face, wishing Domenic was here. "The *Hope* is carrying civilians. Diante Gifted who thought the Republic would cure their elemental attraction. There are little children there." My stomach churns, and I must turn away for a heartbeat while bile rises in my throat. "If I take the *Hope* to the Bottleneck as we've planned, I will sentence them to death. Worse than death if the Republic takes prisoners."

Catsper's brows pull together. "Can they be put ashore?"

"I'd have to swing the *Hope* into the Diante West Corridor to make a safe landing at a hospitable location. The Diante port we'd called on with the *Aurora* is closer, but would take longer to approach given the currents and wind. Either way, I'd be moving away from the Bottleneck when I should be making full sail for it."

"So it's either protect the Bottleneck Juncture or the Gifted."

I nod at the bitter injustice. I hadn't caused this mess, but it was mine now. The confines of the sick berth are suddenly too restricting. "When I discovered my... issue, I forged on because I thought the Diante Empire had a cure. I was going to go there when I could. But they are as ignorant as we." My hand tightens around the edge of the cot, and I lower my voice further. "I don't owe the Diante Empire anything, Catsper. When we'd had some semblance of diplomatic relations, they treated Ashing delegations as if we were some backwater simpletons intellectually incapable of meeting them on equal footing. When we requested aid, they refused. And when the war between Lyron and Tirik grew hottest, they retreated altogether. They wouldn't let the *Aurora* dock for drinking water."

"And you are convincing me of all this because...?" The marine rubs his shoulder. "Have you decided to run this ship by democracy?"

"We are half a day from the Bottleneck Juncture, ma'am." Kederic touches his hat. "No other ships in sight yet."

"Thank you, Mr. Kederic," I say, dismissing the middie and turning to Quinn, who stands at the rail beside me. "I intend to change course to enter the Diante West Corridor."

Quinn looks haunted, as he has since his interview with Price. He pushes his thoughts aside now to give my words his full attention. "You are bringing the Gifted home." He cocks his head in surprise. "Will your royal superiors approve?"

I stick my hands in my pockets. Except for the reference to royalty, it is the kind of question Domenic would ask, and there is an absurd humor in hearing it now from the lips of a Republic officer. "Absolutely not." I stare over the water. "Will your superiors approve of the manner in which your People's Commissioner met his end?"

"Absolutely not."

I chuckle without humor. "Then it appears conscience is leading us both into trouble. Bloody inconvenient."

"Yes, ma'am." Quinn shakes his head before drawing himself up. "You will need to maneuver the ship. I will be out of your way." He takes a step, then turns, finding my eyes. "You likely know this, but in case otherwise... The Diante have an unfortunate view of women."

"Aye. And the Republic has an unfortunate view of nobles." I smile to take the sting out of the words. "I'll manage, Mr. Quinn."

It feels good to say the words aloud.

CHAPTER 20

*T*here are four men-of-war in our path. Or we're in theirs.

"The squadron is flying Diante colors," Kederic says, his voice tight.

I don't answer. It is bad enough my little *Hope* came upon any naval vessels, and it is still possible that the four-ship squadron ahead is actually Tirik, despite their Diante flags. Quinn flew Lyron colors when it suited him. And I am no better with the merchant ensign on my mast. Even if the flags of the squadron before us speak true, we are squarely in Diante waters. Had we been a frigate, our hosts would be well within their right to sink us on sight for violating their territory. But the *Hope* does fly the colors of Lyron League merchantmen, and it's bad form for neutral seventy-two-gun line of battle ships to destroy a civilian craft.

I have a lot of lives riding on faith in manners.

A muzzle flashes in the distance, and the report of a gun cracks in its wake. The warning shot balms my nerves ever so slightly. A Tirik force would unlikely make a fuss in Diante waters. They'd simply sink us on sight. I don't dare let my relief show. It would unsettle the crew to know I've even harbored the doubts and fears. Sometimes command is a game of perception. I turn my shoulder slowly to Kederic and pitch my voice clearly over the deck. "Run up a white ensign, if you please."

Though my glass, I find the seventy-two's name painted on her hull. The *Wave*, if my translation is correct. And she's readying a boat for inspection while her entire broadside is aimed squarely at the *Hope*. With that much firepower, the Diante could blow us out of the sea several times over, if I was stupid enough to resist. Which I am not. If luck is with us, perhaps we might manage to have the Gifted on the *Wave* within the hour and return to the Bottleneck Juncture in time to do something.

I clasp my hands behind my back as the Diante inspection detail rows to us and ties up beside the *Hope*. The sailors are competent, going about the task with not a movement wasted. Unlike my own people, all the Diante wear a uniform—even the six large men with cutlasses have loose burnt-orange trousers and matching sleeveless shirts. Their rust-red hair, all the same length and tied back with identical leather thongs, joins the similar slant of the eyes to give the impression of a single person duplicated many times over. The officers, one in his thirties and the other a boy the twins' age, glow in maroon coats with golden braids. Their perfection sends a jealous pang thought my chest. I look little better than a beggar beside them.

Pulling back my shoulders, I step forward to greet the officer.

He looks through me. "Where is your captain?" the man demands of Kederic. His Lyron is strained but understandable enough.

"I'm Captain Greysik," I say in Diante and hold out my hand. "Welcome to the *Hope*."

He snorts, staring at my outstretched hand as if it is smeared with dirt. "Greatness Bassic, captain of the *Wave*, flagship of the Divine Squadron. Is this a jest?"

I pull back my hand and clasp it behind me. I imagined everything from a pistol in my face to a demand I turn the *Hope* around this instant, but the disrespect still unbalances me. "No. I assure you." Instead of backhanding the arrogant bastard, I bow with cool courtesy. "An honor to meet you, Greatness Bassic. If I may present my first officer, Acting Lieutenant Kederic and the lieutenant of marines, Catsper."

Catsper shifts his weight, his anger palpable.

Bassic's gaze weighs the men and returns to me, the disgust now turned to suspicion. "Are you a ship of war, then?" he asks with a calm voice that fools no one. Bassic is an arrogant ass, but he isn't daft. A Lyron warship has no business here.

I meet his eyes steadily. "Yes. Last night, my officers and I captured this vessel from the Republic of Tirik and discovered forty Diante citizens held prisoner aboard. We came to return them. My apologies for the misleading flag, but I believed it safest to enter thus." I motion for a pair of Spades to bring Neera on deck and step back as the Diante Gifted falls sobbing at the captain's feet, speaking too quickly for me to understand her.

"With your permission, sir," I say over Neera's desperate words, "I'll have two boats take your people to whichever of the four Divine Squadron ships you'd prefer. I wish to have *Hope* free of your waters as soon as I might."

Bassic puts his hand out to silence Neera and turns toward me with a smile that does not touch his eyes. "Of course. But I do hope you would find it convenient to join me aboard the *Wave* first, *Captain* Greysik."

CATSPER VIBRATES with fury as I board Bassic's cutter alone. I give the marine a steady look, and he turns on his heel. Catsper can be as angry as he wishes, but we both know I've no choice. There is very little the skipper of a six-gun merchant would find *inconvenient* when facing seventy-two guns.

The Diante crew rows us to the *Wave* with sure, rapid strokes. Despite my racing heart, I sit tall in the boat, ignoring the hull's violent drops and the sting of salty spray as the bow cuts the waves. Bassic gives terse orders to his men, the same ones I'd issue. We all sail one sea, be we Diante or Lyron or Tirik.

The boy calls out the Diante equivalent of *oars*, and the crew stops rowing to accept a line thrown from the *Wave*'s hull. I rise in preparation to climb aboard, but Bassic holds out his hand to halt me and shouts up to the deck.

I stay put, waiting with mild curiosity, until the realization of what he's doing dawns. This time, I can't help myself. My nostrils flare, and blood heats my face like a furnace. The bloody man is having a bosun's chair lowered for me, as one would for a landsman or invalid.

Go sink yourself, Bassic. Ignoring the disembarkation protocol—not that I even know whether the Diante have the senior or the junior unload first—I brush past my good captain. The waves bounce our little boat with a ferocity that drops my insides with each roll, but it's hardly the worst I've seen, and my body adjusts to the motion with little thought.

I time the play of the two hulls as they pull apart and come together with a bone-breaking crash. Once. Twice. I step forward slightly and grip the metal rungs clamped into the frigate's side. Moments later I climb over the rail, bowing to a confused side party who'd expected to pipe their captain aboard. They snap to attention within heartbeats as a crimson-faced Bassic climbs aboard after me, his eyes glowing with such satisfying fury that the corners of my mouth twitch up.

Before I can fully enjoy the repercussions of my little rebellion, the entire deck, Bassic included, stills as a man in his fifties ascends the companionway. The many gold braids and fancy embroidery of his tailored jacket speak of power and prestige as loudly as the rigid attention Captain Bassic holds. His graying hair is braided and wrapped into a bun at the base of his tanned head. Though his back is pole straight, the man limps slightly on his right foot and the skin of his right hand is mangled, as if from an old burn. He regards me with no sign of emotion, then speaks quietly to Bassic.

I keep my spine straight and my mouth shut.

Satisfied with whatever he learned from Bassic, the older man pivots toward me and inclines his head, angling it slightly. "I am Greatness Tul Addus IV, Admiral of the Divine Squadron. It is an honor to make your acquaintance... Captain." His hazel eyes are questioning, and there is that pause again before my rank. It is as though the Diante all await the punch line at the end of a great jest that will reveal my true position and intention. And I suspect that being female, young, and out of uniform all fare poorly in building status with my new friends.

Which is their problem as much as mine.

Addus is waiting. I wonder if I should bow the way Bassic had, but the gesture feels so absurdly ceremonial and exaggerated that I doubt I could manage it with any sense of dignity. Instead, I offer the formal shallower bow with my hand over my heart, as I would in an Ashing court. A glance at the captain reveals that I gave offense, but Addus flicks his scarred fingers and Bassic says nothing.

"Sir, my ship carries Diante citizens the Tirik Republic captured against their will. If I might see them safely aboard your vessel and be permitted to depart, I would be most grateful." I keep my voice even. The sooner the Diante confirm my claims, the sooner I can stop losing time I didn't have to begin with.

The admiral cocks his head and regards me for several heartbeats. "I am certain you are fatigued from your travels, Captain. Let us share a meal."

I grind my teeth. Of course I'm tired. But I'm not on a pleasure cruise. I bow again. "Thank you for the kind offer," I say respectfully but firmly. "Time presses me, however. My ship is small, but my nation is at war, and my ship's support may help my fleet."

Another wrong answer, apparently. A vein pulses in Bassic's temple.

Addus smiles at me kindly, like a grandfather. His voice is soft. "You misunderstand me, I fear. Your crew's courage is no doubt unfaltering, but the *Wave* does carry seventy-two guns. Which point at your ship."

It is all I can do to keep my anger in check. I did right by these bloody people. I brought their innocents home. And in gratitude, Admiral Addus has made me prisoner in all but shackles. He motions me to the companionway, telling someone on deck to inspect the *Hope* while we dine. Fine. They *should* verify my claims. I force my white-knuckled fists to relax and I follow Addus and Bassic to the admiral's cabin, where a steward quickly sets the exquisite table.

For two.

Captain Bassic, it seems, has not been invited for eating. Instead, he remains stoically standing behind the admiral's chair to offer translation when my Diante falls short. Addus leads a polite conversation that I follow with as much courtesy as caution.

My name is Nile. I am from Ashing. I've been at sea since age eight. I've always loved the sea. I have an older brother and a twin. Another brother had died at sea when I was young. I speak Diante and Tirik. I am a naval officer. I tense here, watching my words with care. The Diante may be a neutral nation, but I am not about to disclose what I know of Lyron fleets.

Addus smiles and pours me more wine as my heart pounds. "What does your father do?" he asks through Bassic.

I take a careful sip and weigh my options. My lineage may carry weight with the admiral, but it may also make me an attractive hostage for extortion. If there is anything left of Ashing to extort. "He helps the Ashing government," I say with a smile. "My mother busies herself with worrying about her children."

"At least someone knows her place," Bassic murmurs.

My eyes flash. A point the admiral does not fail to miss.

A knock at the door forestalls further conversation. At Addus's command, the door opens and the Diante midshipman scurries in to bow to the men and whisper something too soft for me to hear to his captain and admiral. Bassic nods to the boy, who returns to the door and opens it all the way.

The temperature in the berth plummets as two Diante seamen open the door wide enough to drag a man inside. His hands are bound behind his back and his head lolls as the guards deposit him onto his knees on the carpeted cabin deck.

Blood pulses in my head as I watch him struggle to raise his face. Behind the swollen eye and bloody lip, I recognize Captain Quinn.

"I apologize for offending your appetite," Addus says with that same kind tone he used to ask after my family, "but my young gentleman has returned from his visit to the *Hope*. Might I inquire whether this is the man responsible for transporting our Gods touched?"

CHAPTER 21

My attention is riveted to Quinn. I little care if this show is meant as a warning. Quinn is my prisoner. My responsibility. My nostrils flare.

"This is the Tirik officer who was in command of the *Hope* when I captured her." I incline my head toward Quinn as if he isn't tied up and abused. "Captain Quinn, permit me to introduce His Greatness Admiral Addus of the Divine Squadron."

Quinn gives Addus a shallow bow, as I had done.

Bassic backhands him.

Without hands for support, Quinn teeters precariously for a moment before reclaiming his balance.

The wineglass shatters in my hand, the shards cutting my palm. I don't realize what I'm doing until I am up, in front of the Tirik captain. "With due respect, Admiral Addus, Captain Quinn is my prisoner. You've no right to mistreat him."

Addus's brow rises. "Are you not our de facto prisoner as well?" he asks.

My heart is pounding. I'm tired of these games. I meet Addus's gaze straight on. "You tell me, sir. Are you taking my crew and me into your custody?"

"You did violate our waters." Addus's calm, almost deferential tone grates on me even with the translation.

"I did what I had to do," I snarl at him. "For your people and my own sense of decency."

The admiral studies me for a long time. I hold his gaze, vaguely aware of the bleeding cuts on my palm where the crushed glass cut me, my dry mouth, my shallow breathing. When the silence stretches so long I'm no longer sure what it is I'm waiting for, Addus breaks it with a sharp bark of orders.

Everyone clears the room. I fight to keep my surprise concealed as Bassic leaves us as well, closing the door behind him.

Addus points to the spot where Quinn had knelt. "He will not be harmed while I am dining with my guest," he says in very good Lyron. The translation had been a game.

I keep my silence.

"You are... Princess Nile Greysik." It isn't a question.

My face heats as I recall my pointless evasions earlier in the conversation. Of course Addus knew the truth, if not from the *Hope*'s crew, then from Quinn. There had been little point in keeping my secret when the original plan involved pressing the *Hope* into the Ashing navy.

Addus knits his brows. "Why do you protect the Tirik man. Is he not your enemy?"

"His nation is at war with mine," I answer. "Captain Quinn is my adversary, not my enemy."

"And your intelligence people, they will be gentle like you?"

My mouth thins. "I don't know." That is a lie, and I know it. And so does Addus. I tighten my fist. "No. I do not believe they will. But while in my care, I will treat him with the dignity his uniform deserves. Captain Quinn was taking your people to a terrible fate, but he was not aware of it."

"Mm."

Addus's noise leaves much to interpretation, but there is little gain to be had from continued discussion of Quinn and my morals. "Your flag captain dislikes me."

"Captain Bassic finds you rude. Both in your manners and in your decision to claim a naval rank."

"And you do not?" The words are out of my mouth before I consider their phrasing.

"I am a bit older than Bassic. I've traveled more." He points to me. "I studied in Ashing. Saw Felielle, Biron. Ashing seamen are best in the world, I think. Men and women." His smile is genuine, and I smile back, though it is odd thinking of Addus in Ashing ports. More accurately, it is odd thinking of the navy before I joined its ranks. Addus rubs his upper lip. "I was last in your kingdom fifteen years ago now, comparing ship designs. I recall two little children running through the palace like fiends. You and your brother, perhaps? He is well?"

A swallow, the too-familiar mix of pain and fear creeping through me. "He...he attracts metal."

Addus's smile pushes me off guard. "The Gods have touched him, then! My congratulations."

Congratulations. I let my face show my disagreement but say nothing aloud. Whatever the Diante beliefs are, it little changes reality. Ashing, like the other Lyron kingdoms, shuns the Gifted. My twin Clay has been hidden from view for years, as if his existence was the family's dirty secret. "Sir," I say, gathering myself. "I thank you for teaching me the rudeness of blunt requests, but I must beg your indulgence. My ship needs to take her place in battle. If we are your guests, as you say, I beg your leave to depart. Please."

Addus nods, his expression growing serious. "Tell me of this battle you rush to," he commands in a tone I'm used to hearing from admirals. Meeting his eyes, I push my plate away and brief him on the truth, starting with Rima's treason all the way to the destruction of a great portion of the joint Lyron League fleets, to Thad's note about the coming battle at the Bottleneck.

When I am done, Addus steeples his hands under his chin as he studies the chart I've commandeered during my explanation. I can see calculations running through his mind. "There are two fleets readying to fight over the control of Bottleneck Juncture. You believe your little ship will make a difference?" he asks.

I shrug. "The Bottleneck Juncture is a doorway between the Siaman, the Ardent Ocean and the Diante West Corridor. It connects a great deal of water but is narrow enough that even a small ship can make a difference. I intend to position the *Hope* on the Siaman side of the juncture and hold the proverbial doorway closed until other ships arrive."

"I do not believe your ship will make much difference," he says, shaking his head. "You will destroy it and your crew with no impact made."

He speaks without condemnation. An experienced naval officer who has judged the situation and predicted the outcome. And I know he's most likely right.

"I will do what I can," I say quietly. "It is all I have to offer, sir."

His mouth tugs in a smile. "You, yes. But me?"

CHAPTER 22

*A*dmiral Addus offering his ships to support the Lyron League in the battle for the Bottleneck Juncture is as tide turning as it is politically dangerous, and it takes a full hour for the admiral and me to work through the legalities. The Diante Empire is strictly neutral in the Lyron-Tirik conflict, and Addus is not permitted to bring his ships to bear without the Diante Great Emperor's blessings—which we do not have.

"You may not support the Lyron League directly, but you could support the Ashing Kingdom specifically?" I clarify.

"Ashing is a small kingdom, in and of itself hardly significant in the Lyron-Tirik conflict," Addus says with a sly grin at odds with his years and his station. "To fly Lyron colors is a political statement. To raise those of the Ashing private armada is a...gift to the daughter of an old friend."

I am at a loss for words. "You would fly Ashing colors on the ships of the Divine Squadron?"

"If the Princess of Ashing appointed me as an honorary

member of the Ashing armada, it would be an honor," says Addus. "We can make sail in two hours' time and be at the Bottleneck by early evening. It is unlikely we will reach the Bottleneck first, but we will be approaching it from a different direction."

"I do not know how to thank you," I whisper.

Admiral Addus's eyes crinkle at the corners. "It is I who should be thanking you for the opportunity to exercise my men," he says politely, before adding in more solemn tones, "Thank you for bringing home our Gods touched, Nile of Ashing."

Although I will be returning to the *Hope* for our approach to the Bottleneck, I stay on the *Wave* while the Ashing flag is hoisted onto its mast. Whatever the Diante crew thinks of their admiral's interpretation of the law and his decision to defend the Bottleneck against the Tirik, they follow his orders unquestioningly.

The sea of gorgeous maroon uniforms of command staff and the shades of burnt orange and brown of the hands' garb moves with a synergy that resembles Catsper's Spades more than seamen. They move as one, like a swarm of bees keenly aware of one another's presence and role. A helping hand is always there, and no man is left to complete a task without needed aid. They are quieter than the Ashing crews as well. The men know their station and that of their mates, and no words need be exchanged or orders issued.

"They please you?" Addus asks, leaning down to speak to me.

"They've remarkable teamwork, sir," I say with a bow.

"But not too much initiative maybe." Addus points to a set of overlooked carpenter's tools the hands work around instead of putting away until a middie breaks rhythm and assigns two men to the task.

"The *Wave* and all other ships of the Divine Squadron are ready to set sail, sir," Bassic reports to the Admiral. "A cutter is waiting to take our guest back to her ship."

Addus turns to me, his gaze stern. "I would hate to have brought my fleet out to assist the *Hope* only to have her commit suicide. This is a battle, Captain Greysik, not an ego competition. If you disobey and engage any frigate in a ship-to-ship action, I will pull back all my vessels. Is that understood?"

I bristle but nod.

"Very good. Please give my best to your father." Addus claps my shoulder. "One final matter. What signal might I make to your countrymen? Perhaps they will be heartened to know reinforcements sail in their wings."

I hadn't considered the signal until now, but the answer comes without hesitation as I detail the order of flags and pendants to fly up the *Wave*'s mast. *Joining Action,* the flags read. *Ashing Ship Faithful.*

I STAND at *Hope*'s railing, watching the sun journey across the shimmering sky as the *Hope* and the Divine Squadron close in on the Bottleneck Juncture. The sea is deceptively calm, betraying nothing of the battle that has no doubt already begun. Addus had estimated a half day's travel to get to the Bottleneck and we are coming up to the tail end of that stretch.

"Deck there!" Kederic calls loudly from the *Hope*'s foremast. "Sail! Multiple sails! You'll want to see this, ma'am."

I push away from the rail, my heart thumping against my ribs. "Thank you, Mr. Kederic," I manage to say with a calm I wish I felt. I force my breathing to steady as I look up the mast to the lookout platform. It's different this time, I remind myself over the deafening pounding of my pulse. My ankle is healed. I know I can support myself even with half my body disobeying. At least I think I can. I hope I can.

"A year ago, did you climb when the Republic had snipers deployed?" Catsper, who I'd not seen approach, whispers into my ear.

Of course I did. It was necessary. I nod to the marine. Yes, that is another difference between that day on the *Aurora* and now. *The* difference. Today others' lives depend on me. It isn't that I've no choice, I realize as a stoic calm sheaths my nerves. It's that I made the choice long ago.

Gripping that thought as hard as I grip the rope, I push myself into the shrouds. The happy greeting of the wind ruffles my hair, the freedom of movement spurring my feet ahead of my caution. But I still swallow a sigh of relief as I hoist myself deep onto the lookout platform. At least I made it this far.

Accepting Kederic's glass, I scan the waters. The Bottleneck Juncture is plainly visible, the apex of it bubbling with white water. I adjust the focus of the glass on the white canvas that grows closer by the minute. And there is a great deal of canvas. Both Lyron and Tirik.

"We've found the fleets," I tell Kederic unnecessarily. Eight ships from the Ardent Ocean have penetrated the Bottleneck Juncture and are inside the Siaman Sea. Two fly the joint colors of Ashing and Lyron League. Six, the red ensigns of the Tirik Republic.

The remainder of both fleets are still in the Ardent Ocean, much too far away yet to engage. I let myself indulge in a proud smile, seeing that of all the ships supporting this battle for

Lyron, it was the Ashing ships that made it to the Bottleneck first.

Dismissing the far-off ships, I focus on the eight now in play on the Siaman side of the Bottleneck. The battle for control of the Bottleneck Juncture will be fought here. The winner will become the doorkeeper to the Crystal Oasis. The loser will limp home, forced to focus his strength on clearing a path toward an alternative water source. Depending on the severity of the quake's damage, that could take months to years.

Several minutes pass until I can reliably discern the ships. The two Ashing vessels are the *Falcon* and *Hawk*, sixty-eight guns apiece. Not the League's largest, but fast enough to have made it through the Bottleneck before the Tirik frigate sealed it off. Of the six Tirik vessels, five are large line-of-battle ships, and the sixth is a small frigate barely visible behind her larger sisters.

I swallow. The Diante's Divine Squadron is a quarter hour from range. The *Falcon* and *Hawk*, no matter how brave, will suffer horribly at Tirik guns before we get there. As much as I hate Captain Rima, a selfish part of me is grateful for his cowardly tactics that kept Domenic away from this slaughter.

"I know the Diante admiral has forbidden *Hope* from joining the action directly," Kederic says, coming up to me. "But what are we to do, then? I do not believe I have the stomach to sit idle while others die."

"Nor do I, Mr. Kederic." I force myself to smile at him. "We will lend our strength to the boarding parties and pick up any unfortunate souls who find themselves overboard." I hand the glass back to him and brace myself for the climb to deck.

"Captain!" Kederic's shrill cry brings me back to the platform.

"Calm your voice," I murmur in reminder, hooking my arms

securely over the ropes and giving the young man a firm look. "What is it?"

Kederic flushes slightly, but his voice is calm when he speaks next. "That small Tirik frigate behind the seventy-two. The sails shifted, and I just got a good look at her, ma'am." Kederic squares his shoulders. "She isn't Tirik. It's the *Aurora*, and she's been taken as a prize."

CHAPTER 23

*D*omenic.

I climb down.

Catsper moves to stand beside me, his silence a question.

I clear my throat, forcing clarity into my voice—the same as I'd reminded Kederic of just moments ago. "It appears Captain Rima's neck-saving plans have failed him spectacularly," I say, my cheeks devoid of blood. *Domenic.* "The *Aurora* never made it far enough to avoid the arriving fleets. The Tirik have taken her. She's tethered to the seventy-two."

Catsper lets loose a small growl.

I pinch the bridge of my nose, narrowing my mind to nothing but the sea and fleets. It should not take the effort it does. "Get your boarding party ready, Lieutenant." I raise my voice. "Helm! Bear off four points larboard and bring us up beside the *Aurora*. Let us stay out of the frigates' cannon range as we maneuver."

The woman at the wheel nods and spins it.

Catsper moves his finger in a single circle, and the Spades

gather around him, checking their weapons as they listen to instructions with eerie calm. One of the boys hands Catsper a set of freshly loaded pistols and a sword, which the marine weighs in his good hand.

"You intend to board the *Aurora*?" he asks me, stepping away from the others and tucking a pistol into his belt.

"Yes. If we have the strength for it."

He checks the pistols' priming. "I can take the ship, but I can't hold her long, not with the Tirik frigate beside her. We might do better augmenting a Diante boarding party."

I stare at the sea as we skip over the waves, keeping well clear of the large ships. "Rima must have foreseen the possibility of capture," I say, my fingers flexing into fists. "He'd have planned. Kept the most vital of facts to himself as a bargaining chip to trade away for his life. And now he's with his handlers. Storms know what he's told them already." *Storms know what he's done to Domenic.* My nostrils flare, but I know I'm choosing this battle because it's the right thing to do. I trust myself on that. "It isn't the *Aurora* I want, Catsper. It's Rima. And a sword."

Catsper tosses me his.

I LISTEN TO KEDERIC, still on the foremast lookout platform, as he narrates the maneuvers of the large ships. The Ashing crews are superior, firing three broadsides in the time it takes the Tirik to fire two. The large number of sniper shots Kederic reports suggest both *Hawk* and *Falcon* took on large complements of marines or soldiers before sailing. Spades perhaps, or some Felielle soldiers if they were still in Ashing with Prince Tamiath. Despite the Ashing ships' better crews, the sheer number of guns the Tirik point at them takes a gruesome toll. One of the *Falcon*'s masts falls. In my mind, I can see the crushed bodies, the sailors working their axes to separate the damaged rigging from the ship's hull. I will the Diante ships to fly faster. The *Hawk*'s broadside becomes ragged, with too many dead to man the guns in unison.

My chest burns to go to the Ashing ships' aid, though it would be suicide, and I can't. I have to trust Admiral Addus to do his job, while I do mine. So I do nothing but watch, letting the *Hope* swing wide around the battle to come up beside the *Aurora* while the Diante Divine Squadron maneuvers to bring its guns to bear.

"Two minutes," says Catsper with a calm that borders on lazy. The boys around him work hard to imitate, but I see the hands checking weapons a hair more often than necessary and feel the thick silence holding us in place. Kederic, whom I ordered to stay behind in command of the *Hope*, crosses his arms in disappointment but says nothing.

I keep my features schooled despite a dry mouth and treacherously sweaty palms. The hull of the *Aurora* bobs closer, and the Tirik prize crew aboard her realizes what we are about. They split their efforts between severing the *Aurora*'s tether to the large Tirik frigate, now under Diante fire, and readying weapons to fend us off.

I watch them, gripping my own sword.

"Hooks ready," Catsper snaps.

My thoughts jar my muscles. I draw a deep breath and stay close to Catsper, waiting like a coiled spring for the order to board.

It comes, short and crisp. "Go! Go! Go!"

A savage cry erupts about me as hooks clamp onto the *Aurora*'s hull, and our small troop of Spades pours over the rails.

I join the sea of black uniforms, wild energy surging through my blood. When my turn to leap over the rail comes, I take it at a run. My feet hit wood, the impact rushing through my bones, then I topple to my hands and knees. But I don't feel the pain. My focus zeroes in on my old ship. And the blood soaking her planks.

A Tirik cudgel sails over me, striking the air where my head was moments ago. I cling to my sword and roll away.

"Nile!" The desperately familiar voice reaches me through the storm of grunts and cries.

I spin but can't find Domenic in the fray. Most of the crew is missing, likely belowdeck and under Tirik guard. Or dead. Several kneel atop the slippery red decks. Domenic calls to me again, and I finally find him in the center of the deck with several other *Aurora* crew members. He is on his knees, bloody, his hands bound. My chest clenches. His uniform is gone. The latter would have been Rima's doing, not the Tirik's.

I scramble toward him.

Domenic surveys me from head to toe. Satisfied to find me in one piece, his eyes finally settle on mine just as I get close enough to attack his bonds with my dagger.

"Are you all right?" he demands, his warmth seeping into me as I work. The moment one of his hands is free, he pulls me toward him.

All the questions I want to ask about what happened to him bubble to the top of my throat. I swallow them back down. This isn't the time. We can't allow it to be. "Rima betrayed the League," I say quickly. "Where is he?"

"Below." Domenic twists his other hand free of the rope just in time to throw me to the deck while he strikes out at someone behind me.

Just as I scramble up, a Spade shoves me aside again, his

sword already locked with a Tirik. Forcing myself to leave Domenic again is harder than I imagined, but I make myself stay focused on Rima. Racing through the melee, I scamper down the ladders toward the calls of *Aurora*'s crew below. The voices are coming from the Cove, which is barred from the outside. I grunt as I lift the heavy plank from its hinges and step aside as a press of bodies flows into the passageway.

"Where's the captain?" I call to the running seamen.

No one pays me any mind.

I scan the men rushing past me, but the chicken-shouldered bastard isn't among them. Lieutenant Kazzik, however, is. My fists grip Kazzik's tunic as he starts toward the ladder. "Rima," I growl, slamming the surprised man against the bulkhead. "Where the bloody storms is he?"

The man blinks in confusion.

I don't have time for this. "Where is Rima?" I repeat into Kazzik's face.

"I...I don't know. Not with us. His cabin, perhaps?" He flinches as sounds of fighting drift down from the deck. "What's happening?"

Releasing Kazzik, I shove my way back to the companionway. The captain's cabin is one level up, right below the main deck. If the Tirik put him there, he's promised them something already.

I race to the cabin. No bar on the door, at least not from the outside. I step back and kick.

The door flies open. The cabin is empty.

I curse, the blood boiling fire beneath my skin. The traitorous coward is somewhere. He has to be. And when I find him—

Something slams into me from the back. My sword clatters to the deck, and I follow it down, my assailant riding me to the ground. The force of the impact rattles through me. I twist beneath the attacker, turning to see Rima as he pins down my shoulders.

The next heartbeat, Rima's knee descends on my ribs.

I hiss in pain and fury. It's hard to breathe.

Rima releases his knee and straddles me instead. His fist rises high above my face, his eyes burning with hate.

I feel more than see his body shift to put power behind the strike. Rima's weight squeezes air from my chest, but thanks to Catsper's training, the pressure is familiar. Uncomfortable but not debilitating. And counterable. I arc my hips up violently, dislodging Rima's balance before he can swing.

The bump throws Rima forward. He braces out on his arms to prevent his own face from planting into the wood. The weight that once pressed the air from my chest is gone. Rima is still atop of me, but light, unbalanced.

I trap his right arm and leg. Bridging, I twist myself to his trapped side.

He gasps as we flip.

It is Rima flat on his back now, and me on top. "How things change," I growl as I pin his hands with my knees. The excitement of triumph that should fill my soul is not there. Only the rough burn of treason. "Why?" I demand. "Why did you betray us?"

His lip curls. "I betrayed *you*? What world do you live in, chit? The Lyron League betrayed *me* long ago."

I let him struggle beneath me. "The *Hope* was Tirik. You knew as much when you escorted her through our waters."

"There is no Lyron and Tirik in the Siaman passage," Rima snarls. "Just some desperate merchants who think the world owes them. Trade in these forsaken backwaters is sparse enough. I deserve gratitude for helping one more ship cross the passage. One more exchange of pitiful goods between forsaken people."

I study the self-righteous fury on his face. "You don't even know, do you?" I shake my head in disgust. "Don't even care what the *Hope* carried."

"The *Hope* didn't pay for questions."

"No, the *Hope* paid for Lady Rima's lifestyle." Revulsion fills me. Rima's entire mission, likely his entire career, was about dark money. It had always been about money. The danger Rima put his own crew through to make *Hope*'s meeting points, the innocent merchantmen we failed to defend, the kidnapped Gifted in the hold he never bothered learning about.

"Oh, look at yourself, chit." Rima smiles despite his struggles. "You aren't a woman. And you aren't a man. Royal money, and the only berth you could find was in the Siaman. You are worse than useless."

I slam my elbow into Rima's jaw.

He laughs, spitting blood. "Did you not know, Highness? The Siaman is for the rejects. The sons of drunks, and boys too young to shave. And you failed at it even with *that* for competition. Can't haul a rope. Can't manage the smallest of work crews. Gods, you could not even stay away from the grating for a few months, could you? And that was all you, girl. No one helped you fail there. All you and your incompetence. Having you aboard was little better than sailing with a cripple." Rima bucks hard.

My balance wavers. *He's a traitor,* my mind shouts, struggling to drown the echo of Rima's words. *Don't believe him. He thrives on lies. Finish him now.*

But Rima isn't lying, not about my failures. Or my disease. Captain Rima speaks more truth than he knows.

Rima's hand twists free, and his fist connects hard with my

jaw. The startling shock of the punch dazes me for an instant before the pain explodes through my face. I struggle to breathe through it, but Rima's already knocking me off him.

I scramble to reclaim my position, but it's too late.

Rima's on his feet first while I'm still on my hands and knees. His boot cracks into my ribs.

I cry out, toppling to the side. Agony crushes me. Agony and lights. Green lights.

CHAPTER 24

S *torms.*

My heart races, my stomach clenching with fear. A convulsion is coming. Right here. Now. In the middle of a fight for my life. I roll away, seeking nonexistent shelter. Somewhere above us, the air is thick with the clash of swords and fists and pistol shots. Catsper's Spades fight to take control of the *Aurora* as *Hope* watches from afar. The Divine Squadron is engaging the Tirik ships, giving the *Falcon* and *Hawk* some breathing room. Outside, a battle is raging between fleets.

But down here in the captain's cabin, Rima and I are alone.

I try to rise, to run, but I can do no more than flop on the deck as Rima grabs my discarded sword and stalks toward me.

I shout. The sound joins dozens of others and melts into them. My right arm spasms painfully and strikes against the deck.

Rima's boot steps on my hand. The blade above me glistens, hovering impossibly large over my convulsing body. Rima smiles, savoring the moment.

Terror rushes through my veins and rings in my ears. I wish the jerking spell took my mind, as it sometimes does, and wrapped it in cotton. I wish I could watch my death with an odd detachment instead of feeling every instant of the horrible now.

But my mind is very much present. It screams inside the prison that is my body. It wants to fight. It wants to live. I feel my magic roaring its agreement, begging to be let loose. The realization hits me like a pistol shot—I may not have control of my limbs just now, but my magic, that's still mine.

The chair behind Rima crashes first, falling from a phantom wind my magic calls to it. Rima twists around, seeking the culprit over the tip of his sword. But there isn't any for him to find.

The air spins around itself tight and fast. It lifts the chair from the deck, the papers from the desk, the books and medals from the shelves. And it whirls them all.

I focus with desperate intensity on my magic, controlling its flow even as my body flails and my lungs refuse to breathe.

Rima's eyes are wide and wild. The typhoon blows his hair back from his face, and he raises his forearm to block the debris.

I wish I can do likewise. The inkwell flies from the desk and strikes my face. I feel the liquid slither down my shirt as my body tightens and flails. The distraction costs me, and the control on my magic slips its leash. Instead of holding off Rima, my conjured wind wrecks something in the back of the cabin. *No. Forget the ink and debris. Focus on the magic. Keep it alive. Keep it controlled.*

"You." Rima points his sword at me through the wind. "You are doing this, aren't you? What manner of demon are you?"

My body screams. I make myself ignore its protest, pouring all my desire to stay alive into regaining my magic's control. *Focus,* Catsper's voice instructs in my mind. *Focus, Ash.*

"You are an abomination," Rima growls.

Yes. Yes, I am. But I'm an abomination with teeth and claws.

"I made Dana scream when you ran," Rima tells me. "And I keep wondering whether you'll hate me or thank me for it."

My blood boils, and I ride the anger's edge to find my grip on the elusive magic. The second I do, a wind gust slams Rima's chest, lifting him off the ground. A high-pitched crash betrays the shattering of the stern window as he slams into it and slides down to the ground. The glass shards rain down on us both.

Rima moans.

I do too, realizing as I hear my own groan that my body is mine again.

Rima moans again, twitching on the ground in a daze.

My own physical state is little better, but I manage to crawl to a pistol I spot on the deck. Gripping it with both hands, I brace my shoulders against the bulkhead and point it at Rima.

We sit like that. Rima, staying down, half-conscious but aware of the pistol pointed at his head. Me holding the weapon trained on him, unable to do anything more. Even my magic is taking a rest.

Time ticks slowly. Seconds pass. Minutes. More. On the decks above, the sounds of fighting calm. Rima's eyes meet mine, and I know he's heard the difference as well. Neither of us knows which side holds the ship now. So we stay as we are, and wait more.

Footsteps sound just outside the cabin, and I tense, my hands tightening on the pistol's grip.

"Nile!" Domenic's voice booms through the walls.

My chest tightens. "Here," I try to yell, but the words come out as a croak.

Domenic appears in the cabin a minute later, his blood-stained clothes and hair giving him a wildness I've only ever imagined on Catsper. He coolly takes stock of the room, starting with me sitting against the bulkhead and ending with Rima kneeling on the deck.

"The Tirik have surrendered," Domenic tells us both, stepping inside and reaching for the pistol in my hand.

"No." I keep my grip on the weapon. It's an effort to focus. "The *Aurora* or the entire Siaman?"

"Both. Three of Tirik's five frigates are sunk, and the other two are under *Hawk*'s and *Falcon*'s control. Marines and soldiers from *Hawk* and *Falcon* are sweeping all the ships now, to ensure we've no surprises." Domenic crouches beside me, his face taut with concern. "The mystery ships flying Ashing colors turned the tide."

"I'll explain that to you later." It hurts to talk, and I'm fairly certain I'll be throwing up before too long. "Don't you dare," I add, seeing his hand reach for my gun again. Rima is mine.

Domenic's hand changes course in midmotion and brushes my hair away from my face. The warmth of his skin seeps through the layers of blood and dirt between us. "What the hell are you doing, Nile? One moment you're on deck with other boarders, and the next I can't find you at all."

"What happened after Catsper and I left for the *Hope*?" I ask, my attention on Rima.

Domenic shrugs, tugging his threadbare shirt straight. "I was arrested. I'm under arrest still."

"You don't look it." I try to smile, but the humor fails.

"I will look it again soon enough, I'm certain." His voice is smooth and confident, but I see the tension in his bunched muscles. He jerks his chin at Rima. "When the Tirik got through the Bottleneck and found the *Aurora*, the good captain let me out of irons to assist with the fighting." His tone hardens.

"And now the fighting is over. Give me the pistol, Nile. And go up on deck."

"Are you—" My words turn to a gasp as Domenic's body falls limp around me, a trickle of blood snaking from his head and down his neck. Scrambling away, I see Johina stand over us, the bloody handle of a pistol in his hand.

No.

A growl escapes from deep inside me. I turn toward Johina, rising to my feet as I squeeze the trigger of my pistol. The weapon bucks in my sluggish hands, the shot burying itself harmlessly in the wooden bulkhead. Tossing the now-useless pistol to the ground, I lunge at Johina.

My fist connects with Johina's jaw, sending a jolt of pain through my knuckles as the man stumbles back. His eyes widen.

For an idiotic heartbeat, I think Johina's surprise is a fruit of my assault. I realize how wrong I am when hands grab me from behind. Cold sharp metal presses into my neck as a skinny arm surrounds my middle. "Be still, Princess," Rima purrs into my ear. "I'd hate to sever your throat by chance. Johina, secure Dana like the prisoner he is, and tell whoever is in charge of the *Aurora* now that I wish to see him."

CHAPTER 25

I draw a careful breath. My attention swings to Domenic, who stirs as Johina binds his hands and leaves him slumped against the bulkhead. *Alive. He is alive.* That isn't much, but it's something. "What do you want?" I ask Rima.

"Quiet." He says nothing more as Johina leaves.

Agonizing heartbeats pass with Rima's harsh breath at my ear and Domenic's pained struggles just paces away. The wind flows into the cabin through the broken window at Rima's back, the sounds of the sea beyond it deceptively soothing. Then footsteps, and Johina returns with two men. They wear Felielle soldier uniforms and are both athletic and absurdly handsome. Too handsome for the grisliness of the scene.

Idiotically, I wait for them to excuse themselves and leave.

"You are in charge?" Rima demands. "You are no sailor."

"Indeed I am not a sailor," says the taller of the two, a tan man with muscled shoulders cutting a clean angle to a slim waist. From his stance and uniform, I presume he is an officer from one of the Felielle soldier units the *Falcon* and *Hawk* carried. The man raises a manicured brow. "As the issue at hand does not appear to involve seamanship, I believe I'll do. Might I inquire as to who *you* are and why you are holding the lady at knifepoint?"

Rima snorts. "I'm the captain of this ship, and this piece of excrement is one Princess Nile of Ashing." He pauses to let the words sink in and smiles as the Felielle man's eyes widen. "You will pen a document giving me possession of the *Aurora* as compensation for my service to the League. Then you shall let me leave unmolested with my chosen crew. In return," he gives me a slight push, "you may take the princess—such as she is—back to her parents and fiancé."

I try to speak, but Rima's blade at my windpipe quiets me.

The Felielle soldier tilts his head as if weighing the offer. "I must point out, sir, that we are in the midst of a war," he says smoothly, the lapels of his waistcoat lifting in the breeze. "I fear that even if you were to take the *Aurora*, there is no place for you to go."

From the corner of my vision, I see the second Felielle man, this one with short-cropped curly hair, reach for a pistol and slide around the perimeter of the room.

Rima's body shifts, a second knife dropping from his sleeve into the hand that encircles my body. Tearing open the neck of my shirt, he places the tip of the new blade on my exposed collarbone. A high-pitched pain, like a sudden pinch, crosses my skin, and I feel the seeping blood from a shallow cut.

"I will keep track of time in her flesh." Rima announces. "That was minute one. I suggest you deliberate the logistics very, very quickly."

The Felielle's jaw tightens.

Rima's breath is quick against the back of my head, his

desperation palpable. The dangerous desperation of a man who knows that there is nothing but a noose waiting for him should he put down his knife. A man with nothing to lose. Except that Rima had never kept the spoils of his business for himself.

"What of your wife?" I ask, my voice soft as to keep my throat from the knife. The second Felielle man, the one who was creeping along the perimeter of the cabin, is out of my sight now. I have to keep talking, keep Rima's attention to buy him time. "Will you leave her behind and defenseless?"

Rima shifts his weight.

I wonder whether Rima feels the rapid beat of my heart. "She's a famous face in all the courts. Once her funds are traced to the Tirik..."

"She knows nothing!" Rima snaps.

I rather doubt that, but Lady Rima has clearly been his blind spot for years. "Truth little matters, sir," I whisper. "Perception does."

Rima's hand trembles. Another crack in his armor, another pinch of disorientation.

I seize my chance and, grabbing one of Rima's knife-holding hands, slam the back of my head into Rima's face. Rima's other blade cuts into my skin again, but it was never positioned for a grave wound, and the bite is distant and irrelevant.

The others move at once.

The Felielle man who has been speaking with Rima lunges toward me, his body wrapping protectively around me as he pulls me away from Rima. As soon as we are clear, the second Felielle soldier, who had been sliding along the perimeter of the cabin, discharges his pistol.

I hear the fall of a body into water and a wounded scream.

Two screams. One cut off quickly and the other ongoing.

I scramble free of my protector's arms and spin around.

Rima is gone, fallen out the open window with the force of the attack, and the ongoing screaming... That's Johina. On his knees before the fractured window, his hands covering his face. Rima wasn't just his captain and benefactor. He was close kin. *Storms,* I'd be little surprised if Rima's machinations supported Johina's family as well as his own.

Johina's screams stop in a sudden menacing moment. The man rises, enraged grief-streaked eyes taking in the room. Me, standing on wobbly legs beside a bulkhead. Domenic struggling against his bonds. The tall Felielle man surveying the scene with professional caution. His shorter companion, holding a smoking pistol.

Johina's hand moves so quickly, I don't see the pistol he pulls from his waist until it's in his hand and pointed at Rima's killer.

"Aaron!" the man who'd saved me yells, his warning morphing into a strangled cry as Johina fires at his friend.

I thrust my hands forward, a guide for the hard burst of wind I throw across the room.

The gust cuts into Johina's eyes just as the boom of the pistol echoes through the cabin.

Johina flinches back, the gun in his hand jerking as it belches the iron ball.

A red gash streaks across Aaron's temple, the bullet continuing on to bury itself in debris.

A heartbeat later, the tall Felielle fires at Johina, who falls dead to the deck.

I sag to my knees, the last bits of strength failing me. Beyond the shattered window, *Falcon, Hawk,* the captured Tirik frigates, the Diante Divine Squadron, and the little merchant ship *Hope* all fly Ashing colors.

It's over.

The tall Felielle man who'd pulled me away from the late Captain Rima extends his hand to me. "You're Gifted," he says with more curiosity than condemnation.

I rub my face. "I'm Nile."

"Tam."

I give Tam a vague smile, allowing him to pull me to my feet. Other members of the *Aurora*'s complement start filing into the cabin, attracted by the unexpected sounds of gunshots. Catsper. Lieutenant Kazzik. Mic. I don't care. I make my way to Domenic.

He smiles at me despite his wound. This moment is ours to share. I reach for his bonds.

Someone clears his throat. "Begging pardon," says Kazzik's voice. "But Mr. Dana is under arrest."

"No, he isn't," I snap.

Domenic lays a hand on my arm. His brow creases with a mix of apology and regret that freezes my blood. "Yes, I am."

"What—" I start to say, but Domenic's focus is on something beyond my shoulder.

The air around us is tense as, with visible effort, Domenic pulls himself free of my reach and gives a small bow with his head, which must be throbbing. "My Prince Tamiath," Domenic says to the tall Felielle soldier who called himself Tam. "Hello, sir."

CHAPTER 26

*P*rince Tamiath's squadron of soldiers, whom I'd correctly guessed sailed here aboard the Ashing ships, link up with Catsper's marines to take charge. Together, the fighters secure the prisoners and captured frigates, leaving the sailors free to focus on repairs. While the other Lyron kingdom ships arrive and organize, the *Hawk* and *Falcon* hold control of the Bottleneck, promising death to any Tirik vessels attempting to pass though into the Siaman Sea.

None try. Being neither blind nor stupid, the other Tirik vessels turn around upon seeing Ashing's full control of the Bottleneck Juncture. A solid victory for the Lyron League in general and the Ashing Kingdom in particular. I should be ecstatic. Instead, I'm fighting off tears.

Sitting on a sea chest inside Prince Tamiath's cabin on the *Falcon*, I stare out the window at the sea. Instead of the glass water and distant horizon broken by arriving ships, all I can see are Domenic's bound hands as Tamiath's people lead him away to join Price and Captain Quinn in a *Hawk* prison cell. Hurt.

ALEX LIDELL

Domenic had been hurt and they hauled him away to a prison cell anyway. Separated us between different ships. Catsper and Kederic and the Spades were ordered away from me as well, sent back to the *Hope* to ready the prize to sail to the Lyron mainland. Even the overheard news that Kederic would command the captured merchantman on the trip fails to lighten my soul.

Behind me, the door to the cabin opens with a creak. I ignore it.

"I thought you'd be interested to learn that the Diante squadron made sail the moment our position in the Siaman was secure," says Tamiath.

"I imagine Admiral Addus wished to avoid interaction with any Lyron officials," I say curtly. "The Diante neutrality claim was precarious already."

I don't add how I wished to have seen the admiral before he left. Or that I might have, had Prince Tamiath not insisted on bringing me back to the *Falcon*, as if I were an untrained puppy he feared might run away if not leashed.

In his defense, there is decent precedent for the worry.

Tamiath makes a noncommittal noise in his throat. "A dispatch ship is being readied to deliver reports to the main continent. The *Falcon* and *Hawk* will delay setting sail to allow for repairs and arrival of the final reinforcements, so if you wish anything delivered to the mainland expeditiously, this is the time to write it. Will you be doing so?"

"No."

A sigh, then footsteps and the clink of glasses.

"Will you at least look at me?" Tamiath says.

I turn to find him standing beside a wooden table a yard away, pouring wine into two precariously balanced glasses. Despite a body that's no stranger to hard training, Tamiath moves with a slight hesitation along the rocking ship. Felielle royalty go into soldiering, not seafaring, and I childishly hope the choppy seas will be little kind to his men's stomachs.

He extends one of the wineglasses to me, his long fingers holding the glass delicately.

I ignore the wine. "If you wish to endear me into a conversation, you can order Domenic Dana released."

"No," Tamiath replies calmly, "I can do no such thing."

"Can't or won't?"

"Both," says Prince Tamiath, claiming a chair across from me. "He is charged with mutiny."

"Against Captain Rima, who was committing *treason*." I clench my jaw. My only proof that Rima knowingly received Tirik funds comes from Quinn, who is Tirik and thus little credible. No one but me heard Rima admit to the crime. Rima must be laughing in his watery grave just now. The fatigue sways me, and I must brace myself to keep upright. "What are you doing in the Siaman?"

Tamiath lifts a manicured brow. He is about ten years my senior and appears to have spent that decade perfecting a look of intelligent amusement. "I was in Ashing when the Lyron League fleet suffered its defeat. The earthquake that damaged the coastline came soon after. Once the sudden importance of the archipelago in the Siaman Sea became apparent, my men and I chose to join the Ashing ships in the voyage to Siaman. Seamen, the Felielle soldiers are not, but I flatter myself to think we can make a difference with a boarding party or sniper rifles."

I look at the man who wished to buy me just months ago and say nothing.

He settles back into his chair, crosses one long leg over the other, and sips his drink. "Now that I've explained my presence here, might you indulge me with an explanation of yours? I presume our working theory of you having been kidnapped against your will is likely inaccurate." Tamiath's voice is dry.

"Likely, yes." My shrug makes me wince. With the excitement of battle fading, I feel the pain of injuries coming into focus around my body. The cuts on my collarbone, a gash across my forearm, other scrapes and bruises I don't remember getting compete with the too-familiar burn of my ravaged back and the ache of spasmed muscles. I feel the question in Tamiath's gaze, but now that we've touched the heart of the matter, I find myself with nothing further to say. My actions speak for themselves, and I refuse to say anything that may be interpreted as an apology.

"Well," he says after a moment, "it appears you've earned the Lyron League's gratitude for it."

"Did I?" I cock my head. He's lying. There is no way in storms that either Ashing or any other kingdom will publicly admit that a runaway seventeen-year-old bride-to-be negotiated an alliance the Lyron ambassadors failed for decades to secure. Even if that alliance lasted for mere hours.

"Maybe not. The headlines will likely give credit to one of the official correspondences the joint fleet admiralty keeps sending to the Diante Empire." Tamiath sighs and leans back in his chair. "But you've earned *my* gratitude. We were destined for a glorious death before your friends arrived. Now, Lyron ships control the Bottleneck while the Tirik retreat."

"Yet you hold one of the men who made this possible under arrest," I tell him.

"Tam," he says.

"Your pardon?"

"My name." He tastes his wine again. "My friends call me Tam."

I tighten my jaw. "Without Domenic Dana's actions, I

would have failed to get my boats away from the *Aurora*. Not only is Mr. Dana a Felielle subject, Your Highness, but you are also the ranking officer presently in the Siaman. Do not tell me you've no discretion to exercise."

His eyes tighten. "Don't play the fool, Nile. It becomes neither of us." Steel transforms his voice into one of certain command. "From what I understand of the situation, at the time you and your rebel contingent shoved off from the *Aurora*, she was an active duty naval frigate under Captain Rima's lawful command. Commander Dana openly refused to follow the captain's orders and actually *assaulted* him. The only reason the whole lot of you aren't charged with desertion is because, arguably, you weren't close enough to hear Rima's instructions.

"What Dana did, from organizing the escape to physically assaulting his commanding officer, is the definition of mutiny under any kingdom's law." He leans forward, his words crisp. "You are a soldier. Tell me, does the outcome of battle change the military code? I'll offer you one better, Nile. Tell me that you think it *should*. Tell me that military code *should* be contingent on the force's victory or defeat, and we can reevaluate everyone's role in this mess. We'll start, I think, by suggesting to the League's admiralty that Rima and his cronies be awarded medals of honor. After all, had they not been a horrid excuse of officers and human beings to begin with, you'd never have sought out the Diante."

My mouth is dry. I try to swallow and can't. Just as I can't deny Tamiath's words. Damn him. Damn the military code. The court-martial will find Domenic guilty. They'd have to. And execute him. My eyes start to sting, and I dig my nail into the webbing of my hand to keep myself in check. I can't bear to discuss this more, not right now. Not until I've had time to think. *Thinking won't help,* a voice inside me warns. I dig my nail harder into my flesh. "I..." I draw a ragged breath. "May I borrow a clean shirt?"

Tamiath measures me with his gaze and pulls a shirt from a chest. White, tastefully embroidered linen. "It is too large, but it is clean. I will try to find more suitable clothes for you as soon as I can."

Suitable clothes. The Felielle code for *dress*.

I snatch the shirt from atop Tamiath's sea chest. Retreating to a corner of the berth, I help myself to a pitcher and washbasin. The clean water feels good on my skin. I lather my face with Tamiath's perfumed soap, purposely letting it into my eyes.

For long minutes, the splashing sounds are the only thing breaking the silence of the berth.

"Would you like a comb for your hair?" Tamiath asks me. Another of his items. This one he holds in his hand instead of putting down on the table. He's forcing me to walk to him. To take the comb. Because I have to. I have nothing of my own.

I comb my hair quickly and turn my back to him to change my shirt. Privacy is a mythical beast aboard a ship, and I've changed before men without a second thought since I was a middie. Except... Except I'm different now. Mutilated. Even though I have my chest bound, my hands hesitate on the hem of the shirt. *Do it,* a voice urges inside my head. *Show the ruined flesh to the man who's had his thoughts on a marriage bed. End this game once and for all.*

I tense and pull the shirt off with resolve.

The hiss of indrawn breath says the mess of welts and half-scarred gashes have hit their mark. *Good.* My face burns despite my own reassurances. I make myself count to three before pulling the clean linen over my head and turn around as I tuck the fabric into my pants. "It's—" I start to explain, but Tamiath shakes his head.

"I'm a soldier. I know exactly what it is."

I shrug. Then there is nothing for me to say or explain.

"Will you tell me what happened?" Tamiath asks.

Domenic happened. I pull my hair back, braid it efficiently, and tie it with a leather thong.

"Nile?" Tamiath prompts.

"What you see is what it is, my prince." I spit the words. My gaze jerks to pierce his. "The bride you wished to acquire is disgraced, Gifted, and marred. You've all the grounds you need to extricate yourself from this farce, and you need my blessings as little as you had needed them for the marriage."

For the first time, Tamiath's eyes flash in anger. "You seem to think I wished to purchase a royal goat. Pray tell me what I've done since meeting you to support this bloody theory of yours? Keep going as you are, and the treatment you appear to expect of me will turn into a reality."

I take a step back and see the warrior behind Tamiath's groomed voice and handsome face. One who is due more credit than I've given him. I should apologize. But I don't. I *am* sorry, but saying the words sounds too much like surrender. So I tell him the truth to his original question instead. "I refused the first officer's order so that I could conceal my Gift. My back is the price I paid."

Tamiath crosses his arms, his face no longer filled with kindness. "You refused an order. And what price did your ship pay for it?"

I blink. Not *how dare he,* or *why did you not reveal your birth?* but a real, vital question. No, Tamiath is not the Felielle man I thought him. The prince standing before me has enough respect for my profession to call me to task.

"None." I meet his eyes. "The first officer thought a recent fall had made me wary of heights. He'd ordered me aloft in an attempt to conquer the problem. The ship had nothing to gain from my climbing aloft at the time, but I thought the action might expose my Gift."

"Yet you didn't hesitate to expose your secret to save Aaron's life," Tamiath says quietly. He draws a breath and blows it out in a long, slow stream. He reaches toward me and cups my shoulder. "Let me see."

I stiffen.

"It's all right," he says quietly and too perceptively as his fingers raise the back of my shirt and gently brush my skin. "I've seen such marks before." Tamiath's touch is nothing like Domenic's. There is kindness in it and attention, but no passion. No sensuality at all. Tamiath is careful not to hurt me, to touch as little as possible as he examines the wounds, but my body starts shaking nonetheless.

"A couple of the stripes have reopened." Tamiath's voice sounds far away. "They were cruelly laid. I've some salve—"

"No." I jerk away. My chest tightens, my stomach threatening to empty itself right here on the clean cabin deck. Pain and humiliation slam into me so hard that I stagger, catching myself with an arm braced across the bulkhead.

"Nile," Tamiath says with altogether too much understanding, "they are just wounds now. Like any other wounds. Let me."

"No." I wave him off with a casual gesture neither of us believes. "I mean to say I'm quite all right. Thank you."

Tamiath frowns but holds up his hands. A promise not to touch me without leave. "Your Gift... Are you fit to serve aboard ship?" he asks. "I've a feeling I'd have difficulty keeping you from the sea."

He already speaks as someone with control over me, and there is little gained in pretending otherwise. Like someone asking questions about a prized horse. "With due respect, Prince Tamiath, I've a feeling you can do whatever you wish with regards to me."

"For Goddess's sake." His face flushes. "I'd have thought you of all people would know better. There is no royal born on the Lyron continent who can do *whatever he wishes*. But we can help each other, Nile."

I rub my face with the heel of my hand, then count my words off on my fingers. "Gifted. Disfigured. Rebellious. Not interested." I lower my hand and blink. "You don't still want to *wed* me?"

"I did not seek you out on a whim, Nile," Tamiath leans forward, closer to me. "But I did make a leap of faith. And, having met you, I know it was the right one. We need each other. Especially now." He draws a breath and waits until I meet his gaze, see the full intensity of it. "Yes." He holds my eyes, instilling the importance of his words with their fire. "Yes, I do. Marry me, Nile of Ashing. Marry me and I give you my word you shall stay at sea."

CHAPTER 27

I sit, pick up the wineglass, and drink.

He waits.

"The Felielle forbid women in the navy," I say dumbly.

"Royalty does have some advantages." A hint of a smile. "If a commission is as important to you as I now believe, I will make it happen."

"Why?" My tone is sharper than I intend, and I curb it. "We both know you can force this wedding, if you wish. But that's not what you are after, is it? You want my true consent, to desire this union as much as you do." I frown at my wine. "A Felielle prince doesn't vow to turn the sacred traditions of his kingdom on their head on a whim. So, why, Your Highness. Why do you want me?"

"I need a wife."

"Why? You aren't the crown prince," I retort. Like me, Tamiath has an older brother who will one day rule Felielle. "So you don't need an heir. If you simply want royal-blooded children, is there no other princess available?"

"I said I need a wife. You are the one who surmised the rest." He nods to no one in particular. "If you wish to have children, I will oblige you. Is that acceptable?"

Acceptable. Like a concession in business negotiation. I feel the truth bubbling below the surface of the words, just out of reach. Whatever is driving Tamiath, I cannot see it. Not yet. But I must. I set down my wineglass and lay my hands flat on the table. "What do you really need, Tam? Tell me," I ask softly.

Tamiath's perfect jaw tightens, and his gaze locks with mine. "Trust is earned, Nile. And we're neither of us ready to extend it to each other. We can discuss the life you wish. The expectations we'd have of one another. I will give you my honesty. But not my secrets."

"What did you know of me before we met?"

He is silent, and tension lines his brow. "I heard of you as a soldier. I thought we'd make strong... comrades for each other. I still think so."

Comrades. Not lovers. Tamiath does not want to marry; he needs to. At least one question answered, then. "When I disappeared... It gave you reason to put off the problem of a bride altogether, with none able to question your motives."

He opens his mouth, but no words come. Just a hint of apologetic smile.

"I'm sorry to have ruined that plan," I say dryly and lean back in my chair, only to recoil with a hiss as my back connects with hard wood.

"Ah well," Tamiath starts to say, then stops, staring at the space I now leave between my back and the chair. Thoughts blossom in his eyes, and his gaze focuses with disconcerting intensity. "The man who ordered your flogging," Tamiath says slowly. "First Officer Domenic Dana. He is the one whose coming punishment upsets you so greatly?"

I freeze, unable to stop the jolt of anxiety Tamiath's words spark. My thoughts rush to get ahead of Tamiath's too-keen mind, to see the next move lying beyond his words. But his brow twitches, and I know even my momentary silence gave up more than I intended.

"Are you in love with him?" he asks calmly.

I flinch, this time with fear. "What?"

"Do you love Domenic Dana?"

"No. Of course not." My heart races, and heat rises to my face.

He chuckles. "I am ten years older than you, Nile. I've a bit of experience reading such things. I understand." The mirth fades. He taps his fingers together and looks somewhere beyond his cabin walls. Minutes pass in silence while the prince appears to have a conversation with himself, tasting thoughts in his mind and discarding them one at a time until something clicks into place and he nods. "Dana is a Felielle subject," he says quietly. "The Lyron League court-martial will likely have no choice but to sentence him to death. But..." He pauses, pressing his lips together. "*But* the Felielle royal family has been known to grant pardons. During a time of special occasion, few would think much of it. In truth, many would expect a kind act from a new princess."

Words abandon me. He's offering me a way to save Domenic's life. I'd have thought this a cunning trick but for the cards that sentenced Domenic to death having been played before Tamiath ever stepped foot into the game. I bite my lip.

"Will you marry me now?" Tamiath asks again, and for the first time, I see the anxiety chiseled in his gaze. One that's much deeper and more primal than my potential refusal can possibly account for. When he looks at me again, there's a rawness to it. "I need you, Nile. We need each other."

And suddenly, I know. "*You* are in love," I whisper. My thoughts race. Tamiath is in love. Desperately so. And obviously not with me. And yet he wants to marry.

No, *needs* to marry. I jerk with the memory of Tamiath's strangled call when Johina open fire on...on Aaron.

"You are in love with a man," I say slowly. "And it would mean his death should the truth of your relationship become known in Felielle. So...so you did the best thing you could think of. You sought out a girl from Ashing, not Felielle, a girl who you heard was a soldier and little wished for a life of another kind. You sought her out in order to offer her what you know she wants. A commission."

Tamiath's pallor is all the answer I need.

CHAPTER 28

"Yes." One word. One nod. That's all it takes to turn my life officially on its head. Tam kisses my cheek and whispers his thanks. I can't summon words. Nor can I summon the courage to go above deck while the news of our official betrothal spreads like wildfire through the *Falcon*.

It was the right choice, I tell myself. The best choice. The only choice. One that will keep Domenic alive.

The carpenter makes short work of adding a partition to Tamiath's cabin, the biggest on the ship, to create a private space for my cot. Beyond the glass window, the *Hawk* stands in *Falcon*'s wake, finishing repairs before heading to Ashing. The *Hope* and other Lyron ships are already moving about, some heading to the mainland, others to map the best routes to the Crystal Oasis and valuable timber. The Tirik limp home to lick their wounds. With the coastlines ravaged and timber not readily available, it will take them a few months to repair and regroup.

I try to be happy. I really do. Happy for Kederic's command

of the *Hope* for this voyage, for Tamiath and Aaron, for the respite in the Lyron-Tirik war. But each time I follow a thought, it brings me back to Domenic. Alone and hurt and locked in a cell, all because he chose to sign his own death warrant to give me a chance to escape the *Aurora*.

The tentative knock at the cabin door sounds a few times before I register the intrusion. I finally invite the visitor in, forcing myself to my feet only to come face-to-face with Aaron and sit right back down. Curly haired, well muscled, and a bit shorter than Tamiath, Aaron has the air of a lifelong soldier mixed with an oddly beautiful face and lashes that would be the envy of any court lady. Standing with his hand on the now-closed door, he looks ready to bolt right back into the passageway.

Silence hangs between us until I finally clear my throat. "If you need Prince Tamiath, he's been out for about an hour."

"Yes, ma'am, I know." Aaron nods, revealing a stitched but still-swollen gash that Johina's pistol shot left across his temple. "I came to see you."

Right. I hook the toe of my boot around the leg of the closest chair and slide it toward Aaron. Perhaps I should find some wine. I seldom drink spirits, but a chat with my future husband's male lover seems like a good time to start doing so. "Just Nile is fine."

Aaron swallows, his curly hair and hint of freckles reminding me of an older version of Thatch Lawrence. "Nile," he repeats as if tasting the word. "I wanted to thank you for saving my life. Not just back on the *Aurora*, but in what you discussed with Tam. What you agreed to do. If there is something I might do in return... I know nothing will equal your actions, but if I might make your own life more comfortable... I mean to say, I'm at your service."

I rub my face with my hands. "What else did my new friend Tam tell you of our conversation?"

Aaron flushes and lowers his gaze. "Nothing." He sighs and, as if just realizing he is still standing, takes the chair I slid to him. Aaron sits with his knees spread and his forearms braced on his knees. His light green eyes look up at me. "Please do not be angry with Tam. He... What he and I do, in Felielle it is a matter of life and death for me. Not officially, perhaps, but given Tam's station, that is the reality of it. Tam *had to* tell me that you guessed the truth."

And if I hadn't guessed? Would the two of them play me for years? An unfair question. "Who else knows?" I ask instead.

"No one," Aaron tells me, his jaw tightening. "Tam's mother suspects, though. It is because of her that Tam started the whole marriage show to begin with."

"I see."

"I doubt it." Aaron winces. "But perhaps you will once you meet her."

"I see," I say again.

He grips my gaze. "Tamiath told me nothing else of your conversation, though. He is a good man, Nile. And he will keep your confidence. As will I. I know you've little reason to believe just now, but it's true."

It's also mutually assured destruction. I play with the thought of telling Aaron about Domenic, but decide against it. No benefit and too much danger. Plus, I'm little certain I can keep myself together if I touch that conversation. Suddenly, all I want to do is sleep and beg the stars that I don't dream of Domenic. I wonder whether the sudden despair is obvious in my face or if Aaron is simply a keen observer, but I feel him notice the change in me.

Aaron's green eyes narrow on mine, then slide along my

body in such a frank assessment that I shift from fatigue to indignation to curiosity in a span of a heartbeat.

"Yes?" I raise a brow.

"I thought, if you are well enough, we might go on deck and spar."

It's a good thing I'm not drinking wine, I decide. I'd choke if I was. "Shall we be fighting for Tam's affection?"

"Oh, most certainly not." For the first time since Aaron entered the room, I see a spark of mischief. "It will most likely piss him off no end. And that's only *half* the benefit."

"The other being?"

Aaron grins. "That there is a unit of Felielle soldiers drilling there just now. If you'd like to send a message about who you are and how you are to be treated, this is the time to do it."

In other words, enough wallowing.

As we walk onto the poop deck, where Tam and two dozen of his men are, in fact, training with knives and blades, I decide that it would be very difficult to dislike Aaron. Striding companionably beside me, Aaron carries a pair of practice blades and inquires about the different parts of the ship, as if the rigging—and not the new Felielle princess—should be the main focus of everyone's attention.

It, of course, fools no one, and by the time we reach the poop deck, a blanket of silence hangs among the Felielle men training there. Stopping before Prince Tamiath, Aaron gives his commander a formal bow.

"Might we encroach on a bit of your space, sir?" he asks in a voice designed to carry over the unit of men on the poop.

"For what, exactly?" Tam asks, his eyes flashing a warning at Aaron, who appears suddenly blind to subtlety.

"The princess requested I tutor her on the Felielle

swordsmanship style before she joins in the regular training. It seemed a fair request, sir."

I make a mental note to introduce Aaron and Catsper, and then think better of it. If the two of them team up, there will be no defense for anyone.

Tam's face turns to stone, and I almost feel bad for Aaron.

Aaron bows to the prince as if permission had been granted, and tosses me a practice blade. He'll pay for this, I'm certain. In private, yes, but he'll pay.

My body groans as I snatch the weapon from the air. I'm tired and I'm sore. My only salvation is that in the short time I've known Catsper, he's managed to drill the tired-and-sore excuse out of my arsenal. *If you can breathe, you can fight,* he'd tell if he were here instead of helping Kederic. *And if you want to keep breathing, you'd better fight.* Right. Adjusting my hand on the sword hilt, I meet Aaron's gaze in an exchange of salutes that has the soldiers taking a step back to watch.

"If they were sailors, they'd be exchanging bets now," I murmur to Aaron as I open with a low feint to his thighs that morphs into a slice across his belly.

Aaron steps sideways sharply, deflecting the thrust with expert precision. "Oh, they are. They just don't want the prince to notice."

Aaron's blade snaps down hard toward my right shoulder. Hard enough that even if he pulls the blow, it will still come close to shattering bone. *Storms and hail.*

I bend my knees as I parry, the vibrations of the strike making my teeth clank together. Letting the force of Aaron's own blow propel me, I spin around, dropping low and extending my leg as I do.

The ship rocks on the waves, and my heel catches Aaron's ankle just as he fights for balance on the shifting deck.

Aaron swears, recovers, and promptly tries to separate my head from my shoulders.

It's all I can do to duck under the deadly arc of his blade and raise my own in time to block the next attack. The swords slam hard against each other, and only another lurch of the ship keeps me from toppling under Aaron's relentless pressure. Strike. Strike. Strike.

No let up. No reprieve. No quarter.

After Catsper, who openly carries violence with each step he takes, gentle Aaron's hidden fire is a sight of its own to behold.

When the ship jumps on the next wave, I seize on Aaron's heartbeat of disorientation to slide close to him, negating the advantage of the man's greater reach.

He elbows me in the ribs and dances away, circling like a wolf.

My lungs burn, but the triumph roars in my blood. It had worked, using the ship's motion to beat Aaron's defenses. Only for a moment, but still.

A plan forms in my mind, falling into place block by block as the ocean sings its song. With Aaron's greater strength and training, he'd take me down in a moment on land. On the ocean, however, with the moving deck and cresting waves...

Aaron circles again, likely to give me a chance to breathe. His mistake.

Focusing my attention on the ship's movements, I drink in the pattern of waves that I know Aaron cannot read. Crest and valley, crest and valley, each rocking the ship, the deck, the world. I watch the coming waves as I would in a naval battle, waiting for the uproll to give the order to fire. Except instead of firing, when the next large wave crests, I kick.

My foot sinks into Aaron's abdomen just as the deck drops out from below him.

Aaron's eyes widen as he is suddenly airborne. He lands on his back with a thud that's echoed in the gasps and chuckles around us. Even Aaron's own mouth twitches in a half smile as he recovers from the impact.

My victory is short-lived as Aaron rolls backward over his shoulder to come to his feet again. Then he rushes me, his full strength and training and wrath aimed at my chest.

In a blink, I'm flat on my own back, the point of Aaron's blade at my throat.

Right. And that's that.

Aaron grins and withdraws the weapon, offering me his hand. "Not bad for a seaman. And here I thought you lot were only good for giving us soldiers a ride."

"Hear! Hear!" shouts one of the watching Felielle soldiers.

"Enough." Tam's command quiets his men like the report of a great gun. All the soldiers, this time including Aaron, reclaim their wits and straighten before their commander. Discipline thus restored, Tamiath strides toward where Aaron and I now stand side by side.

A show. Aaron and I had put on a show, and I little blame Tamiath for his unhappiness over being neither consulted nor warned. Aaron lowers his face as Tam approaches us. I raise mine.

"Are you all right?" Tam asks me coolly. He is no longer the man I'd met in the privacy of our cabin, but a prince and commander.

"No," I say, meeting him glare for glare. "I'm dead. At least that was my understanding of the somewhat universal blade-at-your-throat signal."

I hold my breath.

Tamiath tilts his head, considering. Finally, after what feels like an eternity, he clears his throat. "I would be pleased if you learned better strategy than waiting for the ground to mystically drop out from beneath your opponent's feet."

"I would be pleased if you learned the difference between mystical forces and waves," I say in matching tone.

His mouth twitches. "We'll teach each other, then." Without breaking my gaze, Tam holds his hand out to Aaron, who obediently surrenders his practice blade to the prince. "Shall we be about it, then?"

It's a long, hard few hours, made more so by everything else I'd put my body through recently. I can barely stand by the time Tam calls a halt. The soldiers are in little better shape, though I know their challenge came from the shifting deck, not the sheer physicality of the fight. I think Tamiath pushed everyone to their limit on purpose, wringing full advantage of the camaraderie that shared misery instills. Either way, I'm obliged to hold on to the bulkhead as Tam, Aaron, and I trudge back to the cabin.

"Not that I mind," I say when the door closes behind us, "but is Aaron's presence here not odd?" My voice, laden with fatigue, sounds half-drunk.

Tam grins. "On the contrary. He's our chaperone, you see."

I roll my eyes and sprawl onto the first piece of furniture I see, which happens to be the sea chest from earlier.

Tam grips the edge of the dining table, as if the wood were any more stable than the rest of the rocking ship. "Once I'm not worried about losing my dinner, Aaron, I'm going to describe the full extent of your stupidity to you. In detail." Tam closes his eyes. "Goddess take me, but I hate waves."

"Bringing Nile to spar on deck was a good idea," Aaron says, crossing his arms as he sits. "It's all perception now, and this—

her with a weapon, us taking her fighting skills seriously—it sent the right message. You are just sore that you didn't come up with it."

"I *did* come up with it," Tam growls at him. "And then I thought one second longer and decided to wait until Nile heals before putting on a show."

"Heals?" Aaron echoes, his brow furrowing as he studies me. "Is she injured?"

I tense, little wishing to explain either my back or the muscles screaming from convulsion, but Tam steps in smoothly, "Nile was part of two boarding parties in a span of two days. What do you think?"

Aaron winces, and I can see the apology I don't deserve forming in his throat.

"I'm quite all right," I say quickly, even as my body reports in with complaints. "And I needed to get my mind off...things." I take a deep breath, allowing nothing but common fatigue to show in my face even as my heart threatens to break. The marriage I agreed to this morning is a business arrangement, and I refuse to burden my two partners with anything more than I must.

The ship's bell rings through the *Falcon*, and I excuse myself to my cot, grateful for the privacy as I collapse onto the sheets. I'm bleeding. Skin and heart and mind. But, on the other side of the partition, another cot groans as two bodies slide onto its narrow frame. It's a small thing, one that lovers all across the world do every day without thought, but one the two men beside me have been denied. If my being here in this cabin makes falling asleep in each other's arms possible for them, then today was well lived. I'll deal with tomorrow, tomorrow.

CHAPTER 29

"I'd like you to have a bodyguard." Tam's words, said with deceptive casualness over breakfast a few days after our official betrothal, have me spilling my coffee.

"You *what?*" I jerk away from the table before the scalding liquid burns my skin, Aaron doing the same beside me. My chest heaves as I stare at Tamiath. First my mother forcing things on me for my own good, then Ana and Domenic. Now Tamiath. It's some kind of Felielle disease. "No, Tam. The answer is, no. I'm neither a porcelain doll nor a dog to be leashed. Your fragile Felielle sentiment be damned."

"It's *your* Felielle sentiment now," Tam snaps back at me, his spine straightening so hard that Aaron subtly maneuvers between us. "And you bloody well will care about its people and their fragile sentiments. We will lead, we will guide, and we will challenge. We will not..." His palms plant on the table beside my place setting. "We will *not* disrespect them or break their trust."

"No one will take an officer with bodyguards seriously,

Tamiath," I hiss back at him, my hands mirroring his on the table. "I would be a doll playing at commander. How can I ask my people to risk their lives while I hide behind someone's back?"

Tam sighs and pushes himself upright with visible effort. "What were you planning on doing about your Gift?" he asks.

"Don't change the topic."

Tam sits, leaning back in his chair. "I'm not. How many people know you are an air caller?"

"You, Aaron, Domenic, Catsper," I say tightly. "A medicine woman in a Diante village. Rima and Johina knew, but they are dead."

"Were you going to tell your parents?" He spreads his hands. "The world?"

"No, of course not." I sit too, my muscles taut. If word of my magic got out, my parents would hide me away with Clay. There would be no going to sea, certainly no wedding with Tam. No pardon to save Domenic's life. "It would end all this."

Tam nods patiently. "And the convulsions?"

"What do you want me to say, Tam?"

He shrugs one shoulder. "Are you concerned?"

Of course I'm concerned. The bastard knows it and is leading me on. I rub my temples. What if the Felielle Admiralty is right? What if I fall to a spell in the middle of something vital and put the whole damn ship in danger? What if I was wrong about Prince Tamiath, and this conversation is the beginning of the end? "If you think I don't belong aboard ship, just say it."

"You *do* belong on a ship," says Tam. "A sniper can remove you from action just as quickly as a jerking spell. And more permanently. I'm not minimizing the danger, just putting it in perspective. Battle, war—none of it is safe. Plus, did you not keep a ship from capsizing? Did your Gift not save Aaron's life?"

I throw up my hands. "Then what—"

"The Felielle are used to royalty being under a bodyguard's protection, Nile, especially female royalty. It will look nearly invisible to them. But the *right* people can get you out of sight if a convulsion strikes, help you keep your magic under control. If you are powerful enough to keep a ship upright, you are powerful enough to tip it over as well. Plus, it will give you a spotter when you climb the rigging, with no one the wiser as to why. Surely the freedom to get around the ship safely trumps self-consciousness over having a guard?"

I stare at him, the words sinking in slowly in the silence.

"He's annoying when he's right, isn't he?" says Aaron.

Tamiath snorts. "The challenge is finding the right people, and I dislike the notion of disclosing your Gift more than we have to. I could certainly find good men in Felielle, but my circles run with land troops, not seamen—and I presume you'd rather not trip over your own guards in action. What of Ashing?"

I think of Thomas. And Mother. "I'll have a spy on my staff quicker than I can call the wind."

Tam taps his long fingers against his cup. "We'll think on it. All of us."

AFTER FIVE DAYS OF REPAIRS, the *Falcon* and *Hawk* finally set sail for Ashing. The captains take the journey very slowly, not stressing the ships more than they must. My passenger status on the *Falcon* would drive me mad if not for Aaron and Tam's physical training, but I feel like myself again only when we approach the mainland after three weeks sail. At that point, I claim a spot on the deck to catalogue the earthquake's damage.

It's...horrid. Even before training a glass on the shoreline, I see the ocean's wounds in the changed colors of the water. Once brilliant blue and turquoise, the new waves rustle in polluted browns and grays. Tree trunks and other large debris float aimlessly on the water's surface, while the changes in the ocean's floor alter the known currents. The *Falcon*'s captain sends a guide boat out before the ship to continually check the depth, further slowing our approach to port.

I shift my glass to the Ashing coastline and cringe. If the rest of the Lyron and Tirik coasts looks like this, no wonder the fight for the Siaman archipelago was so vital. We will need the islands' timber for repair, the Crystal Oasis's fresh water for our barrels, the vegetation for food and medicine. All things we once had aplenty that are now gone or too far to get easily.

"We'll be dropping anchor tomorrow and going ashore the day after that," Tam says, coming over to the rail to summon me for dinner. "After calling on your parents, we will proceed from Ashing to Felielle over land. Are you prepared?"

"Of course not." Giving the wounded coastline one final gaze, I close the looking glass and follow the prince down to our cabin, where Aaron and food already await. The thick aroma of beef stew saturates the air. "I'd rather face a hundred guns of a Tirik frigate than explain my running off to my parents. With the Tirik, there is a chance of victory."

"You are a Felielle bride now." Tamiath holds a chair out for me before sitting himself at the round table beside Aaron. "Your parents can yell, but they can't force their will on you. Not anymore."

"We aren't married yet. If my Gift comes out—"

"It won't." Tamiath's gaze grabs mine, strong and reassuring.

His hand slips across the table to rest atop mine. "I understand what it is like to hold a secret that can destroy your life, Nile. And I'm not going to let it happen to you."

I swallow. "It's not you—"

"You've managed to conceal your magic aboard a ship where you can't spit without hitting three people." Tamiath's voice is firm. "We can manage it for a few days in the Ashing palace."

"I'm going to rather miss this housing arrangement, though," Aaron drawls, lacing his hands behind his head. "Being your chaperone has been the height of pleasure. Especially at night."

My face heats, and Tam rolls his eyes at us both.

Comfortable. Tam and Aaron are so comfortable together, it still strikes me in the gut every time I see it. I take a sip of stew and pick up a ship's biscuit, tapping it against the table to evict the weevils before dipping it into the liquid. "How did you two meet?" I ask.

Aaron throws a quick glance at Tam before answering. "My father was the palace master at arms, so Tam and I trained together as boys."

So straightforward. A fairy tale. Or fate. Me, I met Domenic at a beach, violent debt collectors on his tail and my Gifted twin at my side. By the time we saw each other again, with me lying and him wearing a mask of cruelty, the ship of straightforwardness had long sailed.

"It was not as smooth as Aaron makes it sound," says Tam, studying me.

"Tam..." Aaron says quietly. "She little wants to hear a saga."

But Tam turns to me, disagreement with Aaron plain in his face. "I was a spoilt royal prick," he says, brushing his fingers along his lover's wrist in silent apology. Beyond the window, the waves caress the *Hawk*'s hull with equal tenderness while the sun kisses the horizon. "And I little appreciated the training master's son wiping the sand with my hide every day. Instead of training harder like a smart lad, though, one day, when I was eleven, I decided to play dirty.

"I ordered the servants to let me into Aaron's rooms. Broke all his things. Including a portrait of his mother, who'd died the year before."

My eyes widen, my spoon forgotten in its bowl.

"It gets worse before it gets better," Tam says darkly. "I ensured Aaron knew who ruined his home—knew and could do nothing. It would be my word against his, and the servants wouldn't dare contradict the prince. It was a crude variation to a trick I'd seen my mother use against courtiers who'd displeased her—the woman makes up in pettiness and power what she lacks in wit—and I was proud as a peacock about it."

"What happened next?" I ask quietly.

"Aaron found me in a swimming hole and knocked two of my teeth out." Tam throws Aaron a look of shy admiration. "My guards, who knew exactly what I'd done to deserve it, let it happen. So I went home howling and so full of humiliation and indignation, I did the one thing that no one could undo. I told on them all." Rising, Tam pulls out a bottle of wine, which he pours into three glasses. "The next day, I learned what it really means to be a prince."

My breath quiets, my gut telling me exactly what came next even before Tam speaks.

"Aaron and the guards were all punished in the public square," he says, looking down into his untouched wine. "I watched Aaron's father cry as it happened. Finally understood what I'd done. I still don't know why Aaron didn't throw me out of the infirmary when I walked in to see him."

"Oh, I would have, if I wasn't so bloody scared of contradicting you," Aaron says, his voice tinged with humor that speaks of wounds cleanly healed. "So there I am, bleeding and miserable, when the little prick of a princeling shows up with sweets. Good ones too: chocolate truffles, little lemon tarts, berry pies. The kind of things I had maybe once a year. I swear he robbed the kitchens blind. He gives it all to me and runs off, and then comes back with more the next day. And the day after that. After a week, I started to look forward to it." Aaron stares glumly at a weevil peeking out of his biscuit, and hands the hard tack to me for help dislodging the critters.

"After two weeks, Aaron offered to share," Tam says in quiet wonder. "After what I'd done, he offered to share. I was so stunned, I nearly started bawling. And instead of laughing, Aaron stuffed me with half a pie. He knew the risks better than anyone and befriended me anyway."

"I had a belly ache from the sugar," says Aaron. "Eventually, we started talking and discovered we actually liked each other's company. When I was ready to return to training, we decided that we were only allowed to lose to each other. So if any of the other boys scored on one of us, the other would be challenging him a minute later."

"Made you popular, no doubt," I say.

Aaron chuckles and runs his fingers over Tam's forearm. "Oh, you've no idea. Tam's mother tried to beat the friendship out of him when she found out how close we'd become, but it was too late by then."

"Because you weren't royal?" I ask.

"Because she could sense what Aaron and I only understood when we were a little older," says Tam. "And she hated us both for it."

"Luckily, we were smart enough by then to keep our private

games private," says Aaron, digging into his food. "And when Tam reached his majority and became an officer, he made me his lieutenant and aide. It surprised no one."

"Especially not my mother," Tam said, taking a deep swig of his wine. Yes, the wounds of the past may have healed for Aaron, but Tamiath... Tamiath still hates himself. Still thinks himself unworthy of the man beside him. He clears his throat and looks up at me. "Like I said, it wasn't a clean start."

I swirl my own wine, which I've been sipping throughout the men's story. And maybe it is the alcohol or the late hour or Tam's brutal honesty, but I tell my story too. From Clay falling ill, to the the *Faithful*'s destruction and cover-up, to my life aboard the *Aurora*. But mostly, I talk about Domenic.

Aaron's face grows harder with each word I utter, and when I finish, after the moment of silence that hangs between us in the air, he wheels on Tamiath, his green eyes flashing. "You *forced* her into this marriage with a threat to her lover's life? Are you insane? That wasn't our agreement."

The fury in Aaron's quiet voice throws me back, and it takes a heartbeat before I recover my wits. "He didn't force me into anything, Aaron," I say, meaning it. Tam gave me all the facts he could, many of which—too many—are beyond any of our control. "I made my own choice. For this insane scheme to work, we all have to."

THE FOLLOWING DAY, I finally get to be of use to the *Falcon*'s crew through assisting them in preparations for docking and reprovisioning. Boats go back and forth between the *Falcon*, *Hawk*, and *Hope* in an attempt to come up with a single list of supply requisitions. By midday, our efforts read more like a work of fiction than anything else, with each ship adding mistakes as readily as goods to the ledger. The *Falcon*'s captain and I finally lock ourselves in his cabin over dinner and come up with a clean copy I'm certain will pass the dockmasters' standards when we go ashore tomorrow morning. It's the first time in weeks I've contributed in a naval sense, and I feel a pleasant fatigue as I return at the end of the evening to my cabin.

And find Domenic waiting there for me.

CHAPTER 30

or a moment, I think I'm drunk on fatigue. I step back, hit the solid bulkhead, and step forward again. My heart pounds, the beat echoing through my body.

Domenic is on his feet in an instant, filling the cabin with his presence. He crosses to me in two large strides, his powerful hands cupping my face. His shirt is ripped, patches of smooth skin and glimpses of tattoos peeking from the holes. Safety and need crackle from him like bits of lightning as his thumb traces my jaw.

"Nile." The soft rumble of his voice caresses me, shattering the protective walls around my heart like glass.

I fling myself against him, burrowing my face into his muscled chest and inhaling his sea and brine scent. The heat of Domenic's body saturates mine, as his arms obligingly wrap around my waist and hold me against him.

I can't think. Can't breathe. Beneath my feet, the ship rocks on the waves, pulling the rope tethering it to the anchor while I cling to Domenic. Beyond the grand window, dusk's red and orange hues crown the clouds and spill into the cabin.

After a minute, Domenic grips my shoulder and pulls me away from him. His chest is heaving as if he just ran, and the lingering rays of the sun catch in his eyes, making them sparkle with a starved intensity that tightens my muscles into cords.

"I didn't think I was going to see you again," he whispers.

I don't want to talk. Making a grab for Domenic's neck, I pull him toward me.

He doesn't budge, holding me off by my shoulders even as his throat bobs in apparent pain.

A shiver runs down my spine. "What's wrong?"

Domenic's hands reach around to the back of his neck, gently unhooking my hold. Bringing my fingers to his chapped lips, he brushes a kiss over my knuckles. "I understand you are getting married," he says softly.

My chest tightens, squeezing my ribs. "It... It's complicated."

Domenic shakes his head. "No, it isn't." He raises our clasped hands, sentinels between our two bodies. His voice is quiet as he speaks. "A Felielle lieutenant came to my cell on the *Hawk* this morning. He asked for my parole, a promise that I will not flee pending my court-martial, if he releases me from custody. Once I gave my word, the man offered me a guardsman's position protecting Prince Tamiath's bride, who requires someone with knowledge of both the sea and of her... special attributes."

I let out a long, slow breath. "And was the lieutenant's name Aaron?"

He nods. "I explained that such an arrangement would be *very* short-term, given the rather accurate charges against me. The man, Aaron, seemed to be of a different opinion."

Domenic's face hardens. "Are you marrying Tamiath to secure my pardon, Nile? Is that why you agreed?"

I am going to kill Tam, I decide. It's only a question of how.

The sudden silence between us threatens to pull me under like ballast, and my hands tense inside Domenic's. I long to tell him the full truth of it, but the secrets are not mine to share. "I have my own reasons."

Domenic's eyes flash. "Do not lie to me, Nile," he says too quietly. "Not again. Is my life part of the arrangement?"

I step back from him and cross my arms over my chest. "What if it is?"

"Then undo it. Now." Domenic paces a few steps, like a wolf circling his territory, then stops before a chair. His fingers curl around the chairback in a bone-white grip. "I do not need you to ruin your life for the sake of mine. I do not *want* you to do it. Call off the marriage you so feared that you abandoned your throne, rank, and family to avoid it. I won't let you do it, not over me."

"Let me?" My jaw tightens, my teeth scraping together. "Let me? Who died and made you my keeper?"

"Who made you mine?" he spits back.

"The prince of Felielle," I snarl, not caring that I've just pulled the rank of my birth on Domenic until the words hang between us like a pistol shot.

Domenic is the first to break the impasse, stepping back and offering a perfect bow. "Of course, Your Highness," he says evenly, each note of his icy voice polished to perfection. He straightens before me, places his hands behind the small of his back, and stares straight ahead into the bulkhead. "I am your loyal subject."

I run my hands over my face. "Domenic, I didn't mean it like that."

No answer. Not even a twitch of muscle to let me know he's heard me.

"Please," I whisper, but I might as well be talking to myself. Fine. Bloody fine. I hadn't expected to see Domenic at all, didn't think Tam would wish us anywhere near each other. Domenic will be pardoned, and that was going to be enough for me. It should still be enough for me.

And maybe... Maybe I'd been stupid and selfish and naïve to imagine that Domenic would desire me at all now that I'm betrothed. The storm of problems that sail along with *that* are great enough to wipe out a fleet—and that's before we even start with the issues of my Gift. I shake myself like a dog, shedding my illusions of the depth of Domenic's affection.

"You are not obliged to take the post," I say with a voice too calm and cool to be mine. "The acceptance of your parole is not contingent on your agreeing to follow me around. Please accept my apologies that the lieutenant who made the offer failed to make this clear." I swallow and raise my chin, summoning the trained face I use on the quarterdeck. "You are free to return home to your parents if you wish, or seek other employment on land. The choice is entirely yours."

"Thank you, Your Highness," says Domenic, that mask of impeccable politeness I'd seen him wear on the *Aurora* sliding perfectly across his face.

Nausea rises in my throat, but I manage to keep my face unmoving as I clear the way to the door, a dismissal which Domenic accepts without hesitation. Once the door closes, I curl up on my cot and stay there until whenever it is that Tam returns.

"It did not go well?" Tamiath runs his palm over my shoulders and back. The gesture is meant to be soothing, but the thought of anyone feeling my scars and ruined flesh makes me cringe away.

I sit up, pressing the heel of my hand into the bridge of my nose. The world keeps turning whether I'm ready for it or not. "It is likely Mr. Dana will not be taking the position," I say, summoning a businesslike tone. "Would you be open to offering posts to Catsper, the lieutenant of the marines on the *Aurora*? And...Captain Quinn?"

"Quinn?" The prince cocks a brow. "The Quinn from a nation who wants to destroy our continent in general and kill royalty in particular?"

"He has officially defected," I counter. "There's no going back to the Republic for him. The salient point is that Quinn is familiar with both the Gifted and the sea. That, and I believe he is a good man, if a bit politically misguided."

"Misguided?" Tam throws up his hands. "He's Tirik!" He shakes his head with resignation. "Well, at least he won't have any conflicting loyalties *inside* the Lyron League. We'll ask."

I nod my thanks. "And Catsper?" In the past several weeks, the marine had sent me a few short messages from his station on the *Hope*. The latest of them described Kederic's budding command skills, compared the runty size of *Hope*'s weevils against the superior *Aurora* breed, and inquired as to how he should have the fetters he'd commissioned for my coming wedding engraved. The coward that I am, I failed to rise to the bait of the question. "I should ask him myself, though, or he will never let me live it down."

He shakes his head. "The Spades aren't letting anyone go just now. Give it a month or two until the supply channel with the Siaman Sea is well established and the updated reports on the state of the Tirik forces arrive—make the inquiry then." He gives me a sympathetic smile and stands. "We should get to bed.

Going ashore tomorrow will be interesting enough without adding sleep deprivation into the mix."

Despite my best efforts, the night passes with little sleep—and not just because of Domenic. In the four weeks it took *Falcon* and *Hawk* to complete repairs and make the painfully slow voyage to Ashing, other ships have come and gone from the mainland. Even the *Aurora*, which I last saw setting sail under Lieutenant Kazzik's command for one of the Eflian ports would have arrived well before now.

All that means my father already knows most everything about the Battle of Siaman and today's conversation will focus solidly on scrutinizing me. With that to look forward to, it's little surprising that the morning begins with a convulsion, and by the time I'm washed, dressed, and ready to face the world, I've vomited twice. I am contemplating doing so for the third time when a commotion outside my cabin door shakes the bulkheads.

I open my cabin door just in time to see Domenic flatten Quinn out on the deck with an uppercut to the Tirik man's jaw.

"Explain your presence, sir," Domenic growls at the Tirik captain, who wisely chooses to stay down where he fell.

Quinn wipes the trickle of blood from his mouth. "Do you imagine me to be an assassin, sir? Or a thief?"

Domenic braces his palm against the bulkhead inches from Quinn's face and looms over him. The tight muscles of Domenic's back tremble with a violence I've seldom seen. "I imagine you to be Tirik. "

"How clever of you," Quinn says dryly.

Before I can gather my wits, Tam strides into the passageway, one brow arched in question at the commotion.

"I see you two have met." Tam's voice is dry, but loud enough to grab the men's attention. "Nonetheless, allow me to offer official introductions for their sentimental value. Mr.

Dana, allow me to introduce your partner, Mr. Quinn. Quinn, Dana. You two will find your charge standing behind you."

Quinn pulls himself to his feet and gives Domenic a cold look. The Tirik's effort is wasted. Turning toward me, Domenic straightens to his full height, unfurling his broad shoulders. His expression is stoic, like an officer reporting to a new ship. Only the slight twitch of his hand hints at a human being behind the hard facade. That, and the intensity of his stare.

A million emotions rush through me as Domenic's attention settles on my face. Relief. Fear. Desire. I force them all beneath my own cool mask and schooled voice. "Mr. Quinn," I make myself turn toward the other man, though tearing attention from Domenic takes all my strength. "Thank you for agreeing to take the post. I imagine the duty is unlike any you've envisioned for yourself."

"Nothing about the past few weeks is as I've envisioned, ma'am," Quinn says with a courteous bow. Beside Domenic's large frame, Quinn's average height and slender build make him seem smaller than he is.

"I'm sure." I swallow and shift my focus. "Mr. Dana. A word in private with you if I might."

A retreat of one step puts me right back in my cabin. Domenic follows my course a heartbeat later, shutting the door behind him but taking no further steps inside.

I wait.

He does too.

When I can bear the tension no further, I finally speak. "You stayed."

His brows flick. "Did you imagine I would leave you unprotected?"

Stepping toward him, I put a hand on Domenic's chest. Despite him doing a bloody good job imitating a statue,

Domenic's heart is beating so hard and fast beneath my palm that it's a miracle he can stand still. "Dom—"

A knock at the door has him jerking away as if my palm were aflame.

I draw a calming breath before calling, "what is it?" more snappily than I intend.

"Begging your pardon, ma'am." A middie with a stack of papers edges into the cabin and touches his hat. "The captain thought you might find these newsleafs of interest. They came aboard in yesterday's dispatch exchange, but he only had a chance to review them this morning."

Dismissing the boy with a nod, I pull the first of the printed sheets from the stack and curse as my eyes race over the text. I'd been worried about my parents and Domenic. I should have been more concerned over the dead.

"What's wrong?" Domenic is at my shoulder at once, all traces of chill replaced with concern.

"Please find Tam, Aaron, and Quinn," I whisper, staring at the headline and illustration.

Captain Rima, his face drawn with sharp, confident strokes to evoke an air of courageous suffering, stares back at me from the page.

A Hero's Return, the text beside the portrait reads.

Captain Valeus Rima, the skilled commander of the joint fleet frigate Aurora, *returns home after a near brush with death.*

"The Aurora *was stationed in the Siaman Sea during the earthquake," Captain Rima told the* Lyron Herald. *"Upon learning of the earthquake's damage to the continent, the strategic importance of the archipelago's resources became clear to me at once.*

I immediately dispatched a segment of my crew to commandeer a nearby merchant vessel and use it to contact the

Diante empire, with whom the Lyron Admiralty has had a long-established correspondence." Having dispatched his subordinates to summon aid, the brave captain proceeded to the most dangerous of missions—pitting his lone frigate against the coming Tirik fleet. It was a desperate attempt to delay the enemy until reinforcements arrived—and it worked.

"It was a challenge," Captain Rima admitted to the Herald. "The mission was suicidal, and much of the crew was understandably frightened. For me, though, the training the League Admiralty instilled in me took over. We had a job to do, and by the Gods, we'd do it, or die trying."

Unfortunately, not all the Aurora's officers shared Rima's unwavering bravery. Before the battle, Captain Rima was forced to relieve his own first officer of duty for insubordination and assault.

It is this warrior's attitude that allowed the captain to survive his fall into the sea during the last minutes of the Battle of Siaman. Despite being wounded, Captain Rima fought his way to a friendly vessel.

We thank the Gods, fate, and skill that returned our hero home. And we thank the League Admiralty for their foresight in establishing a relationship with the elusive Diante Empire.

Admiral Wolo of Eflia North announced that he plans to personally award Captain Rima the Order of Bravery, one of the highest honors in the joint fleet.

CHAPTER 31

I shake my head, staring down at the newsleaf as the newly arrived Tam, Aaron, Quinn, and Domenic all finish reviewing the text. "But Captain Rima is dead," I say numbly. "Gone overboard with a shot of Aaron's pistol. I saw it. We all did."

"We never looked for the body," says Tamiath.

"He went overboard," I repeat, as if that should explain everything. "We don't look for bodies at the bottom of the sea."

Except Rima hadn't gone to the ocean floor, but had swum to another Lyron ship, claimed himself a survivor, and returned to the continent. With the time it took the *Falcon* and *Hawk* to get to port, he had plenty of time to poison the water.

"The *Lyron Herald.*" Tam taps the header. "They are Eflian, but the owner, Lady Madeline, has been in Felielle for years, worming her way into my mother's inner circle. The *Herald* even operates a printing press in our capital." His voice twists with ill-concealed disgust. "Madeline tells Mother whatever she wants to hear, and Mother thinks Madeline the embodiment of brilliance."

"Of course." I shut my eyes in dread-filled comprehension. "Lady Madeline—she is Rima's wife. Once Rima managed to survive and get to shore, he returned to his long-standing priority of protecting his own ass. Hence, this." I wave my hand over the newsleaf.

Thad's words from ages ago return to me. *Truth is irrelevant. Perception is what matters.*

"How will this protect Rima?" says Aaron.

I sigh. "Between Rima's trying to weasel out of orders and accepting payment from Quinn, the joint fleet admiralty could charge Rima with treason. By recasting the events to give the joint fleet credit—a heroic joint fleet captain, a joint fleet ship, the joint fleet admiralty's supposed relationship with the Diante —Rima entices the admiralty to stay put. They have been fighting for respect and greater status for years. Rima's fiction grants it to them in one single swoop. The joint fleet won't *want* to raise a hand against Rima now."

I scan the other newsleafs. Some reprint the *Lyron Herald*'s details, others just state facts: the Tirik had the *Aurora, Falcon,* and *Hawk* trapped and would have taken the Siaman Sea if not for sudden aid from a Diante squadron. Speculation varies as to how the Diante became involved, but all agree that Rima's *Aurora* was the only Lyron frigate in the Siaman prior to the Tirik attack, and that the Diante arrived carrying members of Rima's crew.

Keeping my self under control is an effort, and I avoid punching the bulkhead only by reminding myself that my hand will break before the hull does. "I never sent a report," I say, remembering Tam's offer to include my own correspondences with the dispatch boat making full speed to the mainland after the battle. I'd been too upset and declined. "All anyone from *Falcon, Hawk,* or any ship could report were observations from the actual battle, not what Rima did or didn't do before the battle happened."

"If I might say something?" Quinn's soft, confident voice cuts through the cabin.

"No," says Domenic.

I scowl at him. "Yes, Mr. Quinn?"

The ex-Tirik captain clears his throat. Unlike me, Quinn speaks with academic detachment, as if these twisted accounts are of little surprise to him. Propaganda is commonplace in the Tirik Republic, and I've been naïve to think the Lyron League much different. "There is likely a piece to this we are not yet seeing. The joint fleet admiralty might be little inclined to prosecute Captain Rima, but what stops me from forcing the matter by disclosing the payments I made to the captain, or Nile from detailing the actual engagement with the Diante?"

"Your ongoing safety stops you," Tamiath says with a sigh. "If you pit your word against Captain Rima's, Mr. Quinn, by the time the League finishes *interviewing* you, you will be either dead or broken enough to confess making the whole thing up. My naming you a Felielle subject protects you from being questioned as an enemy prisoner, but open your mouth and the joint fleet will find a loophole deep enough to drown you."

I pale, but Quinn nods with little surprise.

"As for Nile," Tamiath continues, "she has been lying to everyone since setting foot on the *Aurora*. Discrediting her will pose little difficulty for the League. Especially when the cronies in Rima's crew come forth to collaborate their kinsman's version of the events." Tam put up his hand, cutting off Domenic who has already opened his mouth to speak. "And before you ask, Mr. Dana, recall you are legally a mutineer. The only place you would be able to provide evidence of Rima's character is at your own court-martial, which we are working *very* hard to avoid having."

Quinn still looks dubious, but I rub my face and set my shoulders square. "*We* may not be able to discredit Rima directly," I tell the men, "but my father and Thad are a different matter. We tell them the truth today and go from there." My memory blinks to another false article, the one that ended my career in the Ashing armada, and my voice darkens. "Whatever else, those two are plenty experienced handling newsies and alternative facts."

With that, Aaron remains on the *Falcon* while a pair of seamen row Tam, Domenic, Quinn, and me ashore. Soon I am setting foot on the cracked remains of what was once a pristine pier.

Domenic shoulders his way to walk directly behind me, a hand on the pommel of his sword.

"Seriously?" I hiss at him. "We are in Ashing."

"If Mr. Quinn and I are here for decoration, get us pretty uniforms," says Domenic, refusing to relinquish the post. "Until then, Your Highness, allow me to do my job, please."

I glower.

Tam snorts and quickens his pace.

An escort of palace guardsmen greets us formally at the pier's edge and ushers us to the palace, moving quickly past the ongoing repairs. Storms, but I little expected this much destruction. Crumpled houses, upturned stones, shattered storefronts. At least the wind dancing across the low shrubbery is soothing, plying us with its salty charms. "Is it this bad in all the kingdoms?" I ask one of the guards.

"The coastline," he says. "Inland was spared."

Felielle is intact, then. Tamiath lets out a breath. He must have left before full reports of the damage came in.

My pulse quickens as we near the palace, the trepidation of facing my father striking against the lies Rima has spread in my absence. However angry Father and Thad are with me, I think they'll help. If not for me, then because it would look good for Ashing to say that its princess negotiated a Diante alliance.

"This place is like a ship run aground," Tamiath says as we step onto the first of many breezeways connecting the Ashing palace structures—mercifully, all intact. Whitewashed walls and columns separate the open space into clean, ordered lines.

The elderly clerk meeting us in the antechamber of my father's study smiles as I walk in, and ruffles around in his desk drawer before standing. "A letter came for you several days past, my lady," he says as if no time has passed since our last meeting. The entire room looks the same, in fact. Leather chairs, low table, refreshments. "Do you wish to have it now? His Majesty will be a few minutes."

I thank the clerk and take custody of the envelope while he offers Tam wine. Domenic and Quinn position themselves at the walls.

Breaking the unfamiliar seal, I find the now-familiar copy of the *Lyron Herald* newsleaf. The note accompanying it, written in a loopy hand, freezes my blood. Quinn had been right to predict that Rima would want to insure himself against my transgressions.

My darling Nile,

I expect you've read the news by now, but I include a copy here for your benefit. Should you choose to lie and contradict the reported facts, I will be forced to reveal your abominable Gift to the world. My congratulations on your coming nuptials.

Your humble servant, Captain Rima.

"Storms and hail," I murmur, extending the note to Tamiath.

His face darkens as he reads the words. Seconds later, Tam picks up a candle and burns the note, putting out the paper's smoldering remains in his own wineglass just as Thad appears to invite us into my father's study.

CHAPTER 32

*W*hatever I thought I was prepared for when I walked into Father's study, his arms wrapping tightly around me was never on the list. We've not hugged in years, and I am uncertain what spurred his affection today. "Storms and hail, Nile," he says, stepping back quickly as if remembering himself, and surveys me.

I study him too, even as my heart bleeds from Rima's words. Father stands as tall as he always has, his chest wide and powerful like Thad's, but there is more silver around his temples than I remember, and the crow's feet touching his eyes are etched more deeply into the skin.

"I am glad you are alive," he says gruffly. "If only because I can now strangle you myself."

That sounds more like him. I bow. The window is open, and a familiar breeze flows inside to ruffle my hair, which I wear down over my shoulders. With whitewashed walls, shelves with workbooks and hanging charts that watch us from their ordered spots, my hair's red is the only bright hue in the room. Not a

233

single painting or plant in sight. A junior officer's tiny cabin has more personality than the Ashing king's workspace.

"What happened in the Siaman?" Thad asks without further preamble, once he and Father exchange greetings with Tamiath and everyone settles into chairs. "We received no report from you and nothing from anyone explaining how the hell the Diante ended up in the middle of our mess."

A fair, perceptive question. One I want to answer. And can't. The threat from Rima's note tunnels through my mind. I probe the words for loopholes and find none.

Rima *can* make my Gift public knowledge. If he does, there will no wedding and no pardon to save Domenic's life. Tam brushes my knee in silent support, as if he knows my decision, understands that Domenic is more than I can risk.

"I've little more to offer on that account, I'm afraid," I say quietly.

Father frowns, his face taking on the familiar grave expression of Ashing's ruler and protector. One who does not take kindly to elusive words or leaps of logic. "Were you not with the Diante when they arrived in the Siaman?"

I swallow a curse. Lying to Father and Thad is nearly impossible under any circumstance, much less without preparation. Having not read the reports Father and Thad did receive, I am navigating without map or compass. "There is a detailed account of the events in the *Lyron Herald*," I say with forced lightness, as if nothing about this conversation is worth their time. "It's accurate."

Thad's jaw tightens. "The *Lyron Herald* can't accurately report a recipe for apple pie, much less a fleet engagement. Is there a reason we are dancing instead of hearing a bloody report from a woman who's trained her whole damn life on how to deliver one?"

I swallow, jolts of fear and shame tingling in my chest. I have to do better. For Domenic's sake. "I was with the party that went to press the merchantman *Hope* into service," I say, making myself meet Thad's eyes. I can't bear to meet my father's. The half-truths and outright lies taste bitter on my tongue. "The *Hope* then traveled into the Diante West Corridor, where we met with the Diante Squadron and delivered a letter from Captain Rima on behalf of the joint fleet. I do not know what was inside the letter. The Diante agreed to come to Lyron's aid. I know little more, Thad. The Diante are not fond of women."

"The *Hope* was Tirik," Thad snarls. "You didn't just press her into service, you boarded and took possession of the damn ship. Did that slip your mind?"

My voice chills. "The *Hope* was a small merchantman, while the *Aurora*'s boats carried a complement of Spade marines. Taking control was a nonevent."

"It's an event when—" Thad starts, getting halfway out of his seat to lean toward me and snarl.

"Oh, shut up, Thad." I'm on my feet in a heartbeat, snarling right back at him. "Last we spoke, shortly after your creative interpretation of *Faithful*'s orders, you informed me that I was more useful to Ashing on a marriage bed than a quarterdeck. Your wish has been granted. Tamiath and I are getting married. That you are no longer happy about losing me from Ashing's officer core is your problem."

Thad's dark eyes flash, his face turning first white, then furious red. "You play vengeful games when the survival of your own kingdom is at stake?" he yells, fully on his feet now, as am I. "The purpose of your damn life is to serve Ashing, you spiteful, traitorous wen—"

"Your pardon, sir." Tam's quiet singsong voice snaps like a

whip. "I must remind you that you speak to my bride and the future princess of Felielle."

"Sit down, Thad," my father says in a voice so cold, I shiver. "Nile, get out."

I open my mouth to throw a final insult at my brother, but Tam wraps a protective arm around my shoulders and guides me to the door. I am desperately glad for the gesture until we walk out of the study and right into Domenic, whose jaw tightens as he takes in Tam's arm.

Untangling myself, I storm out of the antechamber and into the wind.

CHAPTER 33

I make it a hundred yards before Tam, Domenic, and Quinn surround me on the empty breezeway. This part of the palace being on a hill, the troubled shore of the ocean is visible. My eyes stay riveted to the water even as the men speak quietly around me. From the snippets of conversation, I know that Tamiath has filled Domenic and Quinn in on both Rima's note and the audience with Thad and my father.

"If I'd sent a report to Ashing with the early dispatches, I could have prevented this," I say, digging my nails into my skin.

"If you could predict the future, many things would be quite different," Tamiath says firmly. "We'd no reason to suspect Rima was alive, much less busy changing history through the news. More to the point, Rima would have leveraged knowledge of your Gift to protect himself no matter what. He might have been forced to go about it another way, but that's all."

"Are you going to keep rattling off excuses for my ignorance, or do you have a solution somewhere in there, Tam?" I wince in apology over my tone and say more softly, "What are we supposed to do now?"

Tamiath sighs, his handsome face sympathetic. "I can't decide whether I find your simple honesty naïve or refreshing. This isn't the open sea, Nile, where you are a world unto yourself. It's politics and image and power. Given the fact that Rima received a commission to begin with, I wager it is not his first round with manipulating perception. As for what more we are to *do* about this, the answer is *nothing*."

I open my mouth to protest, but Tam puts up his hand.

"Our marriage will ensure Felielle supports the Ashing Kingdom's standing in the Lyron League and keep Mr. Dana from being executed for mutiny. As for the other, if the worst that comes from Rima's unfortunate lack of death is your hurt pride and an Order of Bravery unjustly pinned to an idiot's chest," Tam says, splitting his gaze between Domenic and me, "then we will take it. We'll have the wedding as quickly as we can and keep our mouths shut. We cannot fight every battle we wish we could, and I propose that Mr. Dana's life, the Ashing-Felielle alliance, and the commissioning of Nile as the first female officer of the Felielle armada is more important than taking Rima's bauble away. Agreed?"

Domenic draws a breath, then bows. "Yes, my prince."

Tam twists to me, waiting patiently.

"I don't like it," I say finally.

"It's despicable," Tam agrees. "But focus on the things you can control—which, apparently, include the wind itself." A wry smile touches his face, though his eyes remain worried as he strides on, hair ruffled by the breeze.

"It is very difficult to dislike Prince Tamiath, is it not?" Domenic's voice makes me jump.

I take a breath, choosing my words as carefully as if I were picking eggshells. "He is a good man. Different from what I expected."

Domenic rocks back on his heels and turns his head to watch the horizon. "Does he make you happy?"

I step toward Domenic, meaning to simply grab his attention, but my hand closes around his wrist before I can stop it. The thump of Domenic's heartbeat pulses beneath my fingertips, my own heart quickening in response. Ahead of us, Tamiath walks on with a soldier's quick step, while Quinn, sensing a private conversation, suddenly finds a whitewashed column endlessly fascinating.

"You want to know what I feel?" I say to Domenic, my voice just above the wind's whisper. His face turns to me, and my mouth dries, the words tumbling into the void between us. "My father just threw me out of Ashing. I'm about to join a people who think me a misguided idiot for loving the navy. Magic courses through my blood with every heartbeat, convulsions riding its wake. Meanwhile, a bastard named Rima is rewarded for his cowardice while a man I care deeply for..." I break off, swallowing as I struggle to control my voice. My eyes sting. "You want to know what I feel? Scared. I feel scared, Domenic. Scared and cowardly and alone." I tip my face up, fighting the moisture threatening to fill my lids.

Domenic's hand twists out of my grip, and I stagger back, my own weight threatening to collapse me to the ground.

Strong fingers grip my chin. "Not cowardly and not alone, understand?" says Domenic. "You'll have me at your side for as long as you wish."

"Last night—"

"As your friend," Domenic adds quietly.

"Dom—"

"Stop." He pinches the bridge of his nose. "Goddess, Nile.

You think it doesn't lash me bloody to say those words? You think it takes anything less than every damn ounce of self-control to keep from wrapping you in arms? But the currents of reality don't flow the way I wish. I agreed to protect you, and that means protecting you from myself as well. Prince Tamiath... He's a good man. One who can and will make you happy. I'll do nothing to compromise that. All right?"

I nod, my cheeks moist.

"Say it," says Domenic. "If you want me to stay, I need to hear you say it."

"All right," I say, though the words taste sour on my lips. "You are my friend, Domenic Dana. And I'm yours."

"Good." He takes a breath, his shoulders tightening the way they do when he braces himself. "And one other thing."

"No." I cross my arms. "Whatever you are about to say, I don't want to hear it."

"On the *Aurora*," he says, ignoring my protest, "I once told you that if faced with a choice between you being safe and you liking me, I'd choose the former. That goes double now."

WHILE TAM SETS up travel arrangements to get us and his men to Felielle, I seek out my twin, Clay. Predictably, I find him in a back courtyard, small and hidden from passing eyes. Coarse grass covers the ground, and the hedges are manicured into geometric patterns. A cube, a sphere, a cone. Shapes that catch Clay's attention. We've a single gardener who tends to this oasis, one whom Mother trusts never to leave behind a set of metal shears or carry nails that might accidently spill from a pocket. Nothing metal that might hurt Clay if his magic attracts it by accident.

The magic in my veins stirs as I approach, as if my twin's presence makes it restless. I pause, a burst of excitement brushing my mind. My magic is *reacting* to Clay's. It shouldn't be possible, but it's happening. Just like Price's unusual Gift. Perhaps more is possible than any of us know. Clay and I are twins. A matching set connected in the womb.

"Hello, Clay," I say to my twin's back as he plays with a pack of puppies under the mother dog's supervision. I remember the bitch, who now looks at me with considerate chocolate eyes, from the beach. Dismissing me with a snort, the dog rises and trots over to the edge of the clearing where Domenic and Quinn are stopped.

Clay appears as ignorant of the guardsmen's presence as of mine.

"Clay?" I repeat.

Nothing. No response.

My chest tightens. It's my own fault, though. I'd set myself up for failure sneaking up on Clay from the back. I should have approached him from the front, where he'd have no choice but to see me. I don't know why I didn't. No, that's a lie. I'd wanted to see whether anything changed, if perhaps Clay's magic senses mine the way mine rises to his. We are *twins*. Who knows how magic works with twins.

One of the pups separates from the pack and gallops at me with paws too big for his body.

I scoop up the beast and carry him around Clay, so I can see my brother's beautiful doll face. "Hello, Clay."

Nothing. Not even an echo.

My magic roars its fury.

"He's gotten worse since you left."

I jump at the sudden sound of my mother's voice and wait for my heart to restart beating before turning around and setting the puppy back on the grass. The queen is a bit thinner than I recall, but still stunning in a flowing gown. Despite Mother's guilt-instilling words, her gaze is warm.

I want to throw my arms around her like a little girl, but after this morning with Thad and Father, I limit myself to clasping my wrists behind my back. "Mother," I say formally.

She takes the three steps separating us and wraps me in an embrace so tight, it borders on unladylike.

Relief floods me, and I press my face into her shoulder, only to remember myself and jerk back before her fingers can feel the ridged skin of my back through my gown's thin fabric.

Hard accusation fills Mother's gaze as we separate. "You've no notion what you've put us through," she says, her lips trembling. "Thinking you were kidnapped. Stolen. Violated."

I sigh carefully. Everything on land is a game, words and appearances used as weapons. Ones that can do a good deal more damage than great guns. "Mother. You didn't really think that. Not with my sea bag and clothes missing. When someone wishes to kidnap a woman, they rarely stop to pack first."

Lips pursed, she takes out a handkerchief from her sleeve and dabs at her face. "It could have happened! At sea or on whatever Goddess-forsaken path you might have taken. I had no way of knowing where my little girl was for months. I could not know whether my child was even alive."

Translation: *I had no spies on your ship. That is unacceptable, and you shall ensure that does not happen again.*

I reach out and take her hands. "I've not been a little girl for some time."

Mother's smooth fingers massage my calloused ones, and she frowns, turning my palm over to inspect it.

"Mother..." I say in warning. If she is about to lecture me on appearance with Domenic close enough to hear, I think I might bolt.

She clicks her tongue, but when she speaks, her voice is different. Deep and quiet and intrusively genuine. "Did working with your hands, being on that ship in the middle of nowhere... Did it make you happy?" she asks, her eyes truly seeking an answer. "Did you discover there is more to Nile than the sea?"

I swallow and step back. There is that word again. Happiness. *Happiness and I resolved to just be friends an hour ago.* "I..." Words escape my grasp like slippery eels. "Tam and I would like to have the wedding soon. Six weeks. I know it's in Felielle, but I thought you might wish to help with the planning." Yes, a cowardly course diversion, but sometimes avoidance is the better part of valor.

She raises a brow. "What I *wish* to do, dolphin, is to speak to those two gentlemen over there in guardsmen's uniforms about how they plan to keep you from cutting your leash and running off in the middle of the night like a feral cat. But alas, I shall save that for another time when I can intimidate them suitably."

In the corner of my vision, I see Domenic turn away quickly in a coughing fit. Brilliant. All I need is for my mother and him to team up.

I rub my face and study my mother's lovingly cunning eyes. How can someone I love manage to drive me insane within moments? A talent. Mother has a mystical talent for knowing just what to say to drive me to madness. "I'd like to have a moment alone with Clay, please," I say firmly.

She pats my cheek. "I love you, dolphin. Always. Even when you foolishly think you know better than your mother. I do not enjoy saying that I told you as much, but had you listened to me, you would have met Prince Tamiath long before now. And he is as good a match for you as I've imagined." Before I can reply, she turns in a perfect whoosh of skirts and strides away.

Something warm and wet slithers over my foot, and I turn away from my mother's retreating form to find the puppy who was milling about me now peeing onto my leg. I shudder in disgust and am about to jump back with a squeal when I realize Clay is watching. *Watching*.

The magic in my blood spikes as my eyes meet my twin's. "Clay?" I whisper.

"Clay," he repeats, mimicking my tone perfectly. A pair of metal balls rotate around each other in the air a few inches away from my twin's face.

I move toward him.

The puppy whines, interposing its small self between me and Clay.

Ignoring the dog, I stare into Clay's eyes that look right back into mine. *Want. Give. Touch*, the magic inside me sings without words. Wind picks up around me, rustling the hedges.

"Nile," Domenic's voice calls in warning.

My lungs burn. Realizing I've forgotten to breathe, I gulp a too-big mouthful and choke. However it's happening, the proximity to Clay is playing havoc with my magic.

And I couldn't care less. Not even as a window shatters somewhere, the shards raining down onto the grass. Not when Clay is *looking* at me. Reaching out, I take Clay's limp hand in mine.

The world spins, the magic inside me breaking free of its tethers. Wind swerves into the clearing, bending the hedges and choking my lungs. My heart, racing moments ago, slows. *Lub-dub. Lub-dub. Lub-dub*. A clear steady beat to the tune of another's body.

A voice curses behind me. Familiar. Male. The scent of sea and brine fills my nose. I know I *should* recognize the person who now crouches at my side, his muscled forearm raised against the wind, but the name escapes me.

"Nile!" he bellows into my face.

I ignore him. He doesn't matter. What matters, the only thing that matters, are the clear eyes of my twin that now hold mine.

"Nile?" Clay asks in a voice I've not heard in four years. His own.

Elation and magic course through me—through *us*—drowning out the dog's insistent barks and the men speaking quickly beside me.

"...Yes, her twin."

"...Gifted. Both."

"...Separate them. *Now*."

The last command fills me with panic. I hold tighter to Clay's fingers. Thinking clearly is hard. So hard. Our pulse quickens. *Clay,* I try to say, but the word won't come. It's there, in my mind, but it can't find its way out.

The dog yaps like mad.

"Nile, stop," Clay says, as if my lack of speech has returned the power of his. "I want you safe."

I flail as someone tears me away from my brother and tackles me to the ground. Deprived of contact with Clay, my magic roars its agony, as if all the skin on my palm is torn away with the separation.

"Clay!" I scream.

The dog howls as green lights flash before me, and I dissolve into convulsions until the world darkens.

CHAPTER 34

I awake in a bed. Not my own. It takes me a moment to recognize Tamiath's guest bedroom, decorated gently with the blues and greens of the sea. My dress has been exchanged for soft oversized trousers and a tunic that smells of Tam. My face heats as I wonder which of the four men before me took care of that. Or why it needed to have been done.

"You are in my quarters," Tamiath says in response to my questioning gaze. His voice is hard, and he crosses his arms as he speaks. "It appears you lost control of your magic, your mind, *and* your body when you touched your Gifted twin. Dana and Quinn physically forced you apart from Clay and brought you here. How much do you recall?"

I sit up, rubbing my throbbing head. My arms scream their protest at even that slight motion, as if I'd just spent hours carrying boulders. "I was with Clay, my magic spiked, and when I took his hand, he seemed to recognize me."

"It is possible that the twins' magics reacted to each other in a way that allowed Nile to temporarily absorb some of the strain on Clay's mind, though the strain on her own mind and body increased exponentially." Quinn rubs his upper lip, pacing the room as if it were a quarterdeck. A thousand thoughts race in his intelligent eyes as he weighs me with them. "One of the Institute's theories suggests that magics might influence each other, and I've seen evidence of it to a much lesser extent with siblings before." He pauses. "There is a generous commission for anyone who safely delivers Gifted siblings to the Institute. They've never been able to acquire twins, as far as I know, though the reward offered for that is astronomical."

A growl escapes Domenic's throat, and he steps toward Quinn with enough menace to have Aaron shifting himself between them.

Quinn drapes his hands calmly behind his back. Despite being smaller, he manages to address Domenic as if speaking down to a wayward lieutenant. "I will not apologize for my nation's attempt to find a way for Gifted to live normal lives, Mr. Dana. The Diante think them Gods touched, who should humbly accept anything fate throws, and you in the Lyron League kingdoms hide your Gifted away and pretend the problem is absent. The Institute's methods are deplorable, though the intent is humane."

"That summarizes most of the Republic's agenda," I mumble. "Deplorable means for noble goals."

"Debate politics later," Tamiath snaps at all of us, pacing the room from wall to wall several times before stopping. "What happened, this magical tantrum, is as dangerous as it is irresponsible. The objectives now are safety, secrecy, and prevention, in that order. To Mr. Quinn's point, pretending that Nile's magic simply doesn't exist suits no one."

Domenic opens his mouth, but Tam yields nothing to him.

"Mr. Dana," says Tam, "we will not overlook information

vital to Nile's life so we can protest the means by which that information was collected." Tam turns to me. "Nile, stay the hell away from other Gifted until you understand your body. You almost got yourself killed, never mind discovered. Mr. Quinn." Tam turns once more, examining the ex-Tirik officer. "Given your experience—however you've come about obtaining it—how thorough is your understanding of the Gifted?"

Quinn cocks his head, considering the question. "Perhaps at a midshipman's level, if we were to use a naval analogy. The *Hope*'s mission was humanitarian, and I made it a point to know as much as possible about the patients' needs, but my primary function remained captaining the ship."

"In the world of landsmen, that takes the crown," Tam says darkly. "All right. Between now and the time we reach Felielle, I need the three of you to eat, breathe, and sleep magic. Get this bloody thing under control before someone is hurt." Tam's gaze returns to me and softens. "I'm pushing you, I know. I wish there was time to take things slow, to let you rest."

"I'll be fine," I tell him, hoping that to be at least half true. I don't think I can lift my arms over my head, much less stand.

Tam kisses my forehead. "I'm returning to organizing our departure, then. Let Aaron know if you need anything."

Left alone, Quinn, Domenic, and I stare at each other in silence. I sit in bed, cross-legged and flushed, Domenic hovers nearby with his arms crossed, and Quinn leans with one hand against the wall. The air between Domenic and Quinn crackles.

"Please don't kill each other," I say wearily. "And if you want to yell at me for being reckless, can you do it now and get it over with?"

Domenic glowers. "I'll yell at you in private."

"Wonderful." I rub my face and cut my attention to Quinn.

"Mr. Dana is welcome to take charge of the yelling," Quinn

says practically. "I'll focus on the training. In my experience, that route tends to bring about better results."

Domenic rolls his eyes, and Quinn wisely decides he needs to be elsewhere.

Left alone with Domenic, I shimmy myself to sit more comfortably on the bed and eye Domenic wearily. Quinn may have considered Tam's lecture enough, but I rather doubt Domenic will let the episode rest that easily. If my aching from head to toe and facing a week of punishing training can be called *easily*.

"All right," I say, spreading my arms. "I know you'd still like to lecture me, so go ahead."

"What I'd like to do," Domenic snaps, "is set you to scrubbing decks for however long it takes you to work out just how much you scared me back there. It was as if—" He cuts off mid-sentence and strides to the door, which Quinn had left open. Domenic closes it with a single swipe of his hand, the latch clicking into place on a hidden spring. That quickly, the spacious bedroom is too small, the air stifling. The silken sheets tickle my bare feet as I shift beneath Domenic's stare.

He shakes his head, his jaw tight. "It was as if you weren't there anymore, Nile. The very fire in your eyes dimmed. Then your body arched up so tight and high, I thought you might snap your own spine. And you know what else?" He stalks toward me, a storm howling in his eyes while the wooden floor creaks beneath each heavy step. Stopping at the edge of the wooden bed, Domenic presses both palms into the edge of the mattress. He leans onto his hands, his shirt shifting in deference to the coiling muscles, and brings his face within a foot of mine. At eye level now, he pins me with his gaze.

I swallow.

"And you know what else," Domenic repeats so calmly that

I squirm beneath the intensity of his words. I wish he'd yell or shout, but Domenic refuses to so much as raise his voice. "I am willing to bet my life that you felt your control slipping. You felt it, but you were too intent on doing what you wanted, on getting through to your brother, that you damned the consequences to hell."

The silence that follows his words presses in on me from all sides. I *had* felt the coming danger, had heard Domenic's shout of warning, seen the shards of a window shattered beneath a rogue wind. Yes, I'd sensed—and ignored—it all.

Of course Domenic is angry. He has every right to be.

And I have every right to ignore it.

Except I can't. The force of his fury pins me in place. My mouth dries; my head turns away from his glare.

I shuffle myself to relieve the pressure, bringing my knees up and wrapping my aching arms around them. The large mirror hanging on the wall opposite the dresser shadows my movements. At least I know why I'm so damn sore. Why even my chest muscles hurt if I breathe too deeply. "If it makes you feel better, I *feel* like I've been scrubbing decks. For a very long time."

"Good," Domenic says.

The memory of that particular task from my initial days on the *Aurora*, my first taste of a low seaman's work, won't be fading in the foreseeable future. Neither will the one of Domenic watching me struggle, waiting for me to quit as the sanding stone split my skin and the bosun's mate lay his rope's end across my shoulders.

My body betrays me, and I flinch at the memory. *Storms and hail.* It is as if Domenic's mere presence is enough to shatter my self-control, stone by stone. Face heating, I lower my forehead atop my knees.

The bed shifts as Domenic pulls back to sit sideways on its edge, granting me a measure of breathing room. When my head remains bent over my drawn-up knees, he sighs and brushes the exposed nape of my neck with his fingers.

A jolt of awareness races through me, and I must draw a breath before I can turn my head to the right to look at him through half-lidded eyes.

"Yes, I'm still furious with you," he says, though his fingers rub light circles on my neck. One of his legs tucks under him so he can watch me more easily. "But stern lecture over. All right?"

"Thank the waves," I mutter, trying for a half smile and failing. I wonder whether Domenic knows how easily he could shatter me just now, how stupidly open I've left myself to him.

Domenic's fingers on my neck splay to a full calloused palm, its warmth seeping into me through tender skin. "I was so afraid I'd lose you back there," he whispers quietly.

The heat of his touch rushes through my veins like wildfire, and my stomach twists. It's wrong, how much I want that touch, how my body explodes with the longing for it. *Friends.* Domenic and I are just friends because that is all we can be. The only way to be fair to Domenic, who can never know the secret Tam, Aaron, and I share. No matter how much it kills me to keep it from him.

I can't move for fear of losing whatever touch he is willing to grant me, not even to nod. Instead, I close my eyes and savor each brush of familiar calloused fingers that coax my aching muscles to release.

Domenic's hand slides from my neck to the top of my shoulder and sweeps down my back.

My stomach clenches, a small gasp escaping my lips as I jerk away.

The hand freezes. "Does your back still hurt?" The concern

in Domenic's voice speeds his words. "It should have healed, unless—did the wounds get infected?"

"No." I shift forward slightly, away from his hand. Despite the chilled room, my skin heats like flame. "It's fine. No infection. No pain. Not anymore."

"Let me see." His fingers reach for the hem of my too-large shirt, stopping again when I fail to suppress a shudder, my instinctual drive to keep the scars concealed winning over common sense.

"Who changed my clothes?" I stammer.

Domenic pulls back his hand and blinks. "Who changed your clothes?"

My face burns hotter still, and I bring my eyes back to the bedspread. It's blue and green, like the ocean. "I wore a dress when I went to see Clay. Who took it off? Who...saw me without it?"

He frowns. "Does it matter? Nile, you—" He stops, his eyes darkening as he answers his own question before forming the next. "Your back. *That's* what worries you, isn't it?"

I turn my face away.

Domenic swears softly, his profile sharp against the setting sun's silhouette. "Nile." His voice is quiet. "Look at me. Please."

I turn my face back to him, laying my ear and cheek against my knee.

Domenic's gaze cuts through to my heart. "Why specifically?" he asks. "Is it the sight or the memories?"

I shrug. "Both. I don't know. I've never seen them. It's easier to pretend none of it happened."

A muscle in Domenic's jaw flickers. "It did happen. I know because it haunts me each time I close my eyes." He surveys me, the room, the locked door. Reaching out, Domenic traces his thumb around my chin before holding out his hand to me, palm up. "Come."

"Where?"

"Not far."

The sea-and-brine scent fills me as I let Domenic draw me off the bed. The stone floor is cold beneath my bare feet, and I hiss softly before I realize Domenic has led me to stand beside the mirror. My heart pauses for a moment, then sprints into a gallop. "No," I say, twisting away from the reflection. "No. No. No."

CHAPTER 35

Stepping back from the mirror, I hit the solid wall of Domenic's body behind me.

"Easy," he says softly, the heat of his body warming mine despite the room's chill. The rise and fall of Domenic's chest pushes against my shoulders with each breath.

"What happened..." Domenic's throat bobs as he swallows. "What *I* did to you, it is quite horrid enough without letting its ghost haunt and shun you from your own body. I won't let it."

I shake my head vigorously. "Not now. Later. When... Just later."

Standing behind me, Dominic turns me slightly to catch my gaze in the mirror. "You are getting married, Nile," he says dryly. "That involves activity not usually done with a shirt on."

My face heats. "Yes, well, I'll sort that one out. Let it go."

"No." Domenic's voice hardens. "I couldn't protect you from the pain when it happened, but Goddess help me if I let you fear looking at your own body." Taking hold of my shoulders, he angles me gently to open my back to the mirror's reflection.

My mouth is dry, my legs ready to sprint.

"It's all right." Domenic's voice is soothing as I press my face into his chest. He blows out a long breath. "Come on. You survived the doing of it, you'll survive the seeing too. We both will." The last comes out in a whisper that flickers with vulnerability.

"All right," I say, letting Domenic draw the back of the shirt up and over my head while keeping my arms still in the sleeves. The fabric hangs forward from my shoulders and neck, covering my breasts while exposing the scars to light.

I flinch at the first brush of air on naked skin and shut my eyes. My fingers dig into Domenic's biceps, pressing hard enough to bruise.

Our bodies are flush and Domenic's hand comes to cover my own. We stand like that, angled diagonally before the mirror I refuse to look into. Then his cheek, slightly rough despite his morning shave, scrapes along the side of my neck until his lips hover beside my earlobe. "You look like a warrior." His warm breath fills the inside of my ear. "Honed and strong and feminine. Open your eyes."

The note of command has me obeying, but though my eyes are no longer veiled, it is him I examine in the mirror. Domenic stands beside me, his legs shoulder width apart, his back straight as always. The loose purple shirt of his guardsman uniform tapers to a taut waist, wrapped with a wide swath of golden fabric, its loops ready for weapons. Domenic's eyes meet mine in the reflection.

"You are beautiful," Domenic says quietly, reaching around me to run his fingers fearlessly over mutilated flesh. My body trembles beneath his touch, and he puts his free hand on my hip to steady me. His hand flows down to caress the groove of my spine and the valley of scars. "You deserve to wear these battle marks as badges of pride. That's what the other seamen do, you know." He forces a smile. "On the lower decks, half the men will say you aren't a true sailor until you've survived the grating."

Yes. I've heard that too. And the shame turns my gut. "I fell apart." I whisper my confession quickly, before the words catch up with me. "At the grating. Afterwards. I wanted to be brave and stoic, but I couldn't. I was terrified."

Domenic makes a guttural sound. "I heard you could have given up Catsper and avoided the whole unpleasant business." He snarls softly. "You chose. You survived. And then you saved us all. The *Aurora* never deserved you, Nile. I never deserved you."

I swallow.

Shaking his head, Domenic traces the marks one by one.

Sensitive, I realize with detached surprise. My back with its ridges and marks is oddly sensitive now, numbness and awareness exploding together into a bouquet of forever changing, unexpected sensations.

My eyes now following the progress of Domenic's hands across puckered flesh, I let myself lean against him, savoring his touch. "Doesn't it...." I hesitate, forcing the words past my defenses. "Does it not repulse you?"

Domenic's hand freezes in midmotion. I start to pull away, but he shakes his head and walks around me instead. In the mirror, I see him stop behind me. Wordlessly, deliberately, and very slowly, Domenic lower his head and presses a kiss to the nape of my neck, just where healthy smooth skin meets jagged marks. "No," he says, meeting my eyes in the reflection. "I'd kiss every one of those scars if I could."

My whole body goes taut at that, but this time it's desire, not fear, that heats my blood. In the mirror, I can see nothing beyond Domenic's gaze, the speckles of light reflecting in his irises. Even on land Domenic smells of the sea and stands as tall as if commanding a ship.

A need low inside me flares to life, and I press my thighs together to suppress it.

Domenic tenses and draws a short hard breath. "Nile." His voice is no longer soothing, my name a warning on his lips. He steps back and away.

I twist to face him, even as the wrongness of it screams its warnings. The air between us crackles. Domenic's body is coiled tightly, and he flinches when I press my palms against his chest.

Domenic's large hands brace my hips, holding me away from him. His chest heaves. "Nile," he says again. A caution and a warning and a plea all wrapped into one. "This isn't where—"

He cuts off with a gasp as I push him backward, more and more until his calves thump the bed's wooden frame. My hands slide over the cool silk of Domenic's shirt and the hard muscles beneath it.

"Don't do that," he hisses between clenched teeth. "Please."

A *tattoo*, my memory murmurs. Domenic has a tattoo sneaking between his pectorals, and I want to see it. Now. I shove him, pressing until he falls back onto the bed behind him, catching his weight on outstretched arms.

We stare at each other. Me, standing between his legs, my shirt draped loosely over my breasts, which peak in the room's chill. Domenic sitting on the mattress, his arms trembling with more than his body weight can account for.

Back. I should be stepping back now. To think. To reason.

The magic stirs in my blood. And I don't know whether the

need comes from it or something deep in my chest, but I call my wind and flatten Domenic beneath its force. I'm atop him with the next heartbeat, straddling his hips. His hands rise and tangle themselves in my hair, his own still ruffling in the lingering wisps of my preternatural breeze.

Domenic's eyes widen, and, as if some tether inside him snaps, he pulls my shirt free from my body. He bucks beneath me and turns us over, until it is me on my back and him looming atop me. Domenic's mouth dives toward mine, pressing into my lips faster than they can part for him. After the gentle touch on my back, his tongue inside my mouth is hard and demanding, as if determined to taste everything that I am. Domenic growls softly into my mouth, his voice rumbling against my tongue.

A bonfire flares low inside me. My hips rise up, undulating, rubbing against his hardness.

Domenic's hand slides down to grip my breast in reply. His thumb brushes over a taut nipple. The ache inside grows unbearable. I hiss through my teeth and fumble toward the laces of his breeches, pulling the cloth hard enough to rip.

Domenic's fingers close around my wrist, halting my attempt. He balances over me, throat bobbing as he swallows hard before pulling back. Back and away.

No. *No.* I scramble up after him, getting to my knees before I manage to grab a fistful of his shirt. My lips part in a whispered plea, but Domenic shakes his head, panting as if he'd run for miles.

"I won't bed you," he says, his voice strained. "I want... You deserve happiness, Nile. I won't ruin your chance at it with Tamiath."

Tamiath won't mind. "Tamiath won't know," I say, all my willpower engaged just to keep myself still.

"*You'll* know," says Domenic. His hands press into my hips

259

as he shifts me gently away from him. The moment my weight is stable and my hands no longer clutch his shirt, Domenic is up on his feet, his back toward me, his hands braced on his thighs as he draws slow deep breaths before straightening. In the mirror, Domenic's palm rises to cover his face. His head drops. "I'm sorry," he sighs. "That was... It won't happen again."

Before I can find my voice, Domenic leaves the room.

CHAPTER 36

*W*e prepare to leave for Felielle the next morning. I walk in a daze toward the assembled soldiers, the memory of Domenic's touch flooding my every breath. My face heats, and it's an effort to assure myself that my thoughts are mine alone. Spotting Domenic at the edge of the waiting group, I stumble over flat ground, my mouth suddenly dry. My gaze scampers across the caravan's wagons and horses, seeking out a place to hide until I can look at him without my body tightening.

"There you are," Aaron appears from the crowd, leading a slender dapple-gray mare by the reins. The horse is already saddled, her wide nostrils snorting the crisp air. Long silky hair skirts her legs and feet majestically as she lifts one foot, then the other with a dignity more befitting a queen than a horse. The scents of hay, grain, and leather waft from her like odd perfume. My stomach tightens.

Perhaps I could *walk* to Felielle.

ALEX LIDELL

Aaron flips the reins over the mare's neck and interlocks his fingers into a makeshift stirrup. "Give me your foot."

I bring my boot up. The mare shifts her weight and dismisses me as someone unworthy of her concern.

"Your *other* foot, Nile." Aaron's voice drops. "Do you not know how to ride?"

"Do you not know how to rig a sail?" I hiss back.

"Do you want to ride in the wagon?"

Yes. "No." I let out a slow breath and put my hand on the mare's neck. "I'm not riding with the turnips."

Aaron gives me a look similar to the one the mare had. "Oh, you'll be a delight to speak with tomorrow after a day of riding. And the day after that even more so."

I give him a vulgar gesture as he settles me into the saddle, which shifts precariously beneath me. Aaron eyes me dubiously but silently adjusts my stirrups. "Let me know if you change your mind about the wagon."

"I will not—" I cut off with a gasp as the horse beneath me wanders off to munch on a trimmed hedge. "Turn starboard, stupid beast." I dig my heels into her sides.

She snorts, raises her tail, and poops.

"Trouble?"

I bite my lip at the sound of Domenic's smooth, low voice, my breath halting as he leans over from his own mount to grab my mare's headstall and turn her toward the caravan. The sea-and-brine scent of him makes me dizzy. I bury my hands in the horse's mane and refuse to meet the man's eyes.

Recognizing a higher authority in Domenic's touch, the bloody horse perks up her ears and trots behind Domenic like a pet. My fingers in her mane tighten to keep myself from being bounced right out of the saddle as my teeth click together. "Woahhhh," I beg the mount. "Easy."

Domenic slows to a walk without appearing to move a single muscle. He twists back, regarding me with a mix of surprise and worry. "She *was* going slow. Are you all right?" The many layers of the question turn my gut.

"Fine," I say, my attention firmly on the horse's ears. "Though Aaron foretells I'll feel differently after a day of riding."

"Riding and *other* training," Quinn says, joining Domenic and me. Like Domenic, Quinn too sits competently atop his mount and watches me with some concern. "Did you never learn to ride?"

"My kingdom is a bloody peninsula," I hiss. "I learned to sail. What is *that*?" I point to a set of dark eyes studying me from Domenic's saddlebag.

"A dog," Domenic says with a shrug of a muscled shoulder that brings my mind back into the bedroom faster than I can blink. I keep my focus trained on the dog, noting that Domenic appears to have none of my emotional jumpiness this morning. "He's one of Clay's pups," Domenic continues. "The one who started barking right before... I've seen dogs predisposed to sense certain conditions before they occur. It is very possible this pup shares the talent. We will test it during the trip."

First the horse, now the dog. I appear to be attracting a bloody menagerie.

"Might I suggest we discuss the training plan before Nile falls out of the saddle?" Quinn inquires, leading the three of us downwind of the waiting column to where our quiet words have little chance of carrying back to the soldiers.

Once settled, I fill the two men in on what I've learned about my magic so far, covering everything from the sail-setting analogy I use for control, to the Diante medicine woman's words and Catsper's exercises. It takes a full hour to lay out and order the facts, with Quinn asking thoughtful questions and suggesting hypotheses while Domenic and I pointedly avoid looking at each other.

"Are you two paying attention?" Quinn snaps with a voice reserved for wayward midshipmen, and I flush in realization that I, in fact, hadn't been. Domenic gives no acknowledgment of having heard the reprimand, but the horse beneath him dances uncomfortably. "What I propose," Quinn says, plainly not for the first time, "is to establish how much magic Nile can comfortably control while relaxed, then systematically increase the strain—physical, mental, and magical."

Sounds delightful.

"And the convulsions?" Domenic says, nudging his horse to put himself between Quinn and me.

I sigh. "We let them happen and take them as they come." It's as far from ideal as it gets, but thus far we've found nothing to suggest the damn things can be managed.

The one good thing about the next two weeks—the only good thing—is that by the time Domenic, Quinn, and the damn horse are done with me each day, I fall into my bedroll too exhausted to fret about the undead captain. Each waking moment, I'm either meditating, destroying innocent branches with bursts of air, or clinging to my saddle while the horse decides she's had enough of lugging me around. Despite his quiet bearing and careful words, Quinn turns out to be a relentless taskmaster, possibly because taming my magic is one of the few things the man can do without compromising his odd sense of loyalty to a nation that would execute him if given a chance.

Domenic, on the other hand, morphs into an overprotective wolf ready to go for Quinn's jugular. "This isn't the Republic," Domenic hisses after Quinn's instruction that I call a breeze to help my horse along ends with the mare rearing and me on the ground. "Killing a princess isn't an acceptable outcome."

"Killing anyone should be an unacceptable outcome," Quinn replies with infuriating calm.

I groan and glare at the horse's bridle. "Can we kill whichever sadist thought a six-inch bit in the mouth of a thousand-pound animal was a good idea?"

"The problem was with neither the horse nor her bridle," Quinn says primly, too disciplined to point out that I was doing well enough until Domenic rode by and my attention snagged on him like cloth on a stray nail. "But let us try again."

Being beside Domenic hour after hour, unable to touch him beyond an accidental brush of one body against another, is its own special kind of torment. At first, I try to make those accidental brushes a frequent affair, but Domenic catches on quickly enough and gives me a silent withering look that has me keeping my hands to myself.

The puppy, whom Aaron names Bear in deference to his huge paws and tendency to steal food from closed saddlebags, indeed appears to sense my coming convulsions and enjoys announcing this fact to the world with ear-piercing yelps. Despite my nightly attempts to relocate Bear into one of the wagons, I wake up each morning with a warm black bundle the size of a travel pack snoring softly into the small of my back. After a week, I give up trying and even look forward to waking up with the pup's soft snoring against me.

By the time we enter the Felielle capital city two weeks later, I've little skin left on the inside of my knees and thighs coupled with an intense hatred for saddles. I study my new home through a veil of ache and fatigue.

If the Ashing palace is a ship on land, the Felielle capital is a greenhouse. Flower beds, blooming trees, and stinging bees are everywhere. Instead of the neatly ordered and breezy streets that I'm used to, the city is stuffed with winding narrow alleys, rising stone dwellings, and uneven cobblestones—as if the planner had thrown paint onto canvas and let things fall as they may. Potted plants of all shapes hang from balcony windows, growing from flowers to herbs. Mixing with the aroma of pollen and greenery is the solid stench of manure—some of it left behind by my own mount—which fills the air as thickly as salt does at home. As for people, they are *everywhere*. Crowding, pushing, pointing.

"Third balcony of the red house," Quinn murmurs, pulling his horse up beside mine. "Send a breeze to scatter the dandelions without breaking their stems."

"Now?" We are approaching the stone walls of the palace, green grape vines climbing its sides a testament to the many years of service it granted. The thought of Tamiath's family waiting inside makes nausea crawl up my throat. Like me, Tam is a younger child, not crown prince of the kingdom. Also like me, he little talks of his parents.

Quinn raises a brow.

I clear my mind, pushing thoughts of Tam's family, of our great charade, of Rima's letter into a void. When nothing but my magic remains in focus, I shift my attention to crafting my attack —calculating the distance, motion, natural wind, and everything that will affect the air current I call forth. The mathematics I've drilled for navigation and gun drill obediently lend their services to my new skill. Course thus charted, I release my magic with an exhale.

A breeze rustles the top of my collar and pushes against the balconies not ten paces from us. The flowers bend, white flakes of ripe dandelion soaring into the wind.

"If you two are done playing," says Aaron, maneuvering his

horse beside Quinn and me, "then Nile should come up to the front. It will look well if she and the prince enter the palace gates side by side."

The crowd I'd pushed into the void while wielding my magic returns into focus with a vengeance. Watching. Staring. Waiting for me to trip. To the people of Felielle, my appearance in their midst is mostly entertaining drama. They know little of Ashing's plight and care less. Of all the kingdoms Felielle touches, Ashing is the smallest. The Feliellies' same ignorance extends to the specific lives and deaths that hang on this marriage—Domenic's, Aaron's, Tam's, mine.

Ignoring the galloping of my heart, I nudge my mare to follow Aaron as we weave toward the front of the column. People's voices rise and blend, calling everything from wishes of the Goddess's love to worries over an Ashing savage in their genteel midst. As we approach the head of the procession, where Tamiath sits tall atop his black stallion, trumpets blare their tune across the square.

Ta-DA-DA. The music calls in a musical equivalent of a great gun salute. The crowd parts at once to leave an empty stretch of street between Tamiath and me. Even Aaron veers off to get behind my dapple mare. *Ta-DA-DA.*

Tam extends his hand toward me. With his lithe, tall body, rich brown hair cascading over a gray-and-gold embroidered tunic and a shining blade strapped comfortably along his back, Tam is every inch the warrior prince. Beside him, my blue woolen coat with a high collar, a thick waist belt, and black leggings—all picked out by Tam with more care than I've ever put into an outfit—are a flag of naval prowess. A union of land and sea that plays right into the Feliellies' desire for show.

Ta-DA-DA the trumpet calls a third time, cuing Tam to raise our clasped hands into the air for all to see. As we do, the tension filling Tamiath's body surges into me, the anxiety beneath his beaming smile a beacon in itself.

"What's wrong?" I murmur out of the corner of my mouth, my own smile plastered in place.

Tam's chin moves slightly, almost imperceptibly, to point toward a tall woman in a flowing crimson gown who frowns down at us from the palace balcony.

"My mother," he says, circling our horses to let the whole court get a good view of our joined hands. "She is out for blood."

"I thought your mother *wanted* you to get married?" I ask once the hostlers take our mounts and Tam and I climb the palace stairs to the tea parlor where Queen Leanna of Felielle would like to receive her younger son and his bride. If there is a place with more stairs and hills than Felielle, I'm having trouble picturing it. The palace itself is an exquisitely decorated aboveground dungeon, with stone walls and passages and staircases everywhere.

"She *wanted* to auction me off to a girl of her choice," says Tam. "Politically speaking, Felielle is so centrally located on the continent that my father has greater swords to wield with other kingdoms than his younger son's marriage bed. For Mother's social power, however, my marriage carries greater influence. The only reason I was able to sideline her demands for as long as I had was that my father couldn't care less if I decided to marry a cat, provided it didn't pee on the rugs. But between the kingdom starting to murmur and Mother squinting at Aaron..." He lets the rest go unsaid as we near a hand-painted door with bright swirls and leaflike abstractions crawling along the hinges.

Inside, the parlor is surprisingly cozy. High-backed, softly padded chairs, velvet-swathed walls, candles in intricate holders, soft, warm light that plays off the browns and reds that accent the room. The woman from the balcony, Tam's mother,

Queen Leanna of Felielle, sits at the small round table, a porcelain cup of tea in her fragile hand. Her dark cold eyes are at odds with the warmth of the parlor. She looks me over as if appraising a filly, but her trained voice is perfectly gracious. "Nile, what a pleasure," the queen says by way of greeting. "I look forward to learning all about the young woman who captured Tamiath's ice-filled heart."

"Ice filled?" I blink like a wide-eyed doe. Theatrics aside, what I say is honest. "If that Prince Tamiath exists, I have yet to meet him."

She raises a brow and slides her gaze over to her son in question.

Tam's face is stone, as if he faces a loaded broadside instead of his mother. He holds a chair out for me, pushing it in expertly before taking a seat beside mine. Beneath the tablecloth, I put my hand on his knee and brace myself for danger that remains hidden from my notice. When nothing in the vicinity explodes, I wonder if Tamiath's worry over his mother is more family discord than real brewing trouble. While there is little warmth in Leanna's eyes, there is also little of the keen intellect that Tam wears like a second skin.

"Well," Leanna says smoothly, "let us not discuss the maidens who tried and failed to capture my son's attention and focus on the one who did. I have read all about your ship's adventures in the news, Nile. Thank the Goddess for your captain's good sense. Tell me, did you know Captain Rima before joining his ship, or was it a fortunate coincidence?"

Tamiath stretches out his long arm and drapes it over my shoulders, a protective gesture made no less so by his playing absently with my earlobe. "Since when do you pay mind to military news, Mother?" he asks.

Leanna's lips tighten. "Since you've brought home a girl

from a kingdom that can't seem to tell the difference between the male and female of the species, Tamiath. I thought you'd *appreciate* my welcoming Nile on her own terms."

It takes me a moment to realize that Queen Leanna actually believes her own words.

"Your pardon, my lady." A serving girl at the tea parlor interrupts with a cautious curtsy. "Your other guests are here. Shall I show them in?"

Tam's eyes darken while Leanna's face lights up into a smile. "Ah yes." She inclines her head toward me, her musical voice genuine. "I thought some familiar faces might be welcome for us all."

It is only my quarterdeck training that keeps the tea in my hands from spilling as Lady Madeline and Captain Rima stroll into the room.

CHAPTER 37

My first coherent thought, materializing through a haze of panic and suspicion, is to wonder how long it took the Lady Madeline to dress. Larger than Rima in all dimensions, Lady Madeline is nearly as tall as Tam and wears a flowing gown of sunflower yellow that complements her Eflian eyes. The pattern on the corset of her dress, cut in just enough of a V to reveal the tops of ample breasts, is embroidered with a design identical to the tattoos decorating Rima's cheekbones.

Captain Rima, now in finely cut civilian garb and his left arm in a sling, is of a height with his wife's bosom. Beside her, he seems almost insignificant, except for a cruel gleam I recognize all too easily behind his smiling lips.

Lady Madeline kisses Tam's mother on both cheeks in a gesture of intimate friendship and receives the same greeting in return. "Oh, my most sincere congratulations to you all," says Madeline, her low, melodic voice filling the room. "Your Majesty, might I present my husband, Captain Rima?"

Rima bows and kisses the queen's hand before turning and

bowing to Tam. "My prince Tamiath," he says formally. As Rima straightens, he angles his body such that only Tam and I see the warning gleam in his eyes as he adds, "I do not believe we've had the pleasure of meeting."

Tamiath's body tenses, his gaze ice cold. As Rima turns his attention to me, nausea rises in my throat. I touch Tam's hand. *Nothing.* I remind us both. *We've agreed to do nothing. To let Rima have his life and his games.*

After a heartbeat, Tam nods to Rima but doesn't bother to rise. "We've indeed not met, but your reputation precedes you, Captain," he says coolly.

"Tamiath, really, where are your manners?" Leanna chides, her brows narrowing in a flicker of displeasure at her son before she gives Madeline an apologetic look. "Captain Rima is the hero of the Battle of Siaman *and* the protector of your bride all these months. It is an honor to meet you, Captain Rima." Leanna says the last to the captain directly.

Rima waves off the compliment with murmurs of his unworthiness of all the attention. "I was just doing my duty," he says, holding out a chair for his wife before joining us at the table.

"The newsies will always be newsies," his Lady Madeline puts in, laughing softly. Her message to me and Tam is quite clear: *And they will write what I pay them to write.*

A servant appears with more tea and milk. Cups are filled and stirred, an uncomfortable silence saturating the room. Tam's mother forces a smile to her lips as she eyes me intently. "Do tell us about yourself, Nile." A command.

"What would you like to know, Your Majesty?" I ask.

Lady Madeline gives Queen Leanna a supportive look. "I, for one, am incredibly curious as to how in the Gods' name did you end up in the Siaman Sea," she says, as if making good on a promise to help uncover the secrets of the queen's daughter-in-law-to-be.

"I overheard plans of a marriage to Prince Tamiath," I answer truthfully. "Not having met him, I feared what such a match might mean for me and chose to go into the open sea instead."

"And what changed your mind?" Queen Leanna asks me, her brows narrowing on her son in suspicion. Leanna might be fooled into thinking Madeline her friend, but she knows Tamiath better than to believe him enthralled.

"Love," I reply promptly, then spread my hands. "And politics, of course. An alliance between Felielle and Ashing would benefit my kingdom."

"It would have benefited your kingdom sooner if you'd not run off," says Leanna, her gaze plainly stating that she has plenty of other causes she'd have preferred to receive this benefit.

"How fascinating," says Lady Madeline smoothly. "Do tell us more about your family, Your Highness. You've two brothers, do you not? I remember Prince Thad well, but I confess the name of the other escapes me. Kay, is it?"

The corners of Rima's mouth twitch in a suppressed smile.

"Clay," I say icily, finally catching on to the game. Queen Leanna might think that Madeline and Rima came to support her quest to uncover secrets about her son's marriage arrangement, but the couple's real plan is to remind me of the stakes and demonstrate to Tam and me how close Madeline and the Felielle queen have become.

"Clay, such a nice name," says Madeline, her voice still smooth as silk. "Why has the world seen so little of him, though? He isn't ill, I hope?"

"My twin is Gifted." It's an effort to keep my temper leashed.

"My condolences," Rima murmurs piously, while Madeline smiles at me like a cat closing on her prey.

"How fortunate for Ashing to have a healthy, marriageable daughter despite such tragedy," Lady Madeline tells the queen. "Nile's mother must be so grateful."

I walk out of the tea parlor an hour later, ready to do violence. With a hand on my shoulder, Tamiath guides me down the corridor, where Domenic and Quinn peel away from the wall to follow our progress. Bear, upset at having been left out of the tea parlor audience, prods my shin with his nose. Bear's mother may have been large enough to reach my waist, but the pup has a bit of growing to do yet.

A familiar throat clears behind us. The three men and I turn at once to find Captain Rima alone, rubbing his sling-supported arm. The air around Tam and Domenic vibrates with fury, while Quinn studies the scene with academic curiosity.

"Prince Tamiath, might I have a word with you and your bride in private?" Rima asks mildly, ignoring Domenic, Quinn, and Bear altogether.

With a jerk of his head, Tam leads the procession down a set of steep stairs and through several narrow corridors into a sarcophagus-like alcove. A single beam of sunlight streams through a high window to illuminate a marble bust of a long dead king. Stopping in the shadow around the statue's pedestal, Tam twists to the captain. "What the bloody hell are you doing in the palace?" he demands.

Rima opens his good arm innocently. "My wife and your mother are dear friends. I could hardly refuse the queen's invitation."

"Get out of my city," Tam snarls at him. "We will allow your lies to stand, but I want you out of my sight. Understood?"

Rima sighs. "I'd love to, Your Highness. Unfortunately, I find myself at the physician's mercy while I fully recover. Given that it was your man's misfire that caused the injury, I'm certain you will agree that modest assistance from Your Highness with my physician's bills and recuperation costs are only just."

My fingers curl into a fist. Tam grabs my wrist before I can bury my knuckles in the captain's nose.

"A million gold should cover the expenses, I think," Rima says, running his finger over the marble bust's edge. He examines the dust before rubbing his fingers together to dispel the dirt. "I thought it would be prudent to come to you instead of Queen Leanna with my concern, since, while the queen is generous, she is a woman and does ask many questions. This way we can help each other. A joyful wedding for you and medical care for me. My next physician's bill comes due in two weeks. I would appreciate the funds by then." Before either Tam or I can respond, Rima bows, turns on his heel, and strides away.

CHAPTER 38

"This Captain Rima, will he make good on his threats?" Aaron asks quietly as we fill him in on Rima's new demands.

"He killed a midshipman and beat another to death's door, all for wounded pride," I say, inviting the men into my room. The canopied bed, marble fireplace, and carved armchairs of my suite feel as though they belong to someone else. Someone who is used to dresses rather than uniforms filling her armoire. "As he and Lady Madeline took some pains to remind us upon our arrival, they have both the queen and the press under their influence."

"Plus, Rima has done this before," Domenic adds quietly. Our faces turn toward him, and a flash of grim vulnerability skitters across his eyes. "The reason I served under Captain Rima is because he purchased my family's debt and used my continual service to counteract the accruing interest."

My heart pauses, but I don't dare bring more attention to him than the words already do. I want to pace, but the precious rug is a work of art, and I can't bear to step onto it with my boots. Damn Felielle and their ornamental idiocy. I rub my temple to relieve the growing pressure in my head. When the throbbing continues, I slap my palm against the wall.

"Yesterday, Rima demanded silence. Today it's money. Storms know what he'll want tomorrow," I hiss. "We were fools to think Rima would let go of his advantage. "

Bear whines.

Domenic whirls on me, his eyes worried.

"I'm fine," I snap at man and dog both. "I'll be better when we sort out a way to castrate the bastard."

Bear yaps softly in disagreement as green lights flicker in the side of my vision and familiar panic courses through my veins. Ignoring the damn rug, I stalk across the room to my bathing chamber to enjoy my convulsion in private.

OVER THE NEXT TWO WEEKS, as Rima's deadline for payment approaches, we try and fail to divine a means to castrate Rima's extortion plan. My one hope is that the wedding will necessarily take some of the wind from the captain's sails—at least as far as Domenic's pardon is concerned. Once I know that no noose hangs over Domenic's head, I'll be able to think better. Aside from the wedding preparations, the only other area to see any meaningful progress is my magic training, which emboldens Quinn to press it even further. We go so far as to find a small riverbank about an hour's ride from the palace that offers both access to small sailing craft and privacy.

Quinn, Domenic, and I occupy that riverbank now. Domenic crouches several paces in front of me, his wet shirt clinging to shifting muscles while a wooden practice blade sways in his hand. A tattoo peeks out from the wide open collar of his shirt and my fingers tingle with the want to trace the ink.

Domenic raps the flat of his blade against my shoulder.

I grunt.

"Pay attention," Domenic snaps, his mouth tightening. The somber expression is somewhat marred by his hair, wind-tousled into a semblance of a porcupine. Domenic is neither Catsper nor Aaron with a blade, but the finer points of swordsmanship are of little consequence since I'm bound to a tree.

Standing on the sideline, Quinn shakes his head. The aura of a captain's authority—and disapproval—clings to his straight shoulders and thoughtful, guarded eyes.

I reel my mind back into focus and press the wall of wind against Domenic, forcing him to retreat farther, step by step from where I sit. A trail of sweat trickles from my temple and into my ear, tickling the inside ridges. The wind shifts with my undulating thoughts, and Domenic curses as the force of the gale knocks him to the sand.

I cringe. "Sorry."

Before the word leaves my mouth, Domenic is already back on his feet, striding through an opening wide enough for a horse. I scramble to even my wind out, but it's too late. Another stinging rap of the blade lands on my shoulder.

Domenic tosses the practice sword to Quinn. "Are you ill, Nile?"

"No." I release my magic and sag back against the tree trunk. Domenic is now wet *and* sandy, with river water sloshing from the tops of his boots. Like the sand, the excess of water is my fault. Thirty minutes back, the three of us rigged a small boat that I attempted to propel from shore while Domenic steered. I capsized the craft before Domenic made it four hundred yards.

And now I'm gloriously failing an exercise I'd mastered days ago.

Domenic turns to frown at Bear, who reliably alerts of my coming convulsions before even I know they ride the winds, but the dog is happily gnawing a stick. Twisting back to me, Domenic starts to undo the rope binding my wrists.

"One more time," I say.

"No."

"Domenic—"

"No." This time it's Quinn speaking up. "Mr. Dana is correct. We'll try another day." The rope comes loose, and Quinn offers me a hand up. Except for the minor problem of his political allegiance, he is the kind of officer I'd gladly serve under. Firm without being cruel, and confident in his choices while forever observing and iterating. He turns to Domenic and motions toward the beached boat.

Domenic nods, watching while Quinn trudges across the sand to deal with the vessel.

My shoulder tingles, and I rub out the soreness. "The one thing worse than you and Quinn being at each other's throats is the two of you teaming up."

Domenic says nothing, focusing instead on rinsing his shirt off in the river before pulling the wet garment back on. His movements are slow, as if he is fighting his own muscles. Domenic's gaze flickers to Quinn, who is cleaning up the boat and out of earshot.

Whatever Domenic wants to say, I've the sinking feeling I won't like it.

"I'm sorry I turned the boat over," I say on the odd chance that it's the dunk in the river that has Domenic on edge. "But it's too cold for wet clothes. If you're wearing a soaked shirt for my benefit, you little need to bother. I like you without it just fine."

"What a relief," Domenic says tightly.

I cross my arms. "You say it as if it's a bad thing."

"You say it as if it's a good thing." Domenic closes the distance between us, each step heavy as it presses into the sandy ground. Fire dances in Domenic's eyes, the muscles of his jaw tense and unyielding. "I promised to protect you, but my very presence is placing you in peril. Prince Tamiath isn't blind. Neither is Quinn. You think he fails to notice that your performance improves when I'm not involved in an exercise?"

"I lost my focus today," I say quickly. "I won't again. I'll make sure I don't. And I'll be more careful when Tam—"

"It isn't just Quinn and Prince Tamiath and you." Domenic tucks a stray bit of hair behind my ear. His own hair is tussled from his dunk in the river, and his salt-and-brine scent is plain even far from the ocean. "My presence is a liability. Ammunition that Rima and people like him can use against you. And it's time to ensure you have every advantage to succeed as Felielle's princess."

Ice crackles along my spine. "What are you saying, exactly?"

Domenic's throat bobs as he swallows, but his shoulders straighten. "You need to find a replacement for me, Nile."

I snap back on my heels, my mind ringing as if a great gun had gone off too close to my ears. "What? No." I wonder if I misheard. I must have misheard.

Domenic's gaze flickers to his hand, wrapped knuckle-white into a fist. "I'm sorry."

I taste blood and realize I've bitten my lip. The world spins around me like a carnival's twisted looking glass. "What did I do wrong?" I whisper. "Why don't you—"

Domenic lays a finger against my lips. "Meeting you has been the greatest turn my life has ever taken. You are a dreamer and fighter. While the world navigates known paths, you chart new ones. Great ones. I knew it from the day I met you on the Ashing beach." His voice drops, his words barely audible over the breeze. "I think I fell in love with you before I ever learned your name."

My mouth dries, his words echoing through me. I reach for his face, wanting—*needing*—to feel his skin against mine, but he catches my wrist with one hand. "Please." That's all I have to offer him, and my breath catches on the word. "I'll... Please. Don't leave."

Domenic leans over and kisses the top of my head. "I'm leaving in two weeks," he whispers into my hair. "Right after the wedding."

CHAPTER 39

My mind is still ringing with Domenic's words that evening, my impotence to stop him from leaving blinding me to the changes in Tamiath until he appears unannounced in my rooms. Instead of entering, Tam stands at the doorway like a schoolboy, his face white and his hands clutching an envelope.

"What's happened?" I ask, ushering him inside and shutting the door.

Tam enters with uncharacteristic clumsiness, tripping over the edge of the expensive rug before I grab his elbow and steer him to the sitting area, where he sinks onto one of the cushioned chairs and cradles his head in his hands. "He's going after Aaron."

"Who is? How?"

"Rima." Tamiath stares at the floor. "The deadline for his payment is tomorrow, and he's... he's taking extra steps."

I pluck the envelope gently from Tamiath's fingers and pull

our the message, angling the page so the light from the window illuminates the writing. Instead of the expected note in Rima's loopy hand, I find a printed newsleaf with the words DRAFT sprawled boldly across the text. A picture of Aaron, drawn as skillfully as Rima's had been on a different newsleaf, stares menacingly from the upper left corner. I read the text quickly. Short and to the point, the article describes how one man's *horrific judgment* and *sheer incompetence* led him to mistake the heroic Captain Rima for an enemy combatant and fire a near-fatal shot. The text ends with a call to charge Aaron with attempted murder.

I put my hand on Tam's bicep and find the muscles trembling beneath.

"It's an opinion piece, not a charging document," I say with forced calm. "It has no power to do anything."

Tam shakes his head. "It's a threat, Nile. The only reason to send *me* a draft of an article demonizing Aaron is to demonstrate the author's knowledge of Aaron being someone of significance to me. Rima isn't threatening to get Aaron charged with murder; he is threatening to expose us."

"How would Rima know?"

Tam pinches the bridge of his nose. "Mother. She's suspected the truth about Aaron and me for years. Likely she let hints of it slip with her *close personal friend* Lady Madeline. The viper is likely baiting Mother into divulging all sorts of derogatory information, and Queen Leanna is too self-centered to even notice."

I want to tell Tam that there are other possibilities, that perhaps Rima is simply gambling on Tamiath's wish to protect his lieutenant—but even I little believe it. Not with knowing how Rima operates. I turn the page over to find a small note on the back, noting plans of turning the draft over to the *Lyron Herald* for printing tomorrow evening. A postscript advises that the draft, along with unspecified others, is a copy from a sealed packet in the *Lyron Herald*'s office—to be opened should something unfortunate happen to the Rimas.

It seems Captain Rima likes to insure his funds.

"I'm going to do it," Tamiath says, looking at me with a silent plea for understanding. "I'm going to pay the bastard tomorrow."

At sunrise the following morning, Domenic, Tamiath, and I file wordlessly into the small alcove with the marble statue, where Rima first issued his demands. A messenger to summon Captain Rima to the spot was dispatched an hour past, and Quinn holds position at the end of the corridor to watch for the captain's approach. Heavy silence hangs over us like fog, and the minutes ticking by are infinitely long. Tamiath's strong and beautiful face is drawn, and I pray to the storms that I'm hiding my fear better than Tam is concealing his shame.

Finally, Rima's footsteps echo down the stone.

Domenic steps away from the statue to make room for the captain, who gives Tam and me a mocking bow upon arrival. "Your Highnesses, what a pleasure," Rima says, straightening. The captain's arm is still in a sling, and today the cloth is gold in color. Like coin. Beneath the sling, Rima wears loose trousers and a thick shirt, the ample cloth concealing his scrawny, chicken-like frame.

Tamiath looks down his nose at Rima, as if examining an unusually vocal cockroach.

Rima scowls. "You wished to see me, Your Highness." A demand.

Face blank, Tam withdraws a thick envelope from his inside

jacket pocket. "One million gold crowns have been made available to you through a network of Lyron League bankers," Tamiath says coolly. "You will only be able to draw the funds from outside Felielle and only two hundred crowns at a time. Attempt to take more or try to access the moneys from within Felielle, and the agreement will terminate."

Rima reaches for the envelope, but Tam pulls it up out of reach.

"One last thing, Captain Rima," Tam says softly. "I want you out of my kingdom by day's end."

Rima plucks the envelope from Tamiath's hand, his smile widening as his eyes take in the notes of credit, one after the other, that make up the small fortune Tam has just laid into his hands. It's over. For now. I let out a breath and turn after Tamiath, who is already heading to the corridor when Rima's voice chimes behind us.

"Thank you for this gesture of goodwill, my prince," Rima says easily. "There is one small problem, unfortunately. It appears my shoulder requires greater medical aid than I initially estimated. If you could raise the credit to two million, I would be most appreciative. You will also need to remove this silliness about the funds being unavailable within Felielle. Neither my lady nor I have plans of departing, and it would be the height of inconvenience to have to send riders over kingdom borders simply to withdraw the necessary funds to cover my medical needs."

Tam stops dead. Inside my veins, blood simmers and agitates my magic. There is no escape, I realize. Never was. Rima never intended to settle. He was simply waiting until we bowed to his initial demand before making the next, and the next. Around me, a preternatural breeze picks up and twirls the dust.

Rima clicks his tongue against his teeth and steps around us, making himself the leading figure in the corridor heading away from the alcove. "Take a breath, Your Highnesses. There is little reason to hang on to frivolity on either side. For ones such as you, the money is insignificant. For me, it's but funds for medical treatment you have caused me to require." He bows again and tucks the envelope into the inside pocket of his jacket. "I look forward to hearing again from you soon, before the wedding, no doubt. Until then, by your leave." Without waiting for a reply, Rima strolls away down the corridor.

Storms and hail. I wrap my arms around myself and stare at nothing. He's won. The bastard won. We gave him what he wanted, *twice.* And it still failed to ensure Rima's silence or Domenic's safety or Aaron's fate.

"Excuse me." Domenic's voice breaks through the crackling silence with a quiet surety that stops my breath. When we turn toward him, Domenic steps forward from the shadowed wall and faces Tamiath. "Your Highnesses..." The title encompasses us both, but it is Tam's gaze that Domenic finds. "Given the developments of the situation, I would ask you to accept my official declination of the offered letter of pardon. As is my right, I will be going forward with a public trial."

I blink, my mind processing the words. "What the hell are you talking about?" I say finally. "We've quite enough problems as it is, if you've failed to notice."

Tam nods in agreement with me, though with more composure. "You committed mutiny, Mr. Dana," he says bluntly. "There is but one way such a trial can end—and that is with a hangman's noose. I am unclear as to how it would help the current dilemma."

The light from the window set high in the ceiling plays in Domenic's eyes as he studies Tamiath with a calm as preternatural as the wisps of wind still swirling the air. It's a look I've seen on Domenic before—when the Tirik *Devron* opened its gunports and launched deadly shot at our ship. An armor of confidence and decision.

Tam's brow flickers as he too notes the change in Domenic's demeanor.

"I am quite aware of a trial's likely outcome," Domenic tells Tamiath with equal bluntness. "I am also aware that avoiding said trial is a material matter in several key decisions being made. So I am taking myself out of this equation. There is quite enough to be weighed without my trial or lack thereof affecting issues of state."

Blood drains from my face. I open my mouth to speak, but Domenic isn't finished yet.

"Additionally," he says, looking exclusively at Tamiath, "a public disclosure of Rima's true character will do well to cast doubt on the man's credibility and might prevent him from commanding a future ship to its doom. That in itself is worth my life."

"Domenic," I plead, stepping toward him.

"No, Nile." His voice is calm, his attention on Tamiath even as his words aim toward me. "You are done doing things to protect me as of this moment." With a sharp motion, Domenic executes a perfect bow and withdraws down the hallway, heading in the same direction Rima had disappeared moments earlier.

I start after him, but Tamiath stops me with his arm. "Let him go," he says gently. "Mr. Dana will not change his mind."

I swallow, the truth of Tam's words ringing in my soul. I won't change Domenic's mind. Or Rima's. Or anyone else's. My thoughts spiral in a tightening typhoon until something snaps with a mental crack that echoes through my skull. An image from the *Aurora*, sparked by Domenic's resolution, materializes in my mind, and an eerie calm settles over me.

I'm done asking, done bending to realities others create with lies. It's time to make my own truth.

"Let *me* go, Tamiath," I say, my voice icy as I remove his arm from my path.

CHAPTER 40

I locate Aaron in the training yard, his shirt off and his practice blade clobbering an innocent dummy. One look at me has him pulling away midblow and hesitating only long enough to grab his shirt before following me to the closest place where we can speak privately, which happens to be an empty stall in the nearby stable.

As I detail what I need Aaron to do, his face steadily drains of color. By the time I finish, the shirt he'd been using to mop sweat from his brow and shoulders hangs loosely in his calloused hand.

"You are insane," he informs me finally. "That's not how the rite is used. You are warping the concept into something unrecognizable."

"On the contrary, I'm using it exactly as its spirit intends. It's only unrecognizable because no one has thought to use it this way yet." I harden my gaze. "The debate is beside the point. I need to know whether or not you can find a priestess agreeable to performing it."

Aaron pinches the bridge of his nose between two fingers. "Of course not. If such a person existed—"

"Of course one *exists*. There is always someone who looks forward, in every field." I step toward Aaron, forcing him to meet my eyes. My voice is so low, even I can barely make out the words. "You've lived your whole life hiding a secret. The only way to do that in a nation that would destroy you for it is by knowing the right people to trust. I need you to tap into that network, Aaron. Now. Tonight. If you will not do it for friendship, consider it a royal command."

Aaron's face is hard as he studies me, his green eyes turning a dark shade of emerald in the stable's dim light. After an eternity of silence, the man bows with a hand over his heart. "For friendship," he says.

I sigh in relief.

Aaron smiles and pulls on his shirt. "Friendship, and the entertainment of watching Tamiath kill you when he finds out," he adds before striding off to saddle a horse.

I watch him for a few moments before walking away to locate paper, ink, and a copy of the Felielle legal code.

Aaron is gone within the hour. I wait into the night for his return, only to fall asleep by morning without his arrival. He fails to return the next day as well. And the one after that. My stomach twists itself into knots, but I keep silent under Tamiath's questioning, though he is on the verge of disemboweling me for information. It is safer if Tam knows nothing just yet. I'm done with endangering others.

On the third night of Aaron's absence, I am lying awake in my bed and staring at the ceiling while the night's darkness stands sentinel. The clock in my head ticks away seconds to damnation. With my family due to arrive in three days, and the wedding a week after that, there is precious little time to work with.

Bear, curled up shamelessly in my bed, springs suddenly to his feet. A momentary dread passes over me, replaced by fluttering anxiety as I realize the dog is alerting on an approaching visitor, not a looming convulsion. I close my eyes and listen.

Steps indeed approach my chamber, and they aren't Tam's, Quinn's, or Domenic's. Although the latter is remaining at his post pending the storms-damned trial, he and I have exchanged fewer than three words in as many days. It little matters, though. There will be no trial. Not if Aaron—who I'm certain is the owner of the steps—is back with good news.

The knock at the door has me on my feet in a heartbeat. By the time Aaron enters without waiting for invitation, I'm as awake as if awoken by a battle drum.

"You found a priestess?" I ask, my hand clamping onto the lieutenant's wrist. "Tell me you found her."

Aaron nods, his face tense as he lights a lantern. He looks— and smells—like a man who's spent the past days in the saddle, with exhausted eyes and dirt-streaked clothes. "Yes, I've found one who is willing. But Nile—"

"We are going." I exchange my sleeping chemise for a pair of dark breeches, shirt and a woolen coat. "Get Tam and meet me in the stables."

"Nile." Aaron grabs my boots, holding them hostage until I meet his gaze. "We are going nowhere until I know you've both heard and understood my words." He pauses, waiting for my reluctant nod before continuing. "What you are starting is a direct challenge to the tradition of the Felielle throne. Whatever happens publicly, privately King Hallord and Queen Leanna can and will find a way of punishing you for forcing their hand.

Tamiath will have some protection by virtue of his birth, but you... Crossing the Felielle throne can end very, *very* poorly."

Aaron would know.

I take a deep breath, forcing myself to absorb the full weight of Aaron's words. "I know," I say finally, putting my hand on the man's shoulder. "And we should do it nonetheless." My voice softens. "You need not come, Aaron. I will—"

He snorts and hands me the boots. "Oh, shut up. Of course I'm coming."

A weight lifts from my shoulders, and I grin as I secure the documents I've been preparing into a travel pouch. "Can you bring Tamiath to the stable?"

"Already done," Aaron says dryly. "Just because I wanted to warn you, doesn't mean I didn't know how the conversation would end."

Tam indeed meets us in the stables, looking as bewildered and furious as I'd be in his place. Stepping out of the shadows, he pins Aaron and me with a stare that would send the most seasoned sailor scurrying across the deck. Behind him, however, three horses stand tacked and ready.

"Does one of you want to tell me what's going on?" the prince demands. Although Aaron's safe reappearance has dulled the edge of Tam's murderous rage, his whole body is coiled with violence.

"Yes," I say, meeting Tam's gaze head-on. I jerk my head at his horse. "But en route. An explanation will take more time than we can spare just now. I'm asking you to trust me, Tam."

To Tam's credit, he says nothing and mounts his horse in a single practiced motion. I follow suit, albeit less gracefully, and point my mount to follow Aaron's. With no basket attached to any of our saddles and me uncertain how far Bear can run beside the horses, I decide to brave the night without the pup.

Once clear of the palace grounds, Tam clears his throat expectantly.

It takes me a solid hour to explain the situation—everything from the rite I witnessed between two Felielle seamen on the *Aurora,* to my subsequent crazy notion, to Aaron's efforts in finding a priestess whose location, qualifications, discretion, and worldview matched ours.

The prince's face grows graver with each word I utter. When I finish, Tam reins his horse up in front of me, forcing my mare to an undignified stop.

My chest tightens, but I straighten my back and stare right back at the prince, my chin held high.

"Nile." His voice is sharp, but he checks it quickly. "You are talking about using a loophole in an archaic tradition. This idea is—"

"Brilliant?"

"I was going to say audacious, deceitful, and impudent," says Tam.

"Storms know you had good language tutors," I mutter.

"I've more words where those came from," Tamiath says darkly.

I rest my hands on the pommel of the saddle. "I'm certain you do. But not one of those possible words includes *illegal.*"

Tamiath pauses, plainly running through the same laws in his mind that Aaron and I had considered. Tam's jaw tightens. "It isn't illegal," he concedes finally. "But it is dishonest."

"It will be the most *honest* thing we'll have done thus far," I snap with more rawness than I intend. "Tonight we will choose to be honest with ourselves. And we'll do it in a way not even the King of Felielle can deny. And to save you time and effort, Aaron has already given me the *you shall incur the throne's wrath* speech."

Tam is silent, but in the moonlight, I see the emotions ripple through his usually schooled face. Disbelief. Anger. Wonder. *Hope.* "Let us be honest, then," he says finally, gently. As if he's afraid to believe his own words.

I bite my lip, throwing a quick glance at Aaron, who has considerately moved his horse a few paces away. "There is one other thing," I tell Tam, watching Aaron's straight back to ensure no hint of my words reaches his hearing. This last bit of the plan, I've held back from Aaron to give Tam a true choice. "You can take tonight one step further, you know. If you want to."

Tam freezes, his gaze going to his lover before he can catch himself. When Tam turns back to me, the breath in his chest stills and his face glows with a mix of shock and desire. "You..." For the first time since I met him, Tam struggles for his words. "You...you wouldn't mind?"

"How could I?" I say quietly and nudge my horse away to give Tam space to work through his thoughts.

The ride to the temple—or what's left of one after years of abandonment and disrepair—ends up taking nearly three hours at a pace that leaves me uncertain of arriving with my neck and limbs intact. Tam and Aaron keep their seats with the ease of sailors minding a rocking deck, but I am sore, bleeding, and shaken to the very core when Aaron finally signals a stop. Tam lifts me off the saddle, his arms sliding around me protectively as he sets me to the ground.

"I'm fine," I tell Aaron, who comes up with a worried expression to examine me.

Ignoring me, Aaron looks to Tam.

"She's fine," Tam tells him.

I scowl at them both. But I don't mean it.

The temple's door is long gone, though stone pillars still

stand as sentinels before the entrance. A petite woman in gold priestess robes waits at the doorway, her hands inside wide bell sleeves. Her hair, white as virgin snow, cascades unbound to her waist. A horse, grazing on lush grass beside the small temple, whinnies a welcome to our mounts.

"Hello, then," the woman says, her voice older than I expected.

Aaron bows before the priestess, going to one knee. Tam and I quickly follow suit. Kneeling beside Tam, I can feel his nervous tension.

The priestess runs her cool palms over our faces, and for a moment, I wonder if she might be blind, but then her eyes find mine, and I know she is not. "Rise and come, my children," the priestess says. "We've little time before our absences might be discovered."

Drawing the three of us inside the round temple, she motions to the center, where a hundred candles chase the night from the altar. Age-old dust hangs thick in the musty air, and the flickering candlelight illuminates runes of a forgotten language inscribed forever into the walls. Atop the altar stone, an inkwell, knife, and pair of plain rings already await.

At the priestess's instruction, we kneel on the cold, hard floor.

"Have you the contracts?" the priestess asks.

My heart and breath quicken. Reaching into my travel pouch, I pull out the pair of documents I prepared and hand them to the priestess. She surveys the writing carefully before setting the two parchments on the altar. A knife is placed atop the first contract, and rings atop the second.

My breath stills.

"The Goddess's love is deep and enduring," the priestess intones, looking between us. "There are many who find comfort in limits, strength in tradition. We respect and honor them today. But we also respect and honor the vanguard who will forge a path our children will travel.

"The rite of blood brothers is an ancient one. It was born of battle, when two warriors shared each other's blood and declared themselves brothers. The family of one became the family of the other, to love, protect, and provide for. To this day, in the eyes of the Goddess and the law, the bond of blood brothers is forever binding.

"Three requirements must be met before two people are eligible to undertake the rite. You must be warriors. You must be facing battle and the threat of death. And you must make the choice willingly and knowingly." The priestess pauses.

I reach toward Tam and squeeze his hand.

"Tamiath of Felielle and Nile of Ashing," the priestess says, grasping our attention once more. "You are both warriors—one of land, the other of sea. Thus you've met the first requirement. You are both children of your kingdoms' thrones. Your kingdoms' deadly war is *your* war, now and always. The second requirement has thus been satisfied. As for the third..."

The priestess puts a hand on each of the two parchments on the altar. "I have two contracts here, both of which would forever bind you together. One in marriage, the other in brotherhood. You must make your choice openly and willingly, knowing that by taking one road, you are also choosing against the other. What is your choice?"

"Brotherhood," I say clearly, my voice ringing true as if calling through the fog and report of guns. "I choose brotherhood."

Tamiath swallows. "Brotherhood," he whispers before finding his voice. "I choose brotherhood."

The priestess picks up a knife, its razor edge reflecting the candlelight. "The third requirement has thus been met. Rise, then, and let your blood meet."

I get to my feet, my fingers fumbling as my gaze rivets to the knife's edge. A silly, ridiculous thing to fuss over. My peripheral vision tells me that Tamiath has already complied with the first part of the request, and I will my hands to hurry.

Tam's strong fingers encircle mine, and he gently pushes my hand away as he works my sleeve loose. With my forearm bare, he finds my eyes. "Look at me, brother," he whispers.

I do as he instructs and, when the priestess opens our veins and presses the wounds together, my brother wraps his arms around me and whispers his welcome to a family forged of choice and love.

A warmth spreads from his touch down my skin, a contentment so deep, it settles into my very bones. There is one part missing, though, and I squeeze Tamiath encouragingly. "Complete the family," I whisper back to him. "I want Aaron as my brother too."

He nods to me and pulls away, facing the retreating priestess. "One more moment, if I may?"

She nods and stops.

Tamiath turns to address both the priestess and his lover together. "I'd ask to put Aaron's name on the contract that is still empty."

Aaron's face drains of color. "Are you insane?" he whispers. "When your parents see *that*—"

"They'll have no choice but to accept it," Tamiath finishes. "Just as they will have no choice but to accept my blood brother as legal family." Swallowing, he turns to face Aaron full-on. "It will be difficult. My parents will be furious. Nile and I must still act out a wedding, fake a marriage until the Felielle people are ready for the truth. But for what it's worth, I'd like for the ring

Nile gives me that day to mean something. I'd like it to be yours." He pauses. "The important question is... Will you join with me, Aaron?"

A smile tugs at my mouth, and I watch, mesmerized, as Aaron's dirt-streaked face fills with joy and terror while he accepts Tam's outstretched hand.

CHAPTER 41

The three days between our secretly exchanged vows and my family's arrival at the Felielle palace are heart wrenching. Tam, Aaron, and I go through the motions of pretending nothing is amiss while bracing ourselves for the looming confrontation—scheduled to erupt within hours of my family's arrival, when we reveal the contracts to both sets of royals. Domenic spends his time with a legal advocate. Quinn, observant enough to sense that something is brewing and experienced enough to stay the hell away from it, blends into walls and furniture.

When the trumpets announcing the Ashing royal family's approach finally sound, it's all I can do to keep down my breakfast. Tamiath and I stand together on the balcony to watch them approach the gates, after which I descend to the courtyard to welcome my parents in person. Mother smiles warmly as she steps free from the carriage, and I shamelessly fold into her embrace. To my surprise, the five weeks since I saw her last have felt longer than years at sea.

"Nile." Father's voice is cool and contained. Like Thad, he is dressed in somber blue, with minimal embellishment and decoration. The only gleam to his clothes comes from polished shoes and a golden belt buckle.

I separate myself from my mother and bow to the Ashing king. With a tightfitting blue bodice and wide skirtlike pants of deep purple, I'm already something in between Ashing and Felielle. A child of both kingdoms that fits into neither. And the morning is about to get exponentially worse. "Father," I say evenly. "How was your journey?"

"Fine." His jaw is tight.

I turn to Thad.

He turns his back to me.

"Very mature, Thad," I say to my brother's shoulder blades before twisting back to our mother. "Where is Clay?"

Thad snorts and walks a few steps away, as if even speaking about Clay is an embarrassment to him.

"In the back carriage," mother tells me. "An attendant will wait until the crowds are past to show him out. Or you could, if you'd like."

I squeeze her hand. "I would like to see Clay very much, but there is something Prince Tamiath and I need to speak with you about first."

STANDING outside the royal meeting room, I lean my head back against the cool, hard stone. Inside, Tamiath has both sets of families sitting around the table, and I hear the murmurs of polite conversation. I touch my messenger bag, the two parchments crinkling beneath my fingers.

"Are you all right?" Domenic asks formally. Standing

several paces away, he eyes me and Bear warily. The fact that he's speaking to me at all is a sure sign that I look more frightened than I wish I did.

I straighten. "Quite all right. And there is no need for you to take time away from your preparations to stand outside a door."

Domenic puts his hands at the small of his back. "You are up to something."

"Oh, you have no idea," I murmur.

His voice drops, his eyes flickering with gut-wrenching worry. "Will you tell me?"

"No." My voice is cooler than I intend, but there is little to do for it now. I take a deep breath and clear my mind the way I do before battle. The fear that vines through my chest hits an invisible wall that separates it from my thoughts.

"What are you doing?" Domenic is no longer collected but towers over me. "I know that look, Nile. What are you doing?"

I push past him, open the door, and go inside.

Seven people seated around an elongated wooden table turn their faces toward me. Two kings. Two queens. Two crown princes. Tamiath.

Tam stands and pulls a chair out for me.

"Kind of you to join us, Your Highness," Tamiath's father, King Hallord, says dryly. Despite my three weeks at the palace, it is the first time Tamiath's father has bothered to acknowledge my existence. Hallord looks like a king from a child's picture book—tall, gray haired, bearded, with a gold crown perched atop his head, and dark, calculating eyes. "Tamiath has been keeping us all in suspense. If the happy couple could *now* oblige us with an end to this dramatic gathering, I would be most appreciative."

Well, if you put it that way. I reach into my messenger bag, pull out the marriage and brotherhood contracts, and lay them flat for both sets of royalty to see. Then I take the offered chair, cross my thighs, and start silently counting down the heartbeats to apocalypse.

The wooden table is apparently heavier than it looks, because King Hallord's attempt to overturn it as he thrusts himself to his feet ends with only a slight clattering of the wooden behemoth. What Hallord lacks in furniture-turning power, he makes up for in the murderous blaze coming from his eyes. Across the table from Hallord, Thad's face is turning a steady shade of purple, all the way down to dark, flaring nostrils. Beside him, Father sits like a statue of ice. As for my mother... It takes me a moment to realize that she is smiling. Subtly and only with her eyes, but smiling.

Queen Leanna is *not* smiling. Her severe face regards her son with nothing short of disgust. I'd once thought the two queens a bit similar, both wanting their children to be something we are not. Now I realize the two women could not be more different. My mother's love was never contingent on my choices.

Picking up the brotherhood and marriage contracts, King Hallord crumples the parchments into a wad that he throws to the floor. "I want these two pieces of fiction *burned*," he growls. "After that, you, Tamiath, will declare Aaron a sodomite and rapist. Publicly. He will be executed the morning following the wedding, which will be consummated that very night before four witnesses of my choice. It is only out of great respect for Ashing that I am permitting this marriage to go forth at all. Do not make me reverse that decision."

Hallord's opening broadside is well aimed, loaded, and fired. Tamiath inhales sharply at the mention of Aaron's name. The pleased gleam in Queen Leanna's eyes tells me she helped aim *that* bullet into her son's soul. As for that second volley, about *permitting* the wedding to proceed out of respect for Ashing, that one is for my father's benefit. A reminder of Ashing's standing beside Felielle that has Father's hand tightening with concern.

Tamiath opens his mouth to speak, but I silence him with a hand on his shoulder. This whole plan was my doing, and I shall be the one in the eye of the storm, holding the line. Plus, I've more weapons in my arsenal than Tam does. It may have taken Domenic's bravery to finally open my eyes to the deadly value of truth, but that pyre has been building log by log ever since my father started rewriting history.

I meet Hallord's gaze, my own level and evaluating. Not a common seaman cowering before her captain, but an admiral eyeing her opposite number across a violent sea.

Rising, I pick up the two parchments and smooth them out on the table. Seven sets of eyes track my every move. "With due respect, King Hallord," I say mildly, intent on my work even as lightning crackles inside me, "you will *permit* the wedding to go forward because you've little other choice. Copies of these contracts exist, ready to become public if need be. Given your people's sensibilities, I imagine you little wish for the Felielle throne to receive such attention. You will be doing nothing to harm my brother Aaron for the same reason."

Hallord scoffs, dismissing my words like a bit of excrement clinging to his shoe. "You let me worry about public opinion, girl. We've dealt with greater lies than those written here."

I tip my head at Hallord and smile. "No doubt. I've observed the prowess with the newsies. In both kingdoms."

My father's stare burns into me, and I turn my head slightly to meet the gaze head-on, neither of us giving one inch to the emotions brewing beneath our skins.

"I'm done with these games," says Hallord, striding toward

the door. "You two will burn these contracts, or Aaron's death will be gruesome enough to give your children's children nightmares."

"The problem with rewriting history, sir, is that it doesn't actually change the facts," I say to the king's back. My voice is cold. Deadly. I steel myself to play my final card, the one I've desperately fought to conceal, even while knowing deep down that the need for the truth would come. "The joint fleet didn't hold the Bottleneck Juncture—Ashing and Diante ships did. And I'm the one who brought the Diante alliance into the fold."

Silence cracks as my words sink in. Hallord pauses midstep.

Tam's gaze burns into me. *What the hell are you doing?*

I give him a tight, apologetic smile. "Domenic is right," I tell him softly. "We can press your father with the contracts, and current theatrics aside, the wedding *will* happen. But left unchecked, Rima and Madeline will sink ships. And there is but one way to ensure Rima doesn't endanger another crew or sabotage the war. That message is mine, not Domenic's to deliver."

"What are you talking about, Nile?" Father demands sharply.

"She is talking absurd fiction, is what," King Hallord replies for me. Returning to the table, he braces his palms on the polished wood and leans in to tower over me. "If you are going to lie, girl, do me the honor of conducting basic research and at least *trying* to make your words believable. The Diante would no sooner talk to a woman than I'd put one aboard a ship."

"The idea does have an odd sound to it, does it not?" I say agreeably and, pulling out a chair, invite myself to sit down. "Odd enough to make Captain Rima's version of events more comfortable for the newsies." My voice drops. "The problem is that the truth little needs to *sound* believable. It simply is what it is." I turn to my father. "Admiral Addus sends his best."

"Addus?" Father's eyes widen slowly in understanding. "Storms."

I turn my face back to Hallord, his hands still braced on the table beside me. "The question, sir, isn't whether you or your people would find my story believable. The question is whether you are willing to destroy the goodwill of the first person in a decade with whom the Diante are willing to speak—never mind support militarily." I brace my own palms on the table in a mirror pose to Hallord. "The question is whether the Divine Squadron's decision to fly an *Ashing* flag might be a much greater matter than you wish to admit."

My father taps his finger on the table, studying me thoughtfully. "What I believe my daughter is saying, Hallord," he says mildly, "is that the Diante are under the impression that a special relationship might exist between them and Ashing specifically."

"What I'm saying, Your Majesties," I cut in smoothly, addressing both kings at once, "is that when Prince Tamiath approached Ashing a few months ago to discuss my hand in marriage, Ashing needed Felielle's support and goodwill. Today, all of you need *mine*."

Silence settles again, this time broken by Bear's sudden whining.

I shoot the pup a silencing look, my stomach clenching. *Not now, not now, not now.* "That earthquake changed the field of battle by making the Siaman Sea important," I say in softer tones as I reclaim my seat and try to predict just how much more time my damn body is going to grant me. "The Lyron-Tirik conflict is at Diante's doorstep now, and Lyron needs to sustain a dialogue with them. Right now, that means you need me."

Bear barks, his tail in the air and his front legs bent low to the floor.

Tam shoots me a concerned look, even as my own pulse starts to race and angry glares turn in the pup's direction.

"If that were true—" Hallord starts to say, but I've no time to let him finish the thought.

Pushing away from the table to stand tall, I release the tether on my magic and let a swift breeze race through the room. After ruffling hair, paper, and clothes, the wind narrows into a forceful stream that shoves King Hallord away from me and into an empty chair.

Thad turns his face away in disgust, and Queen Leanna covers her mouth with a delicate hand. The others just stare.

"Captain Rima, Lady Madeline, and the *Lyron Herald* used the knowledge of my Gift to blackmail Tamiath and me into supporting Rima's version of events," I say over Bear's howls. "We can add that to the stack of lies that all end today."

Phantom green lights begin to flash in the edges of my vision, and I step back from the table. Letting my Gift be known is one thing; letting the world watch me flounder on the floor like a dying fish is another. "The terms of my goodwill are conveniently spelled out in the contracts. Now, my dog needs to pee. Excuse us both."

Bear is jumping on me by the time I get the door open. When I step into the hallway, Domenic takes one look at the dog and shoves me into an empty room as convulsions start to take their hold.

CHAPTER 42

J take it we are getting married next week after all," I say dryly the following morning as Tamiath escorts me into the Tulip ballroom, where a formal reception to welcome the bride-to-be's family is in full swing. After my unceremonious departure the previous day, the monarchs had spent hours unraveling the situation. Ultimately, the potential advantage I presented in the quest for a Diante alliance trumped everyone's concerns over Tamiath's choice of pillow mate, and the two families agreed unanimously to move forward with the wedding.

Rima and Lady Madeline had been instructed to depart Felielle in the middle of the night, while an accidental fire consumed the *Lyron Herald*'s Felielle printing press.

As for my Gift... "Have Their Majesties reached a verdict?" I ask Tamiath softly, bracing myself for the inevitable.

Tam shifts his weight, his eyes lowering in regret. "Just this morning, yes."

I sigh. "Spit it out, Tam. I knew what would happen the moment I opened my mouth yesterday."

"I think you knew what would happen earlier than that." A note of gentle accusation modulates his tone. "I think you at least suspected that you might need to divulge your Gift before you asked Aaron to find a priestess."

I shrug.

"Why did you not tell me, Nile?"

"It wasn't a type of weight that becomes lighter by sharing," I say curtly. "And suspicion is not the same as certainty. What did Their Majesties decide?"

"The kings of Ashing and Felielle respectfully request that your ability remains secret for the comfort of both kingdoms' subjects."

"And?"

Tam swallows but meets my gaze steadily. "You've been officially barred from going to sea, Nile. The decision is equal measure bigotry, concern for the crew, and fear of you losing control and killing yourself before your connections with the Diante Empire can be fully exploited. Both the monarchs have spoken, and there is nothing I can do to overturn the ruling now. I'm sorry."

Despite knowing this was coming since I started the gambit, actually hearing the words still takes my breath. I raise my chin and fight back the stinging that prickles my eyes. I nod, not trusting my voice.

"It may not be forever," Tam whispers. "Just until..."

"Until I can prove I am seaworthy, which can never happen since I won't be allowed on a ship in the first place." I put up my hand to stop Tam from uttering false comforts. I'd made a choice, one that will save Domenic and Aaron and the wedding and ships and crews yet to come. One that has other consequences as well. I must take vinegar with the sugar. And I can't talk about this just now.

"How do I look?" I say, stepping back and twirling before him. My gown of blue chiffon floats behind me as I move, as if the cloth and the air around me are one.

Tam nods in melancholy understanding and forces himself to smile. "Exquisite."

"As does the hall," I say, clinging to the silly subject matter as I would a lifeline. The Tulip ballroom really is remarkable. Hundred-candle chandeliers swing from the cathedral ceiling, their lights reflecting in the polished wood of the dance floor. Garlands of fresh tulips, for which the room is named, stream over window arches and drape on the sills. On the refreshment table, flower-shaped ice bowls hold punch, while more candles float in shallow crystal troughs.

I can't release reality completely, though. "Have you spoken to Domenic?" I ask Tam. I've not seen the Domenic since he took care of me yesterday, but Tamiath intended to call on him last night to explain that a trial is no longer necessary nor would it be beneficial.

Tam flinches, and I know I'm in for more disappointment before he even starts speaking.

"Mr. Dana accepted the pardon, but he still plans to leave your service after the wedding. He cited family reasons but..."

"Please forgive the interruption, Your Highness." A liveried servant, one of the hundreds hired for the wedding, is pale faced as he brings himself to address me.

Tam gives my hand a reassuring squeeze before bowing over it and retreating to mingle with the guests while I attend to whatever is the matter. We'd already been whispering longer than etiquette allows, and further conversation must wait until evening.

I force myself to smile politely at the servant. "Not at all. How I can be of service?"

The man steps close to me, lowering his voice to a tentative whisper. "There is a small problem with a young man who, I'm led to understand, is a relation of yours." He shifts his feet. "I was told you'd wish to be informed privately."

"Do you mean Clay?" I ask. "My twin brother?"

The man sighs in relief, as if he feared reprisal for bringing Clay up at all. "Yes, Your Highness. He is having a little bit of an...episode."

I let out a slow breath, my chest tightening. I'd arranged for Clay to enjoy a small garden during the reception, but between the travel and new sights, sounds, and people, it's little surprising that Clay finds the disruption to his world too great to bear. "You were right to get me," I tell the servant, who appears ready to urinate himself from fear, and make a mental note to exclude the man from any further ceremonies. "Lead the way, if you please."

The man scurries to obey, and I follow in his wake, curtly avoiding well-wishers and curious courtiers. Once we step free from the ballroom, Domenic and Quinn peel off to follow, keeping a discreet distance as we move along back passageways.

Just being near Domenic makes my chest tighten, though I couldn't ask him to stay now even if he were willing to live beside Tam and me—not with my landlocked future. The sea flows in Domenic's blood just as it does in mine. It would be unjust for my Gift to tether him too.

By the time I fight free of my thoughts, we've made three or four turns along palace corridors, and I'm no longer sure of my location. "Where are we going, exactly?" I ask, touching the servant's elbow.

He jumps. "Just outside, Your Highness. Master Clay is in the private garden."

"Yes," I say sharply, "but that private garden is in the west end of the palace. We are heading northeast."

The man's throat bobs. "I fear it became necessary to...move him. You'll understand in a moment, I'm sure." He takes a hard turn into a narrow passageway and hurries forward to open the door at the corridor's end for me.

Blinding sunlight hits me. Raising my forearm to block the sun, I wait for Domenic and Quinn to catch up, but their footsteps fail to sound on the stone. I turn back to the corridor, seeing nothing with my sun-blinded eyes.

"He's just there," the servant insists, going so far as to tug my sleeve and point. I turn back, blinking into the outdoors, to find a carriage standing a few feet away from the door.

"Where is the garden you mentioned?"

The servant wrings his hands. "Master Clay was having an episode, my lady. They put him into a carriage to try—"

My muscles tense. Still no footsteps sound behind me, and the servant, instead of getting more comfortable with time, is increasingly nervous at my presence. Without warning, I push past the man and swing the carriage door wide open.

And find Clay wide-eyed, gagged, and bound on a bench opposite Rima.

"Get in, Your Highness," the captain orders, pointing a pistol at Clay's head.

CHAPTER 43

Rima gives the pistol a shake, and my body moves of its own accord. I grip the carriage's frame, step inside, and close the door when instructed. My mind twists like a storm. The magic in my blood rouses at my twin's presence as I slide onto the bench beside Clay, and I am careful not to touch my brother's skin.

Rima knocks twice against the wall separating us from the driver, and the carriage bounces into motion.

"I would suggest Your Highness behaves," says Rima. "I understand the idiot beside you is somewhat unpredictable near guns."

Someone snorts, and I realize there is another man in the carriage, sitting in the corner on Rima's side of the bench. The man's red hair scrapes at my memory. Red. Yes, it's Red from the Red and Bald thug duo who attacked Domenic in Ashing. *Storms and hail.* Rima had hired men to assault his own first officer. *Bastard, bastard, bastard.*

Beside me, Clay whimpers. Amidst my twin's terror, forcing

my mind to function is like moving through a bog. "What do you want?" I demand of Rima once I regain control of my voice. "Last I heard, you were being quietly evicted from Felielle."

Rima's face flashes with answering rage. "Did you truly imagine such an assault on my family would pass without consequences?" he demands. "Did you know that *soldiers* came to my wife's bedroom in the middle of night? That your lies destroyed her life's work in a single torrent of flames? The Tirik are right about the poison running in royal blood."

So that's it. Rima is a coward by nature, but the night's retribution had hit the two things he held most dear: his money and his marriage. The double assault appears to have pushed the captain over the threshold between surrogate violence and direct confrontation. Which means Rima is desperate, and as terrified as Clay. And just as volatile.

I force myself to sound calm and reasonable. "What do you want, sir?" I ask again.

"For now, that you keep your mouth shut." Rima snorts. "Do what I tell you, when I tell you, and there is a fair chance that both you and this idiot will suffer minimal damage."

I swallow what little moisture I have in my mouth and try to get my bearings, but the covered windows keep me from seeing the landscape. "My guardsmen are likely following us already," I say with a calm I feel none of. "Let's settle this before needless violence erupts."

"I doubt it, unless you've found a way to animate corpses," says Rima.

"What?"

"Dana and the Tirik traitor are dead," Rima clarifies with a shrug. "Not officially, of course. Officially, you took the pair with you when you—once again—decided that a marriage to a Felielle prince is more than you can bear. I can see the headline already: ASHING PRINCESS RUNS AGAIN, PRINCE TAMIATH LEFT ALONE AT THE ALTAR."

"No one will believe that story," I say, Rima's claim of Domenic's death ringing in my ears to complement Clay's wailing. Lies. Rima is lying about killing Domenic and Quinn just as he lies about everything else in his life. "Tamiath will look."

"Oh, I think everyone will believe it just fine," Rima says with a growing smile. "Especially when you write all about it to your parents. Now, quiet."

I open my mouth again, but Rima signals Red, who cracks a wooden baton against Clay's shins.

I scream as my twin wails behind his gag, and it takes all my self-control to reclaim my wits. *Domenic isn't dead. Quinn isn't dead. Someone is looking for me. Tamiath. Aaron. Bear. My mother.* For every calming thought I force on myself, its opposite number comes to mind as quickly. Aaron and Tam are busy. Domenic and Quinn are at the very least hurt. Yes, of course my absence will be noticed—but when? Each yard we move from the palace is an advantage to Rima and his cronies.

The carriage bumps to a stop, and the breeze hits me as the door opens. Rough hands pull me outside, and I realize we are at the same river whose banks Quinn, Domenic, and I used for training. A saltless breeze brushes my face. Well away from shore, a schooner holds position atop the sparkling water.

The carriage driver—Bald, another familiar face—pulls my arms behind my back and marches me toward a waiting rowboat. Everything inside me screams the importance of remaining ashore, the danger increasing exponentially each time we shift locations. Taking a breath to steady myself, I drop my weight down and drive my shoulder into Bald's solar plexus. He grunts and staggers back, his grip on my arms loosening.

That is as far as I get before Clay's grunts of pain shatter the small beach, and I freeze.

Standing over my twin, Rima shows me the wooden baton he's just driven into Clay's gut. "You may punish her once we are underway," he tells Bald. "For now, get everyone into the boat and bind her hands."

The boat rocks as Clay is thrown inside, screaming into his gag. I am allowed to step in under my own power, though Rima makes it clear that doing so is a privilege I risk losing. With Clay paying for my actions, there is little I dare try. If I capsize the rowboat altogether, my brother will sink before I can free my hands.

Red and Bald lay into the oars, and the boat glides to the anchored schooner. Once there, Red puts up his oar and catches a rope thrown from the ship. A chair is lowered, and a struggling Clay is wrestled into it and lifted to the deck. I too am hauled up like a sack of grain, denied the use of my arms even to grip the ladder.

The schooner is a smaller version of the *Aurora*. It has two masts instead of three, with the sails rigged fore and aft instead of a traditional man-of-war's square rig, making it easier to handle with a smaller crew. Six great guns, three on each side, are lashed tightly into their ports.

Bald sits Clay beside the mainmast and secures him to it with a rope wrapped around my twin's middle. Clay's arms and legs are free and flailing. He rips the gag from his mouth and wails freely.

"Scream all you like," Rima tells him, though the words are intended for me. "The wench is the only one who cares." He turns to Red. "Bring out the writing desk."

A table and stool are brought forth. Bald shackles my ankles together before untying my hands and forcing me to sit on the stool. Ink, paper, and a pen are placed before me.

The moment my hand closes around the writing implement, I stab the pen into Rima's hand. The metal tip pierces the skin, slick crimson blood flowing over wrinkled fingers.

Rima curses and pulls away. I smile as Rima stomps away but my victory is short-lived as lines of flame cross my back in a too familiar agony. Circling back into my field of vision, Rima thrusts a cat-o-nine tails in front of my nose—this one tipped with metal spikes that rattle like living snakes in Clay's presence. "You remember what *this* is, don't you?" he snarls into my face before tossing the cat to Bald. "Give the boy two lashes," Rima orders calmly, and it is I who wail the loudest as Clay is struck. Once, twice.

Tears stream down my face. I reach toward my twin, but Red's hand presses me back to the stool.

"Perhaps I should have explained the rules better, Your Highness," says Rima, coming around to crouch before me. He wraps a handkerchief around his bleeding hand. "Disobedience will be punished. Twice. First on your flesh, then on that useless idiot's over there. Do you have any questions?"

I stare at him, my jaw clamped tight.

"Very good," says Rima with absurd kindness. "Let us try again, then."

A new pen is brought and handed to me with care.

"You are to copy this text," says Rima, placing a letter on the table beside my clean sheet of parchment. "Write neatly, please. I would little wish anyone to misunderstand your declaration."

I read the message before me, my chest tightening at the words' frightening believability.

I AM Princess Nile of Ashing, the intended bride-to-be of Prince Tamiath of Felielle, and this is my declaration.

I have left the Felielle Court, as I had left the Ashing Court. Do not seek me out. I left of my own free will and will do so again if I am ever brought back.

I am my own woman. I refuse to be a political pawn. My attempts to explain this have met with deaf ears, and thus I must now take action where words failed.

During my time on the LS Aurora, I learned that a cure exists for the Gift my twin brother and I both possess. Clay and I are abominations, unfit for society, and no marriage alliance would have worked long-term.

I have learned, however, that there is an Institute in the Tirik Republic that works toward a cure for people like Clay and me. I have decided to dedicate my life to finding this cure. Even as you read this, Clay and I are sailing for our salvation.

I hope to meet with you once again, when I can look you in the eye and tell you there is no destructive magic coursing through my blood or Clay's. Until then, please do not follow me. I wish happiness to Prince Tamiath, who is a better man than I deserve, and to my family, who I've put through greater pain than I can bear.

With love,
Nile.

QUINN'S WORDS from earlier ring in my memory, and I know there is one truth in the letter Rima wants me to write. Clay and I *are* bound for the Institute, where the captain will collect a great commission for delivering a set of Gifted twins into the science men's hands.

I turn my head and am sick all over the deck.

CHAPTER 44

*R*ima curses at the mess and orders it cleaned, his eyes already gleaming with imagined gold. Yes, delivering Gifted *twins* to the Institute, one of them being an Ashing princess with knowledge of Lyron naval defenses, will make Rima wealthy enough to weather his recent setbacks.

"Don't look so surprised, Princess," Rima says as I wipe my mouth. "Did you truly expect I'd let you come aboard my ship, endanger my people, jeopardize my very life, and then walk away? Cheat me? This is a new world. One where justice rules. And that starts with you. Write."

I consider knocking over the writing desk, but there is little doubt that such defiance will only bring about beatings. Obediently picking up the pen, I evaluate other options. There aren't any. Except one. My gaze resting on the tip of the pen, I gather the rising magic inside my blood and let it roar.

The wind answers my call, and the schooner twists violently in the sudden gale. Controlling the ship outright is out of the question—the last time I tried to do so, I capsized a small sailing boat in this very river—but if I can redirect the crew's attention, I might at least buy myself some time to conjure a better plan. The problem is that calling enough wind to keep the men busy but not so much as to kill us all is a balance I'm little confident I can strike.

The schooner leans precariously, the wide-spread canvas filling with unexpected wind, and the crew rushes to deck at once to trim the sail and reclaim control of the ship. I count five men in addition to Red, Bald, and Rima before my stool topples to the deck and takes me with it. I fling my arms out to break my fall, but it does little good. The desk, pen, and ink fall unceremoniously atop me before sliding overboard with the next buck of the ship.

Clay cries out in terror, and I try to rein in the unleashed storm. Try and fail.

One of the seamen curses as he trips over me. Changing his course, he grabs my arm and drags me to sit beside Clay at the mast, as out of the way as he can get me then.

As happy as I am to find myself mere inches from my twin, Clay's proximity makes the task of reining in the gale infinitely more difficult. The winds howl and dance, bouncing the schooner on growing waves seldom seen on this river. The seaman tending to me uses a length of rope to secure me to the mast.

Unlike me, whose arms are tied down to my side, Clay's limbs are free to flail about. Whenever one of these comes close enough to strike me, my magic rises, as does the wind.

Centering myself on the shifting deck, I try to clear my mind the way Quinn and Domenic have drilled into me over the past weeks. I feel my magic, taste how it moves and flares in response to my will and Clay's presence. *Do you understand any of this, Clay?* I wonder desperately. *Do you know we are in danger?*

"This is your doing, isn't it?" Rima roars, leaning over me. His legs shift in deference to the bucking deck, one of his arms bracing the mast above my head. The captain's other hand holds the cat. Its barbed ends gleam menacingly. With the sails taken in, the schooner's violence has settled to a jostling simmer, and while we won't be turning over, we won't be moving much either. "Stop the wind. Now," Rima yells into my face.

"I can't," I shout back into his.

The whip in the captain's hand swings back, aiming at my head.

My arms try to jerk up to protect my face, but the rope binding me to the mast will not allow the motion. My breath chokes, and I brace for impact as Rima's wrist snaps the cat toward me.

The metal barbs fly and recoil midair, cutting into Rima's own cheek. The captain screams and staggers away.

Twisting my attention to Clay, I find his arms covering his head, his unfocused gaze staring past the screaming captain. An accident? Or had Clay controlled the metal on purpose?

"What—" A crewman's terrified scream has me twisting like a worm and letting out an expletive of my own.

One of the ship's great guns—a seven-hundred-pound carronade—is pulling at its tether, the ropes securing the massive beast to the gunport straining to breaking point. The ship tilts with the waves, adding the pull of gravity to the burden. With a harrowing *snap*, one of the ropes breaks, and the gun—now a deadly mass of moving metal atop a wheeled carriage—rolls wildly across the deck. The barrel crashes into Red's leg, and his blood-curdling scream vibrates the air.

Gaze still focused on nothing, Clay rocks as much as his

bonds allow. Whether or not he'd had control of his magic when he reversed Rima's cat, my twin has lost all control now. Little wonder given how difficult my own magic is being.

"Secure the gun!" Rima hollers. Two of the crew leap onto the rogue weapon, which spins and slides chaotically in answer to Clay's magic and the undulating ship. Even in a calm and natural sea, it takes a team of at least four men to control a great gun, so the two seamen's efforts at taming the magically spurred beast come to nothing. The gun rolls over Red again, quickening the dying man's end.

Rima kicks Clay in the stomach.

The great gun's wildness dies away, but there is nothing to be done for gravity. Still loose, the gun carriage rolls down the sloping deck to crash into the ship's hull with a deafening crack that draws horrified breaths.

Bald, holding on to the shrouds with one hand, points a pistol at Clay's head and cocks the hammer.

"Put that away, you idiot," Rima hollers, and for once, I agree with the captain.

"He's going to get us killed," Bald snarls.

"Kill him, and you are following his body into the deep," Rima tells Bald. "This idiot is infinitely more valuable than your carcass."

My heart stills, but after a moment, Bald uncocks the pistol and puts it away. With the tension easing, I am finally able to get a grip on my wind. We all catch our breath as the schooner responds to the rudder once more.

Clay and I temporarily relegated to the background, Rima's sailors inspect the hull for damage and debate whether we can continue sailing or require a stop for repairs. Clay hugs his knees and shakes, small metal tools popping up and down in rhythm to his sobs.

The crew scurries to secure the metal objects before Clay can wreak more havoc than they can fix.

Rima's boots appear before me again. "Can you control him?" he demands of me, jerking his chin toward Clay.

"No." My eyes flash. "And before you think I'm lying, realize I've as little desire to go down to the bottom of the river as you do. Given that my twin has just sent a great gun on a murderous rampage, you might wish to reconsider your plan."

The enormity of what I just said hits me. How powerful is Clay? I've never heard of a Gifted able to control that much of the element. Quinn told me he's never met a wind caller with my power either. Whatever Clay and I are, we aren't normal. And when we are together... I keep my thoughts to myself, waiting until Rima moves away before sliding my fingers toward Clay's.

We sit half a foot apart, but the inches are endless, my heart pounding harder the closer my bare skin gets to my twin. When I'm but finger's width away, my magic explodes inside me. *Together, together, together* the magic begs me, orders me. *Whole, whole, whole.*

I freeze, the memory of our last connection all too vivid in my memory. The cost of Clay gaining awareness was the loss of my own. "Clay," I whisper.

"Clay," he echoes, his gaze staring at the now-dormant great gun. Blood streaks down my twin's thigh, his perfect doll-like face trembling in pitiful terror. But that gaze is steady. A message?

Did you free that gun on purpose, Clay? Did you deflect the whip? Are you trying to tell me something? Give me some sign. Something. Anything. Tell me what you want before I do something stupid to us both.

Clay stays still.

I study the great gun again. It takes the whole crew to wrestle it back into its port and lash it down with rope. Breaking it loose must have taken every ounce of Clay's effort. An ultimate feat of control, or utter lack of it.

If we *could* break the gun free again and use it against the crew, we could take out the men. Or sink the schooner. I don't know. But I do know that my wind will do little good. I can't blow the crew off deck without capsizing the schooner, and anything smaller will result in Clay being tortured. The very same wind that gives life to a ship at sea is also its ultimate enemy. No, it's Clay's magic, not mine, that can save us. But to do that, Clay needs the presence of mind that I have. He needs *my* mind.

I swallow. We narrowly avoided disaster when I'd surrendered my awareness to him by accident. If I do it on purpose now, will it make things better or worse? Will my hard-won rein over my own magic help or count for nothing? So many variables. So many unknowns. The biggest one, the one that truly sends terror through me, has nothing to do with magic, though. If I surrender my mind to my twin, will I ever get it back?

Before I can reconsider, I grip Clay's hand and entrust my twin with my life. With both our lives.

CHAPTER 45

*A*s my hand connects with Clay's, the now-familiar bouquet of combined power ripples through me.

"Clay." I tug on his arm.

His face turns to me. His eyes are clearing.

This time, I don't dare indulge in marveling at the amazingness of it all. I have too little time before my mind slips and words will no longer come. The wind around us picks up, only my recent training keeping a storm at bay.

Lub dub, lub dub, my heart beats, catching a cadence to complement my twin's. We have one consciousness to share between us, and two sets of magic. And that will have to do.

"We are in trouble," I say, letting my mind yield itself slowly to him, giving Clay the use of my mental focus to orient himself.

"Great gun," Clay says, straining with effort. "Weapon."

So he *had* been sending me a signal. A wave of fear and relief washes over me. Clay has a plan, and the strength to make it happen. All he needs now is my mind.

"Take it," I say quickly. "The helm is yours."

Despite having braced myself for it, the slip into Clay's reality is dizzying. While my senses still function, they report information at an alarming and increasingly disorganized rate, each new morsel competing with instead of complementing the other.

The sun reflecting off the glassy water is so blindingly bright, it feels as though small needles are jabbing my eyeballs. The ropes binding me to the mast burn my flesh to the bone, the searing coming from the inside out instead of outside in. The water lapping the schooner's hull echoes through the whole ship over and over, like strikes of a great and never-ceasing gong. *Baboom. Baboom. Baboom.*

I try to speak but can't find my tongue, as if my muscles have forgotten the nuance of speech. Through the sensory assault, I understand just enough to see the impotence of my own body. The terror of watching my mind slip away, breath by breath, is more terrible than anything I've felt before.

Through squinting eyes, I see a great metal beast pull free of its binding and roll across the deck. It hits a man. He falls overboard. I cringe at the deafening *thud* of his body hitting water and try to cover my ears, but can't. Nor can I protect myself from the chorus of howling breaths, and screaming deck planks, and thumping boots, and cracking fingernails.

The last belong to the boy holding my hand. With his other hand, he's snatched a knife from the air and now struggles to saw through the rope around me, the blade's serrated edge moving quickly. The rope's fibers crackle and screech as they tear. I try and fail to pull free of the boy's crushing grip.

The rope falls away from me, blood returning to my suddenly free and painful limbs. I want to flee but freeze as the deck shifts and the metal beast starts sliding toward me. I need to move. I know I do. But I don't know where. Everywhere is just as loud and bright and dangerous as where I am now.

The boy holding my hand snatches me to the side. My head hits hard, and it hurts. I try to wriggle away from him, but the boy holds fast. He speaks to me, his words low and soothing and steady.

The beast rolls and rolls. Where it hits, bodies fall and splinters fly. Viscous crimson liquid, thick and coppery, pools on the deck. The liquid slithers onto my face like slime. I shut my eyes.

Suddenly, there is a great crash and a bigger splash.

I shut my eyes tighter and hum to drown out the chaos.

"Nile." The boy holding me tugs on my arm. His voice comes in bursts. "Nile, you need to come back. Please. Can't do this myself."

Something pushes against my consciousness, like an invisible hand stanching a bleeding wound. The noises, smells, pressures, and lights around me order themselves into a complete mosaic as Clay shifts the balance of our shared mind. Slowly, I begin to comprehend the hard surface beneath me as the wooden deck of a swaying ship. The beast of metal that rolled wildly before knocking a hole in the rail and falling overboard had been a great gun. The boy beside me, whose awareness I now share, is my twin.

And the scrawny, yellow-eyed man pointing a pistol at the two of us, his tattooed face sprayed with blood, is our enemy.

I send a gust of wind toward the pistol just as it fires. The yellow-eyed man jerks, and the bullet flies high and wide over the waves.

The man's eyes widen, and he curses, throwing down his now-useless pistol. He won't stop, though, I know it in my bones. I know this man, though recalling his exact name is hardly worth the effort, and he is evil.

My gaze takes in the deck. It is bloody, with smashed bodies sprawled across it in gory heaps. Seeing the butt of a pistol tucked into the waistband of what used to be a man, I draw out the gun. It bucks in my hand.

"Sorry," my other half says apologetically.

The yellow-eyed man freezes. "Put the gun down, Nile," he orders. "You aren't a murderer."

"No," I agree. "I'm a naval officer."

I squeeze the trigger and let my other half ensure that the metal ball flies true.

CHAPTER 46

*C*lay and I sit facing each other, our hands and gazes gripped tight, as the joint magic and shared awareness course through our bodies. I know that the moment I let my twin's hand go, something terrible will happen to me. And to him. So we hold on to each other.

The schooner's crew is dead or gone, having abandoned ship when Clay loosed the second deadly carronade amidst them. Now the great gun rests on the bottom of the riverbed, while a steady wind pushes the schooner against the current. We make little headway toward the Felielle capital, but neither are we swept with the current toward the open sea.

Awareness of where we are and what's happening shifts and flows between Clay and me. The wind rises and fall. The only steady sensation I feel is one of unity.

At some point, maybe an hour or a day later, there is a great deal of commotion. Other schooners circle around us like a pack of wolves. People come aboard, shouting and yelling and cursing.

"...bloodbath."

"...impossible."

"...what sort of ship moves *against* the current?"

"...Goddess bless and protect us. Goddess be our keeper."

"...move them gently. We little know how badly Her Highness is injured."

Those last words wash me with fear. These invaders will cleave me and Clay apart. It will hurt, and I will be alone again.

"Nile." The voice beside me is not my twin's, and yet it brushes my soul. The smell of salt and brine fills my nose, and large hands encircle my shoulders. "It's all right."

"This isn't natural, my Prince Tamiath," says a man I've not heard before. Fear laces his voice as others around mumble in agreement. "Look around. All the attackers dead, and the winds themselves moving the schooner against the currents? It—"

"It was the Goddess's own will," a familiar man answers confidently. "The Goddess is claiming Nile of Felielle as her own. Open your eyes, man, and be grateful you are here to witness the signs."

The brine-and-salt man holding me snorts softly beside my ear, but when he speaks, it's with a confident voice that pitches over the deck. "It is as you say, my Prince Tamiath! Nile of Felielle is one with the Goddess and the sea." The man's arms tighten around me, his voice lowering. "She is...injured, sir. Once we separate them..." He trails off into a meaning-laden silence.

No. My grip on my twin tightens.

The man called Prince Tamiath crouches beside me. "Do the best you can, Mr. Dana," he says very quietly. "I'll do what I can about the men's attention." With that, the prince rises and begins to bargain loudly with the Goddess, promising the deity all sorts of things in return for my being permitted to return back to the world of man in Felielle.

Once other voices join in the prayers and bargaining, the brine-and-sea-salt man holding me brushes my ear again. "It's time to let go, Nile. I have you now."

I AM in and out of convulsions for the next week. Domenic is there each time I open my eyes, his face drawn with fatigue and worry. Occasionally, I hear Tam order him to sleep or eat, but even the prince's word has little sway. Between jerking spells, I float in the sea between consciousness and darkness, my body refusing to obey my mind's commands. When that happens, Domenic's voice and scent are my only tethers to sanity, as he talks quietly to me about the sea and waves and wind, the way he had when Catsper tended my wounds.

Clay is so disturbed, he spends the week in a room with no light or noise, unable to bear even the feel of his own clothes. The joining of our magics and awareness had kept us alive, but our bodies now pay the price.

When I am well enough to sit upright, Domenic, pale faced, explains how the corridor I'd been lured down was outfitted with a trapdoor that Rima's cronies took advantage of to block him and Quinn from following. The self-blame in his voice angers me enough to snap at him to stop being stupid, but I fail to make an impact before drifting off again.

When my strength returns further, Domenic supplies me with a newsleaf, the headline TRAITOR FAILS TO KIDNAP NILE OF FELIELLE sprawled across the top. The article begins reasonably enough, explaining how a disgraced and bankrupt Captain Rima attempted to kidnap Prince Tamiath's bride to obtain a ransom. Not exactly true, but close enough. As further details of the kidnapping are described however, my brows begin a slow climb up my forehead. *"Kidnapped and bound, Princess Nile of Felielle miraculously fought off fifteen armed men and weathered a storm on open seas."*

"Rima had seven men, not fifteen," I protest. "We were on a river, not on open sea. And when it came to fighting, Clay did most of the work. Not to mention that I was the one who created the bloody storm to begin with."

"Oh, you are not even to the good part yet," Aaron says tartly from the doorway to my sickroom. "Keep reading." He stands aside to let Tamiath enter the room first. Seeing the two, Domenic bows deeply and retreats into the corridor.

"Sorry," Tamiath says when the door closes behind Domenic. "I've tried telling Dana to stay but... It looks bad, and he knows it. For a while, my being here was the only way of getting him to take food and rest at all. We'll have to work something out about that."

"It might become a nonissue if Nile kills you outright," Aaron says merrily, jerking his chin at the newsleaf. "She is just getting to the good part."

Frowning, I return my attention to the text. Three sentences later, I let out a yelp. *"Nile's survival is a miracle, a gift to Felielle from the Goddess."* My voice rises. *"With the Goddess's hand on our princess's shoulder, Felielle will never succumb to the Tirik Republic.* If this is your idea of a jest, Aaron—"

"Me?" indignation fills Aaron's voice. "Oh no, you have his almighty highness here to thank for all this."

I twist my head so quickly, my braid takes to the air.

Tam flushes. "It wasn't as if I had a lot of time to deliberate," he snaps. Crossing his arms, Tam plants himself in a chair—as close as I've seen the prince come to pouting. "We found you glassy-eyed in the middle of a blood-drenched ship, with a preternatural wind keeping you from being swept with the current. I needed to conjure *some* explanation before the rescue crew bolted or else deduced your Gift."

"And so you came up with divine intervention?" I ask.

Tam shifts his weight. "Quinn once told me that the Diante call the Gifted 'Gods touched.' It gave me the idea. How was I supposed to know the bloody story would catch like wildfire?"

I rub my temples, vaguely recalling the rescue crew's rising speculations, which Tamiath settled with divine appeals. "All right," I concede, "I understand why the rescue crew bought the tale in the midst of confusion. I've seen wilder things in sailors readying for battle or recovering from carnage. But certainly no one else in Felielle will believe this fiction for any period of time."

Aaron snorts.

Tamiath cocks a brow. "You'll be amazed at what people will believe when they want to. If the Goddess wishes to deliver proof of Felielle's coming victory and prosperity, then why *shouldn't* it be you who she chooses as her vessel? You are, after all, an infallible survivor, a princess at the center of an impossible story, and, according to Mother, the only woman ever able to thaw my heart." He grins. "It's certainly more believable than a story of a Felielle prince choosing a Gifted bride who brings no political or financial gain."

Groaning, I drop back onto my pillows. The discussion has drained my strength, and sleep beckons shamelessly. "Wake me up when the madness dies down," I mumble and close my eyes. "They can't keep at it for long."

"Oh yes, they can," Aaron croons as I drift to sleep.

Despite steadily regaining my strength, the next week still passes with me confined to the sickroom and sleeping more than not. Each time I wake, I find a growing heap of letters from Felielle subjects asking me to intercede with the Goddess on their behalf. Aaron fills me in on the new wedding plans, which my mother is taking charge of. "The festivities are getting grander every day," he confides. "Ice statues of you and Tamiath were commissioned yesterday. *Life-size.*"

I am just over two weeks past my ordeal with Rima and three weeks short of the new wedding date when Aaron appears at the doorway and throws a wad of clothing at my chest. "Get dressed," he says, glowing with wicked delight. "*Now*, Your Highness, if it's not too inconvenient."

Abandoning the night shirt I've spent entirely too much time in, I stuff myself into the shirt and breeches thrown to me. Women in Felielle seldom forgo skirts or dresses, but Aaron's addition to my wardrobe is distinctly feminine despite the pant design. Flattering dark blue velvet with gold stitching matched with a ruffled silk shirt, all brought together by a wide sash around my waist. I open my mouth to ask about the clothes, but seeing that he is all but bouncing with impatience, wisely stick to the matter at hand. "What's going on?"

"A meeting," Aaron says, checking the corridor before motioning me out after him. He closes the door before Bear can follow, ignoring the dog's indignant woof from inside the room. "One that you do not want to miss."

I frown. "Who wishes to see me?"

"No one does." Pulling my arm, Aaron ushers me into the servants' corridors, twisting and winding our way into increasingly dubious passages. It's all I can do to keep up until we stop at a spot made remarkable only by a lack of proper light and a multitude of cracks.

"What—" I start to say, only to have Aaron's hand cover my mouth.

"We are right above the royal meeting room," Aaron whispers into my ear as he fishes a pair of old drinking glasses from one of the shadows and holds them against a sizable crack. "The same one you made your grand declaration in."

"And?"

"And, you can hear everything that's said in that room from here—Tam and I found the spot as boys, when we needed to know his parents' plans. Now, if I'm not mistaken, all your parents are talking about something you *very* much want to hear."

Feeling more than a little foolish, I press my ear against one of the glasses as instructed and close my eyes. A moment later, Mother's distinctive voice touches my ears.

"We've discussed this, Hallord. Nile's Gift is too dangerous and unpredictable for sea. I do not see why we are revisiting covered ground."

"With all due respect, Your Majesty, the situation has changed," King Hallord says with exaggerated patience. "The Felielle people see Nile's control of the schooner as a divine message. Felielle's armada *demands* she sail."

"It *wasn't* a divine message, Hallord," Mother insists. "And if you can't find a way to explain it to your subjects, I will."

My jaw tightens as I long to shake sense into my mother. Luckily, King Hallord seems to be of similar mind.

"We are in the midst of a war, madam," Hallord snaps. "If believing the Goddess chose Nile to guide Felielle to victory will embolden my people, then that is what I shall sing."

"She's my child, not your symbol," Mother retorts.

"Nile is a weapon." My father's low, hard voice enters the conversation. "One whose strength we are just now comprehending. If the girl is strong enough to right a capsizing ship and move a schooner against the current, it isn't something

337

we ignore in the middle of an armed conflict. The resources of the archipelago have given Lyron an advantage, but there is a difference between stanching the bleeding and saving the patient. There is more to do."

"We *agreed*—" Mother starts again, but now it's King Hallord who cuts her off.

"Things changed, madam. The Felielle people expect her at a helm, and so does the Diante Admiralty."

I jerk away from my listening post and squeeze Aaron's arm hard enough to bruise. "What are they talking about?" I hiss into his ear.

"A letter from some Diante admiral arrived for you a few days ago. It was sent to Ashing originally and just made it over. Their Majesties thought opening it on your behalf would be...prudent."

The flash of anger rolling through me makes it difficult to pay attention, and I force myself to calm down before returning to the conversation.

"To Hallord's point," says Father, "the question isn't *whether* we will oblige the Diante Empire's invitation, the question is only which flag Nile sails under to get there. As Admiral Addus's letter requests the presence of Captain Nile of *Ashing*, we should respect his preference."

"Nile will shortly be a princess of Felielle," King Hallord insists. "She must sail under Felielle colors."

"Felielle has never had a female captain," Father scoffs. "We will offend the Diante."

"If I recall," says Hallord, "she isn't *in* the Ashing navy. Hasn't been since that *Faithful* disaster."

Aaron tugs on my arm, pulling me away from the listening spot. "They'll be at this for hours, no doubt. We need to go before our absence is noted. Either way, I believe it is safe to say you will be returning to sea."

I'm speechless as we return to the civilized part of the palace, and I follow Aaron blindly for several minutes before realizing that we are not returning to the sickroom but heading to Tamiath's personal suite. Now that I think about it, the outfit Aaron brought seemed much too festive for crawling in dusty passages.

"Where are we going?" I ask Aaron, stopping in the middle of a wide corridor.

"To see Tam," he answers innocently.

"Aaron…"

He raises his hands in surrender. "He—we—have a wedding gift for you. And just now, I think Tamiath has more strength to hurt me than you do, so I am keeping my silence."

Rolling my eyes, I follow Aaron to Tam's rooms to find a small round table set for two. An embroidered purple tablecloth, two covered and steaming plates, a pair of glasses, and an unopened bottle of wine sit cozily together. Tamiath himself is bent over his work desk at the other end of the room.

Without looking up from a slew of spread-out papers, he waves us over. "What do you think?" he says, sliding one of the sheets toward me. "These are rough, but with only two days' notice—"

"Storms." The word escapes me in a half whisper as I examine the gorgeous cross section of what promises to be a weatherly frigate. "What is this beauty?"

Tam's gaze flickers to me and away. "Your new ship. Their Majesties can debate what colors you sail under as long as they wish, but there is no reason to delay the commission of the ship you'll be sailing on."

I trace the drawing with my fingers, words abandoning me

until... "You *knew?*" I glare at Tamiath, who has the decency to look sheepish even while grinning. "You could have told me about the Diante letter."

"I could have," he agrees readily. "But I thought this would be more amusing." His voice softens. "Do you like the plans?"

Launching myself at Tam, I throw my arms around his shoulders and plant a kiss on his cheek. Aaron chuckles behind me. A moment later, a second set of arms wraps around my middle, closing me in a circle of beautiful men.

Of course, someone knocks.

We separate, and Tam sits himself back at his worktable while Aaron piously answers the door. My gaze meets Domenic's, and my breath catches.

"Begging your pardon, Your Highnesses," Domenic says with a bow. "I will come back at a better time."

"Not at all, Mr. Dana," Tam calls over his shoulder. "You are here at the right place and time. I appreciate you answering my summons so efficiently. Have you what I requested?"

Domenic tenses, his fingers brushing mine for a single uncomfortable moment before he strides up to Tam and pulls an envelope from the inside pocket of a worn brown jacket. Brown, not guardsman's purple. "My letter of resignation from Her Highness's guard," Domenic says, looking only at Tamiath. "Effective immediately, as you instructed."

The joy of the past hour dissolves to an icy mist. Domenic was supposed to stay until the wedding, and that's not for weeks yet. And what's this about Tam's instruction?

I clamp my hand over Domenic's wrist, stilling his arm midmotion. "Wait," I tell him before turning to Tam. "Explain."

Tam pivots in his chair. "There is little to explain, Nile," he says, opening his palms. "Mr. Dana was in charge of your security when Rima kidnapped you. It's rather plain that this is not a post he is suited for. I requested a resignation."

My face darkens.

The corner of Tamiath's mouth twitches. "Feel free to refuse the resignation if you think it best, Nile," he says mildly. "I thought that a first officer's commission aboard your new ship might suit Mr. Dana's skill set better, but the choice is yours, of course."

My eyes widen.

Domenic shudders and rolls back his shoulders. My stomach sinks as the miserable look on his face gives away his coming words. He can't accept a commission, not aboard my ship.

Tam beats him to the punch. "What do you say, Mr. Dana, will you accept a commission on my brother's ship? It will be a great deal of work to get her seaworthy, and most of it would fall on your shoulders, I fear—though I understand that Mr. Catsper and Mr. Kederic should be arriving shortly to lend a hand."

Domenic's brows pull together in confusion. "Your brother?"

Tamiath rises and holds his hand out to Aaron, who clasps it intimately, the men's fingers twining together. "Explain it to him, Nile," Tam calls as the two head for the door. They separate before opening it, and Aaron falls in behind Tam—the perfect image of a dutiful aide. "Enjoy your dinner."

"What just happened?" Domenic asks as we are left alone in the privacy of Tamiath's rooms. His focus is riveted to the spot where Tam and Aaron had clasped hands.

I stare at the same spot, my heart galloping. The risk my brothers took for my happiness and the immense sea of possibility that now opens before Domenic and me is both awesome and terrifying. Reaching out, I tentatively brush my hand against Domenic's calloused skin. "Let's speak over dinner," I whisper in the silence.

~

End of WAR AND WIND: TIDES Book 2.
The story continues in TIDES Book 3.
Join Alex's crew to be the first to know when the
book releases! Sign up at
www.subscribepage.com/TIDES

~

Did you enjoy WAR AND WIND? Reviews are an author's lifeblood. Please consider saying a few words about this book on Amazon.

ABOUT THE AUTHOR

Alex Lidell is an Amazon bestselling author of AIR AND ASH (Danger Bearing Press, 2017) and an Amazon Breakout Novel Awards finalist author of THE CADET OF TILDOR (Penguin, 2013). She is an avid horseback rider, a (bad) hockey player, and an ice-cream addict. Born in Russia, Alex learned English in elementary school, where a thoughtful librarian placed a copy of Tamora Pierce's ALANNA in Alex's hands. In addition to becoming the first English book Alex read for fun, ALANNA started Alex's life long love for YA fantasy books. Alex is represented by Leigh Feldman of Leigh Feldman Literary. She lives in Washington, DC. Join Alex's newsletter for news, bonus content and sneak peeks.

SIGN UP FOR NEWS AND RELEASE NOTIFICATIONS AT WWW.SUBSCRIBEPAGE.COM/TIDES

Connect with Alex!

www.alexlidell.com
alex@alexlidell.com

ACKNOWLEDGMENTS

TIDES was made possible by the amazing team of authors, editors, friends, and family who made the journey with me. A special shout-out to my critique partner, Marieke Nijkamp, who followed TIDES's creation chapter by chapter; Rachel E. Carter, who guided my journey; Jenn Stark, whose wisdom morphed TIDES into a series; my agent, Leigh Feldman, who kept me writing; editors Mollie Traver and Linda Ingmanson, who manned the plotting helm; the Lucky 13s, who are always there; the amazing writers in the AYAA forum; and to my mom, who is the most awesome mom ever.

ALSO BY ALEX LIDELL

TIDES

FIRST COMMAND (Prequel Novella)

AIR AND ASH (TIDES Book I)

WAR AND WIND (TIDES Book II)

Untitled (TIDES Book III)

~

TILDOR

THE CADET OF TILDOR

~

SIGN UP FOR NEW RELEASE NOTIFICATIONS

Reviews are an author's lifeblood. Please consider saying a few words about this book on Amazon.

www.ingramcontent.com/pod-product-compliance
Lightning Source LLC
Chambersburg PA
CBHW030656120726
47905CB00001B/242